Wild
Heart
An Equestrian Romance

I0835180

Wild Heart

An Equestrian Romance

by Carolyn Haley

First U.S. edition published by Borealis Books
East Wallingford, Vermont, USA
www.carolynhaley.wordpress.com/wildheart
ISBN 978-0-9887191-3-2
Digital ISBN 978-0-9887191-2-5

Cover design:
Leslie Noyes Creative Consulting, Inc.
Bennington, Vermont, USA
www.lmncreative.com

Cover image:
Copyright © Edyta Trojanska-Koch
www.equine-photo.com

First published as *Into the Sunrise*
The Wild Rose Press, Inc.
Adams Basin, NY 14410-0708
Copyright © 2015 Carolyn Haley
Print ISBN 978-1-5092-0142-6
Digital ISBN 978-1-5092-0143-3

Published in the United States of America

Dedicated to
the Green Mountain Goddesses,
without whom this story would not have survived.

PART I

Cape Cod, Massachusetts
May–June, 1975

"Feminism is the ability to choose what you want to do."

~Nancy Reagan

CHAPTER ONE

There's a poster I've been seeing for years in dorms and gift shops that reads, "Today Is the First Day of the Rest of Your Life."

I used to think that was hokey until the day it became true for me.

Although the accident had only given me a concussion and deep bruises, I was still missing time and events, the past two weeks a blur of disjointed images and conversations. Everything around me seemed off by a few degrees.

The biggest "off" was horses. They weren't supposed to be here. My family had sent me to Cape Cod to keep me away from horses, to avoid temptation while I healed.

For the summer, they wanted me to reconsider my career choice; be exposed to broader experiences and different people; perhaps be tempted by a new idea. If I couldn't find something more productive and less dangerous than working with horses for a living, Mom and Dad would pull the funding that let me train and ride in shows. Losing that support would set me even further back from my dream of competing at Madison Square Garden, maybe even winning a national championship someday.

I hadn't protested the plan, since it had been devised while only half my brain was functioning. Now that the other half was sputtering to life, I resented being manipulated but was grateful for the breather. I needed to make my own plan now. With my job gone, Michael gone, and my dream in jeopardy, I had to find my place in the equestrian world—soon.

That's why I stood beside my older sister, Jona, with our arms folded along the top rail of a corral at a trail-riding stable outside Provincetown on the tip of Cape Cod. I had no memory of exiting the car and walking across the packed-sand parking lot, but I did recall sitting in Jona's Saab all morning as we drove from Connecticut ahead of the Memorial Day weekend traffic.

Before us in the corral, a dozen mounts were tethered along a hitching rail in the center, waiting to take the next influx of tourists across the dunes. All stood hipshot under Western saddles, their heads drooping in the sun and tails swishing against flies. All were grungy, wearing tack as weathered as the barn and fences that sagged around the complex.

My heart ached for them, such unloved drones compared to the pampered pets and pedigreed hunter/jumpers in my chosen world. I wanted to roll up my sleeves and groom every one of them to a shine, then turn them out to pasture for a month to recover some vigor and spirit. But that wasn't my job anymore.

Jona pushed upright and tipped her head toward voices coming from behind a listing barn. "I think he's over there," she said. "C'mon."

I glanced a good-bye at the horses before limping after Jona, delighted that one horse had lifted its head and pricked its ears toward me—a little black mare with a zigzag white stripe down her nose. I wanted to hang back and meet her, to pet and talk to her, but the object of our visit lay ahead.

We passed into shade where the barn hunkered beneath pitch pines and scrub oaks. The breeze still smelled of baked sand with a salty undertone, then ripened to nose-crinkling when a waft of horse manure mixed in. Behind the barn stood a larger corral patched with bright planks of fresh lumber. Only one horse stood inside this one, accompanied by three people and watched by a dozen spectators lining the rail.

Jona and I joined them to see what was happening. Nothing yet: just a fluffy-haired girl in tight jeans, T-shirt, and turquoise cowboy boots preparing to ride a chestnut mare with flaxen mane and tail. Beyond her, an older man stood holding a longe whip at the ready. At her side, a man around my age finished adjusting her left stirrup and cinched the saddle tight.

I recognized his wheat-gold hair and athletic build from the snapshot Jona had shown me of our host, Con Winston. Lots of people knew him as number-two son of Ken Winston, a famous quarterback turned sports commentator turned business tycoon. Jona knew Con through her boyfriend, Dave, who had roomed with Con in prep school. Their friendship had endured through college and led to this summer's house share in North Truro, to which Jona then I had been appended.

We watched Con step clear as the rider gathered the reins and asked the mare to move forward, first with seat and voice and clucking, then with sharp kissing noises and a nudge with her turquoise heels.

No response except flattened ears, a cocked rear foot, and switching tail.

Uh-oh, I thought; *here comes trouble*.

Jona saw it, too, and muttered, "Bet she doesn't last thirty seconds."

"No bet," I replied.

The girl's urgings escalated to kicking and cursing, while the man waved his whip behind the horse's rump. At that the mare shuffled a few steps forward—then dropped her head and lashed out her hind legs in three big bucks.

The girl flew from the saddle. I winced and sucked air through my teeth, reflexively hugging myself against the body slam sure to come. But the girl tucked and rolled to her feet like a circus acrobat, staggering a few steps before brushing herself off then breaking into a grin and flinging her arms wide in a bow.

A few people clapped, while Jona muttered sideways, "Nice trick!"

I couldn't respond, having flashed back to my own involuntary dismount at the show. Fear grabbed me by the throat as I relived hurtling off my horse into a jump, deafened by clunks and clatters as my knee and elbow smacked the rails into a tumble of giant pick-up sticks. The explosion of pain had been cut off by blackness. I learned later that one of the standards had karate-chopped me from behind, cracking my black-velvet hunt cap open like an egg.

A rush of wind and thunder brought me back to the chestnut mare blasting by along the rail in a sprint/buck combination that slapped the stirrups against her sides, spooking her even more. I glimpsed a white-rimmed eye and red-lined nostril before Jona grabbed my arm and yanked me back from splattering sand.

The moment spent wiping grit off our faces helped me reorient. When we leaned forward again, I saw the girl dashing for the gate while Con sauntered the other way after the horse, crooning, "Whoa, girl, easy does it, good girl, take it easy..."

The older man closed in from another angle, using spread arms and his whip to make himself a moving fence. I should've been out there helping—I even bent to duck through the rails—but Jona's hand squeezed a warning into my shoulder. I stopped and straightened too fast, which launched a spin inside my head that doubled my vision and triggered a spurt of nausea. *Damn!*

But this swoon passed faster than any since the concussion, and I hadn't had any other woozies in the last two days. Given that I'd barely moved in two weeks, I couldn't blame my body for protesting an abrupt action.

I leaned against the fence again while the effects passed, just as the girl slipped between the bars of the corral gate and whistled for attention.

"Show's over, folks! Don't worry, that horse isn't part of our string! Your horses are over there, and they're gentle as babies. Now, everybody here for the ride please come with me, and we'll get you mounted up."

She marched toward the stable. Everyone peeled away from the fence and followed in a ragged train, except for me and Jona.

"Owner's daughter?" Jona guessed.

I shrugged. "Maybe she's why Con's working here instead of that resort place where you expected him."

"No," she said. "I don't think so."

We looked back at the corral, where Con and the man had boxed the mare against the opposite side. The man held back a pace, but Con, still murmuring, drifted toward the untied reins trailing from the horse's bit. She shied from him, pressing closer to the fence, but didn't bolt as I expected. He just kept talking and easing closer, not looking at her, until he sidled into reach of the reins and casually grasped them.

She permitted his touch for a few rubs, then tried to dance away. He held her fast, never pausing in his soothing stream of words. For all I could hear, he was reciting poetry, but whatever it was worked: The mare began to quiet. She again allowed him to approach her, and he rubbed her neck up under her mane until she forgot what had scared her. Then he invited her away from the fence on a circuit of the corral.

The older man waited until out of range of the horse's heels, then placed down his whip and hobbled bow-legged across the corral to meet us at the fence.

"You must be the roommates," he greeted.

Jona slid her sunglasses back onto her head. "Yes, I'm Jona Eagan and this is my sister, Linny."

"Tom Adams." He offered a hand. It was thick and rough, grubby like his plaid shirt and canvas pants. Grubby like all the horses.

But he had a kind, basset-hound face scribed with lines from hard outdoor experience. His skin showed broken surface veins that suggested hard drinking, too.

Not on the job, though. He was alert and confident as he looked us over and seemed proud when he hitched back his ballcap and said, "I manage the stable."

"Is this Galeson's Stable owned by the same family of Galeson's Resort?" Jona flicked a glance at me to keep mum.

"Yeah, but they just sold to my brother, Miriam's dad, to get out from under. We're trying to put it back together."

Ah, I thought.

He looked around with a sigh. "The Galesons make a packet from the resort, plus the general store, and now charter fishing and bike rentals—but this place has never done well. My brother picked it up for a song."

"Well, if your other horses are like that one"—Jona thumbed toward Con's mare—"then it's no surprise."

Tom shook his head. "Nope, our string is all old veterans. This mare was never meant for the public. We got her at auction as part of a batch we wanted for fresh blood. She's supposed to be a barrel racer...well, maybe was once, but looks like somebody soured that out of her. She was mopey till Miriam got on her and—well, you saw the rest."

I turned away from him to watch the mare, who was prancing on her toes beside Con, tossing her head, rolling her eyes at every fence post, and shying sideways when she spotted us even though we didn't move. At that point Con acknowledged us, his eyes a blue flash as he nodded.

Whoa! I flinched like he'd stung me with Tom's whip. That blue-eyed glance—it brought Michael so sharply into memory, he could have materialized in front of me from a puff of smoke!

I squeezed my eyes shut to make him vanish, then opened them to see Con steering the mare away from us across the corral.

I released my breath and noticed my hands shaking. *Jeesh*—one little flash, and my knees were liquid! Was this going to happen every time I saw a handsome blue-eyed horseman?

I shook my head clear and rejoined the conversation. Rather, I listened as Jona said to Tom, "Your niece looks like a capable rider. Or at least"—she smiled—"a capable dismounter."

Tom's rubbery face lit up in a laugh. "That gal was born in the saddle. Won herself a lot of barrel races back home. She's got her own horse here but thought this chestnut might work as a spare. Mare went okay for us this morning on the line, but now it looks like she'll need lots of training." He shook his head. "We can't afford to feed 'em if we can't use 'em for something."

That old familiar story brought an ache back to my chest. It usually meant bad news for some innocent horse. For me it might mean good news someday, since the only way I'd ever own a horse was if I got a sound one rejected for bad behavior and therefore cheap.

In this case, I wondered if there was a problem with the mare's bit or saddle, or whether she had been mistreated and become intolerant of riders. *Or all of the above.* By the time horses were sold by lot at auction, they usually had been through a sorry life.

I tracked Con and the mare while keeping an ear tuned to Tom and Jona. The mare was walking better but still rolling her eyes at invisible threats and swiveling her ears when not pinning them backward. She allowed Con to lead her into speaking range of us but planted her feet to stay out of reach.

"Hey, gals," greeted Con while again scratching the mare's neck under her mane.

Jona beamed and sang out, "Hi, Con!"

I mustered up a smile and said same. He returned the smile, bright and white, then we looked each other over.

Up close, nothing about him suggested Michael. Con was bronze and solid, not lanky and dark. I relaxed, chiding myself for jumping like a goosed cat a minute ago. So his eyes were blue. Whoop-dee-doo. They weren't even close to Michael's color—shades of cloud and ocean instead of crystal-clear sky inside a navy ring.

They also said "no trespassing" instead of "come hither." I squirmed at the sense they gave of Con the person peering out through Con the image.

His scan of me was fast but thorough and prompted no expression change. This was unusual enough to tweak my curiosity, since most times when Jona and I were together, people marveled that we were sisters.

Jona carried the dominant family genes that made her round and freckled, with brown eyes and hair and an ample bust, while I was a throwback to early ancestors and came out long, lean, and flat, with blue eyes and white-blond hair.

Because of my hair, most men expected my whole package to be exotic, if not va-va-voom, and were disappointed after first glance. I was just pleasantly plain, with the good luck of being symmetrical and having straight teeth.

Con had a nice smile himself, which he showed while saying, "Nice to finally meet you. How're you feeling?"

"Better, thanks." I wondered how much Jona had told him. "But still wobbly."

He nodded and held my eye for a second before turning back to the horse, who was trying to back up. Upon quieting her again, he said to Jona, "How long have you been here?"

"Long enough to watch the show." She tilted her head in the direction of Miriam coordinating the trail ride.

"Yeah, that was a pretty good flip." He chuckled. "Miriam's a rodeo gal."

I gestured at the sulking mare. "Have you tried her yet?"

"No, but maybe later after everyone has cleared out." He patted the mare's shoulder. "We need to have a little discussion about manners."

The mare tossed her head and flattened her ears, but he kept patting and scritching her neck until her ears came forward.

When he turned to me and smiled again, his face crinkled into lines too deeply etched for someone only twenty-two. Jona had previously told me Con was my age, making us both a year younger than her. She still had smooth skin that would carry permanent smile lines down the road, whereas some of Con's lines already curved in the opposite direction. What did someone so privileged have to scowl about?

"We won't be staying long," Jona said. "Got your note at the house and figured we'd swing by to say hi before grocery shopping—you and Dave left the cabinets a tad bare."

Con transferred his gaze to her. "Sorry about that. I've been, well, busy..." He looked at the horse. "And Dave's been down at the Hole all week. He's due back tonight."

I was still translating "the Hole"—short for a big mouthful, Woods Hole Oceanographic Institute, down at the southernmost point of the Cape—when Tom spoke up. "There's a market on the way into town."

He gave complicated directions that Jona waved away. "I know where it is, thanks. We'll stock up on our way home."

I wanted to look and learn more, but a wave of pressure in my head blurred my vision, accompanied by an urgent need to lie down. But I had enough control to hold myself upright and not bleat, "Can we go now?"—which pleased me, as I couldn't have done that a week ago.

While waiting for the others to wrap up their chitchat, I propped myself against the fence and studied Con's mare. She was a harsh-looking specimen, showing no particular breed type, though a convex curve to her profile reminded me of Iberian horses—Andalusian or Lusitano. It gave her a noble, almost masculine look. But the rest of her didn't match, like the horse equivalent of a mutt. Aside from her suspiciously flicking ears, she possessed a beauty that pleased the heart more than the eye: a coat that would gleam coppery bronze if groomed; strong and square frame with strong and straight legs; mane and tail like flaxen banners. Her eye revealed power, intelligence, personality, and spirit. And her teeth were aiming for Con's shoulder.

He reacted to my indrawn breath by lifting a fist as he twisted so the mare's lips smacked into bone instead of her teeth into muscle. The surprise made her jerk her head back with bugged eyes and a snort. He winced and shook his hand out, then rubbed his knuckles.

Tom laughed and said, "Well, Winston, maybe you can do something with her after all. Sure would be a shame to send her to the glue factory."

Con didn't smile. "It'll never come to that."

Tom's yellow grin didn't waver, but his eyes flickered. "Let's see what it does come to." Then he turned to me as I reconsidered Con, having glimpsed a reflection of myself in his actions and words.

"How about you girls?" Tom drawled. "Wanna ride? You just missed the two o'clock trail, but we go again at four and tomorrow night start sunset rides for the season."

Jona spoke before I could answer. "Maybe later—sounds like fun. C'mon, Linny, we've had a long day and need to settle in."

Con held my gaze and said, "Two hours. On the beach. Right into the sunset."

Now I really needed the fence to hold me up. Riding down a beach into the sunset...my favorite fantasy with Michael! Once upon a time, I had hoped to actualize it on our honeymoon. How cruel to have the opportunity now!

I wilted. Jona glared at Con. "Doctor's orders," she informed him as a way of reminding me.

"You'll lose your nerve if you don't get right back in the saddle," Con reminded me in turn.

I needed no reminder on either point and repressed a spike of temper. Tom's dark-brown eyes brightened in intrigue as he asked, "What, you take a fall?"

"Yes," I stated, while Jona said to Con, "No riding for six to eight weeks, maybe longer."

"Six to eight days at most," I corrected, even though I still craved a nap. I might even be ready in six to eight hours. However, first I absolutely had to rest.

Jona sliced a look at me but didn't argue. Con did same, while Tom, bulging with curiosity, zipped his mouth shut, too. We all turned to watch the trail riders when Con's mare whinnied after them. The group had been getting organized during the conversation, and now set out in single file along a sandy path under the pines.

Miriam led them on a snappy gray gelding with black mane, tail, and legs, which he lifted high in youthful vigor. I looked for the little black mare, hoping to not see her. Nope. There she was, midpack in line, with a preteen girl aboard her. How many times a day, how many times a week—month—lifetime, did that poor horse have to plod through the same routine under different hands?

Con's mare was lucky, having acquired in him a caring rider for herself. I wished that for every horse, as much as I wished for a horse of my own. I also wanted a man of my own to ride beside me; but if Michael was any proof, I'd be better off without one. Horses would not, could not, ever betray me.

"For now," said Jona, "we're off to restock the larder." She rotated me in the direction of the car.

"See you guys tonight," Con called as we moved away.

"Shall I hold supper for you?" Jona asked over her shoulder.

He shook his head. "I'll be in too late—we're doing a dry run of the sunset trail to teach me the route, and time it."

I felt a pang I admitted was envy. Before it could take root, I changed it into determination to ride the minute I felt up to it, rather than wait for someone to officially clear me. Being ground-bound felt like prison; only riding set me free.

One misjudgment, though, could dismount me for good, so I had to be conservative. But the best possible medicine would be taking back control of my life.

CHAPTER TWO

I woke at dawn with muscles itching from pent-up energy. Forgetting to expect pain, I flung back the bedclothes and crossed to the window, my feet tacky against the whitewashed floorboards between pastel rugs. Bruises announced their presence but much less than before, feeling almost like a long day in the saddle instead of damaged joints and tissues. Best, my mind felt connected to my body again, instead of bobbling behind like a half-filled balloon on a string.

Outside the window, clouds were bloated with rain ready to fall, and a gusty wind encouraged it. A muted booming of surf I couldn't see was pierced by the cry of seagulls trailing past on the wind.

I donned a sweatshirt over jeans and tiptoed downstairs to find some breakfast. My stomach gurgled from having slept through dinner, so I tugged open every door in a wall of cupboards painted pale aqua with white seashell knobs until I found the box of Cheerios Jona had bought on the way home. Then I gobbled down a heaping bowl in seconds.

The whole kitchen—the whole place—was a symphony of pastel beach tones, aqua and beige and pink and sunshine yellow, all accented with white—befouled by Con's mucky work boots and jacket. These brought home the fact I was sharing a house with a horseman, an irony that gave me a sour laugh. It also gave me hope. Maybe the winds of fortune were changing direction again, and this time they would blow me back on course.

Shoes and a backpack I assumed were Dave's sprawled on and under a chair. Dishes had been washed and put away, indicating my housemates had gone to bed sober. But probably late, as their bedroom doors remained closed.

I tried not to think about Jona and Dave sleeping together across the landing from my bedroom, and wondered if Con had anyone—that cute owner's daughter, Miriam?—in his room around the back side of the kitchen. Damn, I didn't want to be reminded that I wouldn't be sleeping with Michael again! The breakup had been my doing, but he had given me cause. It still stabbed like a thousand knives.

Refusing to dwell on it, I grabbed a yellow slicker from the hook inside the back door and exited through a sun porch cluttered with wicker furniture and beach accessories. Time to explore my new world.

I hopped off the deck and strode through the bowl the house sat in, my feet leaving beige imprints in the sand. Then I climbed the track up the dune that sheltered the house from the Atlantic. Even on the lee side, the beachgrass rippled and beach-rose bushes danced in the wind off the ocean. It shoved me to a halt as I crested the dune.

Wow! Before me stretched an open vista of roiling clouds and sea, a watercolor wash of gray, deep turquoise, and violet. Whitecaps blossomed then vanished to reappear as waves, frothing and boiling, clouded with sand, rearing and crashing against the shore. I could feel their percussion through my feet.

I hadn't thought to tie down my hair, so it bannered out behind me as airborne grit peppered my face. The bluff I stood on plunged at least eighty feet, as steep and sheer as a pyramid face. It spilled onto a beach that curved out of sight in both directions. A few people walked the strand, miniaturized and hazed by distance.

I recognized the view from a painting back in the living room, a misty-dawn version of the scene before me except the people were on horseback. The work had caught my eye yesterday upon arrival, and I'd been surprised to learn that Con had painted it. After asking Jona to interpret the signature "CSW"—Connor Simon Winston—I had spotted other CSW landscapes, seascapes, and studies around the house as I settled in.

So my horseman host was also an artist. That didn't jibe with what I expected from a football player's son, who also, Jona informed me, had starred on Yale's varsity team.

Was that why he wore a mask?

I shook my head. Not my business. *Don't even get tempted, Eagan.* Woman on the rebound, ripe to make an even bigger fool of herself...I didn't need a second handsome horseman to teach me what I already knew.

More important was seeing if I could make it down to the beach without reinjuring anything. After deliberating for a moment, I rolled up my jeans and glissaded down the dune face. Each sliding step scraped my insteps with buried stones, making me wince.

But my knee held up, delivering me to the crescent beach. Along it ran two tide lines: one near the base of the dunes, a dry snaggle of bracken and driftwood marking the height of winter storms; the other a necklace of black seaweed strands studded with broken shells, dead crabs, and pebbles along the beach's shoulder before it sloped down to the surf. Sandpipers followed the undertow in and out, while gulls either strolled the beach or swung above it on sharp angles, crying.

The sand between my toes was grayer and more granular than the beige dune, like walking through sugar. It grew colder, moister, and firmer as I crossed it, to find the water a slash of ice blades that instantly numbed my feet.

I leaped back at the staggered *boom!* of head-high waves that crashed ashore while curling back into themselves, stained maroon by fuzzy algae swept in with the wind and tide. The undertow might have dragged me under if I hadn't backpedaled out of range. The waves' thunder incited a jubilant tingling like what I felt during spring floods and summer storms, or when straddling a motorcycle or a charged-up horse. Something like it had occurred whenever Michael used to touch me.

For a moment I fell back into memory of his hands, his scent, his wild energy—how when he laughed, the world became a brighter place; and when he rode, his grace inspired poetry. And his kisses...

Just recalling them made my legs sag and heart stumble. But then I remembered how generously he distributed those kisses among other women; how he couldn't keep his pants zipped when opportunity allowed. That jerked me aware, to find myself a yellow speck on a vast gray stage of sea, sand, and sky.

With no place to put my pain and passion, I swung my fist at the air and roared at the water. Oh, for a galloping horse! Only a flat-out charge down the beach with wind ripping through my hair would dispel what raged inside me.

But I was stuck on two legs—both of which were working today, finally!—so I charged back up the dune face. Within three strides I ran out of steam but kept pushing in an all-fours scramble, grunting and gasping. At the top, stumbling over the lip in triumph, I nearly flopped at Con's feet.

"Oh!" fell out of my mouth as it dropped open and I popped upright. If my face hadn't already been scarlet from exertion, it would have further embarrassed me by flooding red. Retreat would only add to indignity, so I flailed for composure while scraping hair out of my mouth and eyes and puffing to catch my breath.

"Pretty good for somebody who's supposed to be crippled," Con greeted.

I couldn't tell if he was being sarcastic or sincere until he tweaked the corners of his lips.

I shrugged for lack of better and flicked a smile back at him. "Well, I did get twelve hours of sleep."

"We noticed at dinner." He flicked a smile back.

I again felt the sensation of someone looking at me from behind a screen. His cool expression, hot gaze, and casual tone of voice didn't align.

I struggled to keep on topic. "I wish somebody had woken me up."

"Jona decreed that you needed sleep more than food."

"She was right, though I woke up ravenous. How was the lasagna?"

He grinned. "Delicious."

"And how was the dry run of that sunset trail?"

"Terrific. You really ought to try it. Especially"—he scanned me up and down—"since you seem to be recovered."

My face continued burning; his study was more blatant than yesterday's. I felt self-consciously female and younger than my years. It didn't help that the wind atop the bluff kept whipping my hair into my face.

I dragged it back and plaited it while talking. "I'm basically healed, but my head's unreliable, and my knee and elbow hurt when I use them. Like… just now."

"So c'mon back to Galeson's and take the sunset ride. In Western, you sit with a longer leg and hold the reins with one hand. And it's all at a walk."

His eyelid twitched. Did he just wink at me? I stared, knowing how Eve had felt in the Garden of Eden when the serpent had offered forbidden fruit.

We stood silent while I tucked my braid inside my collar and wrestled with my conscience. To ride the sunset trail tonight, after having just exhausted myself, meant aggravating my injuries and violating the deal with my parents. To not go meant prolonging other people's control over my life. I was old enough, and now lucid enough, to make my own decisions. After all, I'd be living the consequences no matter who chose my fate.

Con must have sensed me weakening because he prodded, "Tonight would be good—weather's supposed to clear, and there won't be as many tourists as tomorrow."

I slid my eyes around to regard him. His hair was fluttering back to expose his forehead and ears, both as nicely formed as the body under his paint-stained sweatshirt and cutoff sweatpants. Low-riding cutoffs, I couldn't help but notice.

He crossed his arms over his chest. "Be there by six thirty so we can leave by seven."

I met his gaze again, thinking, *If I can't ride off into the sunset with Michael, then I might as well enjoy it for myself with a handsome stranger.* All I said was, "Thanks, but...I've got to talk it through with Jona. She'd have to drive me or I borrow her car."

"You can always bring Jona and Dave on the ride, too."

"Hah! Good luck talking them into it."

"Hey, I've got my charms." He puffed into a peacock pose.

"I'm sure you do." I returned the up-down study he'd given me, lightening it with a smile and a ghost of a wink back at him.

He grinned. That gave me a spark and sizzle, which I instantly shut down. As much as I wanted a new man in my life, it was way too early to open that door. Bad enough that my resistance to horse temptation was crumbling fast.

I put my back to the wind and tried to change the subject. "So you're working today?"

He shook his head. "Not till afternoon. I've got late shift, since we're starting the sunset rides."

So much for changing the subject. In that case: "Would I be able to ride that little black mare?"

He hesitated, forehead crinkling. I clarified. "The one that looks Arab. Zigzag stripe down her nose."

"Oh, Shark. Yeah, she's half Arab. Sure, I can arrange that." He dropped his voice. "So you'll come?"

"I...don't know yet. Depends on how I feel. And how hard Jona resists."

"We can talk her into it, I'm sure."

I shook my head. "She's doing substitute mother duty for the summer, and we haven't even started."

"But she's not your mother. And you're a legal adult now, aren't you?"

I nodded. "But still tied to the purse strings."

"Hm." Con flared his nostrils and looked away. "Know what you mean."

Oh? That was interesting. Well, if he could poke and probe, so could I. "I thought...well, I got the impression you can afford to do whatever you feel like."

Con twisted his mouth. "That's what they all think. Fact is, I was on a short leash until I hit twenty-one, when I came into a little trust fund from my grandmother. Combined with inheriting this house from her, too, and getting a job, this summer is the first time I've been able to do a damn thing I want."

"Ah." I knew all about wanting things contrary to family expectations, and privileges with strings attached. That might explain the mask he seemed to wear. I wondered if I wore one, too, which everybody except me could see.

This was not conversational terrain I wanted to explore. I had come out to explore the physical terrain; no reason why we couldn't talk while we walked.

"Look, if you want to warm up for your jog, I need to cool down before my muscles turn into boards. Want to walk down the beach for a bit?"

"Sure. But we've got to get down there the other way. Supposed to keep off the dunes."

"Why? This is your land, isn't it?"

"Yes and no. The whole outer Cape is a national park now. So there's restrictions about erosion control and breeding birds and all that. Technically, where we're standing is part of my beachfront property, but I try to keep things simple and use that path since it's so close."

He gestured toward the town beach access a few hundred yards away and much lower, where an obvious track was trodden into the sloping sand from the edge of a paved parking area partially blocked from view by the swell of the dune.

"This area around the house is private property, so if you see any kids playing too close or people coming up our driveway, chase 'em off. Once the summer gets going, they'll start parking across the bottom, and I'll have to add more signs and put up a barrier."

I nodded, looking around. He might complain about purse strings, but he owned a mini paradise some people would pay a small fortune for, and he hadn't had to earn it himself. Hard to bleed for him on that front.

But he was giving me free shelter, so I kept my mouth shut, following him back to and around the weathered-shingle house—gray with white trim, like so many on the New England coast—then down the appropriate way. After we found our stride on the beach, we resumed getting acquainted at a near yell above the hammering surf.

"So, how long've you been riding?"

He eyed me as if sensing a subtext, but went along. "Started in prep school. Hunter/jumper, like you; that's all they had. Then I played polo for a few summers during college."

"Polo!"

He chuckled, more relaxed than he had been a few seconds ago. "Yeah. It's like rugby on horseback. Banged me up more than all my years of football! I stayed with it until I had to concentrate on ball."

He scowled. I asked, "Did you ever show?"

"No."

"How old were you when you started?"

"Fifteen."

"Jeesh, I thought I was late at twelve!"

Way too late, I thought for the millionth time. Most champions started before they could walk.

"For a late starter, you must have caught up pretty quick if you're showing," Con said.

"Well...I've been showing almost since I started riding, but this was my first on the A circuit." *And hopefully not my last.* I felt a frown and maybe tears coming on so turned away.

"What happened?" he said. "All I was told was you wiped out and were coming here to recupe."

"I..." God, it was still so humiliating! But I sensed he would not laugh, so straightened and said, "I misjudged my approach and got in too close to the fence. At the last minute, my horse refused, twisting sideways to avoid crashing—and I kept going, off over his shoulder and sideways into the rails."

He winced. "How big a jump?"

"Just a three-six oxer. It was an equitation over fences class."

"Ouch. Couldn't even go down in glory through a six-foot wall! Break anything?"

"No, but got my bell rung real good, and a hard sprain of my left knee and elbow. Deep bruises, too, 'cause I hit a standard and went down in a mess of crossrails."

"What happened to the horse?"

"Nothing, thank God. He just stood there, going, *What the heck?*"

"Your horse?"

"No. And the owner won't let me ride him again. Lost my job, too, though not directly because of that."

"Then why? Seems harsh."

I shrugged to cover my anger. "Because I'll be gone too long. My position can't hang open. I'm supposed to check in with my boss when I get home and 'we'll talk about it,' but..."

His face darkened and he nodded.

I appreciated the sign of sympathy, since I hadn't gotten any at home. In fact, I couldn't believe my luck to be staying with someone who might actually understand my life. It moved me to open up when normally I would clam up.

"Competition isn't just at shows. The Academy is such a good place to work that when something opens, people zoom in to grab it and don't let go. So it's fifty-fifty, at best, I'll get rehired. My mother sabotaged me by calling my boss while I was still half out and telling her my recovery would take at least the summer, *maybe* I'd be back by fall semester. Then she and Dad packed up my stuff from my room in a house share and set me up at home. I was so foggy I didn't notice at first, then so...defeated that I couldn't face calling my boss to speak for myself."

"That stinks." Con shook his head, adding, "You can use my phone any time you want."

I looked at him with arched eyebrows. "Thank you." I'd thought his hospitality to be generous enough, but that plus sympathy plus long-distance calls was a bonus. I warmed toward him another degree.

"Anyway, I lost my hard hat and a lot of memory, but didn't lose any teeth or break my nose, though I had a whopper of a raccoon mask." I smiled then frowned. "The concussion is why I'm grounded."

"I can still see some of your shiner." Con swung into a sidestep to peer at me, then back into stride. We walked for a few minutes without talking, watching the water heave and retreat, squinting against its briny spittle. My braid undid itself for lack of a rubber band to hold it, so I still had to wipe hair from my face. Con did, too, for his hair was collar length and thus too short to be tied back and too long to stay out of the way.

He asked, "What kind of hassle will you have if you get right back on, like the sunset trail this weekend?"

"Probably nothing more than pain, but...problems with my parents if they find out."

"The purse strings."

"Yeah." I paused, then succumbed to the privacy the beach afforded and told him more about myself in a few minutes than I normally told anyone in a year. "They're underwriting my training as part of a deal we made about college. Instead of a four-year bachelor's degree, I did a two-year associate's in equine studies, then had two years to show I could get somewhere in the horse world. We're supposed to renegotiate this fall, but my crash makes things dicey because I justified all their fears."

"Pretty different from football, where they brush off any injury that doesn't put you in a coma!"

I laughed then sobered. "That's what they don't get. My father is a history teacher at the Academy—same one where I work, he's how Jona and I got into the school—and my mother is a social worker. They know all about disaster in theory, yet haven't done anything more physical all their lives than mow the lawn. The thought of risk, even the general dirt of a stable, freaks them out. They knew I'd fallen off before, but they'd never seen it; I never showed off my bruises. But they were in the stands when I went down. For once the event was local, so Jona came home to watch and brought Mom and Dad along in a big gesture of family support."

That's what they had tried to convey, but I'd heard my parents' real message: We're doing this because you're our daughter, and we're trying to give you the same support as to your sister, not because we believe in you or what you want to do.

"Instead," I finished, "they watched me go through a fence and be taken off in an ambulance."

Con made an inarticulate noise while I searched my memory again for any details beyond being moved between ground and stretcher, stretcher to ambulance, ambulance to emergency room. There had been a long blackout before I woke up in the hospital; another blank spot before waking up at home.

Con watched me without blinking, waiting for more. I hesitated, but having a willing listener seduced me into confiding. "They want me to go to back to school for maybe a vet degree, to be on the ground if I insist on working with animals. I can't make them understand that being a vet is gory and risky in its own way; the only real difference is double the classroom time, then the salary you get with a degree."

"A degree ain't everything," he said. "I've got one that's basically useless."

"Jona said art from Yale."

"Yeah, what am I going to do with that?"

"I dunno, be a famous artist?"

Con gave a raw laugh. "That'll be the day! But I'd rather be a starving artist than play pro ball or take over the family business."

"Which is…?"

"You know, Linny—I don't really know. Some fancy managing of big investments and properties. Don't know, don't care. I'd rather shovel horse shit."

His anger sent out a wave I felt above the buffeting wind. The moment felt more honest than any conversation I'd had in the past year. And his mask had vanished.

But he'd mentioned something I'd never thought about—the logistics of being rich and the conditions that might put on children of wealthy families. Nobody talked about such things in my world. The horsey set either took their money for granted or kept its troubles away from the help; and the academic set, represented and reported on by my parents, either complained about money or ignored it in favor of loftier topics.

For me, money was just currency, something everyone needed in order to live. Without my parents' contribution—even with it—I would never have enough to compete at the upper echelons. That didn't stop me from aiming for them, though, because while I couldn't quite believe that old saw about when one door closes another always opens, I *did* believe that where there's a will, there's a way.

I just couldn't see a clear passage right now to anything I desired. All I could do was place one foot in front of the other and hope it led to the right path.

I looked back at Con for a lead to continue the conversation, but his face had closed and eyes veiled, as if a miniature man had drawn the curtains from inside. I must have reminded him of his own problems, so I joined him in looking out at the sea.

It was hard to keep my gaze out there when beside me stood such male beauty. I dared a sideways glance at him, seeking any flaw. Well, he hadn't shaved today…which outlined his jaw in gold speckles. And those scowl lines added age. It must be tough to be traffic-stopping gorgeous; he would never know whether a girl liked the person behind his looks and pedigree. As an artist, that probably stung his soul.

Not much I could do for him except treat him as a regular guy. Which meant he wouldn't mind some interest and support.

"For what it's worth," I offered, "I like your paintings. Especially that big one over the couch."

His head snapped around, and he stared at me. "Uh, thanks!"

What he didn't say but yelled through his glowing face and posture was, *Hallelujah! Somebody likes my work! Somebody cares!*

That wave came across like his anger had. *Wow*, I thought: *Bingo!*—though I didn't know how to react. Artists were a new breed for me. Like many people, I thought of them as weird dressers or struggling neurotics who retreated to aeries to express their genius. That didn't match the privileged boy standing before me with football in his past and horses in his present and God-knew-what in his future. I needed to shift gears, but...which one to be in, where to go at what speed?

Technical seemed safer than personal, so I asked, "Did you copy from a photograph, or sit up here and paint what you saw?"

I swept an arm to embrace the vista, noticing it had become much heavier-clouded than when I'd left the house. The wind was starting to throw moisture at us, signaling a countdown to weather change.

He pulled his gaze away from my face to follow my hand. "A bit of both. I did the sketch, then worked from a photo to get the colors. Added the figures from imagination."

"I don't think you'll get a chance for outdoor painting today," I said as the flying wetness thickened to raindrops. Before he could reply, the clouds unleashed a squall.

We dashed for the house, squawking and laughing as the rain penetrated our hair and clothing. "So much for my run!" Con yelled.

"You're getting it now!" I hollered back.

When we drew up on the deck, saturated, I said, "Jona better have coffee ready!"

"Oh, she will." Con swung open the door. "She's paying her rent by doing the cooking this summer!"

"Yeah?" So much for Jona's assurance of a free ride. "What about me?"

Con smiled through the water streaming down his face. "I guess your cost is physical therapy. We need a lot of help at the stable."

CHAPTER THREE

The cars crowding Galeson's parking lot accounted for the line of people stretching away from a Dutch door open in the side of the barn. Saddled horses dozed at the hitching rail in the front corral, just as they had yesterday afternoon. Some stamped and slapped their tails at bugs brought out by the twilight. I looked for Shark but didn't see her; then added myself to the end of the line with Dave and Jona, scanning for Con.

There he was: shooing a buckskin horse into place, then slinging a saddle atop it. He looked grim and dirty and streaked with sweat. Tom yelled something to him from inside the barn; Miriam, perky and polite, was processing customers.

As the nine people ahead of us peeled off toward the corral, I got incrementally better views of Miriam. The girl looked sixteen, maybe seventeen, made up to appear drinking age—which had been dropped to eighteen four years ago. Her feathered caramel-colored hair ended where her breasts began, making it hard to miss them bobbing beneath her pink jersey. Her hip-hugger bell-bottoms were equally tight, making me wonder how she could ride in them.

I held my tongue and stepped up to the Dutch door when my turn came. Miriam straightened from placing money into a cash box below the counter, then fixed bright hazel eyes on me.

"Next? Oh, you're Linny, right? You guys don't have to pay."

"Huh?"

"Courtesy of Pretty Boy Winston over there." Miriam reached to close the door across the window. Nobody stood behind us, so we stepped back and waited for her to come outside.

She strutted out wearing her snazzy turquoise boots into which she had tucked her pant legs. She also had tucked her hair under a straw cowboy hat and discarded her bangle earrings.

"C'mon, we're running late." She headed for the front corral. "Con says you take Shark and let Uncle Tom know how she responds to direct reining. He thinks she might have been trained once for English. You guys"—she gestured at Dave and Jona—"follow me, I've got some pussycats for you."

They complied, looking like a parody of Roy Rogers and Dale Evans. Dave wore a Stetson atop his frizzy head and a bolo tie with his red-checked shirt and jeans, with cowboy boots he had dredged up from somewhere. Jona's twin brown braids dangled beneath a big-brimmed sun hat, and she wore a red bandana around her neck over a tailored plaid button-front tucked into denim gaucho pants. Instead of cowboy boots, she wore her beloved Fryes.

I was stuck with jeans and a denim snap-front over a T-shirt. I also wore my old paddock boots, which I had packed in a moment of hope-springs-eternal. These gave me real riding shoes for security.

No security up top, however. I'd had no chance to replace my hunt cap, which would look stupid anyway in a Western environment. So I had to ride bareheaded, a vulnerability I'd never known. My teachers and parents had insisted I wear a hard hat. Even though it had ultimately failed me, I still felt naked without it. Best I could do for tonight was tie a bandana around my head and knot it beneath my ponytail. At least if I fell off I would land on sand.

In the corral, Con and two teenage girls were helping customers mount, adjust their saddles and stirrups, and tighten cinches. Con smiled and waved when he saw us, then caught my eye and nodded toward the corner, where the little black mare was tied with a lead rope attached to a halter over her bridle.

I beelined over, slowing as I approached the horse. Shark greeted me with the same forward-pricked ears and curiosity she had shown from a distance. I offered myself for sniffing, then rubbed her poll and the crest of her neck under her mane, babbling friendly words.

As I ran my hands over her body, I noticed taut muscles and fine hair, and the blue-black skin defining true black coloring, as compared to very dark brown or gray. Only her nose stripe and right rear ankle were white. Her proportions promised smooth gaits, good wind, and soundness; and her Arab heritage showed through her inward-pointing ear tips and slightly dished face, short back, and high-set tail.

"What's a nice girl like you doing at a joint like this?" I asked while tightening the crusty cinch. Accustomed to buckles and billets, it took me a minute to figure out the loop knot used with this Western saddle. Shark put her ears back, then swiveled them forward again when I swapped the lead line for the cracked reins looped around her saddle horn.

She was so petite I could have swung aboard from the ground without stirrups—or I could have a month ago. As it was, I strained to hitch my left foot into the stirrup and had to haul myself into the saddle by the cantle and horn. My elbow and knee yelped in protest, but I ignored them, as Shark immediately began jigging. I thought at first the mare was fussy, then realized Con had mounted his chestnut volcano, whose presence agitated all the horses.

Surprised that he would bring such an unpredictable animal out with neophytes, and wondering if he was showing off, I kept my distance. I needed to get a feel for my own mount and the bulky saddle before facing any challenges.

"You guys okay?" I called out to Jona, who sat atop a splashy pinto.

She grinned and waved, waiting beside Dave. He, as far as I knew, was a laboratory worker who never did anything physical. Miriam had put him on an aged bay with a roached mane who looked half draft breed, but which she assured him was as calm as a police horse. Dave still looked tense.

Con and Miriam herded the riders into a line, while the stablehands returned to the barn—both of them looking back longingly at Con. My toes curled in memory of what I had endured with Michael, who left a trail of sighs everywhere he went.

Miriam commanded our attention by raising her arm and calling out instructions. Then she led the dozen riders through the gate and across the barnyard after her. Con brought up the rear, and the teenagers sulked into the barn. Tom, I presumed, was still inside it.

I stuck close to Dave and Jona, us the last three in the line of horses nose to tail. As we ambled into the shadows under the pines, I began to register where I was: back in the saddle!

It was an alien saddle, formed of stiff leather slabs that cupped my pelvis with a tall horn in front. Normally I rode English, atop a light leather shell with slender stirrup leathers ending in slender, arched irons. In this Western saddle, the stirrup leathers were thick flaps ending in rounded wood triangles, at a length and angle that fixed my legs into a more relaxed position. My knee appreciated that, as did my elbow, which I could rest by reining with my right hand.

These reins, unlike the laced straps connected by buckle that I was used to, were skinny leather strips tied in a knot, to be drawn across the horse's neck for steering when weight shifting and leg cues wouldn't suffice. Remembering Miriam's request, I switched to English mode, engaging both hands to steer with finger squeezes and leg pressure. The mare responded to any technique as far as I could tell, since the horses just followed each other through the track in the sand.

"How's it feel?" Jona called back to me.

"Okay, though I think two hours are going to kill me." I pivoted and stretched in the saddle, trusting Shark to stay quiet while I dropped my stirrups and swung my legs. Then I recovered my stirrups and stood before settling back down in the seat.

"I already feel it in my knees," Jona said, having not ridden since she was ten, and only that once.

"Man, my butt is sore already!" Dave exclaimed.

"Wait till we hit the beach," came Con's voice from behind. I looked over my shoulder as he rode up alongside us. "You guys doing okay?"

Instantly better, I thought upon catching his smile. He looked great in the saddle, loose-bodied with tousled hair and sparkling eyes. He seemed more integrated than I'd yet seen him. I couldn't resist smiling back.

"You actually like that beast?" I asked as we bobbed along side by side, the horses' hooves grinding sand while the riders ducked beneath low branches. He nodded, shaking hair away from his eyes.

"Love her. She's like an exotic, rough-tuned car. She'll perform if you treat her right. I think she might have been a schoolie or a rodeo horse, racing barrels they said, but got overworked and beaten and generally used up."

"You've got her in a hackamore!" I exclaimed, amazed that such a raw horse could be managed without a bit. Then again, I'd heard that some hackamores could be more severe than bits, depending on what they were made of and how they were rigged.

"Yeah, that straightened things out pretty quick yesterday. Changed saddles and pads, too. She's way more comfortable, so not fighting so hard."

Nevertheless, the mare kept tossing her head and tugging against the reins, even while responding instantly to Con's seat and leg.

He patted her neck. "Somebody must have trained her once upon a time. I don't know how she ended up here, but it's too bad she did. A horse like this should be privately owned and cared for, used athletically by one person."

"I wonder who," I mumbled under my breath, amazed by the change wrought in the mare and impressed by the person who had wrought it.

We had drifted back from the main group, which allowed more private conversation while the others chattered. Our words carried off behind us on the breeze.

"So what's her name?" I asked, gesturing at Con's horse.

"Klatawah."

"What?" *You mean, someone besides me knows that word?*

"Klatawah. That's what I'm calling her."

"You're kidding!"

"No. It's some kind of Indian name—"

"Meaning, *go to hell*, or *go away*. From that book about diving horses."

This time Con gaped, and I laughed inside. "*A Girl and Five Brave Horses*!" he said. "I thought I was the only person in the world who'd read it!"

"Me too! I handed it to everyone at camp and school, thinking they'd love it. But only one friend was ever interested."

We held gazes for a long moment, me thinking this was a different version of the handsome horseman from what I knew. He looked like he was reevaluating me, also.

Then he looked away with a scowl. "I had to read it with a flashlight under my covers."

"Uh..." What could I say to that? We were wading into too-deep waters in too public a place, but the info was so startling I had to ask, "Why?"

His mouth twisted down. "*Misty of Chincoteague.*"

Another surprise! Not the book—the first horse story I'd ever read, beautifully illustrated, and part of a series for children—but the fact this guy not only had read it but needed to do so in secret.

I waited for him to explain, or not, for which I couldn't blame him. Our horses strode companionably onward, twin cabooses at the end of the train.

Presently he answered, "My dad caught me with it when I was a kid and smacked me for being a faggot, because it was clearly a book for girls."

Oh jeesh. What kind of jerk—I bit back the words, replacing them with, "Aw c'mon. It's just a horse story!"

"Yeah, well, tell that to my dad." Con's face darkened.

My heart hurt for him, while my head realized how good I'd had it. My parents had filled our home with books and encouraged me and Jona to read anything and everything except pornography. Jona was even getting college degrees in literature.

I recovered my tongue and asked, "Did he approve of *The Black Stallion*, which was all boy?"

"Don't know, I never let him see me with anything that wasn't a textbook."

Why are you telling me this?

I said only, "So I guess you skipped *Black Beauty*."

"Yeah, but I read every one of the Black Stallion series, and *Justin Morgan Had a Horse* and *King of the Wind*, all the Billy and Blaze books, then *Man o' War* and *Comanche of the Seventh, Smoky the Cowhorse*, and everything by Zane Grey and—"

"Hey, have you found that English writer, who does mysteries set in horse racing?"

"Dick Francis! Love him."

His face opened up again, and he matched my smile. "Well," I said, "I've got the latest—*Knockdown*—you can read if you want. I haven't started it yet...kinda put off by the title."

"Hm, yeah, I can see how you might." He twinkled. "Sure, I'd love to. Good beach read for the summer. You can pick from my collection if you want."

"Thanks."

We rode without speaking for a few minutes, digesting our conversation. It actually gave me indigestion, because no guy except Michael had ever confided in me, and certainly not on such short acquaintance.

Shark and Klatawah just churned through the sand with bobbing heads, seeming content in each other's company. Each turned an ear back every time we spoke.

Con gestured at Shark. "How do you like her?"

I lifted a shoulder. "Hard to tell just plugging along like this, but she seems lovely. It's weird, though, having so much neck up so close!"

Con laughed in a way that told me he understood my reference. I normally rode hunters that were all or part Thoroughbred, and thus tall and flat-muscled, who carried their heads low on long necks. Shark's neck arched high, and she tucked her nose toward her chest while lifting her tail. I didn't have to stretch to touch the space between her ears.

I could have kept going with horse talk, but Con jogged forward to finish his check on everyone, leaving me to absorb the horse beneath me and the scenery all around. I took the opportunity to trot for a few seconds to catch up to the end of the line.

The trail had woven through oak and scrub pine on a slowly inclining plane toward the Cape's barrier sand dunes, which opened around us. Voices hushed as the dusk deepened, until the loudest sounds were rustling growth, squeaking leather, and jingling bits. Occasionally a horse snorted or a rider slapped an insect. A breeze, as soothing as the sky's pink and indigo, kept most bugs away.

My back gradually relaxed and left elbow stopped throbbing. I tucked it between my hip and waist, grateful that I only needed one hand to direct. Through it I felt Shark testing my touch with occasional tugs and flicking her ears in recognition of the signals I sent back.

She, like all the horses, was strong from daily treks through deep sand. We scaled the slopes without puffing and lurched down the other sides. Our seats thumped the saddles, but we all identified with Lawrence of Arabia as we spread across the slopes, silhouetted against the fuchsia-streaked sky.

I savored the breeze across my skin and the slanted light that picked out the gold in Con's hair and skin, the white of his eyes and smile, as he moved around on his copper mare chatting with the other riders. He rode with the ease of the Marlboro Man, making me wonder how he had learned the Western seat so well if his life had been spent in prep schools and Ivy League college. He'd only worked at Galeson's for a few weeks; could that be enough? I found the transition from English awkward, as well as some of the vocabulary—corral instead of paddock, lope instead of canter, cinch instead of girth—though perhaps if I rode Western daily and had a bit of instruction, it would come more easily. Or maybe Con was just one of those born naturals, like Michael.

I sighed and pinned my attention on Con to keep it from wandering down unwanted alleys. He caught me watching a few times as he and Miriam funneled the group back into line when the dune dropped to join a trail marked by signs and tire ruts, where bridle path and dune-buggy route shared one official track to the beach. Shark jerked up her head and pointed her ears at a grassy knoll ahead, at the same moment other horses whinnied and snorted. The riders muttered and giggled, unsure what lay ahead.

In answer to our unspoken question, an arm of wind swept over the knoll to salt-tingle our noses. The group scrambled forward, to be blocked by Miriam upon mounting the crest.

"Look sharp and sit tight," she told everyone. "Your horses might get excited at this part. Stay in line behind me, and if you all keep control, we might get in a little trot."

We attempted to obey, falling silent as we beheld a broad, flat beach arching out of sight in both directions, fringed by ocean stained to gold-slashed burgundy by the setting sun. My collar and bandana fluttered as I gazed, while all around me the horses bobbed and blew, straining to be free.

Shark started to rev up like a race car—and Klatawah didn't bother revving, just bunched her muscles and shot off in a spray of sand. Con yelped as he lurched back, but his polo reflexes saved him, whereas I had to save myself by grabbing the saddle horn when Shark dropped her head and leaped after them, searing the reins through my fingers. Around us whoops, whinnies, and hollers erupted as the rest of the herd spewed across the beach like buckshot.

Woo-hoo!

In the space of two seconds, I relived my fall yet again while my limbs scrambled for purchase. I had never ridden as fast as Shark was galloping—wind ripping my bandana off and splaying open my shirt—and I'd lost my stirrups at her first plunging stride. But I found my balance and just let the horse go, inhibition having been blown away with everything else. Nothing mattered except the freedom of pounding across the sand straight into the sunset. Behind me lay a helter-skelter of shouting blurs belonging to another life.

Joy brought tears to my eyes, and wind streaked them across my face. I whipped by Con, who had managed to circle Klatawah and regain control. He spurred the mare after me like a cop after a speeder and ate the distance between us with Klatawah's huge strides. I saw a russet shape encroaching from the corner of my eye; then Klatawah drew even, her nostrils gaping and mane streaming as Con stretched over her neck, urging her on. No chase, I realized, but a race!

Woo-hoo!

This was *not* supposed to happen. From the glance he shot me, I knew that he knew, and was throwing responsibility away for a once-in-a-lifetime moment. I caught the same fever and spurred Shark onward, feeling wilder than I ever had in my life.

We veered toward the water, hooting and pumping the reins. Our horses extended beneath us in their own instinctive race, until the beach dropped sharply into the waves. Shark and Klatawah jammed on the brakes to get their hindquarters under them, almost hopping as they adjusted to the slope and the sudden momentum-stopping water. Con and I banged in our saddles, splashed to soaking before we realized we'd be swimming if we angled out any farther. Our race deteriorated into a scramble back upslope, the horses heaving through the wet, gummy sand to the drained, packed sand, and up over the shoulder to the dry beach.

I reined in, laughing, and met his grin while our mounts blew and bucked in circles around each other. He was waiting to meet my gaze each time our horses were pointed in the right direction, and he held it with equal intensity, all masks forgotten, all words that could be said captured in our smiles. For those moments, I felt my heart beat with his and almost saw something reach out between us and bind us to each other.

But then faint shouts broke the connection and brought reality back.

With a sigh, we turned toward the shouts and saw, far down the shore, that the other riders had stopped their horses and stayed in the saddle, though they remained confused and scattered. Miriam crisscrossed the beach trying to round them up. She paused after each success to holler and wave at us. We looked at each other again, no longer smiling—no longer an *us*—then exchanged nods and about-faced to lope leisurely back along the upper sands.

Miriam waited with a windburned face double-reddened by rage, but she kept her mouth shut. Con saluted her and went back on duty, helping herd everybody back to the leeward side of the knoll.

I drew up where Jona and Dave waited, finding Jona bug-eyed and Dave with hair askew and a grin plastered across his face. His Stetson had gone the way of my bandana.

Miriam surveyed the group. "Everyone okay?" she said, her tone chirpy but edged with steel, her teeth clenched in a smile.

We all nodded and babbled in response. Jona drew her pinto alongside Shark and inspected me. "I couldn't tell whether you were running away on purpose, or being run away with."

"Bit of both," I confessed, trying to appear composed but knowing my skin still glowed and eyes still sparkled and chest still heaved, though my heartbeat was finally settling down. "Shark caught me by surprise when she bolted, but I got back in the driver's seat pretty quick. Just couldn't resist racing when Con caught up."

"And if Con ever does that again," Miriam broke in, her eyes stabbing in his direction, "he'll be out of a job before he knows what hit him!"

"Hey, you said last night we could run on the beach." He was flushed and mussed and fighting to smother a smile, to look contrite as Miriam cracked her verbal whip.

"Only if we had strong riders and everyone was in control. That"—Miriam swung her arm back toward the ocean—"was not control! We're lucky no one got hurt, or a horse got lamed."

Since all ears were listening, all eyes were on Con and Klatawah. He didn't apologize, however, feigning a wrassle with his horse. Klatawah arched and pranced to show she had enjoyed the run just as much as he had.

Shark stood square but kept tossing her head and blowing, jolting the reins in my hand. The other horses had quieted, and they stepped into line without prompting as Miriam waved us back onto the trail. Con sneaked a glance at me before retreating to the end of the line, too far back for conversation. Jona positioned herself behind me, and I rode behind Dave.

"That was wild!" he exclaimed over his shoulder.

"How's your butt now?" I teased in return.

He groaned, while Jona said, "I almost fell off twice! Thank goodness for saddle horns! When I got over having a heart attack, it felt like fun."

"Most fun I've ever had," I said, surprised by the realization.

"Now, don't you get any ideas about becoming a jockey!" Jona chided through a smile.

"No, no, but I've definitely got to rethink what I'm doing."

"Well, that's the point of this vacation, isn't it?"

I didn't answer. My adrenaline had ebbed to reveal the effects of that blast down the beach. Both my shirts as well as my jeans, all cotton, were splash-soaked and sand-gritted so they clung to my skin, clammy and abrasive. My hair dripped down my neck and back like wet seaweed, embedding the chill. My joints and muscles yelled at me for exerting too soon, too strenuously. I appeased them by cradling my arms under my breasts and slouching back in the saddle to lift my weight from the stirrups, letting Shark plod along on slack rein.

Rasping hoofbeats from behind announced Con riding forward. He paused beside me and handed me a windbreaker, then—did I see another wink?—moved on to give Dave his hat.

"Where'd you find it?" Dave cried.

"Right where the trail comes out on the beach. You must have lost it when your horse joined the stampede."

Dave punched the Stetson back into shape, popped it on, and called his thanks as Con advanced up the line offering a towel or canteen to anyone who needed them, and a sweatshirt to one lady who was shivering. He pulled them from saddlebags I hadn't noticed earlier, then paused up front to ride with Miriam. I watched their mouths move and hands flap while I wriggled into Con's windbreaker. It could have held two of me but immediately blocked the breeze and warmed me up. *Thanks!* I sent to him up the line.

"How you doing?" Jona asked.

I turned in the saddle. "Okay. How about you?"

"I think I'm going to regret this in the morning."

"I won't, but walking may be iffy."

"Did you hurt anything?"

I took stock. "No. Overexerted, maybe, but no damage. I'll be fine."

"I wish the house included a Jacuzzi."

"That's at the family manse," Con said as he rode into earshot down the other side of the line.

"Snob," Jona said, chuckling.

He smiled back then held out a bag of cookies everyone ahead of us had dipped into. I grabbed one and shoved the whole thing into my mouth. Con held my eye a little longer than necessary. I sensed he was trying to tell me something, but his mask was halfway back in place so I couldn't interpret his message.

I liked him a lot better without the mask, but this was hardly the moment to say so. It also wasn't the time to ask if he'd ever tried to paint the dark rainbow hues streaking the sky above us, or the strangely purple and brown shadows filling the dunes. Maybe we could talk again on the beach when he went out to run. Maybe even we could ride together again and share the elation—motion—madness we had known less than an hour ago.

More likely, in the morning we'd be discussing our employment options. Waiting tables was starting to look probable.

CHAPTER FOUR

Dark had descended by the time we returned to the stable. Yellowish lights, battered by insects, glowed from poles and roof peaks and inside the barn. People milled in the barnyard waiting for the riders, while Tom and the stablehands waited in the main corral. They reached for bridles as the horses entered and led each mount to the hitching rail, aided by Miriam and Con, who jumped down and tied up their own horses the moment they arrived.

I rode Shark to the corner where I'd found her and slid off gingerly to keep my knees from buckling. Then I tied her and fumbled with the cinch. It loosened reluctantly, and Shark heaved a sigh.

I wanted to fully strip the horse and groom her and give her feed and water, but that was somebody else's duty. I was supposed to walk away. But Tom approached me before I could stagger off to join Jona.

"How'd she go?" he greeted, slapping Shark on the haunch.

"Great!" I pushed some enthusiasm through my fatigue. "And, boy, I can tell I haven't ridden in a few weeks!"

"You're smart to get right back in the saddle."

"Some people might disagree."

Tom laughed. "Come back tomorrow, and we'll talk. Rides go out every two hours starting at ten, then nothing between the four o'clock and the sunset. Between any of the rides would be a good time."

He left to help the next rider before I could answer. Miriam popped up in his place, saying, "He's jumping the gun."

"Yeah, I know." I braced myself for a scolding, if not banishment.

She had untied and now led her horse, as if towing a wagon behind her. He was looking around with interest, no threat of resistance or shying.

"You're off the hook as a customer," she said, "but not if you want to work here."

"I...wasn't looking to work here, so that's not a problem. I'm glad nothing bad happened."

"Me too, but we're short-handed and the season starts this weekend, and Con knows you, and it looks like you can ride."

Good grief! Breaking the rules gets me a job offer? "Um, yeah. You mean work for pay?"

"Sure! Won't be much, but you'd get riding privileges."

"I, uh..." Talk about temptation! Hard to take seriously when all of me ached and throbbed. "Well, I'm supposed to use the summer to recover from injuries."

Miriam dropped her gaze down my front then back up to meet my eyes. "That's right, Con said you crashed through a jump. Wouldn't know it looking at you."

"I'm functionally okay but got a concussion, which is the big question mark. This is my first time riding in almost three weeks, and I'm definitely going against doctor's orders!"

Miriam grinned. "That's the spirit! So do you feel okay?"

"So far, so good."

"Then think it over."

I definitely would. For the moment, I thumbed over my shoulder at Shark and asked, "What can you tell me about that horse?"

"Shark? Not much. Some lady whose kid went to college and never came back sold her to us a few months ago, but Uncle Tom never has time to work with her. She's half Arab, you know."

"I can tell." I gestured at Miriam's gelding. "That one looks Morgan."

He arched his neck as if to illustrate.

"Magician's a Morgan/Quarter Horse cross," Miriam said. "I show him Western pleasure, and barrel race when I can. Not much chance around here, though."

"No shows?"

"No gymkhanas or rodeos! Everyone rides English and wants to jump, or else just clop around like this. The only shows I can find with Western classes are dinky local ones, or too many hours away. Maybe next year. We're hoping to build an off-season lesson business so we can stay open year-round."

"Is anyone here after Labor Day?"

"Not many, but it's worth a try. Whatever we can do to revamp the business. My mother's a Galeson, so it's been in my family for decades but always leased out. The last manager ran it into the sewer, as I'm sure you noticed. You should've seen it before we took over! Dad's letting Uncle Tom and me revive it."

"Good luck," I said, seeing at least two years of work and a whole lot of money to upgrade Galeson's to half the Academy's level.

"Luck we'll definitely need. Dad wants to see a turnaround by Labor Day."

"Good luck," I repeated, trying to sound encouraging rather than snide.

Around us, people were still coming and going with horses. Miriam turned to them, saying, "Thanks." Then: "Let me know." Then: "See you tomorrow."

I swayed in place for a moment, then spotted Dave and Jona wandering around on rubbery legs. Con was too busy to do more than wave as we gathered for departure. Dave drove the Saab home while Jona tilted her seat back and I sprawled in the backseat. He revived us all with ice cream, as the Dairy King on the way home had opened for holiday hours.

Back in the privacy of my bedroom, I wanted to lie awake and think about all that had happened, at least until Con got home, maybe go downstairs and talk with him. But exhaustion again claimed me, for another twelve-hour sleep.

I awoke stiff and sore yet buzzing with energy. This time the sky out my window was a sheet of blue, and the air that streamed in was warm. The angle of light confirmed what the clock showed: Morning was half gone. The others must be sleeping in, too, since no sounds came from across the landing or downstairs.

Faint calls and door slams drifted in from below the house, reminding me that the holiday weekend was under way. I showered then trotted down to the kitchen, where a note awaited me on the table. "We're out on the beach," Jona had written. "Join us when you get up."

She had encircled the note with sand dollars she'd found on the shore and plunked a lobster-claw salt shaker to hold the paper in place against a breeze through the open windows. I paused a moment to look out at the dune shoulder that blocked the house from the town beach parking lot, reflecting on the evening's ride.

Oh, Michael—what you missed last night!

I tried to rerun memory of the ride putting Michael in Con's place, matching it against my old fantasy, but the images didn't mesh. Was that good—a sign I was getting over him? Or had I just been distracted by another pretty face?

Looking at the clock then a "Scenes from Cape Cod" calendar on the kitchen wall, I calculated that Michael would be in the middle of competition right now. That hustle-bustle of a show, that vibrating nervousness and excitement, seemed a million miles away from this sandy-floored beach house. I yearned to be in the barn tent, in the arena, at the same time was relieved that I was not. In fact, if I wanted to be honest, I would admit the relief came from escaping a life that didn't really suit me, not just a disastrous love affair.

I couldn't tell that to anyone, though. Since childhood I'd pushed for what I wanted, following a single dream with tunnel vision, establishing my identity around it...so, to suddenly declare, "Oops! Wrong direction!" without being able to say what the right one was would reveal me as a flibbertigibbet who had sucked down an awful lot of someone else's money and wasted many people's time.

Unable to do any better than that today, I gathered bowl, milk, and cereal and reheated coffee on the stove.

While shoveling in food, I scanned the front page of the *Provincetown Advocate*. It presented a world so far from my norm that it held my attention until the telephone jolted me out of a slouch. Two phones jangled in disharmony, one in the living room and one on the wall behind me in the corner of the kitchen. I stood to stare at it, wondering if I should answer. It couldn't be for me at Con Winston's house.

A door clattered and footsteps thudded as Con sprang from his bedroom and grabbed the living room extension. "H'lo?" He dropped one knee onto the couch while tucking the handset between his head and shoulder.

I watched from the doorway, startled to learn he wasn't on the beach with Jona and Dave. But I savored the opportunity to observe him when he wasn't moving. His shoulders were so broad and sculpted that his T-shirt hung away from his back, the cotton long and stretched out to catch against the muscles of his buttocks. The same cutoff sweatpants he'd worn on the beach rode low on his hips and hung loose over his thighs, which were carved like the rest of him. Bare feet with long toes, bare forearms spattered with paint colors. Gold, tousled hair—a streak of green paint there, too—and a flash of blue eyes as he glanced at me over his shoulder.

"Yeah, hi, Mrs. Eagan. How are you?"

I shook my head frantically with bugged eyes and slashed the air with both hands. *No, no, no!*

Con studied me while listening to squeaky-buzzy noises from the phone. "Yeah, she's here." He held out the handset. "Your mom."

I bared my teeth at him. "I'll take it in there." I stomped back to the kitchen, lifted the handset from the wall phone, and waited for the click that signaled Con hanging up.

"Hi, Mom."

"Hi, sweetie! How are you this beautiful morning? Is it as glorious out there as it is here?"

"Gorgeous." I watched the white lace curtains billow.

"We missed you the other day when Jona called. You were sound asleep."

"Yeah, I've been doing twelve hours a night. It seems to be working."

"You're feeling better?"

"Pretty much a hundred percent."

"So soon! That's wonderful. I knew going there was the right thing to do! How's it working out with your…housemates?"

"So far, so good," I hedged, bracing for the question that was coming.

"What have you been doing?"

I paused, thinking, Truth or consequences?

The residue of last night's adventure still lingered, making me stiffen with resistance. Something in my body—my heart—was telling me a truth my mind couldn't quite hear.

I was tired of lying to my parents, which had started the day after I'd rolled into their driveway on the back of Michael's motorcycle. They had been civil to his face, but thereafter, their subtle discouragement of my equine interests had expanded into verbal objection to my choice of men and career.

Decision sank into my belly. I would tell the truth.

"Mostly hanging around, but last night we went riding."

The phone line vibrated in disapproval. "What?"

I plunged onward, knowing that if I didn't cut the strings now, with a swift, sharp knife, I would shred myself from my family beyond recovery.

"Yeah, turns out Con works at the local stable, and got all three of us in free for the sunset trail ride on the beach. It was fantastic!"

Silence for a long moment, then Mom said, "What happened to taking it easy, to trying new things, to giving yourself a chance to heal? What about doctor's orders? What about—"

"It's okay, Mom. I'm fine. We had a great time, and the exercise has done me good. Tomorrow we're going sailing with Jona's friends, and—"

My mother's voice came through muffled, turned away from the phone. "Joe, she's gotten on a horse already. And Jona went with her!"

A clatter followed as my father picked up in another room.

"What's this I'm hearing?"

Mom and I started talking at the same time, our voices rising. My father broke in. "Put Jona on—I want her to bring you home tomorrow."

"No, Dad! Besides, she's not here."

"Where is she?"

"On the beach. But leave her out of it. She's doing her job. She came along last night to make sure I was okay—and actually had some fun, herself."

"If she won't bring you home," said my mother, "we're coming out there to get you."

My control had been slipping with each sentence, but at that I almost shrieked. Instead, after heaving in a breath, I grabbed hard on my temper and modulated my voice. "No, Mom, please—it's a holiday, traffic will be crazy—wait until the visit we planned in July. We can talk about it then, and you can see for yourself everything's fine."

"I'm not hearing you say, 'It won't happen again'!" said my father.

"That's because it will. I can't not ride, Dad—it's like having my legs cut off or my heart cut out!"

Again the line went quiet, save for a faint sizzling. I couldn't tell if it was static or my parents' rage.

"We trusted you, Linny," Dad retorted. "How are you going to get that back?"

"How about by actually trusting me? You've known since I was born that I'm not reckless and I'm not stupid. I know my own body, and I've told you and told you what I want to do with my life. Why do you want to take that from me?"

"Linny!" came both voices from the other end.

I found it easier to speak honestly when I didn't have to face them. "I'm sorry I can't meet your conditions and live up to your expectations. But I'll be a lot sorrier if I live your life instead of mine."

The pause was longer this time, until Dad said, "This isn't a conversation for the telephone."

"We'll be there this weekend," Mom declared.

"No! We just had the conversation that matters—it's the same one we'd have in September, so now we don't have to bother. I knew for absolute sure when I got back in the saddle last night."

"Oh Linnea, you're barely out of the hospital—"

I shook my head even though they couldn't see me. "And I'm okay. Really. Look, I understand if you don't want to invest in my training; that's your right, and I appreciate all you've given me. But Mom and Dad, I need to be with horses. Work with horses. And ride till I drop. It kills me that you don't understand that."

"Linnea—"

"I'll just keep going on my own. In fact, I think I've got a job already. But please don't make a trip out here just to argue. You won't change my mind."

"Linnea—"

"I'll call you next week and let you know how it's going. Good-bye."

I clunked the phone hard into the cradle then stood staring at it, shaking. *Oh God. Oh God. I've really done it now!*

Con peered around the doorframe. "Everything okay?"

"No."

The phone rang. I jumped, then walked blindly through the house and out the back onto the deck. The phone rang twenty times before going quiet.

I heard Con open the sun porch door and felt him watching my back until I turned around.

"Congratulations," he said.

I glared at him, again unsure if he was being sarcastic or sincere.

He didn't give me a lip-tweak assurance this time. Instead he said, "I wish I had the same guts."

If I didn't have World War III going on inside me, I might have questioned that remark.

Instead I sneered, "What, to shoot yourself in the foot?"

Con sniffed a laugh. "Sometimes it's the right thing."

I pressured him with my stare to explain. He sidestepped by saying, "You really do have a job at Galeson's if you want it. Miriam wasn't mad enough to turn down the help we need. And Tom likes you, wants somebody more experienced than a couple of teenagers who probably won't last the summer."

"I might not last the summer, either." I was already thinking about my friend and former student, Allison, who was working at a cushy stable in upstate New York. "Tom and Miriam are nice people; I shouldn't work for them if I'm not serious about staying. Makes more sense to go home and get my car and live off my savings while looking for work at a serious show barn."

"Or earning while you're looking, and trying something new at the same time."

I stood silent, eyeing him.

He said, "Offer Tom through Fourth of July, and see how it goes. That's only, what, six weeks. During which you'll not only help out a nice guy but get all the free pleasure riding you could want."

That spiked my interest. The one thing I'd missed in the show-oriented life was pleasure riding. I couldn't remember when I'd last gotten out on the trail. Maybe I could enjoy some vacation along with my recovery...buy some time to formulate a solid plan.

I needed that time, because a good plan was crucial. Losing forward momentum, even for a summer, would set me back years. I had started at a disadvantage—no riding until my teens, no pots of money or connections, no local opportunity—and if I didn't overcome it, I'd be doomed to serving the equestrian elite I wanted to be. Even without the current setback, I needed extraordinary luck, or a sugar daddy, or exceptional talent to win championships and prize money. Sponsors invested in the people who were performing outstandingly at recognized shows.

Best I could do now was stop the downward spiral. I'd been considering Galeson's only as a way to forestall losing my savings. Con made me think of it as a step toward reinventing my life.

I had been gazing across the hollow toward the dune crest, hugging my arms as I ruminated, peripherally aware of Con watching my face. "I have to go in about an hour," he said. "Doing all the afternoon trails and the sunset ride again tonight. Wanna drive in with me?"

I looked back at him. His gaze was frank yet reserved. "No, thanks. But I'll come in later. That is, if Jona or Dave will loan me their car."

"Tell you what. Drop me off, talk with Tom, do whatever you want for the rest of the day, then come back tonight. I don't think I can get you into the sunset ride twice, though—"

"That's okay, I don't think I can handle it two nights in a row!"

"—so I'll call you after."

"Okay, but...being weak is the wrong qualification for a stable job, Con."

"Don't worry, we've got plenty for you to do that won't hurt!"

I thought for a long minute. Then: "Okay. I'll be ready in an hour."

Con smiled and turned back to his room. I wanted to follow and see what he was painting, but telling Jona about the phone call had to come first.

She saved me the trek to the beach by arriving on the deck before I had cleaned up after my breakfast. Dave followed a few steps behind.

"Good morning!" they greeted, both rosy from sunburn. Jona added, "'Bout time you dragged your sorry self out of bed!" while Dave said, "Hey, it's the Lovely Lorelei of Race Point."

"Actually," I replied, "it's the black sheep of the Eagan family."

Jona stopped and cocked a suspicious eyebrow. "What do you mean?"

"Mom called." I plunked into a chair.

Jona followed, saying, "Uh-oh. Did you tell her about last night?"

"Yes."

"What did she say?"

I related the conversation. Jona rolled her eyes. "Okay, that settles it. In a way, I'm glad we're over the hump. I'll call them later and make sure they don't kidnap you."

Dave shook his head. "I don't understand what the big deal is."

"Me neither," I snarled, while Jona answered, "It's about class."

Dave snorted. "I thought this was the Age of Aquarius. Peace, love, freedom. Make love, not war."

Jona laughed. "You're a few years too late there, but it follows. Equal rights amendment. Feminism."

"Seems to me," Dave said, "that Linny is doing just fine as an independent woman."

"Not if she's shoveling shit for a living."

"What's wrong with that? People built this country by shoveling shit."

"Nothing, except it's a step backward for people who are looking forward. Mom and Dad have worked all their lives to open doors Linny won't walk through. Now that women can get all the education they want and go for every opportunity, why would anyone not want to? Why seek out pain and filth and hardship? Linny's smart enough to get college degrees and fly to the moon if she wants. They're willing to help her in any way they can—as long as she flies up."

"What they don't get," I said through clenched teeth, "is that it's just as sexist to force women into professions they don't want as it is to lock them out of ones they do want."

"Good point," Dave said.

"Equal rights means people, not just men or just women, all having the same chance. But to Mom and Dad, equal means everybody but their kids, who have to be better."

"Oh, Linny, it's not—"

"Oh, yes it is. You wouldn't know, because you naturally go the way they want. Summa cum laude at Radcliffe! Grad school at Brown! You're going to be the next Jane Austen! Or Margaret Mitchell or woman president or whatever!"

Jona frowned while Dave looked back and forth between us. "Didn't some woman just win a gold medal in the equestrian events at the last Olympics?"

"Yes. And that could be me, if I had the chance!"

The flame in my breast subsided as I remembered how badly I'd blown my first chance at having a chance. Now I had to make another one, more or less from scratch.

"This is why," Jona said to Dave, "Linny's here for the summer. They'd be at it hammer and tongs if she stayed home."

"What I need to do is get home and get my gear and my car," I said. "Miriam offered me a job last night. I'm going to the stable with Con to talk to her and Tom."

"Oh brother," said Jona, turning away. She busied herself with emptying her beach bag and prepping the kitchen for lunch. Dave peeled away after tossing a "good luck" and went upstairs to shower. I followed a few steps behind, needing to not just compose myself but also to finish dressing and gather some accessories in case I stayed out all day.

Jona came upstairs and thumped her bedroom door shut. When I went back down to the kitchen, Con was ready to go. He wore jeans and a chambray shirt with the sleeves rolled up, along with his work boots, and had a canvas-and-leather day pack slung over his shoulder. I was garbed and equipped similarly, and about to go to a similar work environment, but I felt like I was embarking on a safari in Africa or something equally strange and unknown.

But I felt a lot better than I had since months before the accident. I felt like, maybe, I was finally getting a chance to be me—whatever that was.

Con might be the first person to know the new me. I liked that idea and followed him to an orange Mustang convertible with a white top parked next to Jona's Saab and Dave's Plymouth on the crushed-shell flat below the house. I had to smother a laugh. *Mustang.* Of course. What else would he drive?

I'd wanted a Mustang myself since they came out a decade ago, and would have settled for a more practical Dodge Colt; but family budget had given me Jona's hand-me-down Datsun econocar. I would miss it a lot less if that meant getting around in a Mustang all summer.

Hey, who says I have to stay here for a summer? With my dream of being a national champion now off in the stratosphere of unreality, I could move to the Cape if I wanted. Or take off tomorrow and hunt up Allison, or any other opportunity. It would be a lot easier to make a plan with options to choose from!

But first I'd check out Galeson's, see what might be possible there.

Con apologized for the mess as I cleared his black vinyl passenger seat of paperbacks, food wrappers, an empty Thermos and Gatorade bottles, two cameras, multiple towels, sunglasses, crusty socks, and Adidas running shoes. The car started with a throaty rumble and made me jump when the radio blared on. Con hastily turned it down, then pressed a button. The top opened and folded itself back behind the rear seat.

"Cool!" I exclaimed. He grinned, then hooked the four-on-the-floor into reverse and swung around to descend the driveway nose first.

After weaving around incoming traffic to the town beach, we headed for the Mid Cape Highway, also known as Route 6. It served as Cape Cod's spine, running from Provincetown to the Cape Cod Canal, which separated the peninsula from the Massachusetts mainland, then on to the California coast. For our purposes, it was the fastest route to Galeson's.

With air buffeting around the open cockpit, Con told me about his Mustang, a hand-me-down from his older brother, Alex, after Alex had received a brand-new Datsun 240Z upon graduating from college. He too had inherited a house from their grandmother, in Maine, when Con got the house on the Cape, but he was using it as a vacation home for his brand-new family.

"There's a house in my family," I decided to tell him, "that's behind my trouble."

Con cocked an eyebrow but kept his gaze forward.

I continued, having to project my voice above the road noise. "My mother inherited her parents' home and sold it to build our college fund. Then she tapped into it for her own career, getting a bunch of advanced degrees when Jona and I didn't need her at home anymore. Once she started working, I was finally able to get riding camp and some lessons during the school year."

"I don't get it. You mean your mother took your half of the college fund?"

"No, no, it ended up divided by three instead of two. It was still enough to put both me and Jona into any school we wanted. Jona has used up all of hers by going to top colleges for bachelor's and master's degrees. I just did my associate's and saved the rest for showing and training beyond what I could earn from horse-related jobs."

That's where things got ugly, I didn't say. A college degree to work in a barn.

"The one thing we agreed on," I said after a silence, "was to not buy a horse. I mean, the cost of a good one plus boarding and training would buy me years of training for myself. Because I was able to ride lots of different horses through school and jobs, it made sense to wait until I landed a working-student deal and could really focus and know the best horse to buy."

Con's silence made me nervous. Was he pondering what I'd said or had his thoughts wandered elsewhere? Damn that mask, it made him so hard to read!

But then he said, "It makes sense to me, too. Having more horse than you're up to can sure make you learn in a hurry! It can also kill you, or you might ruin the horse. It's probably better in the long run to be able to ride anything, so when you do get a great horse, you can develop together and really go somewhere."

I swiveled to stare at him, so unused to being taken seriously. The flare of surprise gave way to gratitude, a softening which undermined the nerve that had kept me going. In seconds I backslid days by becoming weak again and almost weepy.

Damn it! Too many unexpected things were coming from too many unexpected directions. My injuries might be healing fast, but my internal strength still flagged.

The best I could reply was, "Um...true."

Con slid a quick glance at me. "So now they're backing out of your deal?"

"Yeah." I recovered my poise. "Because of my accident, and...other stuff." I definitely wasn't going to tell him about Michael. "It boils down to the fact that I think equestrian skills and business form a valid education, and they don't agree."

Con made a commiserating noise, then turned into Galeson's stableyard. I looked at it in dread, feeling myself getting sucked further down. Then I hoisted my chin and pushed myself out of the car, knowing I'd be a coward and a liar if I backed out now.

I needed to finish what had happened in the show ring. If I'd just fallen off instead of crashed, I would have climbed back aboard, circled around, and jumped the obstacle.

Now I faced new obstacles, but the idea was the same. I had to get back in the saddle, no matter how different. The alternative was to abandon all I had worked and suffered for, tuck my tail, and return to school to become someone else.

CHAPTER FIVE

My first day employed at Galeson's came right after the holiday weekend. It happened to be Con's day off, which meant I had to go in alone.

My anxiety about it vanished after spending the two days between interview and start on a thirty-two-foot sailboat with Jona, Dave, and their friends. That was so foreign and unnerving, I might as well have been on Mars. Not just the nautical part, but seeing Dave—whom I'd only known as a science nerd, deep into getting his doctorate in marine biology—bare chested and grinning as he worked the sails and helm and anchor while Jona and I, and a woman named Lucy, fried ourselves on deck and ate and drank too much.

So upon entering Galeson's Tuesday morning, I felt almost at home. All that mattered to me that day was having horizontal, unmoving floors and air perfumed with hay and grain instead of a harbor's half-rotted fish and seaweed, spiced with diesel exhaust. Out on the water, it had been fresh and briny; but the inescapable sunshine and wind had dehydrated my skin and eyes.

I gratefully stepped into the stable's shade and paused outside Tom's office. He was on the phone booking rides and waved me in. He'd left clear the same chair I'd sat in for our interview on Saturday. I approached it hesitantly, still worried about triggering an avalanche if I sneezed. Desk, shelves, and walls were buried under schedules, calendars, invoices, barn policy notices, the time clock, and crooked photographs of Tom and Miriam winning trophies in various states. I perused them again until he hung up.

After pulling out a clipboard and adding a family to the four o'clock ride, Tom plunked his ballcap back on over his bald spot and grinned at me.

"You look like a lobster."

I smiled. "I feel like one."

"Good day on the water, eh?"

"Two days. Woods Hole to Nantucket; slept in the harbor, then came back. How'd the weekend go here?"

"If you hadn't been out on a boat, I would have called you. Full capacity, all rides. Nice boost to the coffers. Heck, every business owner on the Cape this weekend was ringing the cash register. If the weather holds, it'll be a good summer."

"Great! So what can I help you with now?"

He extracted a scribbled list from the center drawer of his desk, then put his feet up on the surface in a dent in the paper pile. "Well, until you can lift feed bags, water buckets, and full wheelbarrows, you get all the busywork nobody else wants to do."

I stiffened until he opened, "Inventory. Tack, equipment, feed, tools, meds. Label it all—legible and waterproof—then log the information in here."

He flipped a spiral-bound notebook across the desk at me. I snatched it before anything landslided.

"Then replace all those stained and faded labels on each horse's stall, tack, and card showing their grain allotment. We've got thirty head, and nobody can keep anything straight. Figure out a way to stick the labels on so they don't fall off, but we can change them when we need to."

Yikes, I thought, but then, *Okay*. I was good at organizing and welcomed that over the phone answering and supply ordering and scrubbing I'd expected. My elbow was especially thankful for not having to clean tack.

"I've bought a bulletin board I'll put on the wall outside here," he continued, "so we can post the work and ride schedules. And anything else that everyone needs to know."

I opened the notebook, pulled a pen from my hip pocket, and started jotting. He watched me for a moment then added, "Starting next week, ride one trail a day so you learn the routes and the horses. Someone will help you saddle until your arm is ready."

"Thank you. Can I work with Shark when she's not on duty?"

I crossed my fingers, low and out of his sight.

He kept his promise from the interview. "Sure, as long as you remember that her first job is trail rides. As well"—he pulled down his feet and sat up—"you get Klatawah, too, since Winston bought her yesterday."

I went still in surprise. I had guessed Con would buy the mare but not so soon. Then again, he probably had to save her from getting resold at the next auction.

"Um, okay," I answered, not wanting Tom to know I was afraid of the horse. "What will that entail?"

"He didn't tell you?"

I shook my head. "Haven't seen him in two days. Probably won't until tonight."

"Then just make sure she's fed and watered when he's not around, and nobody messes with her, and she doesn't mess with the other horses. Work on handling her if you dare." He smiled. "Me, I'd just whack her on the head with a two-by-four."

I pretended to think that was funny and asked, "Has anyone fed her today?"

"Yeah, I tossed her some hay when I got in."

"Okay, I'll check on her, and work with him on the specifics. What on this list do you want me to do first?"

"Start with inventory. And break when the rides come in so you'll learn that routine."

He waved me away with a final, "Be sure to clock out for meals and when you leave for the day. I've written you in for starting at ten this morning."

Before he went back to his business, I made sure he understood I considered the job to be a mutual helping out while I sought full-time employment elsewhere, and I might depart at a moment's notice. He claimed he didn't have any problem with that, to the point where I suspected he doubted I'd go anywhere before summer was over.

I wasn't so sure. But there I was, and time to make something of it.

I walked into the barn to orient myself. I could hear two stablehands mucking stalls down the aisle, so I shouldered my day pack, tucked the notebook under my arm, and headed toward them to get acquainted.

"Hi, I'm Linny. I'm new here. What's your name?"

A big-framed, busty girl with dishwater-blond hair hanging in her face straightened from her labors and scoped me sideways. "I'm Priss. Short for Priscilla. Nice to meet ya."

I recognized her as one of the young women who'd been mooning after Con the night of my sunset ride.

She said, "You Con's new girlfriend?"

"Ah, no. I'm staying at his house for the summer with my sister and her boyfriend, but that's all."

"Living with him! Oh, Miriam's gonna love that!"

I felt color rising under my skin. "I think she already knows. No big deal."

Priss ignored me and called to someone out of sight. "Hey, Sylvie, you were wrong—he ain't a fag. The trick is to be blond and skinny!"

That made me steam. Before I could decide how to react, a scrawny dark girl appeared in the aisle and studied me with limpid brown eyes. "He's your boyfriend?"

"No," I repeated, squelching my annoyance with a smile. "Hi, I'm Linny. And you are?"

"Sylvie." Presumably short for Sylvia. I could have picked her up and tossed her with one hand, and I was only five foot six.

The way the girls stared without asking questions or making small talk told me that as new mare in the herd I would have to nip and kick my way into acceptance. So I offered, "Tom's hired me part time to do some paperwork and organization, and help around the stable. I'm recovering from an injury so can't handle any weight yet."

"Then what good are ya?" Priss said, snapping her gum.

I hung on to my stiffening smile. "My job is to make yours easier."

"What, you some kind of manager?"

Priss, I thought, *you are cruising for a bruising*. Should I nip and kick now, or keep trying to be nice?

"No, I'm an extra pair of hands during busy season. Next week I'll be helping you guys on the trails. I understand things start getting real lively soon..."

"Nah, not until the kids get out of school." Priss leaned on her pitchfork.

Sylvie had yet to speak but had been studying me without blinking. "What's it like living with him?"

Oh jeesh. "Don't know—I've only been around a few days, and he's spent most of them here."

"With that crazy horse," Priss inserted. "Which he says only *you* can handle when he's not here. If that ain't lovey-dove, I don't know what is."

I shrugged. "It's just 'cause I've dealt with horses like her before."

Total lie, but at this point I wanted to get out of the conversation without making enemies. These girls were pulling me back into the hassles I'd had after winning Michael.

"Yeah, well, he could've asked me." Priss shot me a glare. "That mare's a peach compared to some I've known."

"Talk to Con, then, if you really want to work with her," I said to her back as she resumed scooping and raking. "For now, where's the tackroom?"

"Over here." Sylvie led the way.

I braced myself for more questions about Con, but she'd withdrawn into herself, perhaps even gotten the message to back off. At least she was willing to be civil.

Once alone in the tackroom, I tilted my head back as far as it would go, mentally moaning, *What have I gotten myself into?*

Then I focused on assessing the room's contents and writing them down.

Horses, I kept reminding myself. This is about horses, not people.

At least there was one interesting person around, who had thrown an interesting horse into my equation. Even if Klatawah was a rogue, she was more honest and uncomplicated than any human. Like Shark, she offered a professional challenge as well as a personal bonus. I decided to introduce myself to Klatawah before any more people.

That had to wait until I'd made some progress on my inventory. Didn't get far before the first trail came in: Miriam on Magician leading a party of five.

I helped tie up horses and assist riders in dismounting. Tom, Priss, and Sylvie then saddled up an additional five for the noon ride while I loosened cinches and slipped bridles on the set going out again, after refreshing them with hay and water. It surprised me no one gave them a good lookover after their exertions, so I took it upon myself to do so—starting with Shark.

"You really like that one, eh?" came Miriam's voice over the fence. She had just returned from chatting with the last of the departing riders while someone else attended to her horse.

"She's lovely," I answered, patting her neck, "but I like them all."

"You might not after riding some of them. We still have a few pigs to get rid of, but we'll probably keep them for the season."

I didn't know what to say to that so kept silent. Miriam avoided my eye and talked on. "I'm still looking for another barrel racer to take back to Colorado when the season's over. Haven't tried her yet." She stepped through the fence and stroked Shark's nose, tracing the white zigzag. "Looks like she went pretty fast the other night, racing Klatawah."

Her smile jabbed like an elbow into the ribs, reminding me how much trouble I could have gotten into but didn't, thanks to her tolerance.

"Yeah, she's got short-burst speed, but Klatawah outran her easily."

Then I realized that was the wrong thing to say. A barrel-racing horse only needed sprint power, not endurance. It did not serve my interests to point Miriam toward the horse I wanted for myself!

"We'll have to find out," she said. "I'll set up some barrels, and we can see how she handles them. You might want to try it, yourself."

"Um, maybe later."

"That's right; you're supposed to be hurt."

"No 'supposed to be'; I am. But improving so fast I'll be helping with trails next week."

"Good! I'm sick of doing so many a day. Glad I'm not on again until two. You had lunch yet?"

The subject change startled me. "No, but I brought a sandwich."

To my relief, she did not insist I join her. In fact, her eyes dimmed as her thoughts flitted to something else. She gave Shark a final pat and turned away. "I've got to run into town, see you later."

Off she drove in a black Camaro. I heaved a sigh and finished my inspection of the horses, then retreated to the barn.

Sylvie and Priss finished their meal break and led the noon ride into the dunes, leaving me to hold the fort while Tom dashed out for his lunch. That gave me opportunity to visit Klatawah unimpeded.

Hoping the phone wouldn't ring in my absence, I walked around back to the pen Con and Tom had fashioned for Klatawah in a corner of the turnout corral, adjacent to the riding corral where I had first encountered them. Beyond it was a round pen for individual work, which appeared to be falling down.

The turnout corral offered shade and piped water. Klatawah had her own little run-in shed, trough, and hay rack to avoid competing with other horses. Or kicking and biting them, as the case may be. She was dozing under a pine along the fence when I entered bearing a brush bucket. At first creak of the gate, her head snapped up, and she tensed for flight.

I clamped down on my nerves and started nattering like she was my sister. She took this in with bugged eyes and pivoting ears. When I got close enough to touch her, those ears flattened and her nose thrust forward as she clapped her teeth. I kept out of range while letting her sniff the grooming kit. Then I selected a brush and started cleaning the day's sand out of her coat with my good arm.

At intervals she swung her head at me, but I held up the brush in time and let her bunt her lips against its wooden back. Or else I pressed my foot against the coronet band around her hoof, or thwacked her on the neck or haunch—anything to create a sting that distracted her when she tried to bite, and avoided touching her head.

I left the fun of cleaning her feet to Con then imitated him by scrubbing the crest of her neck under her mane. By then she had accepted me enough to lean into the sensation, but she let me know I hadn't won her over by pressing back her ears and swinging her head toward me every few seconds. No more threatening with teeth, however. I considered that progress and warmed in pride.

Now I had something positive to tell Con. I decided to quit while I was ahead and get back to my duties in hope of winning Tom's favor, too.

Miriam returned for the two o'clock ride but didn't talk to me. She'd cut it close enough that she had to rush saddling up a boarder's horse—a bright palomino Quarter Horse mare named Cube—then led a group of eleven with Sylvie at the rear. Priss, who worked opening shift, had left upon return with the noon ride. She was replaced by a young woman named Julie, who introduced herself, then ignored me for the rest of the day. She took the four o'clock ride alone, since only four people showed up.

When that trail came in, I grabbed Shark from her rider and settled the mare for the evening. I'd held up so well all day that I thought I could handle untacking her—a painful surprise when the saddle came full weight into my arms. I managed to haul it to the now-labeled rack in the tackroom without anyone noticing my wince and stagger.

Before punching out for the day, I checked on Klatawah, who rolled an eye at me and turned back to her hay.

It felt appropriate to say good-bye to Tom, but he had vanished. During the day it had become clear everyone came and went without announcement, and nobody showed any concern about what I was doing, so I escaped to the Saab and drove back to the house.

Jona was on the deck reading a fat romance novel, a glass of Blue Nun in her hand. The open bottle stood on the round glass-top table beside her, along with an empty glass waiting for me. Lack of a second glass suggested Con would not be joining us.

I swallowed back disappointment. I knew he was home because his car was parked on the crushed-shell pad. Maybe, I thought, he ran in the evenings on his days off. He'd skipped the ritual this morning: His bedroom door was still closed, the beach empty of joggers, from dawn until I'd left for work.

Jona closed her book and looked up with a smile. "Hi. How'd it go?"

I plopped into a web chair beside her. "Pleasantly dull. How was yours?"

"Less grimy, for sure." She looked me over. "I plugged away on my thesis, walked on the sandbars, and chatted with Con when he came up for air."

"Where is he?"

"Last I saw, locked in his room with headphones on." Jona thumbed behind her, at which I came aware of muffled, vaguely musical sounds through the walls. "He's on a painting jag." She filled my wineglass.

"Thanks," I said, followed a moment later by, "That explains it."

"What?"

"I expected Con to be hanging around waiting to hear about my day. But I forgot he needs to paint, and has only one day off a week to do it."

"Or late at night."

"Hmph. With the energy he puts out all day, I would expect him to sleep." I shrugged. "Guess my expectations were off. I thought he put horses first."

"Might be equal weight—he's probably in there painting horses right now. He sure puts more time into them! Kinda like someone I know." She smiled. "So…how'd your body hold up in all that pleasant dullness?"

"Good. Barely sore, aside from straining my elbow carrying a saddle."

"I thought they promised no heavy work."

"They did. It's my fault." I described my actions, then lowered my voice. "I can deal with all that, but then I got blindsided by the handsome-horseman syndrome."

At Jona's raised eyebrows, I explained. "Things might be worse here with Con than they were at home with Michael."

Jona placed down her glass. "What do you mean?"

I picked up my glass and took a slug, not a sip. "Con. He's as good-looking if not better than Michael, and I'm living in his house. The girls added two plus two and came up with us as an item."

"So? Just tell them the truth."

"I did. They didn't buy it. Then Con had Tom assign me care of Klatawah when he's not around, which makes sense to me and Tom but not to girls who have no evidence that I can do anything. Looks to them like special treatment for Con's bimbo blonde."

"Guess you'll just have to ignore them, or quit now before it gets out of hand and do something else. Like, maybe, the original plan of spending the summer with me."

I cringed in guilt, as she intended, then shook my head. "Remember I didn't make that plan. And now, with this one, I can't quit before even starting!"

Jona rolled her lips between her teeth to restrain her words.

"No," I said before she unzipped. "I've got to make lemonade out of lemons. This job will help me get fit while I'm looking for something to replace the Academy. I've lost so much ground already that anything horsey will help."

"Hmm."

We sat quietly for a moment until Jona mused aloud, "What are the odds against two such 'handsome horsemen' crossing your path in a lifetime, never mind back to back?"

"Astronomical!" I raked my fingers through my hair. "It's double unfair because Con and I are a figment of other people's imaginations. At least with Michael it was real."

So real, my wounds were still throbbing and seeping. Our split had been one thing; the preceding two years of jealous glares and false smiles was another. Women of all ages had sharpened their verbal claws on me when not meowing behind my back, some finding sport in telling me about Michael's affairs—real or imagined, past or present—while others attempted to be the next one.

"At least you don't have to deal with the real part this time," Jona said.

I twisted my mouth, not sure whether to be insulted or relieved. I found Con attractive enough to want him to respond to me, but the thought of rerunning the Michael experience made me feel sick.

"It's funny," Jona said, "from the academic viewpoint, that is, that your love life would be a career liability. I mean, lots of people think a woman doesn't need a man when she's got a horse between her legs, or that most horsewomen are lesbians."

I emptied my glass. "Both untrue. The real problem is the shortage of men—at least in the East Coast hunter/jumper world. Out west? I doubt it's the same."

"Rodeo," Jona said. "Ranches. Both very male, with women as an anomaly."

"And racing and polo around the world. But in my corner, men are mainly owners, trainers, judges, and directors. It's so rare to have a guy just working in a barn that one like Con makes girls go cuckoo."

"Then where do the guys who win the Olympics come from?"

"Originally the military, but these days same place as the gals—schools and camps, and upscale private stables. But in camps and schools, which are still mostly separated by gender, we don't get to see them much outside of shows."

It used to be, I didn't add, that men ruled the entire horse world, through war and industry. But since machines had taken over horses' jobs, they had become pets or luxury recreation; realms where women dominated.

The two schools I'd worked for were strictly female, with little trouble unless there was a male instructor. That's how Michael had gotten into hot water. He'd had to switch to boys' schools, but even there some of the young men loved him too well. If not them, then their sisters or mothers, or headmasters' wives...

Jona poured herself another glass and held the bottle toward me at an angle. I slid my glass across the table toward her, and she emptied the bottle into it.

"So what you're saying is that being associated with Con has put you back in the hot seat."

"Yeah."

"Well, if you can't deal with it, then you really do have to rethink your career."

I stood and paced the deck. "Why can't I just work with horses without people making it so complicated?"

"Maybe because...the world is full of people? And people own horses?"

I curled a lip at her. She sneered back. "It's the same everywhere, Linny. Doesn't matter if you work in a barn or an office or a factory or a lab. Just figure out how to manage it and keep going."

I slumped down in the chair and sulked, knowing she was right and not wanting to accept it.

But I did have to consider something that had bubbled into my mind during the conversation. If I went back to the Academy, or anywhere similar, and dove back into the show world, I would encounter Michael. I never wanted to see him again, but how could I avoid it if I stayed my course?

That shifted my thoughts back to logistical problems. If I wanted to stay with horses and didn't want to play the same games, then I would have to change environments and fabricate new goals.

My heart screamed protest, for I'd gotten this far by following a dream, and needed that to sustain me. Approaching life from a defensive position felt cowardly and defeating.

So what did I *really* need, what did I *truly* want to do?

Ride wonderful horses. Win ribbons and acclaim. Have a wonderful man beside me. Earn a living. Avoid nasty people.

Galeson's wasn't going to provide all of those, but it beat working some other minimum wage job or sitting at home or going back to school.

And it was different enough that maybe it might spawn a new dream from something I had never considered before.

CHAPTER SIX

In the morning, I waited for Con on the dunes.

Not sure if he was out ahead of me, already running, or still to come, I stood at the edge of the town beach parking lot adjacent to the house. A bluff rising on my left hid the house from public view, though I could have shouted to it and been heard through open windows.

Below, I saw two joggers on the beach, fading off to the right. At the base of the angled path stomped into the dune face, three families staked their claims with towels, umbrellas, chairs, and coolers. Off to my left, a dog walker headed away from people so he could remove the leash; and beyond him, a lone surf caster waited beside his rod planted into the sand, its line stretching past the breakers.

Then Con appeared from around the curve he had immortalized in his painting. I was sure it was him even before I could discern any features. He jogged easily, reminding me of a horse with his efficient motion.

He grew larger while behind me more cars came in and deposited people with sharp, happy voices and armloads of gear. I debated whether to stay in place and let him run up to meet me, red-faced, like he had caught me on the first morning, or to trudge down the path behind the beachgoers and meet him on the strand, or to slink back to the house and take my walk another time.

Indecision left me still in place when he heaved up the footpath and huffed to a stop before me. I smiled a welcome, admiring his sweaty and muscled physique. He grinned back with, "Good morning! Are you coming or going?"

"A bit of both. Figured I'd take a walk and work out the kinks."

"I'd go with you, but too late now—got to hit the shower." He blew off some steam and shook out his arms. "How did your day go yesterday?"

"Pleasantly dull," I repeated, "with some new-mare-in-the-herd nipping and tucking."

He grinned. "Who won?"

"It's a stalemate," I said. "But you could help me with it."

He yanked the sweatband from around his brow and eyed me uncertainly. "How?"

"Um, by being aware the stable girls have marked you and me as a couple, and doing what you can to discourage that idea."

He laughed. "Shall I beat you and berate you?"

I relaxed, now assured I had not offended him. "No, but please avoid any more things like giving me special privileges with Klatawah, and never be more than brotherly."

He sobered. "I had no intention…"

"Understood." I waved a hand. "But they don't. Con, I want to be friends, but the assumption we're a pair got in the way yesterday, and I've had the problem before and don't want to repeat it."

He studied me with puckered brows, finally drawling, "Oh-kaaaay."

"Thank you." I relaxed, then lightened my tone. "What I really want to say is congratulations on buying Klatawah."

That brought his grin back. "Thanks. Never thought I'd own my own horse. And definitely not one like that!"

I reflected his smile. "What are you going to do with an ill-mannered mare you only ride trails with?"

"Not a problem, since I don't plan on doing anything but ride trails." He paused then added: "And she's not that ill-mannered. She just gets bored and has been mishandled for so long she doesn't know what she's supposed to do. The only real problem is she's a biter."

"Yeah, I noticed."

"She didn't get you, did she?"

"No, but she tried a few times. I think she got over it, and we've established a truce."

I described the grooming session.

He smiled again. "Good! She's already going better under saddle since I put her in the hackamore and started leaving her out at night. Later I'll try her in a box stall—those straight ones might be too claustrophobic. Or she just has too much energy. She definitely calms down once she's been run out..."

"I'll take your word for it."

"C'mon, I'm hoping you'll ride her."

"Maybe, but not until I'm stronger. Besides—" I shook my head.

"What?" he persisted.

"Never mind."

He turned his face half away and viewed me aslant with cocked eyebrow. "You sure?"

I gave an embarrassed laugh. "Yeah. It's just..." My heart was thumping dangerously.

He tipped his head toward the house and started walking. I strode beside him, already tired.

"Just..." he prompted.

I shook my head again.

When we walked up the driveway to the parked cars, he stopped. "Okay, I get it. Riding Klatawah will make it worse with the girls?"

"I think so."

He tightened up. "Sorry. I wasn't trying to start something. I just wanted somebody to cover my back with the horse. I thought you'd be willing."

"I am. And I understand your reasoning. It's just that other people don't."

His face darkened. "That seems to be a common problem."

I wanted to pursue that loaded remark but needed to finish what I had started. "Look—Con, we've got to get something else out of the way."

He put on a serious face, but his eyes had resumed twinkling. I met them with a lift of my chin. "I like you, and I think you're really handsome, and I like looking at you. Can we just take that as given and...move on?"

He threw back his head and laughed so hard it came out a bray. It stunned me to rigidity, unsure whether to laugh with him, cry, or run.

"Oh, Linny." He grinned and placed both hands on my shoulders. "You've made my day. You're the first woman to ever put it to me straight. Thank you!"

"Uh..." I sure wasn't expecting that reaction! "You're welcome, I guess."

"And just so we're even, I think you're an Icelandic goddess, and I'm dying to paint you. Can we take that as given and go get some breakfast?"

"Uh, yeah, sure." *Icelandic goddess?* I felt a bit dizzy as I matched his grin and stuck out my hand. We shook. His mitt was hot and still damp from his run, its long fingers strong enough to crush mine. That power made my insides flutter, especially when he held it back and gently squeezed.

"Deal," I said, not withdrawing my hand as fast as I should have.

We resumed walking. I waited several strides before asking, "So how did *your* day go yesterday?"

He slipped a sideways glance at me. "It went good. I got a lot done."

"Can I see some of your work sometime?"

He shrugged and averted his eyes. "Eventually. Nothing's finished that's good enough yet."

I wanted to say, *How do you know it's not good enough? Can't we judge for ourselves?* but decided not to challenge him. His pinkened face told me he wanted to hold off exposing his talents until he was sure of them. While I could understand that, I was still dismayed he wouldn't trust me.

I reminded myself that this was a guy who'd had to hide horsey books to avoid punishment for being sissy. I couldn't tell him not everyone thought male artists were pansies without making things more awkward, so I segued into a more comfortable subject.

"Okay, when you've got something you want to show, I'm interested in looking. Anyway, I wanted to ask you about Tom. Do you think he'd part with Shark? It kills me to watch her go out over and over with those ham-handed novices. I want to buy her for myself, like you did Klatawah." For now, I'd ignore the fact I couldn't afford her and had no place to put her.

"Hm. I doubt it, at least during season. She's a good-natured, reliable thing and way more refined than Klat. So she'll cost a lot more."

"I figured."

"And not being a hunter type, she's probably the wrong horse for you, if you can swing only one."

I sighed. "I know. But..."

I hated to admit this, but he might be the only person I could talk about it with. "I don't really want a hunter type."

He arched his brows. I braced myself for the "why" but it didn't come. Instead he fell silent, brows now creased while thinking, as we walked around the house to the deck.

"Maybe wait a week," he suggested after we'd dusted the sand off our feet, "so Tom can get a feel for how valuable you are as a worker. Then ask his price and offer to take your wages toward Shark. That'll keep him from overusing her, and make sure Miriam doesn't get any ideas."

"She's already got them. But I can try to beat her to the punch. Depends on whether I can land a job for the fall. What does Tom do with the horses at end of season? I can't believe he'd keep thirty head without any business to pay for them."

"He'll probably hold about ten and sell off the rest. I'm trying to talk him into leasing a string next year, makes things a lot easier."

"So maybe I could buy her at the end of summer."

"Yeah, but tell him your interest now so he doesn't make plans that include her."

I stood for a moment, then said, "I'll have to make a lot of phone calls first."

"Go ahead." He opened the door. "If I see anything too extreme on the bill, I'll let you know and you can pay up."

"Thank you." I smiled and peeked up at his eyes. They were waiting.

"You're welcome. But make sure you can stand working there before you tackle Tom."

"I'm already not sure. But with Shark as the prize, I can make myself stick it out."

I hoped. Everything was so new—my thoughts, the horse, the stable, the people—that I had no idea what was possible. I knew only that, since the sunset ride, my equestrian fantasies didn't involve jumping in arenas anymore. Rather, I dreamed about riding here and jumping there, bareback or under saddle, in the woods, in the spotlight, alone across meadows or with the blurry outline of a man riding at my side on the beach.

The horse in my dreams had become black and curvy-necked instead of ghostly gray with long neck and legs. Whatever horse, I had to find a home for it if I wanted dream to merge into reality. Which meant that I needed a job that would pay for it.

Calling around wouldn't be as easy as I'd first thought—lots of dialing Information, since my address book was at home. I would have to wait a few days, anyway, before calling my best contacts for fall employment, because they would all be in Pennsylvania at the Devon horse show—same as Michael. I wondered who would be sleeping with him now that I was out of the picture.

I suppressed a sigh that would signal to Con there was something more, then lightened conversation until the day's demands split us up.

After that I had little chance to dwell on Michael or any other problems, because work became a consuming routine. With the arrival of summer season, Galeson's business picked up, and daily affairs centered around Con's shining blond virility. He drew the attention of everyone who saw him, staff or customers, male or female. Me too, watching him over the top of my notebook as I went about my tasks.

Sometimes I felt like a researcher comparing Specimen B of handsome horseman against a standard established by Specimen A. The comparison showed, after a week, that the only traits Con and Michael shared were good looks and horsemanship.

Michael had always perked up and moved closer at any signal of interest, be it feminine spark or masculine competition or opportunity for alliance. But Con showed the same friendly indifference to all. His face seemed almost frozen into the mask I'd noticed the day we'd met; always pleasant, always remote, with eyes keenly watching. Men either strove to establish buddy-buddyhood or kept chilly distance, while women minced and lifted their tails.

His reserve struck me as weird; what man could resist a female smorgasbord? Was he, in fact, gay, as Priss had implied? Or was he simply in the permanent defense mode of a person under siege?

His treatment of me—the same smile and helping hand as from a big brother or Boy Scout—defused the girls' focus on me as chosen woman. Con and I underscored it by coming and going in different cars. This was less a ploy than a factor of different hours; his full time to my part time kept us out of commuter sync on most days. I thus had to work out arrangements with Jona.

These proved viable, so I made it to my first Friday with few bad moments. I was sweeping the aisles clear of dribbled muckloads from someone's wheelbarrow when Con stepped close to me in passing and muttered, "I need to take reference shots of Klatawah during dinner break. Will you help me?"

"Sure," I answered, startled but flattered. The supper hiatus was the only time we could be alone. The day's last trail had come in, the weekend's first sunset ride was yet to start, and the other staff was out grabbing something to eat.

Con and I wolfed down the sandwiches we had brought, while the horses munched their dinner or dozed. Shark was still under saddle for the sunset ride, while Klatawah prowled around her pen. Con and I leaned on the rail, studying her.

"So you're not taking her out tonight?" I inquired.

He shook his head. "Tomorrow. Maisie for me, this time."

"I wish I could go."

"Maybe tomorrow night. The ride is full, assuming the weather holds; with me and Tom taking it out, that would be a good time for your training run."

"I hope so."

After cogitating for a minute, Con asked, "Have you asked him yet about buying Shark?"

"No. I'm still trying to get a lead on fall work so I can talk money. Left a message with my old boss, who won't be back until next week, and my friend Allison must have moved—her phone's disconnected."

"Where does she work?"

"Some big stable out Albany-Saratoga way, I don't remember what town. Or the name of the place. It begins with an S, I know that much, and is two words. Shadow Hill, maybe."

"Not Shallowkill, by any chance."

"Could be. You know anyone there?"

"Sort of. An old classmate was son of the owner. I can at least get you the number."

"That would be great—thanks!"

"Meanwhile..." He pushed off the fence. "Let's get this done before everyone gets back."

We entered Klatawah's corral with Con bearing her halter. I followed holding his camera. After greeting and petting the mare, who still flattened her ears at me though she had stopped trying to bite either of us, we swapped positions: I held Klatawah by a lead line, doing my best to set her square. Then I ran her through her paces on a longe line while Con clicked off shots from all directions. Although he hadn't explained his motive, I was certain he needed them for a painting. I also became certain no one at Galeson's knew about his artistry.

The first of the staff drove in just as we finished. First sunset ride customers followed shortly, and the evening duties began. My job on this night was to cover the barn with Tom until Con and Miriam returned with the sunset ride, then learn the routine for closing up. All other hands had the night off.

The next night I got my sunset ride. Tom led on a muscular bay named Big Buddy; Con followed the dozen riders on Klatawah, while I rode Paint behind Tom so he could teach me the trails. At the same time, I was to study how he and Con engaged the customers in general chat or Cape Cod lore, and observe how they enforced the rules in a friendly fashion.

Unspoken was: No galloping down the beach.

We plodded all the way to the ocean. The pace made me chafe but gave my healing muscles a chance to reacquaint themselves with a horse's motion, and learn how to settle comfortably and balanced in the Western saddle. Shark was off rotation for a few days, so I'd picked Paint as the starting point for learning every horse in the stable. He was a nice, sturdy fellow with a choppy stride and strange coloring: black and brown splashes over white, a black tail that looked like it had been dipped into a white paint bucket, and a black face with a white ring around his right eye, which was blue while the other was brown. Almost all the children wanted to ride him.

Sorry, kids, my turn tonight.

Out of the woods and under the bowl of sky, I saw the clouding-over promised by the weatherman. It captured us in a buggy calm in the dune valleys, though there was enough breeze on the summits to blow pests away. We saw the sunset before reaching the water because it painted the overcast. On the beach, fiery streaks seared between cloud banks of deep, blurry pastels.

Most of the guests gazed at the scene as they rode above the swishing surf, or photographed it from stationary clusters while Tom looked on. Con and I held back to savor the glory as we talked.

"Probably going to rain tomorrow," he said, his eye caught by some sandpipers chasing the undertow.

Good timing for my day off, I didn't reply. I felt lucky to miss being stuck in the barn with the girls, or handling sodden, sand-gritty horses if anyone turned up for a ride.

I nodded with a "Mm-hm," not expecting the topic to go anywhere. He surprised me by adding, "Miriam wants to race us on the next rainy day."

What the heck? "Out here?"

I looked away from the ocean to Con's face, already in half shadow as the sky faded fast.

"No," he said. "Takes too much time to get here. There's a bowl in the dunes with a long flat stretch, much closer. I heard her ask Tom if she could do sprints there on Magician against Shark and Cube. Wants to know which is faster, under controlled conditions. On a rainy day, we can take the break and find out."

"If you mean tomorrow, Jona and I are going into Provincetown. I still haven't seen it."

"I do mean tomorrow, if you want to join us."

"What did Tom say?"

"He's the one who suggested Cube. Owner wants to sell her."

"Jeesh. Well, if we can do it before or after my outing, then sure. That is, if I can ride Shark."

"I think we're going to rotate, see if weight and rider make any difference."

"Hmph. There goes my idea."

"What, holding Shark back to make her less tempting?"

Humor glinted in his eyes. I smiled. "Am I that transparent?"

"Sometimes." He turned away.

I was saved from having to respond by Tom waving for our attention. Con acknowledged with a lifted hand and swung Klatawah around. We rode back toward the gathering group.

Before passing into their earshot and out of ours, Con tossed back over his shoulder, "You'll just have to beat Miriam while riding Magician. That ought to take care of it."

Hah! But I liked the idea. What I should do was bow out, but I wasn't at the Academy anymore. Galeson's was proving to be my Wild West, and I was ready for a shoot-out.

We made it back to the stable before the rain started, but it continued through the night into the morning. Just a gentle, annoying drizzle, enough to discourage most tourists but not cancel rides altogether. Jona and I went into town for shopping, touring, and a lobster lunch, agreeing to call Con at work before the two o'clock ride to determine whether she should drop me off there on the way home.

"So you're going to race?" she asked while driving along Route 6A, the shore road into town. This two-lane was lined with color-matched vacation cottages, between which we glimpsed Cape Cod Bay. The Cape itself curled around the bay like a flexed arm defying the Atlantic, with Provincetown as its fist and Truro the wrist.

"Yeah, Miriam wants a backup horse for her barrel racing, so she's setting up a match race between the two fastest and hers."

Jona rolled her eyes and changed the radio station. The latest hit from the Eagles sang out. She said, "I guess since Daddy owns the joint, she can just take her pick."

"Problem is, one of the candidates is the horse I want."

Jona darted a look at me. "Which one?"

"The little black mare I rode on the sunset trail with you guys." I carried on about Shark and my hopes until the shore road divided and we entered town.

Jona took the one-way main drag, Commercial Street, which was passable now that the weekend crowds were dribbling home. It comprised a single lane with houses, boutiques, and galleries crowded up to the roadway, leaving barely enough room for traffic to pass the cars parked along the curb on one side. Pedestrians, cyclists, and skaters still wove through the traffic. Between the elbow-to-elbow buildings, flower gardens were starting to bloom.

Jona parked in the town center on Macmillan Wharf—home of the fishing fleet that had helped build the area. I'd already decided I would like the town better off-season, when the population shrank back to a handful. I wondered how Galeson's or any business could survive three-quarters of the year without tourists.

While disassembling lobsters and dipping them into butter in a wharfside eatery, we mapped out the things we'd do on my Sundays off, with and without Dave. Jona was counting down the minutes to his return.

Then we found a pay phone and called the stable. Tom answered, and when I identified myself, he said, "You're on."

Oh! I hadn't really believed the race would happen. We never did such things at the Academy, or anywhere else I had ridden. Excitement and competition took place only in the show ring.

"I can't believe a manager would sanction this," Jona remarked as we hiked to the car.

"Me neither. Then again, making Miriam happy is part of Tom's job."

"Yet she's the one who objected to your race down the beach with Con."

"That's 'cause the public was involved. This is totally private. Off the clock, out of sight."

"With a boarder's horse."

"I'm pretty sure they've got permission," I said, not sure at all.

CHAPTER SEVEN

We pulled into the parking lot, empty save for Con's Mustang, Miriam's Camaro, Sylvie's VW bug, and Julie's Nova. Tom's old Ford pickup was parked in front instead of out of sight beyond the crooked house that came with the property, where he lived.

"I'm not sure they'll let you come along," I told Jona, "but…we'll need a starter or a timer or something. C'mon, let's see."

The stableyard was as empty as the parking lot, only half a dozen horses saddled up in the corral just in case customers wandered in. Not likely, since the drizzle was now driven by wind. In the barn aisle, Cube stood cross-tied being tacked up by Sylvie. Con and Miriam were outside with Shark and Magician in the back corral.

Julie leaned against the doorframe to Tom's office as he gathered up his stopwatch and rain jacket. She and Sylvie, I gathered, were staying behind to mind the store. I stepped past Julie to snag Tom regarding Jona. He barked, "Ride with me in the truck," and strode out.

Jona gave me a bug-eyed look, then spun with snapping braids to follow him. I last saw her jamming on a vinyl rain hat, her slicker flapping behind. I finished donning my own weather gear and took Cube's reins from Sylvie. The girl fixed her round, dark gaze on me and whispered, "Good luck."

I thanked her and meant it, knowing I'd need some kind of luck to keep Miriam from deciding Shark was just what she needed. My best hope was the chunky gold mare I led out into the wet.

"There you are!" Miriam exclaimed, pink-cheeked and bouncing. "Ready to go? Care to make a little bet?"

Yeah, I thought: If I beat you on any horse, I get Shark.

All I said was, "Yes and no."

"Party pooper," Miriam said, and offered a bet to any takers.

Tom hollered, "Save it for later, Miriam," and finished lowering the tire pressures on his truck so he could drive on sand.

I stepped into my stirrup while Con mounted Magician and Miriam readied to get on Shark. Tom rumbled out the trail through the pine forest, with a blurry Jona waving behind the passenger window.

The three of us followed them, walking then jogging to warm up the horses. Cube had a jouncy trot and carried her head low. As a Quarter Horse, she was built like a dragster—low in the front, big power in the rear for explosive starts and sprints. I expected her to outrun both Magician and Shark.

Con looked cool and virile on Magician, even in a yellow slicker and sou'wester hat. The young gelding's Quarter Horse/Morgan blood made him a nicely balanced, handsome, all-purpose horse sized to suit his nicely balanced, handsome rider. Miriam, in a nylon jacket and a cowboy hat pulled low, had a compact, energetic, feminine form that matched Shark's. I looked appropriate on Cube: a blonde on a blonde.

We rode for fifteen minutes, then turned off the trail when it opened onto the dunes. Tom and Jona waited for us in a narrow valley where the trees petered out but the dunes still contained soil and gravel, packed firm on the valley floor. I couldn't tell its length but guessed a quarter mile. Maybe four horses could travel it abreast.

The dunes sheltered us from the wind, so all we had to endure was drizzle. The horses knew something different was about to happen and danced in place while Tom drove to the end of the valley with his stopwatch.

Jona, left standing in the rain, watched us line up, then counted down and waved us off. Con and Magician leaped out in front. Miriam and Shark scorched after him. I, having never done a fast start before and still out of shape, was left in their sand spray. But Cube must have raced sometime in her life, or else the urge was bred into her. She dug in and shot us forward with her rocket-launcher hindquarters, catching up to both horses before they settled into stride.

They had swerved together, racing shoulder to shoulder, so I had to either go around or push through. *Why not*, I thought, getting bold and stupid from adrenaline, and drove Cube between them like a flying wedge.

We left Con's and Miriam's shouts behind and shot past Tom before I'd registered we were a length in front. *Damn, I should have made that bet!* Cube slowed at a touch, while Magician and Shark had to be hauled back to a walk.

"This is the horse you want!" I called to Miriam, grinning.

"Let me on her!" she called back, jumping from the saddle before Shark had stopped. As Miriam grabbed Cube's reins, I hopped down and went for Shark before the mare got wise and headed for the barn.

Con had already blocked her and dismounted to hold both Shark and Magician. He was flushed and smiling as we swapped reins. I held his gaze, sure he was remembering our blast down the beach on Shark and Klatawah. My already hammering heart did a little kick-skip-jump, but no time to think about it—back into the saddle as fast as we could. We swung aboard our new mounts in sync and jogged back to Jona, the horses snorting and frisking.

As soon as everyone had adjusted stirrups and checked cinches, Jona sent us off again. This time Con on Shark won, with me a nose behind on Magician. Miriam hollered and battered Cube's sides with her heels to keep up. Con, Tom, and I exchanged glances, but no one said anything. We jogged back, swapped horses, adjusted equipment, and raced again.

And again the results shifted: Con on Cube beat Miriam on Magician, with me on Shark behind her. By then, Miriam's grins had downgraded to gripes.

By then, too, the rain had intensified, but Miriam insisted on one more trial with Cube. This time she won, though Con, I suspected, did what I did and checked his mount's speed. We had switched horses again to duplicate the race Miriam had lost on Cube, and came in neck and neck behind her.

Then we headed back to the stable, not talking as we huddled into our hats and slickers. Our jeans and shoes got saturated into a chilly chafe. The discomfort brought an isolation I needed, because the race had pumped me into a frenzy I had to struggle to tamp down.

I'd only let go like that once—careening down the sunset beach with Con—carefree and rebellious. Fun like that never would have been allowed anywhere I had ridden. If I'd grown up with horses, I might have known play on horseback, through Pony Club or 4-H, gymkhanas, or just cavorting with friends and family. I'd met one girl who used to jump her horse over cars when she was ten!

The feeling I'd just experienced in the match race gave me a big, belated clue about why Michael loved competitive jumping. It required a controlled madness far from the staid perfection sought in hunt seat over fences. I had always been excited but frightened when watching jumpers, especially when they were racing the clock. Now getting a taste of sport horse for myself, I recognized how wildness could turn someone on.

Try explaining *that* to my parents!

I had always assumed that thrill would come when I reached the higher echelons of equitation. Why else would people devote their lives to attaining ribbons and medals at the biggest and most important shows? The mastery involved in equitation and dressage was its own challenge and reward, its own turn-on. That was nothing, though, to the zest of running wild and free.

Back at the barn, I snatched Shark from Con, who handed Magician off to Miriam, who passed Cube's reins to Julie. As I untacked and fed my mare, Miriam jabbered to Tom in the background about setting up barrels for more test riding. I whispered to Shark while brushing the sand and water from her coat, "I sure hope you stink at barrel running!"

The mare half turned her head to look at me while she crunched. "If not," I added, "this would be a good time for you to go lame."

She didn't respond to that one.

The leather saddles and bridles we'd soaked needed cleaning and oiling, which kept us there until suppertime. While Con, Miriam, and I tended to that in the tackroom, the others hovered in the aisle so we could talk back and forth.

"Cube's definitely the fastest." Tom recited her times. I tuned out the rest of the discussion, caring only that Shark wasn't the clear-cut winner. More interesting were the looks from Con I kept intercepting—which I also caught Jona tracking. The three of us said a lot to each other without words, and I couldn't wait to get home to learn what those looks translated into.

But that chance never arrived: It was still my day off and Con was on the clock, so he had to stay and close up while Jona and I returned to the house. I had just emerged from the shower, and she had just slid a casserole into the oven, when the telephone rang. I hoped it wasn't Con saying he was going out to dinner with Miriam.

Jona picked up the phone on the fourth ring. I knew instantly from her words and expression that our mom was on the other end of the line.

They chitchatted about the weather while I buffed my hair semi-dry, then Jona said, "Here she is, hold on a sec," and stretched the handset to the end of its cord.

Scowling at her, I took the phone and turned my back. "Hi, Mom."

"Oh, I'm so happy to hear your voice! How are you, darling?"

I thawed. "I'm good. Better than expected. This vacation is really working for me." The truth of that spread through me as I spoke.

"That's such good news! Jona tells us you're already back to work and doing your horsey business."

I shot Jona a look, wondering when she'd had that conversation and why she hadn't mentioned it.

Mom's voice held a bright falsity that normally raised my hackles. This time it brought a lump to my throat. She was trying to embrace our differences—practice what she preached—swallow a painful truth I'd hurled at her. How could I hold a grudge against that? I owed her the same grace and respect.

So I spoke as if nothing had happened between us. "Yeah, it turns out the stable Con works at needed help for peak season, so I've taken a temporary job that I can expand or end as I please. For now, it's just administrative stuff..."

I rattled off a synopsis of the past week, not mentioning our little match race. I could hear my father's breath on the other extension, but he didn't speak.

When I finished, and there was a pause when neither Mom nor Dad knew what to say, I sucked in my gut and said, "I'm sorry I yelled at you last time. But all this is important to me, and it's doing wonders for my health."

Before either could respond, I reported on my headaches (only one, which had lasted only twenty minutes); my elbow (sore as heck, as there was no way

I could avoid lifting and carrying); my knee (functionally fine, though still throbbing from the race); and the fact I'd been off painkillers since arriving.

"That's wonderful! I guess we've overreacted from worrying. I hope you'll show us your stable when we come out next month. In the meantime, you and Jona make a list of things you'd like to do when we're all together."

Well! I would have appreciated a direct apology to match my own, but this was good enough. It looked like I could be myself and still have a family. Losing their money was a small price to pay for accepting each other as adults.

A hot squirt of tears into the corners of my eyes made me stammer through sign-off, then flee into the living room. I sat on the couch below Con's painting and picked up the novel I'd been laboring through—*The Pretty Horse-Breakers* by Barbara Cartland, a homework assignment from Jona to help with her thesis ("Evolution of Women's Roles in Literature, as Evidenced by the Romance Novel: 1740 to 1975")—but the words were a blur.

I closed the book and slapped it onto the coffee table, noticing that the *Knockdown* I'd left there for Con had disappeared.

It irked me to sit there listening for the rumble of his Mustang. *Jeesh!* Already, fresh off losing the love of my life, I was yearning for another guy? I didn't like what that said about me. Nor did I like the fact Con's painting on the wall behind me was so damn good. I didn't want to be housed with someone special and stimulating. At the same time, I wondered if he would paint today's adventure. Tomorrow would be a good opportunity: Rain still spattered against the windows and was forecast to continue into his day off. Maybe he'd even let me see his next work. What did I have to do to earn that trust?

Jona entered the living room bearing wineglasses and a bottle. "Thanks for how you handled Mom. That went a long way." She sat and poured.

I shrugged. "Maybe we can be more honest with each other now. Getting money off the table should help."

I still kicked myself for throwing away that support, but the liberation made up for it. And I now better understood another facet of Michael, who'd never had any familial or financial support. He'd had to get sly and assertive to acquire it from strangers. Adding that to his love for women…

Con's arrival ended that train of thought. Jona pulled out the casserole, and we devoured it while talking about the race and speculating on how Miriam and Tom might handle the outcome. Jona surprised me with her interest in Galeson's affairs. For some reason, today my family had decided to accept what they couldn't understand.

It gave me a glow that didn't last long, for I kept remembering how many times I'd tried to do the same with Michael. Eventually I had learned some things just can't be accepted, understand them or not. I was sure that if I were still seeing him, tonight's phone conversation would not have happened or taken a very different course.

It was my turn for doing dishes, so Con and Jona withdrew to their quarters for the rest of the evening. After drying my hands, I resumed making calls toward finding autumn work. Everyone on my A list either didn't answer or someone told me they weren't available; I got partway down my B list and stopped after multiple "sorrys."

I went to bed with a sigh and lay awake a long time debating whether to cash in my savings bonds to buy and board Shark. Jona and I each had received the same amount at birth, from our grandfather, who was long deceased; and we were supposed to pretend they didn't exist so we'd have them at life's milestones—getting married, buying a house, sending our children to college. Nobody in the family considered buying a horse an important milestone. I couldn't get the bonds without parental cooperation, because they were in a safe-deposit box to which only Mom and Dad had the key.

That was another apron string I would have to cut.

Another sigh led into a string of them that finally put me to sleep.

Back at work, I didn't have to worry about losing Shark right away. Miriam zeroed in on Cube, and either rode her on trails or set up barrels in the back corral to run when off duty. The weather had cleared to sunny and warm, so all rides were full and all of us hopping. I went out with two of the day's four rides, getting to know different trail loops while riding Vanilla and Peppermint.

Con hadn't emerged from his bedroom by the time I'd left for work, but he was out on the deck with Jona when I got home. Both were half reclined in chaise longues, he nursing a beer and she sipping something red in a tall tumbler;

he in cutoff sweatpants again and a T-shirt with the sleeves hacked off, both spotted and streaked with paint, while she wore a white sleeveless polo and a skort. Both of them had bare, sandy feet.

I clunked into their conversation still in dirty paddock boots, jeans, and button-front shirt with the sleeves rolled up. Pulling up a web chair beside the table bearing the sangria jug, I noticed papers attached by clothespins to the back of another web chair, overlapping each other and ruffling in the breeze.

"Hi," both greeted, then resumed their conversation. I caught "birthday" before doing a double take at the pictures and almost dropping my jaw. Yesterday's match races galloped across four watercolor sketches—one from the front, side, back, and three-quarter views, each a different race. I recognized the horses instantly, though the riders weren't as precise. All the sketches caught our general sizes, shapes, and features, however, and the clothes we'd worn.

I looked at Con, who was already looking at me in a stiffly casual posture with half-closed eyes. *This is a test*, I realized. *I'd better say the right thing!*

"Perfect," I declared, meaning it.

"Looks like what I saw," Jona added.

Con's face relaxed. "The question is, Which one to give Miriam for her birthday?"

My enthusiasm waned. I was glad he'd said that before I asked if I could have one.

"When's her birthday?" I said in the same voice my mother had used on the phone.

"Coming up soon," Con replied. "Her eighteenth. Tom wants me to give her a diamond ring, but I'm looking for a way to avoid that." He gave a lame smile.

I stared at him. He held my eye for long enough that I felt he'd conveyed a message, though as usual I wasn't sure what it meant. Jona pretended to ignore us but was covertly watching while she tipped the sangria jug into her glass.

I decided to stake a claim. "Can I have whichever one of those you don't give her?"

He shrugged. "She's not getting any of these. They're studies; I'm going to work up a full painting from the best one."

He ratcheted the back of his chaise upright and leaned forward. "So which of them should I use?"

I sat back. "The one with her winning, of course."

Which was the sketch of her on Cube in three-quarter view, with me and Con eating her sand.

"That's what I thought. Thanks." He unclipped the clothespins and tucked the thick, rippled papers under his arm. He walked inside to deposit them in his lair, leaving Jona and I to figure out dinner.

Conversation over the meal was as stilted as the previous night's had been spontaneous and excited. Something had changed, but I wasn't sure what.

The next morning Con had finished his rituals and departed for the stable before I'd finished breakfast. Jona dropped me off at Galeson's a few hours later and picked me up again a few hours after that. Since the weather had been cool but decent, I'd seen little of Con except where our duties overlapped. But he had left the three sketches he didn't need on the kitchen table.

Jona and I divvied them up. I took the one with me winning on Cube and posted it in my bedroom, and she used cute little seashell magnets to tack the other two onto the refrigerator.

They inspired us to cook up a hot and hearty dinner fit for a hungry man. While chowing it down, Con asked between mouthfuls, "Either of you know a guy from Connecticut who rides a Triumph?"

My fork stopped halfway to my mouth. Jona shot me a look, while Con watched.

"I thought Triumph was a car," she said, all innocence. "As in Spitfire."

"Well, they also make motorcycles," Con stated, still looking at me. I was helpless to stop the blood draining from my face. Carefully, I placed down my fork, keeping my gaze on it, then picked it up again and poked a potato, and made as if interested in eating it.

Jona bought me a moment to recover by saying, "Why do you ask?"

Con pushed his empty plate away and sat back. "Because a guy rode in today and I wondered about him. He was in the barn when we got back from the four o'clock, talking show jumping with Tom. He looked me over real careful. Then Miriam came in and tried to sell him on the sunset ride this weekend, if not her own little self. He said he would try but had a rough schedule between the Devon and Ox Ridge shows."

He waited for me to say something, but the wires in my brain were sparking and hissing.

Jona shook her head. "Doesn't sound like anyone I know." She turned to me. "But maybe that guy you met at your first job? I remember somebody giving you a ride on a bike once."

I flashed a grateful glance at her. "Maybe. But he had a Harley." I shrugged to cover the lie, still unable to look at Con. But I felt his focus on me.

He let the subject drop, thanked us for supper, asked for an update on Dave, then withdrew to his quarters, presumably to work on the birthday painting.

Jona and I remained at the kitchen table, looking at each other through narrowed eyes.

"Well," she said, rising to remove dishes. "What do you make of that?"

What, indeed, I thought, feeling light-headed from my heart pumping so hard.

"All I can think is...who did you tell we'd be at the Cape?"

"Just my own friends, who I can't imagine know him." She ran water to fill the dishwashing tub, swishing soap with her hand.

I shoved back my chair and brought my leftovers to the counter, clunking the plate down too hard. "Well, somebody told somebody"—I remembered leaving a message for my former boss with a girl whose name I didn't recognize, and mentioning that the number was long-distance to Cape Cod—"and he figured out the rest if he's here casing stables."

"Doesn't mean he's looking for you."

The blood returned to my face in a spurt. "Why else would he be here? There's no other reason. It's a huge waste of time he should be spending with his students or training."

With Ox Ridge right around the corner, I confirmed with a glance at the "Scenes from Cape Cod" calendar. Michael had to go to that show—multiple classes for him and his students, points toward a championship, prospects to cultivate for future work.

This weekend was the only time he could ride sunset before then. *Oh no*—I would be on duty. And he would know that, because the staff work schedule was posted right outside Tom's office door on the new bulletin board.

Jona shook her hands and wiped them on her apron, pivoting to lean against the counter. "All right, he's looking for you. I'd've thought you'd be happy."

I balled my hands and paced. "I don't know what to think. I told him it was O-V-E-R. He's done nothing to change my mind. I'll never forgive him for…everything. If he walks into that stable, I should just kick him in the balls!"

I halted and faced her. "Most of all, I just don't want to see him. There's nothing either of us can say. So it'd be a whole lot easier if he just stayed gone."

"Con didn't say anyone actually said you work there."

I shook my head and explained why that wasn't necessary.

"Can you change your schedule?" Jona asked. "Or just quit?"

I sighed. "I can't just quit, you know that. Well, technically I can, but I need a better reason than not wanting to face my ex-boyfriend turd!"

"Mm, you've got a point."

Jona turned to the sink to apply herself to dishwashing. I went silent, haunted by a fuzzy memory of my family mumbling in the background during the first and worst days of my recovery at home. I'd never quite caught the words and couldn't remember a particular day or circumstance, but the ghosts were enough to make me ask, "Are you *sure* he never called or came by after my accident? Are you *absolutely sure* there was never a card or letter?"

Jona's back stiffened, but her tone was neutral. "Not that I know of."

Her hesitation before replying convinced me that somebody had withheld something. That didn't surprise me, but it hurt: frosting on the cake formed by Michael's turnabout. He had paid me back for dumping him by never responding to my injuries that same day, which anyone who'd claimed he loved me and wanted to marry me ought to do.

It bothered me that everyone in my horsey set had known I'd wiped out, but none of them knew anything about Michael. During my convalescence I had managed to learn that he'd been seen in the usual places at the appropriate times, but no one had engaged him in conversation. That was hard to believe—half the equestrian sisterhood tracked him like Mission Control tracked Apollo space flights. And if anyone had seen him with That Girl, they'd not said so. I could understand the omission, even if I didn't like it.

Then again, maybe they weren't talking because everyone knew I was out of the picture and Michael was single again—and the stampede was on.

I gagged at the thought. Then why would he bother chasing me down? To give something back that I left behind? To beg my forgiveness? That was something I doubted I could give.

But I should let him try, if only to find out why he had reversed so abruptly. Only a week before the show, he had wanted permanence between us. For two years until the morning of the show, he had been my mentor and friend. From the way he had made love from day one, I had believed I'd won his heart. Then why oh why had I found him making out with my main competitor, their hands up under each other's clothes?

To Jona I said only, "Well, Con's description was pretty vague…maybe it was some other guy."

Jona slung a look over her shoulder. "Perhaps. There are lots of men in Connecticut who ride motorcycles, and probably lots of those own Triumphs. Probably not so many who ride horses, too, though who are we to know. Go ask Con what the guy looked like, or if he noticed the license plate number."

I cringed at the thought. "Maybe later. I'm going for a walk, try to figure out what to do if he really does show up. Tomorrow or for the sunset or anytime else. I can't have him blindsiding me in front of everyone, when the last thing I said to him was 'Go to hell, you two-timing tomcat'!"

Jona emitted a muffled laugh-groan. She waited until I had left the room before adding, just loud enough for me to hear: "If you don't kick him in the balls, then I will!"

CHAPTER EIGHT

By daybreak, my nerves had absorbed the certainty that Michael had followed me. I lay rigid in bed like a jacklit deer, unable to move out of danger. The feelings I had suppressed broke their bonds and surged to paralyze me when I should have been getting up and ready for work.

But I was stuck in the past. It had taken all my nerve, all my guts and pride and self-respect to cut Michael off, and I couldn't face the prospect of seeing him again. If I looked into those eyes, I wasn't sure I could resist them. I hadn't fought being shanghaied to the Cape because out here on the fingertip of a peninsula it took time and trouble to get to, at a lowbrow Western stable, I could reasonably expect to get through the days without encountering Michael Dixon. Once again, I had been wrong.

If I didn't fight back now, I would be a worse sucker than I'd been the first time. Naïve and stupid from the start. By the time I'd begun showing in earnest, I had heard of Michael Dixon, the sexual prize among women of the northeast A circuit; but I'd never seen him, so had no clue who he was the day I was cleaning stalls in a show barn—supporting other people while still hoping to ride at that level one day—and happened to look up as somebody passed in the aisle.

He had glanced into the stall at the same time, and his zircon gaze had struck me with something electromagnetic and thrumming that had dissolved my will and awoken an animal fire. My mind had locked onto a single thought: *You're the one I've been waiting for.*

The feeling had struck him, too, and we'd stared at each other for a long moment of suspended breath. Then my heart had taken off like a Thoroughbred at the starting gate. I could have thrown down my pitchfork and followed him to the nearest hayloft, leaving a trail of clothes behind—and would have done so had my boss not popped into the stall flapping her arms and saying, "Hurry, hurry, saddle up Trooper! They changed Nancy's class, and it's in twenty minutes!"

That broke the spell. But he had found me two days later, back in my home barn at the Academy. That time, I had followed.

We'd kept it quiet for a few months, but working and training and showing soon exposed us as a couple. I had tried to wear my status proudly, but it seemed the world was determined to punish me for it. Not just lusty women, but my family, who had categorized Michael as dangerous upon first glance and urged me through words and gestures both subtle and direct to move on from him pronto.

Nobody had understood—because nobody knew—that we had a deep and private intimacy that bonded us like welded metal. We knew each other's secrets. We shared each other's dreams. We fit together physically as if archetypes of male and female, destined to mate for eternity. Yin and yang, forming one.

With that resonating in my mind, I couldn't face Con tomorrow. He would surely ask because he had seen my shock over dinner. I couldn't fool him face to face under pressure. I shouldn't have to, because he was my friend; but that queer undercurrent between us would make him want to know and made my distress impossible to explain. No way would I tell another guy about the ecstasy and despair Michael had brought me through, even if he wanted to hear it. It wasn't anybody's business, anyway.

My business was planning what to do if Michael walked into Galeson's. I had no way to know whether he had run back to Connecticut or taken the week off to search for me. Now that he'd found me, would he pass right by upon seeing the juicy plum of Miriam, or challenge me in front of her and Con—Tom—Priss—Sylvie—Julie—the customers?

Psychic exhaustion sent me back into the daze that had gotten me through the night. I heard the thumps and squeaks that signaled Con going out for his run. I had only to keep abed until he returned, then left for work.

That would leave a brief window before Jona arose, so I concentrated on being functional by then. Jona might pretend nothing had happened and leave me be; she might also open the day with an interrogation. As I felt like I had no skin, I could not endure even a curious glance.

That meant either staying in my room for the rest of my life or getting out while nobody was around. Neither was the bold choice of a confident modern woman.

Finally I heard Con come back, run the water for a long shower, and rummage in the kitchen. At last, the Mustang growled to a start and rumbled away. The house sank back into silence. I dragged my limbs under me and slithered out of bed.

To my surprise, my legs held me up. And to my relief, I recalled having arranged with Jona to have the Saab for today's commute. So I skipped my shower and just dressed and hastened to the car, driving myself to the Howard Johnson's on Bradford Street—the two-way arm of the Y where the shore road split into Provincetown. There the chance of running across anyone I knew was nil.

I slumped at a corner table with a book my eyes didn't focus on, and re-stoked my furnace with a heavy breakfast and complete pot of coffee. By the time I arrived at Galeson's, I was externally composed. Inwardly, though, I struggled to remember who I was supposed to be, how I was supposed to act and speak, what I was supposed to do.

Con zeroed in on me within minutes of my arrival. "Good morning," he said cautiously.

I mumbled same, darting a glance at him to see his mask was in place, his eyes asking questions his placid expression belied. In a flash I understood him, knowing my own face showed a similar schism.

"Missed you this morning," he commented when we passed during morning chores. "You okay?"

"Just fine," I lied, and moved away, wondering if his bedroom wall against the kitchen wall had allowed him to eavesdrop last night.

For once I welcomed the separation from him a normal day at Galeson's brought, as well as everyone else's interfering company. The schedule favored me that day: When he was out on trails, I wasn't, and vice versa. Since my hours were shorter than his, I was able to slip away and zoom home when he wasn't looking, though that left me open to Jona. However, she stayed conspicuously occupied, leaving me free to take my beach walk in solitude before dinner.

Then Con came home, and we all stiffly discussed topics unrelated to my affairs. Afterward Con retreated to his room after a suspicious look at me, and Jona withdrew upstairs to bang away at her typewriter while I cleaned up.

The next day, I had to drive Jona to Macmillan Wharf to catch the ferry to Boston. She had previously planned a trip across the bay to visit libraries for research. That left me the Saab, allowing me to travel separately from Con.

He honored my Keep Off signals both at home and at work, even in the car when Jona was back, and Con and I drove in together on Friday. In that bubble of privacy, I waited for him to ask why I'd stopped walking the beach in the mornings. But he didn't, despite the curiosity and resentment I felt pulsating from his direction.

I'm sorry, I thought toward him. It's really nothing about you. Except the fact that you've reactivated what I thought I'd escaped.

I kept hoping he would live up to his looks and act like a hero, insisting I cry on his shoulder. Instead, he was playing tit for tat. *Goddamn him!* I had to admit I deserved it.

Knowledge did not equate power, though; all week, I just couldn't make myself behave as I knew I should. It was as if two Linnys occupied my body. Grown-up Linny, carving her own niche in life, responsibly attending to her duties, investing in her own future; and adolescent Linny, wishing she could go back in time and immerse herself in a lost passion, still hoping it might somehow be refound, at the same time ashamed she had given away her soul along with her body to someone who didn't deserve them.

While these two battled, a third Linny had been running the show: little Linnea, thwarted in all her desires, hiding her thoughts and feelings because they failed to match what was expected of her, turning a cold shoulder to all who offered warmth.

These personas used to coexist inside me. Yeah, they took turns, but grown-up Linny had come to prevail. Or so I'd thought.

Maybe that concussion had done more damage than I realized. Maybe Tom thought so, too, because like Con he pointedly ignored my sudden aloofness. All that mattered with him, I suspected, was that I do my job. Which I managed to, somehow.

Miriam and the stable girls seemed oblivious to any change in me because we chatted as little as possible on ordinary days. But I couldn't fool the horses. They all fussed under my hand or rein, reminding me of how I'd unbalanced my mount at the show and caused the chain of events circling back now to revive my misery. *No—Michael started it.* I had just reacted. Badly. I could blame myself for that, but not for causing what I'd reacted to.

The horses, though, assured me that at least one of my choices was sound. Shark and Paint and Maisie, and Vanilla, Big Buddy, Cube, Peppermint... all minded their simple horse business while loyally, patiently, nobly serving us stupid humans. Even Klatawah did her part, though Con stopped inviting me to help handle the cranky mare. I wasn't sure if that was punishment for my cold shoulder or good sense because my smarts had flown out the window.

His gesture made the point I needed to jab me back into focus. Before handling any of my charges, I started calming and centering myself; and when aboard, I enhanced my awareness of fence posts and irregular ground and equine body language, to prevent ever again driving my mount into trouble.

Meanwhile, Michael's name failed to appear on the sunset-ride reservation list. But that meant little. There were always walk-ins, and the weekend might bring more than usual because the weather forecast was iffy. So all that cloudy Friday I kept my ear tuned for the sound of his bike above the background traffic. It never dawned on me that he would travel in the gas-hogging pickup truck he used for pulling horse trailers. Thus he slipped into Galeson's parking lot with sound indistinct from the muted rumble.

Unaware, I was eating my supper sandwich while watching Con work Klatawah on a longe line. He liked to let the mare buck out her kinks before he rode her, and I always liked to watch. The other horses for the sunset group were already saddled and eating their own suppers. A half hour remained before riders would start arriving, and the forecasted evening thundershowers continued to hold off.

I heard Tom in the barn greeting somebody like a long-lost cousin. Moments later, Miriam hailed me from behind.

"Hey, Linny—"

I turned, and there he was. Miriam was leading him by the arm like she'd won a trophy, cornering me against the fence.

"This is Mike Dixon from down your way. Mike, this is Linny Eagan, our newest hand. She rides hunter/jumpers, too. Maybe you even know each other from the show circuit?"

"That we do." Michael held out his hand.

I didn't leap back screaming when he finally materialized in front of me. The adrenaline shot that had near melted me when I'd turned around had flash-frozen me to ice just as fast.

I gave him a basilisk stare long enough to kill any ideas he might have, then softened into a bored smile, ignoring his hand. "Hi, Michael, nice to see you again. How did you fare at Devon?"

He struggled to hold his smile, the glitter in his eye fading. Before he could reply, Con appeared at the rail behind my shoulder. Miriam turned to him, glowing. "Hi, Con—remember Mike Dixon? He's riding Buddy tonight."

That was my cue to head for the barn and saddle up the big bay Tom used for himself and strong riders. I took the hint gratefully, not pausing to hear Michael's answer about the show. I didn't need to, since he always won a string of ribbons that would decorate his home-barn office. Often something ornamental and silver to go with them.

Striding into the barn, I passed Tom watching the trio through the big open doorway. "Might that be..." he drawled after me, "the ghost you've been looking for over your shoulder the past few days?"

I stopped and pivoted. He held his gaze out the door.

Damn! I thought, scrolling through twenty possible replies. Finally I said, "That's a good way of putting it."

Tom waited a beat then asked, "Anything I should know in case he takes up with my brother's little girl?"

My chest started to ache as my internal ice thawed from the heat of my anger. I doubted I could hold together much longer. "Yeah, I could say plenty, but Miriam can probably handle him better than I could. Just don't try to stop her—that'll only make it worse."

He didn't reply as I continued down the aisle to prepare Big Buddy. The horse was eager to go out and playfully bunted me as I moved around him. I struggled to respond warmly, being fuming inside over Michael's game. He had tried to play straight by acknowledging he knew me, but by doing that publicly, he put me on the spot. He should have tried to approach me one to one, not back me into a corner to see what I'd do. I was glad I had frosted him but not confident he wouldn't bounce back.

By the time I led Buddy out into the front corral to join the string, Tom had joined Michael, Miriam, and Con waiting at the rail. Priss and Sylvie had come back from break. They had noticed the new arrival and were carrying their chests a lot higher while tossing their hair. Both Michael and Con ignored them to watch me tie Buddy at the end of the line then hasten back into the stable. Before disappearing from their view, I looked daggers at both men in lieu of giving them the finger.

Inside, I heard door slams signaling the arrival of more customers. My stomach was threatening to reject my sandwich, so I headed to the bathroom to deep-breathe. When calmed enough that I could risk leaving the toilet, I returned outside to resume my duties.

Tom was collecting payments at the window, while Miriam and Con were helping riders mount. Michael was already on Buddy, pretending he knew how to adjust Western stirrups. I stifled a snigger and turned to the next newcomers, who had been assigned Paint and Rocky. Michael flashed me a look I couldn't read before Miriam scurried over to help him. He gave her his innocently seductive smile, and she transformed before my eyes into the idiot I had been.

When all twelve guests were lined up and ready to go, Con pulled Klatawah out of her corral and swung aboard. I saw his eyes search for me and held his gaze a moment before moving to Shark to pat her rump. The little black mare was carrying a rotund, middle-aged lady who had never been on a horse before. I pitied Shark and wondered if I should make a bid for her tomorrow and gamble I'd be able to afford her upkeep later.

Then I dumped the idea, unsure whether I would even come back to the stable tomorrow. It had failed to provide the refuge I needed.

Neither Michael nor Con looked back as the group moved out. Once they were beyond hearing range, Priss sidled up to me and said, "Oh my God, what a hunk! You actually know that guy?"

Jeesh! Has Miriam told everyone already? "Yeah, we overlapped on the show circuit," I admitted.

Her dreamy eyes hardened to points. "Why are you so lucky, knowing the two dishiest guys on the whole East Coast?"

My anger flared so hot and fast, I almost backhanded her. Enough control remained to squash the impulse, so I merely said, "It just happened. Why don't you take up English so you can be in Mike's life? He'll be out of here after the weekend."

"What, and lose Con?" Priss replied, ramping up my steam again.

I wisely abandoned speech and went back to work. We had thirty horses to feed, water, and bed before we could go home.

I started grooming those who were off rotation and cleaned the stalls of the ones out on the trail. Priss and Sylvie worked on the rest while Tom mucked the corral the riders would return to. Con would have to finish his share—plus Klatawah—after the ride returned. Miriam only had to tend Magician.

Instead of visualizing the courtship dance surely happening between her and Michael while I shoveled manure, I considered a different life for the first time.

If I caved in to my parents' wishes and went back to school, I would find ordinary guys in abundance, especially at a nice brainy college like Tufts, where I could pursue bachelors for my M.R.S. degree while pursuing a bachelor's degree in something academic.

I snorted at my little joke and continued shoveling and raking. When the evening chores were done, I moved to my standing project list to fill the long two hours until the ride came back.

The tasks calmed my mind, but my heart started ka-thunking again as arrival loomed closer. I was at full stomach boil with shaky hands by the time I heard the first snorts and jingles on the woody trail.

Tom, Priss, and Sylvie went outside to meet the riders. I followed, dragging my feet. The lead horse—Magician under Miriam—emerged from the trees into the barnyard dusk, with Michael right behind her. A string of singles, friends, and families followed, ending with Con.

Everyone except Con was smiling.

Tom greeted them heartily, and like an emcee led them into tales about their beach adventure. "No sunset but great" was all I heard, but I observed that half the horses had sand-crusted legs and bellies while the rest were clean and dry. Big Buddy and Klatawah were among the wet ones.

After noting where Michael parked Buddy, I aimed for the horse farthest away. The riders chattered through the dismount ritual, then slowly wandered off into the darkening eve.

I thought I had evaded Michael, but while I was leading Shark to her stall to untack her, he appeared behind us in the aisle.

"See you tomorrow," he said low in my ear, trailing his finger under my jaw on his way out.

My feet rooted to the floorboards. Shark kept walking and got jerked to a stop. She looked back at me with flicking ears.

Michael smiled and snuffed a little laugh. "Unless you want to meet me somewhere tonight and talk."

"We have nothing to talk about," I said, glad the barn light was dim so I couldn't really see into his eyes.

"Yes we do," he said, still gentle and patient, and now trailing his finger down my arm.

I swatted his hand away, my already fractured heart now crackling into pieces. "I've already told you: It's over. Thanks for the memories."

I attempted to tug Shark away. Michael grabbed one rein. "You've had your say, but I haven't had mine. You owe me equal time."

"I owe you nothing. You—"

Miriam and Priss clattered into the barn with their horses and peered avidly at us while shooing the horses into their stalls.

That provoked me back into action as Michael melted away. I finished my task like a robot, then hauled Shark's saddle and bridle to the tackroom while the mare shoved her nose into her feed bucket. I passed Con coming in with Lucky as I went back outside for my next charge. He slid me a look but did not speak.

I finished my chores before he did and drove home in the Saab. Dave's car had appeared in the driveway, but Jona's room had the lights out. I went straight upstairs and into the shower, then closed myself into my chamber for another sleepless, wet-pillow night.

The next morning I waited for Con on the beach at dawn.

CHAPTER NINE

Con faked me out at first, having run in the opposite direction from usual. I gave up expecting him to jog into view around the distant bluff and decided to walk in that direction.

Before starting off, I glanced up and down the beach to gauge the population. That's when I spotted him drawing closer from behind me, splashing through the shallows over the sandbars exposed by the tide.

It was a humid, breezy morning and my hair snapped like a bleached pennant in the wind. I wore a tank top and short cutoffs, showing my long, tanned arms and much paler legs, and hoping he would notice.

He wore nothing more than split-side nylon running shorts and a browband. His contoured body, similarly tanned and pale, gleamed with sweat as he trotted into hailing range. *What a god*, I thought, glad I'd had that conversation with him about his looks so I could frankly admire him. It was a break for him, I knew, to be appreciated without demand.

More than once I had wondered what it would feel like to kiss those lips and wrap myself around that body. But unlike the women who panted after Con, I'd already had a gorgeous hunk to roll around with, and hunger for another had not yet come. The pain Michael had caused just cut too deep. I felt it had become part of my bone marrow.

A new hurt had been layered on last night by how near yet so far Michael had finally come. Even knowing better, I had dreamed he would drop his pride and rush to me, sweep me into his arms, apologize and promise, and take me away—back to the future I'd once believed we could share.

I had accepted the impossibility as soon as he'd walked up to me with Miriam.

Now I merely hoped Con would tell me Michael had headed back to the mainland for good after riding my beach fantasy without me. If he would just exit my life permanently, then maybe my heart could start healing, and catch up with my elbow, knee, and head.

Con drew closer, watching me with no expression change even though I gave him a shy smile.

"Good morning," he said, winding down to a walk.

"Hi," I returned.

We looked at each other through our masks until I dropped mine. "How did it go on the ride last night?"

He hesitated before saying, "You mean, was he an asshole or a gent?"

I flushed. "Something like that."

He dropped his own mask with a grin. "He either rode up front with Miriam or gave pointers to the beginners. Then left them with Miriam to join me with the capable group for a run down the beach." He paused, then added straight-faced: "Klatawah blew away Big Buddy, even though he's almost two hands taller."

I wrestled back a smile. "How'd Michael take that?"

"Like a gent."

I was sure Michael had acted gentlemanly while seething inside. He didn't lose very often. I appreciated somebody showing him up, so said sincerely, "Thanks."

"No problem, m'lady. Your turn to do it tonight."

My eyes bulged. "What do you mean?"

"He wants to ride the sunset trail again."

"Oh *crap*!"

I turned away, half sick, half furious. At the same time, I was relieved, having feared he would come by the barn during the day, or try to lure me into a rendezvous after work. More, I worried that he would track me to the house.

"And this time," Con broke in, "he's going to ride Klatawah."

"What?" I spun back around to face him.

Con laughed at my open-hanging mouth. "Yeah, he wanted a faster horse. I offered him the fastest we've got."

I closed my mouth with my fist to stuff back a hysterical giggle. That led me to a practical matter. "What did Tom say? He won't want the responsibility if someone gets hurt."

"My horse, my problem."

"Stable's ride and reputation."

Con looked away with twisting lips, then back at me with a suppressed smile. "Actually, Tom loves the idea. Just said, 'You'll take care of it if there's a problem?' I said yeah."

"Should be interesting," I concluded. "He won't get much of a race from the rest of us."

"But he'll win," Con said.

"If he stays on," I retorted. "Somehow I doubt you're going to give Klatawah her usual warm-up beforehand."

"Whatever gave you that idea?" Con batted his eyelashes in mock innocence. Then he stepped back into a jog and ascended the dune.

I stood for a minute, lips pursed, trying to decide what to make of this development. It took an entire walk to even form the questions.

Was it a peacock thing, with Con trying to outdo Michael as a macho horseman? Or a gallantry thing, Con trying to protect me—and Miriam—from the attentions of a rake? Did he consider Michael a rival or a nuisance? Or entertainment? Was he working with Tom to humiliate Michael enough to stay away, so they wouldn't have to discourage him directly?

Wondering which head game was in force allowed me to return to the stable and sweat through another day of suspense. Jona and Dave had still been in bed when I returned to the house after my walk, allowing me again to escape without grilling.

I wondered about that, too...was my sister deliberately giving me space to dig out of my own mess, or just wrapped up in her own affair? Either way, I would be in the hot seat tomorrow, on my day off.

This work day was plenty hot—an early-season steam bath where sand dust stuck to skin and the horses were lethargic. I wished I had some lightweight pants, for jeans overheated me despite venting my body through a sleeveless top. Everyone donned hats against the sun, and girls whose hair was long enough pinned it up. Con stuck with his browband and drove the female hands and customers into swoons by going shirtless around the stable and wearing a sleeveless T-shirt out on the rides.

Every ride was full, giving neither hands nor horses relief. Tom instructed ride leaders to use the long loop trail through the trees. That granted shade, but the air was stifling. I ended up taking my two o'clock ride out on the dunes for a bit, in order to catch some breeze.

The four o'clock ride got cut short by a thunderstorm. Thereafter, the sky cleared and air turned fresh, ideal for the sunset ride.

I dreaded it not only because of Michael, but also because I would be paired with Miriam. She and I had not achieved more than civility, but since yesterday Miriam had begun making wide circles around me and watching me through slitted eyes.

I wanted to wear a sandwich board that declared in capital letters: I AM NOT CON WINSTON'S GIRLFRIEND on one face, and MICHAEL DIXON IS A WOMANIZER—DON'T JOIN THE CROWD! on the other.

But Miriam was younger than I had been when I had fallen under Michael's spell, and she lived somewhere on the bayside in a vacation party house. Chances were good Michael had slept there last night, if not all week.

Miriam confirmed this by turning coy and confident when Michael arrived half an hour early for the sunset trail. As before, I didn't hear him drive in, and Miriam intercepted him before he reached the barn.

She led him to the back corral, where Con was waiting with Klatawah. Michael glanced around casually for me, or so I suspected, but I held back out of his sight line as Miriam, Tom, and the hands lined up at the fence.

I had made sure all the horses were ready early so I, too, could watch from the background. Michael and Con shook hands like visiting dignitaries, then Con introduced the mare and explained how to ride her using a bitless hackamore bridle. He spoke in a manner I hadn't heard from him before: half big-shot professional and half guy-to-guy.

Michael listened intently, following Con's face rather than his words and hands. Interesting; normally Michael would have focused on the horse. But this, I believed, was the first time he had encountered a fellow horseman more studly than he was, so he wasn't sure whether to view Con as a peer or a rival.

Their brunet and blond juxtaposition inspired an idea that made me chuckle. Take a good photo of the pair, use it in billboard ad for the stable, then sit back and watch the female customers roll in all year long.

Real customers began arriving, so Tom peeled off to greet them, gesturing for Miriam and Priss to follow. They hung back to watch the moment we'd all been waiting for—Michael swinging aboard the crazy mare.

As with Miriam the first day, nothing happened. Klatawah just stood with flattened ears and switching tail as Con adjusted stirrups. When Michael asked for a walk, Klatawah moved out properly, even easing into a jog for several circuits of the corral.

I couldn't see Miriam's face, but I bet it was flaming. The girl might be a great rider, but she lacked Michael's relaxed weight in the saddle and his calm authority. I recognized and envied both, and my heart gave a slow roll.

Sighing, I headed around the barn to take up my duties. I heard Miriam call out to Michael, "Stay there until we're ready to go, then ride up front with me," as she strode from the back to the front corral to organize the group.

Tom sidled up to me and muttered out of the side of his mouth, "I want you on Big Buddy tonight in case Mr. Dixon needs a ride home."

Smothering a curse, I dashed into the stable and for the second time saddled up the bay gelding for advanced riders. Upon joining the group with him, I saw Tom had added Priss to the ride and put her on Shark. I cursed again.

Miriam was already on Magician and into her welcome-and-rules spiel. Con had released Michael and Klatawah from the back corral, and they hung at the fringe of the group as I mounted up.

Michael sat calmly while Klatawah pawed with one foreleg and tossed her head. He scanned until he caught my eye and tweaked his lips in a knowing smile.

I allowed myself a moment of indulgence, gazing into those eyes and seeing the love I had once believed lay within them. The heat they ignited between my legs made me look sharply away.

At Miriam's command, the dozen customers and we three staff moved out into the pine barrens, single file. I tossed a glance at Con leaning on the corral fence, impassive, before tree trunks blocked him from sight.

Then I focused on the line ahead of me. Miriam led as usual, with her straight back, red bandana, and turquoise cowboy boots. Klatawah pranced sideways behind Magician on a loose rein. A mix of couples and singles followed, held safely back from Klatawah's heels by Beetlebomb, who could never be induced to change his pace. Priss formed the midway point on Shark, ahead of a quartet of teenage girls from the same institution who had grown up riding together. Then came a father and his jittering preteen daughter, with me and Big Buddy lagging behind.

We rode for fifteen minutes before the trees opened onto the dunes. The riders spread out and collectively sighed at the painted sky.

I had been shooting eye-bullets at Michael's back as he chatted with Miriam, so I was first to see the eruption of sand as Klatawah leaped sideways into a classic bronco corkscrew that sent Michael soaring. He thumped flat onto his back with a honking *whoof* as the air was slammed out of his lungs, and Klatawah galloped away.

Horses scattered and riders cried out. Miriam leaped off Magician, closely followed by Priss, and ran to Michael's aid. I, already knowing he wasn't hurt, spurred Buddy into rounding up the rest and assuring them everything was okay, the horse had just spooked, the rider was uninjured. Indeed, by the time I had organized the chaos, Michael was sitting up with arms around his knees and drawing shallow breaths. When he could take a full one, he started to laugh.

"That crafty witch! Waited until the first second I was distracted, and launched me to the moon!"

"Which is about where she is by now," Miriam snapped.

One of the riders bleated, "Does this mean we have to go back?"

"No, no," said Miriam, springing back into the saddle in sync with Priss onto Shark. "You'll get your sunset."

She wheeled her gray gelding to face me. "See if you can catch her. If not, go back to the barn and tell Tom. Mike, you take her horse."

"I can't deprive the lady of her ride." Michael looked at me with a hangdog expression.

"You can and you will—that's why we bring spares. Linny, we'll pick you up here if you're still around on the way back. Same with Klatawah."

"Okay." I kept a stone face as I dismounted and handed the reins to Michael. He took the moment to burn a look into my eyes.

I turned away and headed off after Klatawah's hoofprints. The group resumed progress after two horses finished relieving themselves, and headed off toward the sea while I hiked the other way, up a dune.

Once out of sight over its crest, I could release my laughter. "Perfect, just perfect!" I said to the mare waiting on the other side. Klatawah stood four-square and rigid, looking back over her shoulder with forward-pricked ears. As I drew closer, she dropped her head and shook it so hard her whole neck and mane flapped. Then she snorted and trotted just far enough to stay out of my reach.

But I had a secret weapon: Canada Mints.

Con had discovered early that Klatawah loved mints. He'd been offering carrots or apples as treats after a good session, placing them atop fence posts or buckets or whatever was handy instead of hand feeding, to augment her training not to bite.

She'd bit him hard anyway one day, trying to get through his pocket to a roll of Certs breath mints. Thereafter, he stopped carrying or eating anything minty before handling the mare. But when she was good, he put a few of the big, pungent, pink disks of wintergreen Canada Mints in the same places he'd put the carrots and apples.

And happened to mention the fact to me.

I knew where he kept his stash, so when I'd gone into the barn to saddle Buddy, I had snatched up a box and jammed it into my hip pocket. My foresight met with good luck when I found myself upwind of Klatawah on the dune slope. Instead of pursuing her, I sat on the sand and slowly extracted the box of mints from my pocket. It was squashed, so I squared it up before shaking it. Klatawah's head came up at the rattle, and she whickered with fluttering nostrils.

I tumbled two mints into my hand and held them up to the breeze. Then I bit into one and crunched it with my lips open while exhaling, hoping to emit a minty cloud. I wasn't sure whether it would drift far enough for Klatawah to smell it, but the process caught the mare's attention.

I stood and walked perpendicular to Klatawah's return path rather than toward her, and placed two mints atop the sand instead of tossing them, so they wouldn't roll or sink in. Then I turned my back to the horse and headed for Galeson's.

I was only a mile or so out, so the hike didn't faze me. On entering the gloom under the trees, however, a shadow fell upon my spirit as well as my body. There I was, horseless and obeying orders like a servant, while damn Michael rode the damn sunset beach with damn Miriam. And even though Klatawah had delivered a perfect comeuppance, it had failed to humiliate him—even enhanced his desirability to other women as a hero who had survived danger.

Not good enough. I wanted to backstab him through the heart and scar his soul, as he had mine. But how?

By starving and insulting him. Just walking away. Let him reap what he had sown. All I had to do was keep on walking, straight to the car, and drive away until I found better.

One foot in front of the other. The twilight mile I walked felt ten times longer. It drew me back into memory of another twilight, only a year ago, when Michael and I had escaped the hubbub of a show weekend and withdrawn to the shadows, that time a field edged by woods beyond sight and sound of the tents and trailers. We had made love in the grass beneath the stars in a way that had filled my heart to bursting.

Now it felt like my heart had ruptured and was leaking a trail of droplets behind me. The tears I still needed to shed pressured my chest, sinuses, and eyes. I had to stop and mash my hands against my face to keep the tears from spilling. I was too close to Galeson's; already I could see the yard lights through the trees. If I started sobbing now, I wouldn't be able to stop before arrival. And I refused to halt and let anyone come upon me weeping in the woods.

A muffled footfall and squeak of leather shocked my tears back in as I gasped and spun around. Then I relaxed upon discerning Klatawah's murky silhouette. The mare stopped when I did, equally on guard.

Sighing into a chuckle, I tossed down a pair of mints then wiped my eyes and resumed walking. At least I had done something right!

How much better it would be if I could ride her into the stableyard with everyone watching. But I dared not try, lest I end up on my head or skewered into a tree. It was enough to emerge into the open yard, where light and color still bloomed, and see Con straighten from cleaning the front corral. He put down his shovel and headed to meet me at the back corral, where I opened the gate for Klatawah, closed it behind her, and left a trio of mints atop the gatepost. The mare was lipping them off and chomping as Con came into speaking range—Tom close behind.

"What happened?" they chorused.

I had recovered my composure. "It went as you expected. Klatawah dumped him as soon as we reached the dunes. Knocked the wind out of him, but otherwise he's fine. Miriam put him on Big Buddy, and if nothing else has happened, they should be on the beach by now."

"Are you all right?" Con examined me through a squint.

I looked away to hide my puffy eyes. "Just sweaty and tired. Oh, and thanks for the tip." I tossed him the mint box, which rattled with the leftovers. Klatawah's ears swung toward the sound.

Tom, leaning on the rail, said, "I got no problem if you want to go home early."

I looked at him in surprise, finding compassion in his weary eyes.

"Thanks—I just might," I said, more grateful than he would ever know.

I turned away before Con could cross gazes. It had come to me when first seeing him that there lay the answer to my dilemma. If I acted out what everyone thought was already happening, and became his babe, it would rub in Michael's face that he could be replaced by someone handsomer, stronger, and a better rider, who left just as long a contrail of drooling females.

But that would just be another head game. Besides, Con didn't deserve being messed with, and I needed him as a friend more than a tool for revenge.

He started unsaddling Klatawah, but Tom stopped him. "Winston, get back on that horse and go check on the group. Looks like we got away without any casualties, but there's miles yet to go."

Con nodded and retightened what he'd loosened, and checked the contents of Klatawah's saddlebags. I stood limp against the rails beside Tom and watched.

Once mounted, Con said to me, "See you in the morning?"

"Yeah, I guess so."

"You got a flashlight in them bags?" said Tom.

"Yeah, I'm all set."

He rode off into the twilight. I wondered what dark thoughts would accompany him alone in the woods.

CHAPTER TEN

After another near-sleepless night, I parked myself atop the tallest dune to watch the sun rise.

Its pastel beauty didn't lift my heart as I'd hoped; it was not a new day dawning in a new life, but just a rerun of my old one. I still had the same problems, just in different clothes, in a different place.

My perch was far enough from the house that Con couldn't see me when he came out, but I would see him running. I wasn't sure if I wanted to intercept him, though I was desperate to know what had happened last night.

I had taken the coward's route by going home early. At first I'd been pleased to find the house dark—Jona and Dave still out at the Wellfleet Drive-In—allowing me to avoid conversation and try Con's bedroom door for a sneak peek at his art. The door remained locked, as I'd guessed it would be. I had cursed and gone to bed.

Sleep had swallowed me early, so I didn't hear anyone come in, but then it left me wide-eyed for hours. At the first gray hint of daybreak, I had dressed and gone outside.

Con jogged across my field of vision along the shoreline. I wished I had brought binoculars so I could watch him up close. When he shrank to a dot before rounding the bend, I started my slide down the dune face—defying the rules and coming down from the top instead of the public access.

On the beach I found and followed Con's footprints, which led me straight into his return route like two approaching trains fated to collide on a single track.

"Good morning," he said upon entering range.

"Hi," I mumbled.

"Is it not a good morning?" He cocked his head.

I shrugged. "No different from any other."

He walked past me with a bump on the shoulder to prod me into pace alongside. "I would think this would be a good morning."

"Why?"

"Because you got away without having to deal with your boyfriend, who, as far as we can tell, has returned from whence he came."

My shoulders dropped an inch. "That would be nice."

"Problem is," Con continued after I didn't elaborate, "he may come back again because he got thwarted. What are you going to do then?"

"I'm hoping he got the message and will stay away."

"And what message is that?"

"I, uh—that I don't want to talk to him, to see him."

"Mmmm, I don't think that's the message he's receiving."

"What do you mean? How can you miss 'It's over' and 'good-bye' spelled out in capital letters?"

"You can if you're one of those guys who thinks no means yes. He might believe you're playing hard to get. Like, *Gee, Linny's mad at me and doesn't want a public scene. I'll have to figure out some way to talk to her in private.* And keep after her until she does. Maybe even find where she's staying and corner her there."

"That's—absurd," I said, hearing my voice sounding like a Victorian schoolmistress. Then my pride collapsed. "God, he better not!"

"Is this the first time you've fought?"

"Yes. But it's not even a fight. He did me wrong. I'm not forgiving him. Period. Take a long walk off a short pier."

"I...don't think he gets that."

"Apparently not."

"If he did, he wouldn't have come back the second night. And now he's got to show you how cool he is, not losing face from Klatawah dumping him, the mighty champion, when he thought he was going to ride down the beach with you into the sunset."

"Thank you, Klatawah!"

Con grinned. I strangled the urge to smile back.

"If you want to show him up…" Con suggested, waiting for me to look at him. I didn't.

"…next time ride Klatawah yourself."

My head snapped up, and I halted. "No! I mean…maybe later in the summer." *If I'm still here.*

Already today I had vowed to keep calling my old boss and Allison every day until I caught them, or just steal Jona's car next time she went off for a day with Dave and drive back to the Academy. A trip home would let me collect my savings and back issues of horse magazines so I could read the classifieds, plus have people in my segment of the industry to talk to. That would allow a real effort to get my job back or find another one, and properly start a new life.

"That would put sand in Miriam's eyes, too," Con added, still talking about Klatawah.

I liked the idea but had no intention of setting myself up to fail. I would rather never enjoy the victory of riding Klatawah than risk the humiliation of being bucked off like everyone else. If it were possible to ride the mare in private, I would take the chance. But not in the public arena of Galeson's, and double-especially not in front of Michael!

"Klatawah likes you," Con said.

"No, she doesn't. You're the only human she can stand."

"She followed you back last night, didn't she?"

"That was 'cause of the mints."

Con shook his head. "She wouldn't have bought the bribe if she really wanted to take off, or didn't trust the person bribing her."

"Then she came back because she wanted her nice corral and food. And you."

"I'll bet you can do it."

"I don't want to find out the hard way I can't. Remember, I've already had one concussion this summer!"

We walked a few strides before he said, "Think about it."

I already was. I wouldn't mind riding Klatawah for my own sake, but not for anyone else's.

We walked on. Presently I said, "Riding Klatawah is one thing. Putting up with the garbage I'll get from Priss and Miriam is another."

"Mm."

"That's the girl part of the equation you guys don't get."

"Hm."

We walked for several more minutes before Con said, "So are you going to tell me the story?"

"No."

"Why not?"

"It's too…embarrassing. And none of your business, anyway."

"You're going to have to talk to him, you know. Otherwise it'll never get fixed."

"I don't want it fixed. I want it over." And erased from my memory, but that was something that couldn't happen until it really was over. How rough would I have to get before Michael understood the message?

Con stopped. "He really hurt you, didn't he?"

"Duh!" I snapped, halting a stride ahead. Then, after a hesitation, I turned and said, "I'm sorry. I shouldn't take it out on you."

"What are friends for?" he quipped.

I felt tears prick my eyes again. *No*, I commanded them. *Not now.* Not ever.

"This is more a girlfriend subject, anyway." I resumed walking.

He matched my stride. "I don't get the impression you're confiding much in Jona."

"Haven't had a chance. I'm sure she'll make up for that today."

"What's this week's day-off plan?"

I shrugged. "Uncertain. She's got a list we're working down."

"So you don't need my car."

"No, we'll use hers. Thanks anyway."

We neared the base of the pathway up the dune. I stopped and said, "So what happened after I left?"

"Nothing much. The ride came in, everyone drove away."

"Did Michael leave by himself, or with Miriam?"

"Separate cars at separate times is all I know."

"Did you talk with him?"

"Sort of. He thanked me for offering Klatawah and said he appreciated being reminded that he's slacked off on his training."

I rolled my eyes. "That's rich. He probably won ten classes last week on horses twice the size of Klatawah and at least one of them crazier." I thought of the roan he often rode in open jumping, which could leap tall buildings in a single bound and spent the rest of its time in a frenzy.

"He did mention he has no shows after Ox Ridge."

Uh-oh. That left him a few days before he had to travel. So had Michael actually gone home or was he hunkered down somewhere nearby—hopefully not at Miriam's—and waiting to torment me as soon as I went to work?

"If he comes back," Con said, his tone serious and eye contact unrelenting, "tell him to his face what you just told me. A non-negotiable good-bye. Or else he'll keep thinking he can win you back, it's just a matter of persistence."

I eyed him. "Sounds like you're speaking from experience."

Con looked away and shrugged. "Not really. I've just seen the same things happen over and over. And I'm pretty good at keeping people from getting at me in the first place."

I gazed at him, guessing he'd never had an intimate, long-term affair because too many women had pressed themselves upon him too many times for one-nighters and short, shallow affairs. If he didn't have a voracious appetite, then that would be oppressing instead of kid-in-a-candy-store thrill.

"Better yet," he said before I could think of a reply, "call him and tell him off. That way you won't have to worry about being surprised."

I shook my head, no more willing to call Michael now than when I'd been laid up. He had been the wrong-doer: It wasn't my job to grovel for an apology or take the offensive. I had sent him ice in lieu of fire, thinking it more civilized. If he kept after me, I would switch to fire.

But what I really wanted was for everything to not have happened and to be home in his arms like it used to be.

Jona disabused me of that fantasy the next morning. "So what do you want to do today?"

I shrugged and shook my head at the same time. "Nothing, really."

Con and Dave had gone off to work in their opposite directions, leaving me and Jona to occupy my day off.

"Unless," I continued, "you want to drive home so I can get my car."

Jona groaned. "I wish you'd mentioned that earlier! It's too late now to go and come back in one day. You need to get a decent night's sleep and go to work tomorrow, and I know I can't do a five-hour trip back to back."

"You can always stay over, and I drive back. I really need my car."

"Either way, you have to deal with Mom and Dad."

"Not if we time it right, and they're both at work."

"Oh Linny, it would hurt them terribly if we snuck in and out with intent to miss them. Let's just plan it for when we can both stay overnight."

I couldn't argue, and felt like a skunk. With effort, I mentally combed my schedule to find a comfortable time slot for the trip. "Not until after Fourth of July," I concluded.

"That might work better. Maybe when Mom and Dad come for the holiday, you can talk one into driving your car while the other tows the camper. Then they can continue on to Maine together, and you'll have your wheels."

Still a few weeks away. I didn't want to wait that long. I wondered if one could rent a car in Provincetown or take the ferry to Boston and get on a bus, and how much either of those would cost. There was an airport out at Race Point, but I was pretty sure I couldn't afford to fly.

Jona watched me for a moment then said, "Let's call them later and get the ball rolling. What do you want to do today?"

I snorted. "Something that has nothing to do with men and horses!"

Jona laughed. "No problem!" Then she sobered while we cleaned up after blueberry pancakes and bacon, presently asking, "Does going home have anything to do with Michael?"

"Indirectly," I confessed. "But more it's about independence and flexibility. This job isn't going to last much longer, and I need to get around to interview. I also need some stuff, and to stop hogging your time and wheels."

"I'm fine with that." She poured herself another cup of coffee and sat again at the kitchen table. "So...have you spoken with him yet?"

I joined her at the table and related all that had happened in the past days.

"Oh brother," Jona said when I finished. "I think Con is right: Stop dodging Michael and face up. Get his story, and accept it or reject it. Then move on. Otherwise he'll drive you crazy."

"He already has," I growled.

Jona's face twitched from an obvious attempt to hold back her opinions.

"I just..." I started, but couldn't finish.

Jona plunked down her mug. "Linny, open wounds never heal. You need to clean the dirt out of this one, stitch it up, slap a big bandage on it, and let time do its magic."

"I know. But I can't get out the dirt. I might have if he wasn't trying to keep it open. I can't figure out what went wrong, Jona. We had something really precious. I know he loves me and wants me back. But why can't he—what's wrong with him—that he just can't resist other women?"

"There are a dozen possibilities. It's a really old problem, Linny. You're not the only one to suffer it. Lots of men think it's perfectly normal and acceptable to have one true love then all the dallying they want on the side. They have some mental divider between a personal relationship and a physical one. Some women do, too, but not as many."

"But why?"

Jona shrugged. "Who the hell knows. What you have to do is accept that it is."

"I want to at least hear his excuses," I said.

"Then do that and send him packing."

"I already did! That's the real problem. Doing it again. If I give an inch, he'll take a mile, then I'll be sucked back into his arms and start the whole thing all over."

"In that case, you're right to just blow him off now."

We sat in silence for a few minutes until Jona shoved back her chair and stood. "Okay, let's take it from the top. What do you want to do today? The options are walking one of the park trails, exploring the Audubon sanctuary in Wellfleet, renting bicycles and riding the dune paths out by Race Point—"

"No dunes," I said.

"—going to the flea market in Wellfleet, noodling around Provincetown, going deep sea fishing—"

I half groaned, half laughed.

"—miniature golf, checking out some of the other beaches, visiting Dave in Woods Hole, exploring all the little villages in between…"

"Or staying home with a good book."

"That always works for me," Jona said with a grin.

"And maybe taking a nap. I barely got any sleep last night."

"Fine. Why don't you finish that book you were going to give me a synopsis of for my paper? I was hoping to have three from you by now, but thanks to all your adventures, I've not gotten even one!"

I flushed with guilt. "Okay, we'll stay here and get things done."

First on my own to-do list was making calls while Jona was in the shower. I phoned the Academy office and again missed my boss. On top of leaving the same message to return my call as three times previously, I asked for a good time to call back.

"Oh, any time, she's always here."

Right, I thought. "Do you have her home number?"

"Oh, she never gives that out."

Right. I had the number in my address book—at home.

So I tried Allison at Shallowkill. Con had provided that number a few days ago, but I had forgotten about it while fretting over Michael.

"Good morning, Shallowkill Farm, may I help you?"

"Allison McKenzie, please."

"I'm sorry, she's schooling at the moment. May I take a message?"

I felt a zing of excitement. Finally, Allison in reach! "Yes, have her call Linny Eagan at this number." I enumerated the house line. "I'll be around all day today but only in the evenings afterward, for the next week."

I wished I could take personal calls at Galeson's. But Tom was adamant about that, allowing only brief scheduling contacts or bona fide emergency calls.

Still, I'd made progress. It took the edge off my tension, so I was able to enjoy an R&R day with my sister as if nothing was awry.

Enjoyment faded when Allison failed to call back, and Con neither came home for supper nor rang in to announce his change of plans. I tried waiting up for him but conked out on the sofa. I therefore missed when he did return, tiptoeing past me in the living room. I awoke at the sound of his shower.

The house lights were all off except those illuminating the stairwell and a crack showing under his bedroom door. I guessed he wasn't coming back out, and didn't think "Where have you been!" was good reason for me to hammer on his door. So I retreated to my own room to try again on the morrow.

That opportunity failed, too. By the time I had to leave for Galeson's, Con still hadn't emerged, and Jona was still squinting into her first cup of coffee. I gathered my things and drove away in the Saab. While my mind was sure about how to handle things at the stable, my heart wasn't certain at all.

I got through the first round of chores and the morning ride, small enough to lead on my own, before getting cornered in the tackroom by Miriam. By then the noon ride was out with Priss and Sylvie, and Tom had gone out for lunchtime errands.

"Too bad you missed my party last night." Miriam leaned on one arm in the doorframe with one leg crossed to rest the tip of her turquoise boot against the threshold.

"What party?" I said without turning around.

"My birthday party. Uncle Tom and Con took me out to dinner last night."

That explains it, I thought, but only said, "Belated happy birthday to you. Did you get your first legal drink?"

I turned around to meet Miriam's feline smile. She said, "That's why Con drove."

"Smart." Then I remembered his watercolors of the match race. "Get any nice presents?"

She tapped her head, atop which was a turquoise cowboy hat that matched her boots. It looked adorable on her. "My dad sent me this. Uncle Tom gave me a belt buckle." She tilted her pelvis forward to show me a big silver-and-turquoise piece of Native American design. "Con gave me a cute picture of us all racing. Some friends got me a case of booze."

She grinned. I flipped a smile back at her, thinking, *Cute*. That's all she can say about a personalized painting that's really good? Or so I assumed, since I hadn't seen the finished work and she hadn't put it up anywhere in the barn.

"Sounds like a good party."

"It was okay. Going out to dinner is kinda dull with two old guys."

Jeesh. Con was only a few years older, but to her he was probably a fuddy-duddy. That had never stopped her from draping all over him when opportunity allowed.

She doffed her hat and toyed with the feather in the braided hatband. "But the real party is a week from Saturday. We're combining it with a Midsummer Night's Eve bash."

I was about to say, "That's nice," when Miriam added, "Here."

"Here? Why not at your beach house?"

Miriam shrugged away from the doorframe. "Neighbors." She waved a hand to indicate the Galeson property. "Nobody near here. And since Uncle Tom lives on the premises, we've got a built-in chaperone."

"So a barbecue or clam bake or something," I interpreted.

"Yep. And you're invited, since everyone at the stable is coming. And all my friends."

"Okay, thanks. After the sunset ride, I assume."

"Well, people will be coming in all afternoon, but yeah, once the customers clear out, we can get rowdy."

"Sounds like fun," I lied. "Can my sister and her boyfriend come, too?"

"That girl with the braids? Joanne? Sure, why not."

"She probably won't, but you never know. She and Dave like…new experiences."

That was probably untrue. I expected their many years in college had let them see it all, and by now they found bacchanalian revels boring.

"Thanks, I'll try to stop by after the ride. Is there a rain date?"

"It isn't going to rain."

I bit back a laugh and a snide, *Oh, so you've got an in with Mother Nature?* Then shrugged: fifty-fifty chance she'd be right. Didn't matter to me either way. What did matter was, "Have you invited Michael Dixon?"

Miriam narrowed her eyes. "Yeah, but he's got a show that weekend."

I nodded and turned away to hide my relief and confusion. Con had said Michael had said no shows this month after Ox Ridge. Now Miriam said Michael had one on the docket. Who was lying?

I really wanted to leave the tackroom but would have to either shoulder Miriam out of the way or ask her to move. She straightened and planted her feet, shoving both hands into her jeans pockets. "So...what's with you and Mike, anyway?"

I had known some version of this question would be coming and rehearsed my answer. "We were an item once, but not anymore."

"So he's free?"

"As far as I know, yes."

"Then why did he come here looking for you?"

"Just making sure it's really over, I guess."

"And is it?"

"As far as I'm concerned, yes."

Miriam shook her head. "Boy, are you stupid."

I stiffened and squared my shoulders, flaring my nostrils. If she said that again, I would slap her.

"I mean," she added hastily, backing a step, "he's such a hunk, and he's really nice. Why would you toss someone like that?"

"I'm sure you'll find out for yourself," I said through clenched teeth.

Miriam laughed. "Maybe not. I'm a long way from husband hunting."

"Then I'm sure you'll do just fine together."

Miriam smiled and flipped her hair, then plopped her hat back on atop it. I stood with clenched fists until she cleared the doorway. Then I slumped as tension drained out. Congratulations to me for getting through the confrontation. But it had achieved nothing except to make me wonder what Michael really had on his calendar for the summer solstice.

CHAPTER ELEVEN

Later that week, I finally got through to my former boss.

"Oh hi, Linny, how are you doing?" Betsy exclaimed in a too-cheerful voice.

"Completely healed. In fact, I've been working since I got here. What's going on at the Academy?"

"Wow, you bounced back fast. Terrific! Well, at Devon, we…"

Betsy recited show results and personnel changes. When she ran down, I ventured, "How does it look for the school year? I can come back any time, but definitely after Labor Day."

Betsy paused long enough that I knew what she was going to say. "We'd love to have you back, Linny, but I'm sorry—it turns out your sub is able to stay on, so we're fully staffed for at least the semester. But check back with me over Christmas break—things always change around then. And please—stop by when you're back in town."

I felt a dull thud in my stomach. "Okay, I'll do that. Can I use you as a reference?"

"Of course!"

"And do you know anyone who's hiring?"

"Not off the top of my head." Pause. "But I'll let you know if I hear anything."

Yeah, I bet you will, I said to myself, with an understanding that dropped through my heart like a stone to the ocean deeps. Until I could achieve something as a rider or trainer, I would be a disposable stable lackey. And as a stable lackey living off a pitiful paycheck, I'd have a pitifully small chance to achieve something as a rider or trainer.

The Academy job had been my lucky break. But the school remained an institution obliged to put its business before a stable lackey's needs. I had expected, because the riding department was small and I'd spent years at the school as both a student and a reliable worker, plus had a family connection, that I would be granted a second chance.

Guess not. Thank you, world, for pouring that bucket of water over my head.

But I still had friends, evidenced by the phone ringing while I sat there, cheek stretched against the heel of my hand. More from reflex than any hope, I picked up the receiver.

"Hey Linny!" came Allison's cheerful voice.

"Allison! Great to hear from you!"

"You, too. Sorry I haven't returned your calls—I moved, and have been too busy to remember everyone I needed to tell."

Didn't matter; she was here now and already lifting my spirits. We launched into updates covering the two years since we had last seen each other. Allison had been one of my first students at my first job during college. She had graduated a year ago and gotten her own first job at Shallowkill Farm, a plush hunter/jumper stable in the Hudson Valley region of New York.

"And I finally got my own horse!" she exclaimed.

I made happy noises then asked, "What is he?"

"She. A big dappled-gray Thoroughbred mare. Eleven years old. Never raced, never bred, but lots of show experience. She's teaching me more than my trainer!"

"What's her name?"

"Her registered name is Tricky Sister, but I call her Trix."

"I'm so happy for you! Can't wait to see her. I'm working on getting my own horse, but can't put out an offer until I secure a means to keep her."

I recounted the short version of my Galeson's and Shark story and brought the subject back around to the possibility of working at Shallowkill.

Allison said, "You'll have no problem getting a barn job here on short notice because we have an awful time keeping people." She lowered her voice. "The barn manager is a terror. Those of us with our own horses get a board and lesson deal that makes it worthwhile, but Caryl's attitude spills over onto the other staff and chases them off."

"Ugh, just what I don't need!"

"But it's a great place if you can tune her out and stay on her good side. All depends on how bad you need a job, eh?"

"Well, I don't need one until fall, though I'd love to have a new one tomorrow. Should I send a résumé right now or later?"

"Might as well send it now. If something comes up before fall, can you quit without a problem?"

"Yes."

"Then do it. Oh Linny, it would be so great to ride with you again!"

I thought so, too, and that evening borrowed Jona's typewriter to create a new résumé. I had to fiddle a bit to make Galeson's look better than it was without lying, aided by Jona. I retyped it with no errors using a carbon so I could make a clean master later for copying.

"Is there a print shop in Provincetown?" I asked Con on the way to work.

We were driving in together that day, and I had requested leaving a few minutes early so we could swing by the post office. There was no mailbox at the house, and I dared not leave my letters in the office outbox at Galeson's.

"I don't know." He nodded at the stamped envelope in my hand. "A Dear John letter to Mike Baby?"

I shot him a slitty glance. "No, a lead for autumn work at that Shallowkill Farm you gave me the number for."

His brow puckered while his lips smiled. "You hooked up with your friend?"

"Yeah." I told him what Allison had said, concluding, "Working there would put me back on track, and give me a place to take Shark."

Con shook his head but didn't speak. I added, "I'm not going to talk to Tom about her until I hear something back. They might just say 'go away.'"

He nodded and changed the subject. "You going to the Midsummer's Eve party?"

"Maybe." I shrugged. "A token stop-in, I guess. Miriam did invite me directly, so it would be rude to ignore her."

"True. What about Jona?"

I laughed. "She threw back her head and hooted, saying 'Let's see. Saturday night in bed with Dave, or being bored half to death by a bunch of stoned kids playing music too loud. Tough choice!'"

"Heck, I'd rather spend Saturday night in bed with Dave, myself, if it's that bad!"

I grinned at his grin. Then I sobered. "So you're not going?"

He matched my expression. "I didn't say that. Of course I'm going. It's my job."

"Hm, I didn't think of it that way."

"You don't have Keep Miriam Out of Trouble on your duty list."

"True. Right. So we'd better not go to the party together. I'm sure Jona will let me have the Saab that day. Oh, by the way—"

I told him about the plan for my parents to come to the Cape with my own car the day before the Fourth of July holiday weekend.

"That'll help," Con said, his voice turning sullen and mask sliding into place.

I looked at him in question, wondering what I'd said to make him withdraw, but he kept his gaze on the road.

I returned my own gaze forward and sighed. It had been nice, for a few minutes, being the girl in the jazzy convertible with the handsome rich guy, cruising the streets of a summer resort town with everyone watching us pass. In truth, we were just roommate-friends and colleagues, stopping at the post office on our way to work.

Remember that, Eagan. You already have man troubles enough!

At least Michael was out of the picture for the rest of the week, thanks to the Ox Ridge horse show. Knowing I should be there with him didn't hurt as much as it used to. More, I was relieved at being able to ride the weekend sunset trails without having to worry about him.

On Friday night, Con and I were paired to lead, and we had a good group so were able to race all together along the shore. The reckless freedom again pulled a smile from my heart I couldn't stop; but this time Con's expression didn't match. His own smile faded too fast, and during the gallop he had driven

Klatawah to pull far ahead and spray sand and water in everyone's faces. On the way back, he flirted with a cute redhead who was one of Miriam's friends.

Huh? What brought that on? Con had been nothing if not consistent in his conduct at work.

He didn't follow up with the girl, however, and resumed his normal neutrality to all upon return to the stable. I didn't buy it; and in watching him over the following days, I found his mask so obvious from across the stableyard that I couldn't believe nobody else noticed. At home he became politely monosyllabic during meals—Jona noticed that one—and locked himself in his room the rest of the time. He even stopped his morning runs on the beach.

He might as well have been a mirror, showing me the male version of myself after being poleaxed by Michael's return. What the heck had done it to Con? And should I react as he had, giving me space when I'd wanted him to shake me by the shoulders, then bear-hug me in strong arms? Or should I make a grand gesture instead, hoping he didn't really want space?

If he were a woman, I would have just asked what was wrong. But he was a guy who'd given me enough mixed signals that I worried about stepping on a landmine if I got too close. Having sent out more than a few mixed signals, myself, I felt no right to confront him.

Someone had once told me that women and men could not be platonic friends after puberty, and I had not believed them. Now I suspected they might be right.

So I gave him back what he had given me: many covert looks, one attempt at a direct inquiry (rebuffed), then pretense that everything was normal. We went on that way until three days before Miriam's party, when it started to rain.

And rain. So much rain that ride attendance went to zero, and Tom started to sweat fear. I worked up a sweat of my own by cleaning tack and grooming until my weak elbow got inflamed. A break came when Miriam set up barrels in the back corral and informed me, Tom, and Con that it was time to test Shark, Cube, and Klatawah against Magician.

"Oh man, in the rain?" I griped, followed by, "I've never run barrels before, no fair."

"You don't have to," Miriam said. "Just hold the horses in between."

"You're not riding Klatawah," Con stated. We all turned to look at him. His face was flat and eyes on Miriam, with a quick dart toward me then away.

"But she's the benchmark," Miriam whined.

"And you couldn't stay on her for ten seconds," he returned.

"That was weeks ago. You've done a great job settling her. I'm sure—"

"Forget it. If you want a benchmark, I'll ride her for time."

"Have you ever run barrels before?"

"No."

"Well—" Miriam punched her hands onto her hips and stomped away to get Magician. Tom nodded at Con, who left to throw a saddle on his mare.

And that kills any chance I'll ever have to ride Klatawah. Damn! I should have accepted Con's offer to ride the mare back when he made it; now I would deserve all the trouble I got if I ever hopped on Klatawah—and stayed there—in front of Miriam.

Just as well, I supposed. Time to remember that this was a job, and my task was to tack up Cube and Shark.

Outside, rain peppered the roof and trees. It sounded heavier than it actually was and drained through the sand so that footing was surprisingly secure in the corral. The sand was well packed yet soft without being slithery, and we agreed that conditions were safe for a fast pace with sharp turns.

To emulate a real barrel race at a rodeo, we lined up the horses outside the corral and swung its gate wide open so Miriam could get a running start to the timing line. Tom manned the stopwatch, while I held Shark and Cube. Con jogged around the yard on Klatawah, who had gotten spooky when she saw the barrels. Somewhere in her past either a barrel or someone associated with it had given her an experience she refused to forget.

Miriam went first on Magician to set her own baseline. It took half a minute for them to run the cloverleaf pattern at full tilt. Miriam seemed attached to the saddle by only her tailbone, arms and legs flying as she impelled the horse and managed her constantly shifting balance; Magician bunched and reached and swung around, ears flat and nostrils gaping, exploding into a sprint back through the gate as Miriam pumped him and yee-hawed.

Tom had to yell out the time over our whooping and clapping. Only after it quieted did I notice the rain. Then I forgot it again to trade off Cube for Magician, walking him to cool while leading Shark on my other side. Miriam reentered the corral at an easy shuffle to let Cube investigate the new scene. Nobody knew if she or Shark had run barrels before.

Apparently Cube had: Her time was fractions of a second behind Magician. Shark, who got the same warm-up, surprised us all by splitting the difference. Before I could worry about this, Klatawah showed us how it was supposed to be done by beating Magician soundly. Con could have been racing barrels since kindergarten. He made me want to take up polo so I could develop a seat that good.

Afterward we cleaned up and wound down just like after the match race. The excitement had restored us all to good spirits, and for the first time I felt like I belonged to the crew and was glad I had taken the job.

That warmth chilled when Miriam and Tom started talking about the party. That brought my thoughts out of the moment and into the morrow, reminding me that Michael remained unaccounted for.

A poster I had seen sometime in the past year sprang to mind: If you love something, set it free. If it comes back, it's yours; if not, it never was.

Well, "it" had come back, then disappeared again, leaving me no more certain than I'd started about whether it/he was mine or not. The romantic in me wanted Michael to make the grand gesture and come back and try again; the cynic in me wished he'd fall off the planet and leave my life open for another chance at love. The coward in me didn't want to face the verdict.

And then it was the summer solstice, longest day of the year. Miriam's forecast proved correct when the rain cleared out and brought us a perfect summer day.

I watched for Michael's bike or truck all afternoon as people began arriving for the party. The parade began with Miriam's giggling housemates driving a mix of parental gifts and hand-me-downs, followed at intervals by guys toting coolers and kegs in pickup trucks, muscle cars, motorbikes, and a VW Bus. Tom directed them to park tight on the far end of the stable's lot and walk to the house on the sand path through the trees.

The house stood well-concealed by those trees—a good thing, I thought, for it was so stark and scabby that it looked abandoned until one noticed Tom's truck parked around the side, accessible via an almost hidden driveway. He and Con had wrangled the two horse trailers over there, along with Miriam's Camaro and Con's Mustang. Other staff vehicles remained spread through the lot among customer cars.

Muted music floated to the stable all afternoon, and occasionally girls and boys came over to look around or take a ride. Few were appropriately dressed to do so. Most of the girls wore mini dresses or micro shorts and halter tops, sandals and flip-flops; and all, in my opinion, wore too much makeup. Their tote bags—too big to call purses—bulged with supplies.

A raft of beach boys followed them around. Each had sun-streaked hair and wore splashy, baggy shorts and muscle shirts or wild Hawaiian-print button-fronts hanging open to show hairless chests. They were shadowed by what I thought of as the long girls: long straight hair, long floaty dresses in eastern prints and batiks, long bangle earrings and jangle bracelets, long multicolored beads.

The rest—male and female—wore some combination of denim, T-shirt, and big-name shoes.

Around sunset, some tough guys came and went in loud cars, wearing tattered jeans and leathers over shirts sporting racing logos. At that point the music swelled in volume, and Tom had to go over and yell at them to turn it down until all the customers were gone.

Con, exempted from the evening ride, left work at the dinner break to start up the charcoal grill in Tom's pocket-sized backyard. Tom was staying in the tiny, dirty apartment above the barn as an absentee chaperone, making sure nobody burned the place down but otherwise not interfering. "If they're old enough to drink and vote and fight," he said, "they're old enough to do whatever they want." But he wandered around conspicuously all day and evening, flushing out anyone who skulked in the bushes smoking dope or necking, and shooing them back to the house.

Sylvie and I took out the sunset ride; then, after cleanup and close-down, took turns washing up in the barn's cramped bathroom and changing into the clean clothes we had brought to work. I wore my favorite Western-cut plaid shirt with contrast piping, slim jeans, and Jona's Frye boots. I let Sylvie go to the party first, so I could delay as long as possible.

I was last to leave the barn, aside from Tom now upstairs; and hung for a moment in the shadows before crossing the divide between worlds. Upon stepping into the open around the house, I paused for another moment to watch people pass back and forth behind its windows. All sashes were raised to the mild air, and through the downstairs windows, I heard the bright brass of Chicago's music, while from upstairs some Steely Dan was turned up so loud the bass made the air pulse. Around back, a radio played the same Top 40 station as ran constantly in the barn.

A dozen or more people hung around outside within the illumination thrown by exterior lights and windows. I emerged into the glow and approached the front porch, which wasn't actually falling off, though it was dubious enough that I wouldn't try sitting on the railing like some of the guys and gals waving Budweisers and Marlboros as they talked and laughed. I thought I smelled pot but couldn't see which cigarette glows might be a joint. Just as well if I didn't know.

"Hey, blondie—lookin' for me?" greeted one of the shaggy-haired railing-sitters.

"Nope." I gave him a mix of glare and fanged smile and kept walking. The girls on the steps turned their knees aside so I could pass, and another guy waved at me through the open front door into a living room almost solid with smoke, noise, and people. As one, the crowd registered my arrival and scanned me up and down without missing a beat of their conversation.

The weight of their attention threw me back into a dream I'd had as a child, of standing on stage before the entire school in my underwear. *No, think of the show ring!* I lifted my chest and tossed my mane while shouldering into the throng, aiming for a food and beverage table I spotted between bodies.

"Wanna beer?" yelled a slinky girl in a leotard and leather mini skirt.

"Got any soda?" I yelled back.

"Maybe in the kitchen," the girl shouted, and slithered away. I helped myself to some carrot sticks and crackers, then grabbed a tall paper cup and ladled what looked like fruit punch into it. A sip revealed it to be tart and refreshing, so I gulped it down while wriggling through the room toward a promising doorway.

It was suddenly blocked by a basketball player, or so he seemed from his gangly height, who smiled and drawled at full volume, "Howdy, cowgirl. You work here?"

"In fact, I do. I—"

"She's our newest employee," blared Miriam, popping up from behind and nearly flattening me with her Charlie perfume. "This is my friend Peter."

I nodded and bellowed, "Hi." Before I had to come up with more, Miriam steered me away by the elbow, leaned close, and dropped her voice. "Con's out back with most everybody from the barn. If you need a bathroom, it's down that hall."

Then she vanished back into the crowd trailing veils of fabric. I looked around for a route to the backyard and decided to retrace my steps rather than negotiate passage by Peter. I stopped by the drinks table and ladled some more punch—noticing, when I turned back to the room, that Michael was heading upstairs toward the now Pink Floyd music.

The shock planted my feet to the floor for a moment, but then I recovered. *Of course he's here. Why are you surprised?* True to form, he had slipped in when nobody was looking. My lip curled, and I took heart: Maybe tonight I would finally end it. The trick would be doing it without becoming a floor show.

I started after him but was hemmed in by a quartet of young machos before I could escape the living room. But the prospect of dodging, feinting, and parrying didn't discourage me as usual. Let Michael—and Con—suffer my indifference while I flirted with other guys!

Tossing my hair again, I commenced mingling. The silvery sheaf hanging down my back, rippled from having been braided wet that morning, attracted pawing admirers. Although I rebuffed their hands, I accepted their compliments and punch refills. It felt great to be a simple, foxy lady without the baggage of romance.

Within an hour I was laughing shrilly and flaunting my figure as well as

Miriam. In fact, I so enjoyed detracting attention from Miriam that I almost forgot my original plan.

I recalled it when Con appeared in the doorway I'd not yet managed to get through; caught my eye and tipped his head; then retreated. That reminded me I had last seen Michael going upstairs. I should find him and get it over with before joining Con.

Pivoting to locate the staircase, I wobbled enough to wonder if I could get there. What was in that punch I'd been sucking down? My stomach was sending up queasy signals that advised me to fill it—fast. Michael would have to wait while I dipped into the barbecue around back.

Detaching myself from a stringy dude in leathers who called me "Annie Oakley," I wove my way to the nearest doorway. It led into the kitchen, where the smoke was a little thinner, the light a little brighter, the noise somewhat dimmer; and where at last I found my cowboy counterpart.

Con didn't notice me leaning against the door frame, as he was leaning close to that curvy redhead he'd flirted with on last weekend's sunset ride, while keeping his back to the male trio drooling in his direction. I had hoped to find him manning the grill. I did find bowls and bags of chips on the counter, but all that remained in them were crumbs.

I really needed food—my queasiness had graduated to nausea. But food, I realized with a spurt of fear, might not stay down. I'd better get out of there while I could still walk, but walls of people barred every doorway. Miriam had pointed toward a bathroom down a hall, but a hundred oblivious people blocked my way.

I'd better try for the barn. But turning around looking for the back door made my head whirl. No time to make the stable—it would be a race to the bathroom before I puked. I might be able to make it outside, but the nearest exit meant staggering past Con with my hand clamped over my mouth.

I groped out of the kitchen the way I had come, bumping off shoulders and elbows, stepping on feet. That landed me in a foggy hallway pulsing with bass beat, but it was lined with people and had too many choices of door.

I yanked open the first one, which gave way without resistance into a utility room. A light bar sliced across a couple embraced with tousled clothes.

They gasped and jerked apart at the sudden intrusion. I instinctively shoved the door closed but then jerked it open again, my brain having caught up to what my unfocused eyes had seen.

"No," escaped my mouth, as if I spoke through gravel.

"Oh *shit*!" yelped Michael, swatting Priss away.

The shock hit me as the jump poles had at the horse show: clanging and banging and searing pain as my chest and head—and the room—fractured into fireworks. My stomach lurched into my throat, sending me reeling back into the hallway. My last sane action was slamming the door in Michael's face.

Half the partiers in the hallway scuttled clear while the other half pushed me toward the bathroom, where I caromed off the locked door and thumped onto the floor. I rebounded and hammered the door panels while people gaped at my raucous pleas. A blurry kaleidoscope overtook my vision. Then the door fell open, and I flopped forward at someone's feet.

Shoes jumped over me as hands came up from behind and hauled me to the toilet. I vomited through tears, heaving and twisting until my guts felt inside out, and I slumped to the tiles in a fetal ball.

The hands then pried under my armpits and knees and heaved me up against a chest, against which I jounced on the rapid trip to and through the front door, down the porch stairs, and across the yard, where I was propped against a vehicle. My ears hummed in the sudden quiet, and I gulped cool air wishing it were water. Before I could identify the man fumbling with car keys, he scooped me up and plopped me into the passenger seat, buckled me in, then jumped in beside me and drove away.

CHAPTER TWELVE

Lights streamed and flickered past for minutes? hours? while my head joggled against the window. The motion revived my old headache, but the cool glass eased it at the same time. At each bump in the road, my stomach clenched, but nothing more came up.

Presently the world stopped spinning, and I could fixate on details. White knuckles on the steering wheel. Canvas headliner. Detritus on sandy floor, black vinyl upholstery. I was in the Mustang with Con.

Memory rushed back and I whimpered. Con's head snapped around. "You all right now?"

I nodded and made another noise, hiding my face.

"Here, sip this." Con handed me a half-empty Coke, warm and flat from sitting in the car all day. Its sweet cola syrupy-ness went down like nectar. I wanted to pour it into my eyes, too, to stop them from seeing what played constantly before them: Michael again in another woman's arms, Michael again betraying me, while I flounced around thinking fruit punch was an alcohol alternative then half-poisoning myself in another humiliating public display.

My heart seized in a fist so tight I could hardly breathe, then bump-started into working again at a sudden quiet. The car had stopped running. We were parked below angular shadows defined by star-spangled sky that indicated the house. A yellow square beaming from inside meant Jona had left a light on for us. A dark lump next to the Mustang suggested Dave's car, meaning the couple was asleep—or otherwise—in the darkened upstairs. I relaxed a bit, glad that I would not have to account for myself to my sister.

Con unsnapped his seat belt and swiveled to face me. I started fumbling for my own belt, but he put a hand on my arm.

"Wait here a minute," he said. "I'll be right back."

"Huh?" I'd half expected Mr. Hero to carry me inside.

"I'm getting some supplies for a little picnic."

"Picnic?" I croaked. "It's the middle of the night!"

"A beautiful moonlit night. And just right for walking off a bad drunk."

He got out of the car and left me there to sulk in a dizzy doze until my door jerked open and he pulled me upright. "C'mon, time to move."

I staggered the first few steps, leaning heavily on him. Then I found my balance and trudged in step with him around the house, through the hollow of whispering grass, and onto the dune crest.

The exertion cleared my head and revived my muscles. I halted beside Con to gaze upon the eerie but beautiful sheen cast over the sand by the moon, and the sea glittering in competition with the stars. An aircraft's light blinked silently across the sky, answered from the horizon by an invisible ship's beacon. The wind sighed over us with a gentle, cool kiss.

I had to stretch my mind to recall what had brought us here; why Con stood ankle-deep in sand with me tucked under his arm. The longer we stood, the more conscious I became of that arm's weight across my shoulders. My side exposed to the air broke into goose bumps, while the side pressed against him was warm and matched contours as if I had been cut to fit. A crazy desire rose within me to kiss him. The sour taste still in my mouth, however, killed the urge.

For a while we walked along the dune edge, listening to our feet swish the sand, then Con veered and began the steep plunge downward. I balked then followed, feeling a hair's breadth away from careening into space. I stumbled at the bottom, but he didn't reach to catch me, instead waited for me to fall into stride with him at the water's edge.

Walking on a slant in the spongy sand against the wind, before the surf's hypnotic hiss, dispelled tension between us. Abruptly Con changed angle, strode up-beach to the dry sand, and sat, drawing up his knees and looping arms around them. He waited for me to settle into an identical position before he slipped off a teardrop backpack I hadn't noticed him wearing and unloaded a packet of Saltines and bottle of Gatorade.

"Eat," he commanded, while unwrapping and paring some Velveeta cheese with a penknife.

"I can't. My stomach is twisted as a pretzel."

"This will make it feel better." He handed me a slice of the rubbery orange non-dairy product so hated by Jona but so beloved by me, Mom, and Dad for mac-and-cheese supper and grilled-cheese sandwiches. I slugged down some Gatorade straight from the bottle then made a little sandwich with the cheese and crackers, washing down each dry, gummy bite with the sicky-sweet juice.

"I take it," Con said, "you're not used to drinking."

I finished chewing. "Not that much."

"No swinging Academy parties?"

"Sure. But I don't go to many. And I usually stick to beer." I busied myself with more mini sandwiches.

"So you've never gotten shitfaced before."

I turned a shudder into a shrug. "Well, too many beers on an empty stomach once, and our whole family gets tipsy on wine at birthday and Christmas parties."

"Not quite the same as tonight. How much booze did you have?"

"I don't know. I thought the punch was, well, punch."

Con laughed. "That stuff was loaded!"

"Didn't taste it." I looked at the Gatorade bottle. "In fact, tasted kind of like this." I tipped back a swig.

"But something else happened," he stated. I could feel him looking at me but evaded his eyes, unwilling to tell. The act of throwing up had cleansed my heart as well as my body. I finally felt severed, permanently, from Michael and didn't want to think or talk about him anymore.

But Con would not let it go. "Did one of those guys hassle you?"

"No."

"They were all over you."

"I could deal with it."

"But I saw you running like hellhounds were after you."

"I had to puke. Would you rather I did it on your shoes?"

"You were shrieking, Linny."

I felt my face get hot and took refuge in more Velveeta and Saltines. Presently I admitted, "I opened the wrong door and...walked in on somebody."

"Okay. So what? It was a party. People grope each other in dark corners all the time. And sometimes in not so dark corners."

I had noticed plenty of that and remembered feeling a mix of disgust and envy. "It wasn't like that," was all I could say.

Con sighed. "So what happened?"

My back stiffened and I remained silent, nursing the Gatorade bottle. *To tell or not to tell? Do I want to risk losing him, too?*

Con persisted. "Was it Miriam messing with somebody?"

"No." I almost would have preferred the girl to be Miriam; I already knew Michael had latched on to her. But yet another girl, so soon? On Miriam's own turf, with me there at the same time? The door unlocked? Did the guy want to be caught or something?

"Then was it Tom with some girl?"

"No. Forget it, Con—I—it's none of your business."

"But it is. You're living in my house and working beside me at my job. Jona trusted me to look after you—and I didn't tonight, and you found trouble. I'm sorry for that, but it doesn't change things. I can tell that something ain't right, Linny, and I need to know what it is."

I sighed. "Thanks, that's nice of you, but there's nothing you can do and no reason for you to get involved." *And besides, you won't tell me what's troubling you!*

He changed tack. "Then something did happen."

I spit out a breath. "No. What is this, twenty questions?"

"Who frightened you? What did you see?"

"Back off, Con!"

"Were you reliving your accident?"

"No! Yes! I mean—I—I—"

I choked on tears. Con fell silent and rubbed my neck with fingers that amazed me with their strength. I squirmed free and stood. Con pulled me back down. "C'mon, Linny. Give!"

"Goddamn it, it was Michael!" I blurted, twisting away from him.

Con released his grip on my arm. "What?"

"Michael. He came back."

"But Miriam said—"

"Well, either she lied or he did. Or his schedule changed, and he was able to get away. I'm not sure Miriam even knew he was there. But Priss did—that was her with him in the closet."

Con rolled his eyes so hard it tilted back his head. "Shit."

Some molecule in my mind noted he'd taken to swearing instead of censoring himself.

"It was just like at the show…" I said in a tiny voice, feeling tears rising again. I struggled to suppress them.

Con stiffened. "What do you mean?"

"He did it to me at the show. And before. But that was the last straw."

"Wait a sec. You mean the show you crashed at?"

I nodded. Con cursed again, adding softly, "Jona didn't mention that part."

"That's because Jona's big fun in life is keeping secrets. And she's in league with our parents to keep him away."

"Why? No, never mind, I think it's obvious."

"You don't know anything."

"Not unless you tell me."

"It's none of your business," I repeated, desperate to tell all.

"I told you—this *is* my business. And you're jerking me around if you don't explain."

I squeezed my eyes shut. The indignity, the insult, the mortification were still so fresh.

Finally I uttered, "It's a long story."

"I'm not going anywhere."

I cast a glance at him, solid and stoic as a rock. I didn't, didn't want to tell him, but I so wanted release!

It took me a few minutes to organize my thoughts, while he waited without moving. Presently I inhaled and, mentally crossing my fingers, told him my tale.

"He was the one, Con. My first and only. And though I was hardly his only, I was the one for him, too."

Con snorted.

I said sharply, "I don't expect you to understand. Nobody does. But since none of you were there, you'll just have to believe me."

He grunted assent and surprised me by placing his hand on my shoulder, giving it a little shake, then withdrawing back into the same position. I took that as a signal of faith and carried on.

"I knew his reputation. But when we got together, he stopped messing around. It was just us. Or so I thought for the first year. But then there were signs…little things…people's hints. But I knew him to be true so kept believing in him. What I think now is that he really meant to be faithful, and kept it up long enough to be his new norm. He just couldn't hold out indefinitely against temptation."

I sighed. Con remained still until I said, "He's got the same problem you do—women crawling all over him"—at which point Con twitched—"but he doesn't brush them off. He loves it, and has mastered this utterly seductive way of saying no and yes at the same time."

"Lothario," Con muttered.

I nodded. "It got to the point I had to warn him; that if he didn't knock it off, we were through. That made him turn up the flame, to the point where we were talking about buying rings this summer. But then…"

I squeezed my eyes shut and swallowed a lump. Took a deep breath. "The show. We were both there with our schools, lots of colleagues and students, everyone sharing hotel rooms and motorhomes, bunking in the tent barn, so he and I couldn't sleep together. Fine. But I was nerved out about the next day—my first A show, what I'd been working toward—he was supposed to coach me in the practice ring before the class—so I got up real early. Went for a walk to warm up my body and calm down my head. Was coming back from the bathrooms and took a shortcut between the trailers. And there he was, pawing up my main competitor."

Con flinched. I sucked in a final breath exhaled, "I guess they thought they were safely out of sight. But I saw them and they saw me; all I could do was walk away. He yanked me back to 'try to explain.' I just slapped him as hard as I could and told him to get out of my life."

"Good girl," Con said.

"Yeah, but there I was with still hours to go before my class and having to pretend to everyone that nothing was wrong. Then to ride against that girl with my parents watching. Well, I couldn't pull it off—or, rather, I did until in the ring. Then I was just so hurt and distracted, I fouled up my horse and got him off stride, and—"

The poles rushed at me again and I heard them, felt them, clunking against me. I pressed my hands against my eyes, but that didn't stop the memory or my words. "That was almost worse. Completely my fault. I didn't just blow the class and break a win streak—I disgraced myself in front of everyone who matters. Nobody destroys fences on dry ground in equitation! They're not high enough, they're just there to challenge your form. I might as well have forgotten to tighten my girth and turned upside down during a sitting trot. And you know what? While I was out cold in an ambulance, she won the blue!"

I gnawed my wrist to keep tears from escaping. The hole in my heart burned just as hot now as it did those weeks ago. Yet something in this night's silvery glow let me take a step away from it. As if it had happened to somebody else. As if I might get over it. As if something better was possible, someday before I died.

I glanced at Con, who with elbows on updrawn knees had pressed the heels of his hands against his cheekbones and was watching me with an expression I neither liked nor understood. After a moment he said, "So your parents stashed you here to keep you away from him?"

"Sort of." I looked back at my feet half buried in sand. "They don't know about the Michael part, they only know I was upset, and witnessing my fall upset the hell out of them. I got knocked out and hauled to the hospital, kept in a few days for observation. But they've been against me seeing Michael since they met him, and maybe a week before the show they told me to drop him or they'd pull my funding."

"Did you?"

"No."

"Did they?"

"Yes, but not till I told them I rode the sunset trail with you."

Con fell silent. Then he said, almost whispered, "Do they really think there's going to be a repeat with me?"

"No, otherwise they wouldn't have agreed to me staying here. Jona made sure they understood you're a perfect gentleman. In fact, she told them you might be queer, so there would be no question."

He laughed. "As if that would stop me."

I flashed a look at him. He went sober and silent again. I sat the same way while many waves splashed and retreated against the shore.

Finally, wanting to get something back for my confidences, I asked him, "What about you?"

He tightened. "What about me?"

"Who did you make a fool of yourself for, and how?"

"None of your business," he mimicked.

I lashed back, "Come on, with looks like yours, they've probably been lining up with their skirts hiked since you were twelve!"

"Earlier than that, if you really want to know," he snapped back.

"I don't." Oh yes I do!

Our next silence crackled. I bundled up the food and capped the bottle. Con stuffed them into his pack, saying too casually, "The first one shoved her hand down my pants when I was ten."

I cringed, too easily seeing it happen. But I didn't dare ask for details.

Instead I offered, "Guys made passes at me that early, too. It grossed me out. So I was a late bloomer, not even being kissed until Michael entered my life."

"So he swept you off your feet."

"Worse than that. I just lay down and spread my legs. Then discovered too late that I was just a car on a long train."

"Yet he followed you here."

I shook my head. "That's what I don't get it. He totally betrayed me; he never came to the hospital or the house after the accident—never even called—"

"Maybe he regrets what he did and wants to make up."

"By screwing around with somebody else right under my nose?"

"Did he know you were at the party?"

I shook my head again, though this time in bewilderment. "How could he not think I'd be there? And even if he didn't, it was his best chance to intercept me without having to ride again at the stable."

"Sooner or later, if he still wants to talk to you, he's going to follow one of us home." Con stopped and swallowed. "It better not be me."

"Or me. At this point, I don't think I can limit myself to a slap."

Con chuckled. "You may have to get in line. Miriam's not going to take this kindly."

I scoffed. "Who's going to tell her?"

"There were enough people in the hallway that somebody will say something that will get back to her. I wonder if Priss will still be employed tomorrow."

I shook my head. "I don't want to go back and find out. I wouldn't, if I'd built up any money yet. But right now I can't get farther than back home—where I don't want to be just as much."

"A rock and a hard place," Con said.

I nodded.

"Know what you mean," he added, leaving an inviting silence.

I stepped into it. "What do *you* mean?"

He leaned back against his straightened arms, stretching his legs into the sand. "I can't go home, and I can't go where I want to be. So I'm stuck here, too."

"I don't get it."

I wriggled around to look at him. The moonlight angle hooded his eyes in shadow.

When he didn't elaborate, I prodded, "You own the beach house and have a trust fund or something, plus what you make at Galeson's. And rich parents. You've got a car, you're done with school…what can't you do?"

He flicked a glance at me. "Pretty much what you wanted. Not the Olympics or anything at that level, but a dream I can't afford."

My heart quickened with interest. "Like what?"

He shrugged. "A ranch in Montana. And being as good a Western artist as Frederic Remington or Charles Russell."

I resisted an impressed whistle. "That'll take some work. I mean, I don't mean you're not good—from the little I've seen, you're terrific. But yeah, you'll need some experience of that life to get the same realism." I waited a beat then added, "Why don't you just sell the house and go?"

"Can't," he said with an edge to his voice, gouging his heel in the sand. I held my breath, hoping the reason would follow. He continued staring at the water and said, "Not until I'm twenty-five."

"Ah." I remembered our conversation on the dune my first morning. "Those strings attached."

"Yeah."

"What are they attached to?"

"A couple million dollars."

"What!"

"Yeah. Enough to buy and work a ranch while I paint the rest of my life."

I felt envy stab me like a hurled lance. Millions of dollars! I could buy a horse and even a farm and train full time for ten Olympics. Or go the other way and build a sanctuary for old and abandoned horses. Or both. *Oh, lucky, lucky Con!*

I also shared his frustration. How maddening to be stuck on hold for years in the prime of your life, waiting for a particular big thing to happen that would give you the dream you wanted!

His face remained stony, moving me to look for a bright side. "That's only, what, three more years to go? Not so bad."

"Hell, it's an eternity of suspense." He pulled in his arms and legs to sit cross-legged. "I might not get the money, so I can't sell the house until I know."

"I see." But I didn't. Struggling to be neutral and polite, I waited for him to explain instead of machine-gunning him with questions.

Still not looking at me, he eventually said, "Kind of like you, I have to play their game. The money is a combination from my father and his father. Dad has his share no matter what; my brother Alex got his already, and I get mine on my twenty-fifth birthday. But until then Dad has complete control, and he can shut me off any time he wants."

"Why would he want to?" At this point, I considered Con a prince and couldn't imagine why a parent would think otherwise.

Con squirmed. "Because of what I did to him. Because of what he did to me and Alex and Mom. He's a bad man, Linny, and I beat the crap out of him as soon as I was big enough to do it. We would have killed each other if my mother hadn't broken us apart."

I went mute in astonishment. Con sighed and turned away, waiting for me to ask the inevitable. Though I was dying to know what dear-old-daddy had done that could provoke my prince to violence, I didn't want to sidetrack Con or have him clam up. Better to show I could respect his privacy, since he was clearly confiding, and I wasn't sure I wanted to know all the gritty truth.

"She dragged in the family attorney," he continued, "who calmed everybody down to a stalemate. We each got our own deal, and mine is, I don't expose his dirty secret as long as he releases that money on time, and I fade away quietly afterward. But he can take over the money if I don't toe the line before that date. Meaning, doing nothing to embarrass anyone in the family and living according to their rules."

He swallowed back a rage as old as he was, then said in a calmer voice, "That let me off the hook on pro football as long as I played through college. Since Dad's alma mater has a good art program and a great ball team, I could study there without attracting attention while keeping up the necessary image."

I nodded, knowing he'd done exactly that. "How did they take you working at Galeson's?"

He shook his head. "They don't know yet. Gram—my mother's mom—died last year, and I got the house just before finishing school this spring. Went straight from graduation to here. Gram knew her daughter was a rat and had married somebody even worse, so she made sure their kids would have a home and enough income to get by once they were old enough to get out. Alex got the place in Maine, and I got this one. So here I am, out of trouble as long as I don't go bohemian with the artsy-fartsies in Provincetown and attract attention. Just as well, because I need time to put together a portfolio. Gram's money is enough that I don't have to work as long as I live on peanut butter and jelly, so I wasn't planning on getting a job right off. But I couldn't resist the chance at Galeson's. Or Klatawah. Now I can build up some Western riding and training experience before moving west."

I sat connecting the dots I had noticed during our short acquaintance. His story reminded me of mine in an oblique way—the big difference being that I had cut the financial umbilical cord and he had not. He didn't need to, and with that huge pot of gold at the end of the rainbow, he could hide out here and mark time with his living expenses covered—a luxury beyond me, save for his charity in letting me stay in his house for the summer.

That grated, but I was grateful.

"Does working at a hack stable count as stepping out of line?" I asked.

"Not sure. But Galeson is a big name out here—they've got that marina and resort and all those other businesses, with the stable being a sort of embarrassing leftover. I can always let my parents think I'm working at the upscale end. Yachting is 'acceptable.' So is any business in a resort area. They're not likely to drive here and check out what I'm doing, especially this summer because they're in Europe for most of it. I can lie through my teeth as long as nobody tells them anything different that might embarrass them."

I shook my head in commiseration, though I felt a lot better about my own decisions. And warmer toward my parents, who had done nothing except want me safe and happy—according to their definition. But even if I tattooed my whole body or got pregnant or went to India to study transcendental meditation, when the shouting was over they would still love me and always welcome me home. I could not imagine physically fighting them over something morally wrong. I hoped Con would trust me enough to tell me what had happened, while hoping I never had to know.

I realized then that he had distracted me from thinking about Michael. He also had not mentioned anything about girls.

He straightened his legs again and looked at me. The moonlight sculpted his face into planes and blocks, capturing his beauty in stark geometry that made my breath catch in my throat.

I really, really wanted to kiss him but knew that would backfire. I would seem like all those hussies at Miriam's party, crawling over him for his money and looks. He had rejected those easy lays to help me, a scorned and heartbroken friend and little sister.

No—a kiss, no matter how sincere, would send the wrong message.

Still, I wanted to ease a bit of his pain; to assure him I liked him for himself, maybe even loved him. But his confession showed me how little I knew him, and how far apart our desires and worlds.

I lay back to think about it, keeping sand out of my hair by crossing my arms behind my head. It felt damp and cool under the length of my body. I wished Con had brought a blanket for our picnic, then corrected myself: Maybe that was a good thing, because of what a blanket would allow.

He stretched out on his side next to me with one hand propping up his head and the other scooping and trickling sand like an hourglass. I said, after a long stare at the stars: "Too bad we can't ride on this beach. It's a perfect night for it."

"Maybe someday," he murmured in a dreamy tone.

"If we'd been thinking, we could have trailered Shark and Klatawah here and no one would notice."

He sat up at the idea; I followed suit. He slid his arm around me again. I relaxed and leaned in. "Yeah," he said, "I could've snatched Tom's keys to the truck. Hitched up. And while everyone else was partying, we could have been galloping down this beach."

We shared a sigh and watched the breakers rear and paw like iridescent horses. When I looked up and down the beach, imagining the thrill, I realized it could happen. There was not a soul in sight; nobody to see us drive in, unload, and ride by. In fact, nobody on the planet knew where we were.

The thought broke over me like a wave: I was truly free. At this moment, no one could tell me what to do or judge me for it. I could ride through the moonlight with this lovely man if I wanted; or run away from it all if I wanted; or make love with him on the beach if I wanted; or just lie back and sleep.

Without thinking, I turned my face toward Con's hand resting over my shoulder and kissed his fingertips. He stiffened but did not speak. I felt my face flush, but in the moonwash no color showed. Con and I were just forms composed of pales and darks, with intermittent gleams for our eyes. The beach was soft contours of neutrals, the ocean a constantly moving glitter and sparkle going swish, thump, hiss.

I pressed closer, heart thudding and abdomen throbbing. I could feel his heart banging against his ribs.

Nobody but the moon and stars watching.

We were both romantic fools...how foolish would it be to...?

No.

No. I needed a friend, not another lover. Someone big-brothery to lean on, like I was leaning on Con now.

I sighed again, wishing he'd never mentioned his inheritance. I would not be able to forget that. The knowledge brought a different urge, to ease away; but that would signal rejection—another wrong move. He needed a friend, too. I could at least give him that.

So I picked up where he'd left off, saying, "Doesn't this beach wrap around to Race Point, where we ride the sunset trail at the other end?"

I felt him nod.

"So maybe we could leave from the stable and turn the other way, ride down here and back. It can't be too many miles."

He considered then said, "Let's try it next full moon. If we get caught, say we're testing the idea of a possible night ride for the stable as an extension of the sunset trail."

"Who would catch us? Are there really cops in dune buggies patrolling the beach?"

"I...don't know. Probably now and then. We might get fined if caught, but nothing worse." He paused while we thought about it, then shifted and said, "Assuming we can do it without getting arrested, are you game?"

I turned my head and smiled at him. "That would be really cool!"

More than that, I didn't say. It was a new fantasy that would keep me going for many a day and night.

He smiled back, then heaved himself to his feet, holding out a hand. I took it and accepted his hoist.

"You okay enough to head back now?" he asked, so blandly that I presumed he was ignoring the little shock that jittered between us upon contact.

I tried to ignore it, too. "I guess so, but no hurry."

"Okay for you, but I'm on duty tomorrow. Early. So let's go, if you've recovered."

"Yeah, thanks, I feel fine now." I stepped out to prove it. We walked back toward the house along the water's edge.

Con had not released my hand, and I made no effort to withdraw it. It felt so nice to have that big warm hand around mine, that big strong body protecting me, that big warm heart caring for me. All so far from where I'd begun the evening.

In fact—I realized with a start—during all the time I'd spent with Michael, he had touched every part of my body but never held my hand.

Con continued holding it as we slogged up the dune face, using the lower public trail to the parking lot. He held my hand as we stood on the sand-swept pavement debating where to park a horse trailer and whether to try. Then he steered me by the hand to the driveway for the last ascent to the house. Hand in hand, we walked around to the back deck to avoid the squealy front door.

He released me only for the ritual of brushing sand off our feet, moving quietly to avoid waking Jona and Dave with our thumping. With a final, deep sigh, I reached for the door handle, then hesitated. I turned back to Con and said, simply, "Thank you."

He acknowledged with a courtly bow. Then, eyes on mine in a dark glitter, he took up my hand again and lifted it to his lips like a suave European gentleman. He kissed my fingers as lightly as a butterfly.

I felt a bonfire light off inside. I gaped at him, vibrating, as he drew me closer and touched his lips to mine, pulling away before I could respond.

Then he returned my hand to me with a one-cornered smile and said, "Good night," reaching past me to open the door and shoulder me in.

I stumbled witless through the living room toward the kitchen-light beacon while he turned into his bedroom. If I hadn't heard his door lock click, I would have followed him in.

CHAPTER THIRTEEN

Depletion knocked me out as soon as I hit the mattress. But after a short, dreamless sleep cycle, my eyes popped open and my mind launched into a Con/ Michael/Con/Michael loop that exhausted me all over again.

Dawn came and went. Grateful I didn't have to get up and face it, I rolled away from the windows and opened my eyes again at one twenty-five in the afternoon. *Whoa!* I'd never slept through half a day before!

I rubbed my eyes and arose, slipping on my terry robe to creak and groan across the room and look out. *Not worth getting up for.* The gray sky wept, barely casting shadows. Window panes rattled intermittently in the wind. I didn't envy Con having to work today.

Yet I considered heading to the stable...he might just be hanging around, given the low demand for trail rides. But first, a trip to the bathroom, a turn in the shower, and a hot breakfast into my curdling stomach.

Through the bathroom floor I heard voices downstairs, the words masked by background radio, but their tone rising and falling, sometimes sharply. One was Jona, the other rumbled like a man. At first I presumed it was Dave, though Jona had said he'd be heading back to the Hole this morning. Maybe he was waiting for the weather to clear before hitting the road. Maybe Con had come home for lunch.

That prospect moved me to ramp up the shower and let the hot water blast the grubbies and squeamies away before I ventured into public. I donned a soft sweatshirt and jeans instead of going downstairs in my bathrobe, but kept my hair in a towel turban.

At my footsteps on the stairs, the voices in the kitchen stopped. I swung around the corner to find a red-faced Jona standing at the counter and a pale, shadow-eyed Michael hunched at the table. Both of them watched me with taut eyelids as I froze midstride.

"Good morning," Jona said coldly.

"Afternoon," Michael corrected.

My mouth opened and closed a few times before I managed, "I... cannot...deal with this...without coffee and food."

I cannot deal with it at all! I pivoted and groped for the Mr. Coffee machine on the counter. Jona must have anticipated my arrival from the shower noise and brewed a fresh pot, putting out a mug beside it.

"I can make you some breakfast," she offered as I gulped down the caffeine. The offer was genuine, I sensed, but her eyebrows were still lowered, her voice still frigid. She looked away from Michael but did not turn her back to him.

"I can take you out for breakfast," he countered.

"On a bike in the rain? Forget it," Jona sneered.

"It's not raining right now," he snapped back.

I inserted, "My helmet is at home, anyway."

A tense silence reigned while I drained my mug. Then I plunked it down and turned to him.

"Michael, what are you doing here?"

"Trying for the six hundredth time to talk to you." He slung a fierce glance at Jona, who bit her lips.

I exhaled hard. "How did you find this place?"

"He followed me home," Jona said. "Dave dropped me off at the stable to fetch the Saab."

I cringed, remembering why the car had been abandoned and realizing that Con would have had to tell Jona a thing or two about the previous night. But she kept her expression straight.

"And since I knew Winston took you home sick," Michael continued, "and guessed that someone would pick up your car today, I just waited until it happened."

"What, hiding in the bushes?"

"Just about."

Michael held my gaze with eyes like zircon drill bits. I hardened myself against their penetration. That caused his gaze to dart toward Jona, who caught the look and sneered. "If you want privacy, go somewhere else. In my car if you have to, no bike. If not, Linny, cereal—now—and Michael waits for you outside."

Michael's lips pressed tighter. I glanced at Jona, surprised she hadn't just kicked him out.

Michael interpreted the glance and said, "I already told her I'm not budging until you talk to me."

I believed him. He looked as immovable as a boulder in his wet black leathers and helmet-flattened dark hair.

I yanked the towel off my own damp hair and said, "All right. Wait for me in the parking lot. I'll be down as soon as I've eaten."

I needed time to wake up and think. A run into town for breakfast would buy me some time, as well as get me off Con's turf and away from Jona's eye. But compressing myself into a vehicle with Michael would introduce its own complications.

Another glance out the window showed the sky was blowing and spitting, which would keep an outdoor encounter from running on too long. That was the best bet. I had to get it over with—now.

Jona busied herself with pulling out food for me, while Michael departed. I heard the screen door screech on its hinges and his bootheels on the railroad-tie stairs. Then he was absorbed into the mist as he hiked down the driveway to the town beach parking lot.

Jona left me to my sustenance, her own heels loud on the kitchen linoleum, then muffled on the braided rug in the living room, where they stopped.

I shoveled and slurped, mind whirling and heart hammering. Then I grabbed a slicker and went out barefoot, thinking to walk with Michael on the beach then send him home.

He was waiting at the top of the path, bareheaded against the moisture that wasn't quite rain and not quite fog, looking down at the ocean. My bare soles across the empty parking lot let me get close before he sensed my approach.

He spun and glared with darkened eyes and flared nostrils, looking like the hero of some literary tragedy in all black against the stormy sky. I tried to freeze my heart, but it rolled over with a thud.

He opened, "I want to explain last night, among other things."

"I bet you do." I glared at him, exulting in my anger.

"Linny, don't make this more difficult!"

"Why? You've never made anything easy for me!"

He glowered. "I thought you loved me."

"I do. At least, I did. But that doesn't mean you can walk all over me! Love's supposed to be a two-way street."

"I want it to be. Linny, I'm sorry. I'm sorry a thousand times over, for everything—especially last night. You were so late, I didn't think you were coming."

"So that gave you an excuse to mess around with whoever was handy?"

He shook his head. "I—"

"And lying to Miriam about coming at all?"

"No lie. I thought I wouldn't be able to. But then things changed last minute. I drove straight from home, but you were out on the trail when I got there."

I wondered where he had parked his bike and whether keeping it out of sight had been intentional. I certainly had looked for it.

But I didn't interrupt as he said, "After seeing how that place operates, I thought it would be better meeting you in the chaos of a party than interrupting you at the stable again."

"Leaving me yet another chance to interrupt you, instead!"

"Aw c'mon, I—that girl was throwing herself at me. We were both drunk. It didn't mean a thing."

"It meant something to me!"

We turned away from each other, steaming. He flung up his hands then started down to the beach.

I called after him, "Funny, you need privacy to talk but not to mess around with a stranger!"

He stopped and called up, "It's not the same thing."

I crossed my arms over my chest. "Pray, do tell—what's the difference?"

Michael shrugged. "One is just…fun. The other is…important."

I wanted to scream, How can sex be meaningless with one person and important with another?

"You know that song." He jammed his hands into his pockets. "Love the one you're with, if you can't be with the one you love." He grinned.

I snarled back, "And I've never understood it."

"Then what are you doing living with one of the world's most eligible bachelors while claiming you love me?"

"Nothing! Con is my host and friend, Michael. I was oh-so-kindly coerced into spending the summer with Jona, and this is where she's staying. Her boyfriend is an old friend of Con's."

"And you're completely immune to his charms—and money."

My face flamed as I recalled a late-night beach scene. But the memory gave me power. "Unlike you and Priss and Miriam, Con and I believe there's more than one kind of relationship between the sexes."

Michael snorted. "Maybe. But I haven't seen it happen yet!"

"You're looking at it now."

Michael laughed and finished his descent to the beach. That forced me to either wait for him to come back, leave the confrontation unfinished, or follow.

Damn! I hesitated, pulling hair out of my eyes, then scurried down the path to catch up with him at water's edge. He knew I'd do it and was waiting with, "Look, Linny, I'm trying to play it your way. You said you wanted to get married but weren't ready yet. That means we're both free to play the field before—"

"You play the field like a bee pollinating every flower on a hundred acres!"

"I told you, it's just fun—people getting close and enjoying each other. 'Make love, not war.' Some of us can do it without strings attached."

"And some of us can't."

"Then I guess I'm not ready to get married, either."

"That's obvious."

I spun and strode down the beach, making him catch up with me. "C'mon, Linny—"

"C'mon, yourself." I planted my feet and punched my hands onto my hips. "Why didn't you come see me after the accident? Why didn't you even call or send flowers? Then you come out here flaunting your lovers in my face and—"

Michael gaped. "What are you talking about? I followed your ambulance to the hospital. Your parents froze me out of the waiting room, so I tried to sneak in later, but they were always there. And when they weren't, they told the nurses to watch out for me, and they kept me out of your room. When you went home, your guard dogs wouldn't let me in the door and dodged me on the phone—'Linny's sleeping, she can't be disturbed, we'll have her call you when she feels better'—until they just hung up when they heard my voice. Next thing I knew, you were gone."

I went mute and hollow. Some part of me had suspected this, and I knew Michael was speaking the truth.

He added, "I asked everybody I know until someone mentioned they'd heard Jona was summering at the Cape. You had to be with her since you weren't anywhere else. So I checked every stable from the Canal out to here, knowing you'd find your way to horses somehow."

The way his voice softened moved me to look into his eyes. Mistake—because I fell into them, as mesmerized by those vivid blues as when I'd first seen them. They seemed now to be spinning like my mind, a mass of love, resentment, wonder, worry, anger, fear, excitement, despair. My body hummed as it always did in his presence. But this time, the flame reignited my mind instead of my heart.

Looking up from beneath my brows I said, "That doesn't tell me why you abandoned me at the show. You were supposed to coach and critique me, not cheat on me."

Michael spat out a sigh, looked away then looked back again. "I was doing you a favor."

"What!"

He angled forward and dropped his voice. "Suzanne had been slinking around me for months, real pushy at the show, finally asked me to help her get ready. I knew she would beat you, so I took the chance to disrupt her balance, tire her out if she'd go all the way. If nothing else, I could make her late. Instead, I distracted you so much that—"

He stopped. I wouldn't have heard him anyway. Truth hit me like ice water poured through a hole in the top of my head, seeping down through my face, my throat, my heart to congeal in my belly like a glacier. It didn't matter if Michael loved me and promised to be faithful for eternity. With rationalization like his, I could never, ever trust him again.

In that moment, I could have cried icicles. Instead, I reversed and headed for the house as fast as I could walk in deep sand.

Michael caught up and grabbed my arm. "Hey, Linny, come on—we can't leave it like this!"

I stopped so fast that he stumbled. "Then how do you want to leave it?"

"I don't want to leave it. That's the point."

I would have laughed in his face had I not glimpsed fear in his eyes. "You're gonna have to leave it, Michael, because as I told you before, we're through. I can't play it your way, and you can't play it mine."

"Linny!" He dogged my heels, then caught my arm again to halt me at the base of the path. "Linny, please, I'd marry you right now if I thought you would forgive me. Your denial makes me crazy. Give me your heart, and I'm yours."

I stared past him unseeing, disconnected from my body. He was finally saying what I wanted to hear. But it was too late.

I said in a graveyard voice, "I gave you my heart, and you walked all over it. I'm taking what's left of it back, and you can't have any more."

His grip fell limp. I snatched my arm away and trudged up the dune. At the parking lot—mercifully still empty—I turned back and looked down at him upon the strand. A black form dwarfed by steely clouds and surging seas, he looked so forlorn and alone that I started to cry.

During the minute I lost sight of him by wiping my eyes, he ran up the slope and stood again before me. Red-faced and winded, with his hair battering his face, Michael finally appeared daunted.

"Linny, please. Just hear me out. You've got to believe me. But I'm not good at words. I can only express feelings through my body, my hands."

Then why have you never held my hand? I wanted to scream.

But that sounded so pathetic, I couldn't speak.

His chest heaved. "Linny, living without you, worrying about you these weeks, has convinced me I want only you. Those other girls—yeah, they ease my frustration, but every minute I'm wishing they were you. I can't be faithful until I've got you to be faithful to! All of you. I need to know you love me, in a language I can understand. I mean it about getting married. If you want a ring, let's go into town and buy one. I don't want to fight you or hurt you, I just want to love you. Is that so hard to understand?"

I stared at him, desperately measuring. Every syllable of every sentence rang so true, I had to believe. His body underscored his words with awkward, abrupt movements. When Michael was in command—and/or lying—he had a dancer's poise.

An image of Con flashed through my mind. I shoved it aside, but not before realizing that if I gave in to Michael, then I'd never have a chance to kiss Con.

The thought made my want to slap myself. I shut my eyes and shook my head to clear it. Michael read the gesture as "No."

"Linny, please!" He stepped closer and held out his hands. "I came here to ask you in person, knowing you'd never believe me otherwise, and not knowing what lies your family has told. And I'm staying at Miriam's only because it's free, and I can come and go all summer between shows."

"Paying her rent with your dick," I sneered.

He didn't deny it.

I stood silent while the wind flapped my hair and stung my cheeks red. Then I leveled my gaze at Michael and pronounced, "I believe you, but that doesn't matter. What does is that I don't trust you as far as I can spit. I need that from my partner, and you can't deliver. Forget it, Michael. Good-bye."

Before he could speak or touch me, I strode across the parking lot and back up the driveway. Wind buffeting my ears prevented me from hearing if he followed.

I stomped inside, grabbed my purse and Jona's keys without looking at her, then stomped back out to the Saab. Michael had parked behind instead of beside it, so I shoved his bike over to clear the way and blindly backed out, turned, and headed down the driveway.

I meant to drive through Provincetown to the rotary at Pilgrims' First Landing monument, where a breakwater arched out to the last sandy spit of the Cape. It ended at the Long Point lighthouse; a long, remote walk where nobody would think to look for me. But as my headstorm cleared, I caught up to what my spirit had known from the first: I needed to ride my horse across the empty dunes to the emptiest possible shoreline.

The car had already made the turn toward Galeson's. When I drove in, the stableyard was almost empty: a few saddled horses standing rumps to the wind in the front corral, and the usual employee vehicles parked alongside the barn. I sat in the car for a moment, panting hard and waiting for my legs to stop shaking. The tumult inside my head was less willing to subside.

Thankfully, I didn't have to explain my presence. Nobody was bustling around. I heard Sylvie and someone chatting in the tackroom, and Tom in his office on the phone talking a four o'clock customer into riding tomorrow instead of today. Of Con or Klatawah I saw no sign.

I bridled Shark and led her into the yard, hopping aboard bareback. It took all my willpower to refrain from kicking the mare right into a run. Instead we walked through the trees, then eased into a trot, followed by a canter when the trail opened onto the dunes. I slowed again before the first gradient to save Shark's wind for later climbing.

When we reached the highest point between stable and ocean, I conceded that riding to the beach would be miserable even wearing my slicker, as wind whipped raw drizzle against my already chilled face and hands. If the clouds let go, I would get soaked, just like after the match race. Shark's coat had already become slippery, and flying sand wedged between her back and my legs.

Anyhow, I was tiring, and a sofa in a warm bungalow seemed a smarter place to mourn.

Except that fresh hoofprints wove through the sand beneath Shark's nose, heading beachward. From my lookout, I saw the printmaker riding back. He rode with chest and chin thrust against the gale, sitting as proudly as the horse bore him. But he stiffened upon spotting my silhouette.

I considered wheeling Shark and galloping off. In the next breath I admitted that I had hoped to find him out here, so I stood my ground. But I had no idea what to say to him.

He crested the dune and drew up beside Shark, greeting, "What brings you out?" as if nothing had happened between us. When I didn't answer, he lit up the afternoon with a grin. "I thought you'd be hung over in bed all day!"

I returned a feeble smile and shook my head. "No hangover, but I did sleep past noon. Then, things got—difficult—and I had to get away."

Con frowned. His face then disappeared as Klatawah pranced a circle, to return wearing the same grim expression. "Jona wasn't mad when I last saw her, so what happened?"

"Michael followed her back to the house."

"Oh." His voice dropped.

Klatawah surged forward, so I couldn't see his face. I pivoted Shark to follow, abandoning my plans to gallop down the beach. Klatawah's wet, sand-spattered legs and Con's sodden clothes showed that they had already done so.

"Miriam was wondering," he projected above the wind when I caught up, "where Mike had gotten off to. He was supposed to meet her at the stable hours ago."

"She must have given up, 'cause I saw everybody's car but hers." *Thank God*, I added silently. Followed by: *Good luck, Miriam. Let this be a lesson to you.*

"So where is he?" Con fixed his gaze on my face, trusting Klatawah to pick the way.

I kept my focus between Shark's bobbing ears. "Last I saw, sulking on the beach below your house."

"Huh?"

"That's where I left him. He's probably gone by now." Oh no—what if he comes here again? I should've walked out the breakwater!

After a long pause, Con said, "Interesting."

We rode in silence for a few minutes before I added, "We quarreled."

"So I figured."

I darted a look at him and saw a suppressed smile. He dropped it as soon as we crossed gazes.

"So…" he prodded after another long moment. "Who won?"

"I did." I squeezed Shark into a jog. "I'm giving him enough time to be gone before I go back."

Con jounced up beside me. We rode until the next hill loomed, then slowed for the climb, resuming conversation at the top.

"You'll be glad to know," I said, "that I gave him his walking papers."

"You're right."

"I can't say I'm glad, but I'm relieved it's over." Indeed, my heart felt several pounds lighter inside my chest.

I gazed ahead as Shark walked and Klatawah pranced and the wind moaned around us. Upon descent into the quiet shelter of trees, Con pulled Klatawah to a halt.

"How did he take it?"

"Almost like a gent." I tweaked a corner of my lip. Con, recalling the same conversation, tweaked his lip back.

I dared look at him then, seeing his face tauten then relax as he struggled between holding his mask and being himself. I wanted the real guy talking to me, so helped him let go by telling more than I should have.

"It just became so obvious," I said. "He was pouring his heart out, telling me the truth, but I could see the manipulator in the back of his eyes and finally understood he could never escape that."

"You're right again." He paused then added, "It comes with the plumbing in some folks."

"Well, in his case it probably overdeveloped from survival instinct."

"What do you mean?"

I nudged Shark forward. "He started from nowhere and got far by grabbing any opportunity and parlaying it into better ones."

"How nowhere?" Con brought Klatawah alongside Shark.

"Opposite side of the tracks from you. And…" I hesitated about elaborating, then realized I didn't have to keep Michael's secrets anymore. "His parents were violent drunks. When they happened to be around, that is. He ended up getting shunted between foster homes, most of which were as bad or worse, except for one lucky stretch with a wealthy family. They got him through school, taught him manners, and introduced him to horses. But the father booted him out after catching him with the underage daughter. At that point Michael was old enough to support himself."

"As what?"

"A gypsy rider. Stable to stable, teacher, trainer, worker, competitor, hoping to charm his way into a sponsorship but usually just getting temporary room and board. He became smart enough to avoid wives but had a magnetic effect on daughters and spinsters, who were all too willing to lend him their big-ticket horses. Usually some irate father or boyfriend chased him off each gig, or a lonely woman or young man got too emotional and scared him away."

I shuddered even now from remembering the story and realizing I might have trodden a similar path without the generous, loving parents I'd been lucky enough to have. I used to feel deprived because I hadn't been born among the well-heeled horsey set, but these days I was becoming more grateful for my privileges. Michael's life in comparison was part of why I had forgiven him so much.

But I recognized now that I had met him too late; beguilement was too deeply ingrained into his nature to just slough it off like an old skin. Even if he wanted to change, he didn't have the discipline or even the understanding of how to do it—and I didn't want to be his teacher. Or guinea pig. I just wanted a partner to grow through life with, not one I had to drag along by a nose ring hoping we would eventually find conflict-free balance.

"Gotta give him credit," Con said. "That's a hard way to live. And you've got to be a smooth operator to pull it off."

I met his gaze and read in it an anger that surprised me. He surprised me more by saying, "And you've got to give him credit for trying. He knew enough to love you, that you're a special creature outside his world. But in order to have you, he had to maneuver, to second-guess, to cover his tracks because you wouldn't want who he really is."

As I sat on Shark with my mouth open, Con pressed Klatawah onward and kept his back to me as we rode the rest of the way single file. I let the space between us widen so I could ponder, now as unsure about Con as I'd been about Michael. Things had changed overnight again, leaving Con...what?

My friend? My big brother? Just my co-worker? Or my next lover?

No, I would not bounce to him on the rebound!—and probably never. I didn't want his Montana dream. Nor would I deny it to him. Likewise, he didn't want the life I had mapped out for myself and wouldn't deny it to me. That gave us nothing to share beyond this summer.

Could that be what he was mad about? The way finally made clear for him, yet nowhere to go?

I wouldn't have entertained the thought if he hadn't kissed me. Unlike Michael, I couldn't brush off a move like that! I needed to know what it meant before I could sort out how I felt about it. As a double whammy, there was that money problem he'd revealed. Why had he told me? A test? It must be. How better could he measure a woman than by how she reacted to a multi-million-dollar prospect?

Mr. Moneybags was in the office talking with Tom when I rode in, so I took care of Shark in slow motion to give Con a chance to intercept me. He didn't. Stifling a sigh, I went out to the Saab and drove home. *To Con's house*, I corrected myself; *the residence I'm staying at until time to return home.*

Michael's Triumph was gone when I got there, though he'd left a big scuff in the sand from wrestling it upright. I exhaled in relief spiced with satisfaction. He'd probably rolled it down the driveway before starting it up, as Jona had neither heard the bike leave nor noticed anyone through the window. She had been intent on scribbling in her notebook, propped up cozily on the couch listening to her favorite Joni Mitchell album.

"So did you get everything squared away?" she asked, her tone light but her gaze intent and muscles tense.

I flopped into an armchair, then sprang back up upon recalling I was damp and sandy and smelled like horse. "He knows not to come back again. But..."

I paused to lean with feigned casualness on the doorframe to the kitchen. "He told me something I didn't like hearing about you."

Jona lifted a brow. "Oh?"

"Yeah. He said that you, Mom, and Dad prevented him from seeing me at the hospital."

Jona looked away. I added, "And you wouldn't let him into the house. And you didn't pass me his messages. Eventually you just hung up on him when he called."

After a long silence Jona admitted, "That's right," and swung her gaze back in a challenging stare.

I pushed upright and stamped my foot. "Damn it, you lied to me! And you think you're better than him. How dare you!"

Jona shook her head. "We had the right. You were injured—and he caused it."

"How did you know? I hadn't told you yet!"

Jona closed her notebook, slowly and carefully. "But I saw."

I clapped my mouth shut. Jona pulled her legs down to sit square on the couch. "At least some of it. I went to the show grounds early to bring you breakfast. Wanted to hang around and watch the whole rigmarole. Your events were always while I was at school, so that time I came home the night before and, as you know, was planning to bring Mom and Dad a few hours later to watch. But I thought it would be cool to see you in your own element, surprise you with my interest."

"I sure would've been. But I never saw you."

"That's because I saw you first. I was wandering around looking for you and attracted by the shouting. I saw you crack him one across the face and storm off. It was a toss-up whether to follow you for comfort I knew you wouldn't accept, or see what he and the girl did. Well, I'm sorry to say, after he rubbed away the imprint of your hand, he and the girl started laughing and retreated to a nearby trailer."

I stood with clenched fists and a stabbing pulse in my head. "Did you tell Mom and Dad?" I asked through clenched teeth.

"No, they just hate him on principle."

"So what else didn't anyone tell me?" I asked the room. Then I flung at Jona, "You're all a bunch of rats! You know what else he said to me? He was 'doing me a favor'! Just like you!"

At Jona's arched brows, I explained Michael's rationale for canoodling with Suzanne. Jona rolled her eyes and said, "Convinced yet?"

"Oh yes. More than ever. And so, so embarrassed that I ever bought his act."

My eyes smarted from suppressed tears. I still wasn't sure how much of my private time with Michael had been an act. Now I would never know.

Jona stood. "I'm sorry it worked out this way, Linny, but please understand that we didn't want you to be hurt anymore and didn't know how else to prevent it."

"Nice thought, but it didn't work, did it?"

I stomped up to my bedroom, tore off my clothes, and again cranked up the shower. There I could really cry, hiding the tears from even myself.

CHAPTER FOURTEEN

Since the next day was Con's day off, I didn't have to worry about facing—or dodging—him as I went through my morning rituals. And since Jona never got up before I departed for early shift, I could operate without stress.

Before leaving the house for my beach walk, I studied myself in the mirror. Sleep had relaxed my skin and muscles so I looked normal again. That made it time to return to normal life.

I strolled along the dawning shore, studying the dunes and sea and early beachcombers, wondering how much I would miss it all once I left. I wished I had started an hour earlier so I could walk all the way around the curve and see if the rumored "nudie beach" actually existed. Con had claimed he'd never seen anyone swimming or sunbathing naked, but that struck me as the kind of fib a guy would tell.

And Con, I thought, was still a regular guy regardless of the trappings he wore and baggage he carried. He had proven that by kissing me in the moonlight. I knew I should respond to that but found myself unwilling. I resented him for destroying the comfort I had felt with him. Now he caused as much turmoil in my heart as Michael had.

I should just purge them both from my life and take my chances with that stable Allison worked at. Then, instead of hanging out with my barn colleagues during off-hours, I could start looking for the places where guys like Dave hung out.

A Dave was what I needed. His heart was as big as his face was homely, and his mind an even match for Jona's. They shared the same sense of humor and liked to do the same things. He'd been a good friend to Con, and he accepted me for myself. Who wouldn't want a guy like that?

Me, I thought morosely. I wanted all Dave's qualities *plus* a horseman. *Plus* good-looking. *Plus* an income that made up for lack of mine.

Such a gem was figuratively sitting in my lap, but I just couldn't envision Con as a lover or lifetime partner. His artsy side and family secrets made him uptight and dual natured. I'd had enough of that, though I could sympathize with his position. He was an ideal friend, and, someday down the road, perhaps a good connection. I needed to keep thinking of him that way, or else I'd unsettle myself even more.

Firm in my resolve, I drove the Saab to the stable and clocked in. The first thing I noticed was Shark in one of the box stalls reserved for private horses, like Cube and Magician. Klatawah would have gotten the third stall if Con didn't keep her outside in the pen with the run-in shed.

Normally my little black mare was saddled up with the string, or loose in the turnout corral with the off-duty horses, or in her own narrow tie stall. I thus assumed Shark was ill or injured and hastened into the stall to check.

But she seemed fine and nosed me for treats. I looked around, confused, for Tom.

"He's not in yet," said Sylvie, passing by with a saddle in her arms.

"What are you doing here?" I asked. "I thought Priss was on this morning"—which I had dreaded but sworn to endure without losing my cool.

"Priss got sacked," Sylvie said with a smirk. "Miriam caught her at the party messing with your old boyfriend."

Uh-oh. "Is that why Shark's in here?" I asked, fearing the answer.

"Didn't they tell you? Oh right, yesterday was your day off."

My voice shot up. "They're selling her?"

"Oh, no. She's Miriam's now."

I flinched. *No-no-no!* "I thought she would pick Cube!"

"Naah. Shark is prettier and almost as fast. Much more trainable—less to unlearn. And Miriam can just have her without having to buy her. Cube's owner wants too much."

I moaned. Sylvie added with relish, "And…she's talked Mike into taking Priss's place, at least part time, around his schedule, until we find somebody else. He'll be staying here"—she pointed at the cobwebby ceiling to indicate the barn apartment—"since the Cape is pretty much No Vacancy from now through the end of summer."

Sylvie smiled at my expression, which must have been blanched and slack because my face felt like melted rubber. Then she scuffed along down the aisle. I turned to Shark and hung on her neck, gnawing my lips to keep back tears.

This is the end. Right now, right here.

A big thunk occurred in my chest. At first it ached, but then faint relief began to ripple out. I'd known something was going to happen, suspected that this chapter of my life would end badly, but I had hung on, hoping. What, really, had there been to hope for?

Just a longer reprieve from reality. Which was over now, unless I wanted to fight a battle I couldn't win, with no ammunition. Fair game on losing Shark: I hadn't made my move fast enough. But rubbing Michael in my face on top of it? *No way!*

I stomped back to Tom's office—still empty, no sign of him in the stableyard—so I looked at the schedule outside his door. It gave me another kick in the chops: My hours had been doubled, but only during the week; all sunset rides eliminated. Michael hadn't been written in yet, but that didn't matter. I wasn't going to hang around to find out when he started.

I pulled a pen from my pocket, scribbled my name off the schedule hard enough to tear the paper, then clocked out and strode into the tackroom to grab a brush box. Shark was going to get her last thorough grooming as a good-bye gift to us both.

While cleaning her dainty hooves, I recited every four-letter word I could think of and fantasized about spiking Miriam in the eye with a hoof pick when she came in. Instead, the person who filled the stall opening when I straightened was Tom.

He looked at me with his basset-hound face. "Sorry about this, kid. But you know how it is: When girlie pulls the daddy card, there's nothing I can do."

"I understand," I said, proud of myself for not expressing what I really thought and felt.

He cussed under his breath and looked away. I heard another car pull in outside. Tom gathered himself to deal with it, saying first: "I owe you a day's pay for Saturday."

"That's okay—save it, you'll need it."

So would I, but waiting around while he wrote that paltry check was more than I was willing to do. Regular payday had been Friday, and I still had that check in my pocket.

"Thanks, it's been good working with you," he said without smiling.

"And thanks for giving me the chance."

He slapped the top edge of the stall door with both palms. "Good luck to you, then."

I nodded, and he walked away. I gave Shark one last pat, one last hug, one last carrot, then let myself out of the stall. The mare turned back to her feed bucket as if I wasn't there.

That really stung, from the horse who had lifted her head to welcome me the day I had arrived and carried me through some of my happiest moments. "Hope you like barrels," I said to her, then snatched up the daypack I had dropped in the aisle, dug to the bottom for the rest of my Canada Mints, and went out back to place one atop each fence pole of Klatawah's corral.

She started toward them before I'd finished and gave me the eye.

"Take care of him," I bade her. "I'm sorry we didn't get to know each other."

She, at least, watched me walk away.

I got to the Saab before meeting anyone else and headed for the bank driving fast, then back to the house driving slowly. When I walked in, Jona was caffeinating herself at the kitchen table over a book. I had hoped to avoid her but knew it wasn't possible unless I drove off in the car I didn't own and abandoned all my belongings.

I had hoped to avoid Con, too, but his car was in the driveway. He could have been on the beach or in his room; all I cared about right then was his absence from the kitchen.

Jona looked up in surprise. "What, did you go in on the wrong day?"

I shook my head. "Wrong place. Wrong time. Wrong everything." I dropped my pack on a kitchen chair, then stopped and faced Jona. "I quit."

"Oh." Jona closed her book with a thunk. "What happened?"

"I got shafted." I headed for the coffeemaker.

"Um, can you be more specific?"

I banged my mug and the pot and the refrigerator door as I assembled my coffee. "Miriam stole Shark, fired Priss, hired Michael, installed him in the barn apartment, and cut my hours so I can't ride the sunset trails anymore."

"Oh." Jona sipped her coffee, eyeing me above the rim.

I continued, "And it isn't worth trying to do anything about it."

"I don't see what you could. What did Tom have to say?"

"That his hands are tied because Miriam's the boss's daughter."

"Oh."

"So, since it's supposed to be a minimum wage temporary job, not a big soap opera centered on my personal life, I left."

"Can't say I blame you."

I didn't blame me, either, though surely others would. Too bad for them: I would move on. Starting with: "Please take me home. Today."

Jona placed down her mug, looking sidelong at me, who stood holding mine. "Can't you give it a day to calm down? Won't you consider having the summer vacation we originally planned?"

"You and Mom planned it, not me. I just went along because I was in no shape to do different."

I flumped into a chair across from her and glugged my coffee, avoiding her eye. Then I smacked my empty mug onto the table and held her gaze in challenge. "It looks like whatever invisible power that rules the universe has decided Galeson's isn't where I should start my life over. Restarts don't count, I guess, until you've been stripped down to bone and nerves. Well, that just happened. So there's no reason to stay."

"None?"

Con appeared in the living room doorway.

I gulped and forced myself to look at him. Fresh out of the shower with his hair slicked back, wearing only cutoff sweatpants, he looked like a publicity shot for a movie star or model. His stormy-blue eyes, however, threatened thunder and lightning.

"Well, I don't mean—" I stopped and turned red. "Nothing personal."

Liar! If he were the only element of the equation, I would stay put.

So I told them both the rest of the truth. "I can't afford to hang around for a summer. I need to work—and I won't work with people who play games with me. So I've got to get back to where I have contacts and a car and gear and possibilities."

"Why not just waitress for the rest of the summer?" Jona said. "You'll make more money doing dinners in Provincetown than you will in a year working in a barn."

"Yeah, that's probably true." No *probably* about it, and the prospect of a real paycheck tempted me. Why not make a living doing something else and afford my own horse—skip the whole crud of working at a stable?

Because it would take too long to execute, and be too miserable in the process. I didn't want to work with people; I wanted to work with horses, today as well as tomorrow. "That's my backup plan in case of total failure," I told Jona. "And while this episode takes me closer to failure, I haven't exhausted all possibilities yet."

I chucked her car keys onto the table. "So since I'm starting over again ten years too late, I really need to get moving."

Jona snapped a look at Con, then sighed. "Okay, give me a chance to pry my eyes open and put on some clothes." She rose and headed for the stairs, then stopped. "But only if you promise to spend at least one night with Mom and Dad."

"Fine. Whatever. Thank you. I can be ready in half an hour."

"I can't, but I'll do the best I can." She clunked up the staircase, leaving me alone with Con.

He slid into the room and sat in Jona's chair. I glared at him then turned away. "Would you at least put a shirt on? I don't need a naked god in my face right now!"

He laughed, tinged with acid. "Yes, ma'am." And departed while I refilled my mug.

It struck me, minutes later, that he was taking a darn long time to grab a T-shirt. What, had I offended him so bad that he'd left?

No: He sashayed back into the room wearing hiked-up sweatpants, laced-up boots, a squall jacket zipped up over his chin, and a woolly hat pulled low on his brow. "That better?"

A hooting laugh fell out of me. And tears almost followed. Hastily I jabbed my eyes. "Ah, yes, that's just fine. Thank you."

He sat with a snarly grin, tugging off his beanie. "So tell me the rest. I only caught part of it."

I recited the morning's events, much calmer now. At the end he said, "And you don't think Shark is worth fighting for."

"Doesn't matter—I have nothing to fight with. Even if I'd gotten my dibs in first, I still don't have the means to keep her, or ship her, or a place to board her. Maybe if I'd stayed the whole summer it would've worked out, but nobody factored in Michael. I'm not going to put up with his and Miriam's crap for a horse I can't afford!"

Con nodded then said, "I'm surprised he decided to stick around."

"Me too, but that doesn't matter, either. He's not getting anywhere near me again. This time I'll make sure nobody knows where I'm going!"

Con shook his head. "The horsey set is a small world."

"Well, if he ever approaches me, I'll do what Jona suggested."

"What, knee him in the nuts?"

"She put it differently but yeah, same idea."

Con winced and folded his hands over his crotch. "Remind me to never make a woman angry."

I gave a lame smile, which faded when he said, "Now you've left me understaffed with a hornet's nest in the stable. Thanks!"

"I'm sorry. But you signed up for the deal before I was in the picture, so don't try to make me feel guilty." Even though I did.

"Yeah, but you made it a lot more fun."

I met and held his eye. He meant it, I could see, and deserved a better response.

Thawing, I reached across the table and touched his hand. "I'm sorry I have to hurt you to stop other people from hurting me. But I can't just run around kicking and punching them all just to get even!"

"You could always take the high road…"

I laughed harshly and shook my head. "I'm not that big. Maybe someday I'll be in a better position and able to be more gracious, but this job isn't how I'm going to get there."

"I can't argue that." He shrugged and looked away, unzipping his jacket. "So…what's your plan?"

When he looked back at me, his mask was firmly in place. I felt my lower lip starting to protrude in a frown. By taking my stance, I'd lost him, too.

I pulled my lip back in, inhaled, and lifted my chin. "Make calls. Visit people. Arrange interviews."

"Starting with Shallowkill?"

"Maybe—at least I've got a friend there who will let me sleep on her couch. But she's already warned me that their barn manager is a problem. It would be stupid to walk straight into another situation I'll have to walk out of! I need to find someplace that works."

"Good luck."

I couldn't tell from his voice whether he was wishing me well or being sarcastic. So I fudged with, "Yeah, well, thanks," then stood. "I've got to pack."

I didn't want to part from him but could find no basis for lingering. His slouch in the chair suggested he wasn't about to leap up and say or do something to prevent me from going. *Just as well*, I thought, trudging up to my bedroom. I needed no more complications; rather, needed to roll with the strip-down-and-simplify syndrome. There wasn't a better choice. Not if I wanted to sleep at night.

Besides, it bugged me that he had choices, too, yet was sticking with one that wouldn't get him anywhere. And maybe blame me for how much harder his life was going to get. Perhaps if we'd traveled farther down the road to romance, I would be willing to stick around. But at that moment, I could see no gain in doing so. The whole wasn't vital enough to self-sacrifice for. Still, I wanted to cry.

Packing took longer than expected though I was ready before Jona. I gave the room a final glance for overlooked leftovers, saw nothing but the pastel-mint walls, white floor and furniture, and white curtains that had greeted my arrival.

None of the artwork on the walls had been done by Con except for the watercolor sketch of me winning the match race on Cube, which I had tucked flat between books in one of my bags. I wished I had the sketch showing me on Shark; Jona had put that one on the refrigerator. Would she mind if I snatched it?

I went downstairs to try, clunking my bags against the stairs and walls, to find Con waiting in the kitchen. He was back in shorts and T-shirt, and standing between me and the fridge.

"Want help?" he said, even though he already held three flat rectangular packages wrapped in newspaper and securely taped.

"I'm okay, thanks." I moved for the door as Jona started down from upstairs. Con shouldered the screen door open for me and held it with his foot as I passed through, then followed me down the railroad ties to the Saab. He placed his packages behind the driver's seat while I loaded the back.

We caught up to each other outside the passenger door, where I hesitated before opening it. Jona slid in on the other side and started the engine.

"See you in a day or so?" Con said to her, leaning in through the window.

"Yes. I'll call."

"And you'll call Dave."

"Yes."

"Have a good drive, then."

They waved each other good-bye. Con straightened and faced me, his smile gone. I gazed into his eyes, which reflected my uncertainty. We had barely known each other a month, and only touched each other one night, which seemed both surreal and unreal in this morning's blazing sunshine. So a brotherly-sisterly hug felt...wrong. A kiss? Too easily misunderstood. Shaking hands? So stilted.

My hands lifted anyway, in a helpless shrug; he caught both of them in both of his then lifted one all the way to his lips to kiss my fingers. My heart unclenched a fraction with that reminder of the moonlit night, but I remained mute and rigid.

Then he stepped forward, almost in a formal dance position with one hand still holding mine and the other on my waist. He paused to let me back out if I wanted. When I didn't, he bent to kiss me.

That's more like it! I parted my lips in welcome. His touched mine with the same softness as before, but lingered to taste them, and part them a little further, and tease them with his tongue, asking and inviting and apologizing and hoping.

I answered in kind, releasing some of the love I'd been strangling back. Then I withdrew before it flooded out and fired me up to grab him and devour him while Jona twiddled her thumbs in the car.

He released me at once, stepping back while still holding my hand. His eyes had turned darker blue and sagged around the edges, but he managed to quirk a smile while sliding his fingers away through mine.

"Till we meet again, Miss Eagan," he said in a deep voice, not letting my gaze escape.

I gave him a wobbly smile. "Um, yes. God knows when that will be. But, well, thanks so much, for—everything."

I ducked into the car and tugged shut the door, glancing up at him a final time through the open window. He stood with arms crossed and waggled a few fingers. I returned a two-fingered V. He smiled.

Then the moving car took him out of sight. Part of me remained behind in the sand at his feet.

Jona slewed the Saab down the driveway. Once settled on the road, she sneaked a look at me and said, "What, did he kiss you or something?"

"Yes," I answered, back stiff as a pole, eyes fixed ahead.

Jona laughed. "You finally figure out he's in love with you?"

"What?" I swiveled to stare at her. "Where'd you get that idea?"

"The way he looks at you."

"And what way is that?"

Like the way he just left me.

"Well, it's more about how much attention he pays to you, and how cranky he gets when you don't pay enough back. Remember, I spend his off time with him."

"I—we—c'mon, Jona, I practically lived in his pocket for weeks. We share the same interests. He's been a really good friend. I don't have too many of those...especially lately."

I heard the falsity in my voice, even though the words were true.

"I've also seen his paintings," Jona said.

I stopped mid-inhale for my next words, remembering the wrapped rectangles Con had slid into car. I twisted to pull them forward between the seats.

"Careful..." Jona said. "They're not framed."

I couldn't quite wriggle the big one into my seat so left it and just addressed the small one. Two small ones. With shaking hands, I untaped the wrapping.

Out came a watercolor portrait of Shark, showing her zigzag blaze and ears like pointy parentheses. Her dished face and the pink spot below her left nostril. The bright curiosity in her warm, brown eyes. Even her whiskers before I had trimmed them.

I choked back a sob and opened the next package. This a colored-pencil sketch of Klatawah bucking, not in angry retribution but joyful frisking. Her coat was the correct shade of old penny and her mane the proper palomino blond. Con had even caught the oddly uniform pale-ash color of her hooves.

I stared between both as the Mid Cape Highway rolled away beneath our tires. Jona left me in silence, fiddling with the radio as we drove in and out of broadcast ranges. Finally I rewrapped the pictures and inserted them between backseat luggage. When I sat forward again, hands clasped in my lap, Jona asked, "What do you think?"

"I can't. Think. I'm too overloaded. I don't dare look at the big one. He bombards me with mixed messages. I can't—I don't need this. I don't know how I feel. I don't know what to do."

"That about covers it," Jona quipped, suppressing a smile.

More miles and minutes passed. We crossed the bridge over the Cape Cod Canal, at which point I blurted, "He can't love me so much if he let me go without even a whimper."

Jona tipped her head toward a shoulder in a half shrug. "Well, maybe he's seen the same poster we have. *If you love something, set it free...*"

I snorted. "That's B.S. Michael came back, and he sure ain't mine! And never will be."

"At least you know where Con will be if you change your mind."

I snorted again, but this time didn't speak. I knew I would not change my mind. If this abbreviated, man-complicated summer had taught me anything, it was that one's head had to rule one's life, not one's heart. I would be better off dreaming about what might have been than gambling on a slim chance and then blowing it. I did not need another handsome horseman. I needed a job that would pay the bills and let me be a horsewoman.

That meant climbing back into the saddle, changing leads, and cantering off toward the next hurdle. Con and Michael could jump their own—or crash into them—just fine without me.

PART II

Hudson Valley, New York
June–October, 1975

"[I]n the marriage union, the independence of the husband and wife will be equal, their dependence mutual, and their obligations reciprocal."

~Lucretia Mott

CHAPTER FIFTEEN

"Linny! I am so happy to see you!"

Allison launched herself into my arms with a squeal and a bear hug. I staggered back with a laugh pushed out of me and clamped my arms around my friend's back.

"Me, too!" I stepped back to hold her at arm's length. "You look great."

The gangling teen had become a tanned and taut young woman, her terra-cotta hair a dusky flame atop her head and eyes a sparkling hazel.

"Thanks, you too. I didn't expect to see you till end of summer. What gives?"

We finished crossing Shallowkill Farm's parking area toward my sun-faded yellow Datsun, packed to the headliner with my belongings. "That temp job finished earlier than expected. So I'm on a job-hunting tour, figured I'd stop in and see you first."

"Well, you can stop touring right here—we need staff desperately. I've missed the last two shows because there was no one to cover for me."

"I can certainly do that. And I need work desperately, so it's meant to be!—unless things are as bad as you said last time we talked."

"I dunno, some can take it, some can't. Are you here for an interview? I mean, did you ever send your résumé?"

"Yeah, but if they answered, it hasn't gotten to me yet."

We leaned against the car fender, still warm in the June sun. I said, "I tried a bunch of times to call you, but you're never home."

Allison rolled her head back with a dramatic sigh. "God no, I freakin' live here! And yeah, I got your message, but I'm so fried by the time I get home, I keep forgetting—or else just fall asleep."

I smiled. "Which is why I finally called the barn to find out when you'd be on duty."

Allison matched my grin. "You timed it right—here I am, and everybody you need to see is around, too. Want to meet 'em?"

"Sure, but I'd like to look around, first." I had already seen a big outdoor ring enclosed by white board fencing and bracketed by bleachers, adjacent to a schooling ring, surrounded by acres of white barns and outbuildings and white-fenced turnout pastures. "When can you break for more than two minutes?"

Allison wiggled her mouth. "I've got a lesson in fifteen...why don't you just help me get ready. I'll introduce you to my instructor, and you can jump right in."

My mood bubbled up to match my friend's. I helped Allison tack up her mare, Trix, then followed the tall, silvery-dappled horse as Allison led us through the showpiece barn into a connecting arena.

Ye gods, I thought, almost pulling up short. You could fit two Academy arenas in here!

"Nice, huh?" Allison buckled on her schooling helmet.

I shook my head at the well-lit cavern—thinking, *This is more like it!*—then tightened Trix's girth and slid down the stirrups on a saddle so beautifully made and buttery soft that I almost salivated. It felt good to have my hands back on fine-crafted leathers and buckles after Galeson's battered tack, so crude and heavy in comparison. My doubts and regrets began to dissolve.

I gave Allison a leg up and stepped back just as a woman came up behind us. Her steps had been silent on the arena floor, which was soft yet firm, fluffy without being dusty, moist without being wet, freshly raked since the last riders.

The woman looked to be in her early thirties, slim and fit and poised. She kept her bronze, jaw-length hair back from her face with a tortoise-shell band, and wore the Shallowkill uniform.

Uniforms! I thought, privately shaking my head again. Allison wore the shirt—a navy-blue polo with "Shallowkill Farm" embroidered on the left chest pocket above a jumping horse and rider—over her schooling breeches, while the woman wore it with the crisp khaki pants, two-tone belt, and leather ankle boots I had seen on half a dozen people since arriving.

"Hey, Allison," the woman greeted, nodding to me. "All set?"

"Yep. Mary Anne, this is my friend, Linny Eagan. She was my teacher when I was at Mount Bradbury. Linny, Mary Anne is our resident trainer. Another gal, Cindy, comes in three days a week."

Mary Anne extended her hand. "Nice to meet you. Didn't we get a résumé from you recently?"

My pulse skipped. "Yes, I sent one a few weeks ago. But I've moved on since then, so if you answered, I didn't get it. Part of why I stopped in today."

Mary Anne nodded. "We can talk later. It's Allison's time now. You can watch, if you'd like, up there."

She gestured to a viewing deck along the length of the arena, both sides, with a glass-fronted viewing box on the far end. I nodded and sauntered off as if such features were part of my everyday world.

Then I leaned forward and focused on Allison's hour of private coaching. To have the same package, I would willingly shovel many tons of manure.

When the session was over and Allison was leading Trix back to her capacious box stall with nameplate on the door, Mary Anne signaled me to follow and left the arena through the viewing box, which opened into a lounge then the business office. Mary Anne had her own little office within, into which she led me and closed the door behind us.

Upon sitting at her desk and gesturing for me to sit in a corner chair, she said, "How does Allison look compared to when you worked with her?"

"Terrific," I answered. "She's left me in the dust."

Mary Anne nodded and leaned to open a file drawer in her desk. "If I recall...you were riding Western this summer."

She swiftly tabbed through hanging files and withdrew a folder. After riffling through the papers, she pulled out my résumé. "Galeson's Stable, in Provincetown."

"Yes."

Mary Anne looked up with studied blandness. "Rather short stint there..."

I held my practiced relaxed posture while saying, "That was the intent. It was an informal pitching in while they were short-handed, and I was building strength up after injuries."

Mary Anne cocked an inquisitive eyebrow, then winced after I explained. All she said was, "You're completely recovered?"

"Yes."

She nodded. Then, after a pause, she asked, "What were you doing, then, at your previous job?"

"Stable work, teaching beginner lessons, exercising school and boarder horses, training for show."

"This was at Old Avon Women's Academy?"

"Yes."

"And you'd been a student there?"

"Yes." I took the hint for more background and summarized my riding experience: summer camp from age twelve to fourteen, then the Academy's equine program during my high school days, then: "I started showing Junior at C-level hunter/jumper shows, kept at it during college at UMass. Taught lessons at Allison's school during semester and the summer. Then I got a chance to go back to the Academy for full-time work and helped show one of the students' horses. I was just starting the A circuit when I had my, er, mishap."

Mary Anne digested this. "So where are you looking to go from here?"

This was the question I'd been dreading. I had practiced an evasive answer that was still honest, but Mary Anne seemed like such a genuine person that I wanted to be straight with her.

"I'm not sure. That fall was a big setback and made me reconsider my direction. I've dreamed of being a champion since I was a little girl, but got such a late start that I had to work harder and focus more manically on making up lost ground. I'm starting to realize I don't have what it takes and am trying to come up with a better plan."

Mary Anne kept her gaze on me, steady, and let me take my time. I liked her all the more for it.

"This place appeals to me," I continued, "because it caters to different schools of riding. Or that's the impression I get. I want to settle somewhere with diverse training and events to watch and participate in. Otherwise I'll just be wishing for the impossible the rest of my life and keep suffering setbacks."

Mary Anne regarded me for a moment with slanted brow. "Interesting."

I held her gaze and volunteered nothing further, silently pressuring her to take the lead.

She responded, "Do you have your own horse?"

"Not yet."

She nodded and shuffled her papers. Then she looked up and said, "All we have open is barn work. But that may be a good way for you to get back into the swing of things. Your impression is correct, in that we have people riding pleasure as well as showing in hunter, stadium jumping, dressage, and cross-country. Many of us belong to the local hunt. Our riders who compete do so independently, and mainly for fun. Just last year, though, we formed a show team around them to give us a higher profile and the riders a more economical and enjoyable way to travel; it's what Allison is doing now. But while our riders are enthusiastic, they're not rabid about showing, and their careers don't depend on it."

"That sounds ideal." I said it casually, with a light smile, but internally I was stomping down excitement.

Mary Anne must have sensed this, for she softened her businesslike tone and leaned back in her chair. "I showed heavily through Junior in the Medal/Maclay program, and quit when I was on top because I'd burned out. I wanted to go to college, get married, and have a family. Now I've done all that but never left horses. It's worked out nicely: a steady job doing what I know best and helping other riders, without the madness of competition life. Our traveling trainer, Cindy, is still competing at a high level, and she works mostly with the boarders keen on showing."

"I want to do something competitive," I admitted, "but the hunter circuit...doesn't suit me. It would be great to have people to talk about options with."

Mary Anne smiled. "We offer good pay and benefits for barn work, and opportunity over time to move in different directions. But...there is a downside, and you'll need to discuss that with Allison then get back to me."

I was pretty sure I knew what that downside was so said only, "Assuming that can be dealt with, what's the next step?"

"Meet with our barn manager, Caryl Ballard." Mary Anne dropped the gaze she'd held throughout the conversation, and her forehead wrinkled. "I can mention we've talked and get you an appointment. When would be convenient?"

Whew! I'd been lucky to catch the main players at home rather than off at a show, so I said, "Tomorrow, if possible. I expect to stay with Allison tonight, so can talk with anyone tomorrow. If that doesn't work out, I can come back any time—just let me know when."

Mary Anne smiled again. "Call me tomorrow morning around nine. I should have information for you by then."

"Super. For now, can you tell me when Allison comes off duty?"

"Not for a few more hours. But I'm willing to look the other way if you want to work with her. That will give you a chance to feel things out. I don't have time to give you a tour this afternoon, but if anyone challenges you, tell them you have my permission."

I smiled and stood and held out my hand. "Thank you."

Mary Anne mirrored my actions, and we shook.

"See you in the morning, then," Mary Anne said, and departed. I followed her outside, then paused to gaze around, bemused, for a few moments, before seeking Allison and exploring what I hoped would be my new world.

When I caught up with her, she said, "Sure, I've got a couch you can use. My trailer is small, but it's like a boat, with everything folding up and pulling down and all sorts of nooks and crannies for storage."

"Thanks. I'd much rather stay with you than at a motel!"

"What motel? You'd have to drive thirty miles to find one. That's why most of us live here."

"Most? There's got to be at least twenty employees here!"

"Well, I mean barn staff. When we walk around, you'll see. That house across the road is divided into apartments. Then there's a bunch of trailers and cabins all over the Farm, and apartments over garages and barns."

"So everybody else drives in?"

"Yeah, some commute from Albany and Saratoga, but most anyone with a house lives in Beverwyck or Horatio, or one of the little villages nearby."

"Where do the owners live?"

They were Desmond and Clarissa Burlingame, I recalled from my trawl through *Chronicle of the Horse* and *Practical Horseman* when I'd been compiling lists of stables and people to contact. Con had gone to school with their son, but I had not picked up his name.

Allison waved a hand. "Down the road a ways. They have a huge estate. And one in Florida, I think, too."

That figures, I thought, as I helped Allison finish her duties. She tossed information over stall dividers or when we passed in the aisle, or while bringing in horses from turnout, walking side by side.

"There's no rentals near here, for housing or visitors…though there is one old lady a couple miles away who has a little cabin. I stayed there my first months…you can probably get that place because the girl who quit last week had it, and none of us grabs it when available because it's so cold in winter. Rent's really cheap, though…but you have to mow the lawn and weed the garden, and help with her animals. Two dogs, eight cats, and two retired horses, last I knew. She doesn't work the farm anymore, so makes her money renting to us and leasing half the land to local farmers…lets the rest run wild. We can swing by there on our way to supper."

Which we did, me driving so Allison could have beer with her pizza. I couldn't see the cabin because it was tucked behind Mrs. Edwards's timeworn farmhouse, but I got the idea. And loved it: a little place of my own, in the country, supported by a job at a real equestrian facility, which would rebuild my funds and set me back on the right path. Whatever that was. And no guys around to disrupt my head and heart.

While waiting for the pizza to cook in the village twenty minutes away from the farm, I was feeling a sadder, more seasoned self and ready to get down to business. But then Allison leaned back in her chair and said, "So things didn't work out with your Michael, huh?"

I suppressed a cringe. "No."

They might have, I didn't say, *if I had given in*. I declined telling Allison more, since there was no law that decreed I must announce that I'd made a fool of myself.

"I'm not surprised," Allison replied, "given his reputation."

"Richly deserved, I'm sorry to say. At least I got two years out of him before he reverted."

"Hey, that must be a record."

"I hope I can go down in history as someone *other* than The Girl Who Kept Michael Dixon Monogamous the Longest!"

We laughed. I found the stricture in my chest loosening a little, followed by a surge of warmth toward my friend. It chilled when Allison leaned forward across the table and said in a stage whisper, "What I really want to hear about is Con Winston."

I groaned and rolled my eyes. "Oh no, not you, too!"

"I didn't get it at first when you mentioned you were at his place. You were so casual, like he was just a regular guy, someone else of the same name."

"Well, that's what he's like."

"Then I realized he's son of that rich and famous guy. How'd you ever hook up with him?"

"We weren't 'hooked up,' if you mean 'together.'" I explained the chain of sister to sister's boyfriend to Con, emphasizing that the plan had been rehab, but things had taken on a life of their own.

"And a short life, at that," I concluded. I withheld the fact that Michael had come on the scene and blown everything, saying only that Galeson's had gone sour to the point it had cost me more to stay than to leave.

Allison didn't question this, leaving my promise to myself unchallenged. I had sworn that, unless Michael went loco and tracked me here, I was done with talking about him, done even thinking about him—done, done, done.

My bigger problem was what to think about the other guy I'd left behind.

No, I reminded myself: My biggest problem is getting and keeping a job.

It took no effort to divert Allison onto horsey topics. In exchange for details about Shallowkill daily life, as well as what she knew about other area farms, I described my great-circle plan: a loop covering equestrian establishments across New York State and Pennsylvania, applying for jobs in person.

"I thought about just hopping from show to show," I said, "to hit the greatest range of people from the greatest range of stables. But that gave too much chance of running into people I *don't* want to meet."

Allison grinned. "There's plenty else to choose from around here."

"That's for sure!"

I hadn't realized until my magazine search that the Hudson Valley and Capitol Region were home to many show barns, racing stables, breeding farms, and hunt clubs; old money, new money—a business sector rivaling that of Kentucky and Virginia.

I could surely find a place at one of them. If not, I could always move south where the pickings were richer. If that failed, I would know for sure I was following the wrong dream and must find another niche in life.

But Shallowkill was good enough for now, and better than I expected. That reminded me of Mary Anne's hint about downsides, so I said to Allison, "Tell me about Caryl Ballard."

Allison twisted her lips and held from answering until the pizza server came and went. Between mouthfuls she answered, "Caryl runs the horse part of the facility and is the one who would actually hire you. She's a brilliant organizer, but..." She looked around and dropped her voice. "Well, to put it charitably, she doesn't do well with people. If you're a lackey, she chews you up and spits you out laughing. If you're a bigwig, she sucks up so obviously it either makes them laugh or throw up. Problem is, the Burlingames are, for the most part, absentee owners, and they're very nice and very important among the rich folk. So no one's willing to tell them bald-face that they hired a dud."

"But the stalls are full; wouldn't the boarders bail out if she was a big problem?"

Allison shook her head. "They get their butts kissed. The peons who complain sound like complaining peons everywhere, so we're ignored. People come here for Mary Anne and Cindy, as well as the events we host; and lots of stablehands try it out because the money is way better than other places. If you don't get on Caryl's downside, you can do pretty well."

"So what puts you on her downside?"

"Who knows? The moon in Sagittarius. The stock market. Her time of the month. You"—she pointed a pizza slice at me—"could go either way, unique enough to catch her interest, but she might also see you as a threat."

"Threat? To what? No way would I want her job!"

"That's not it." Allison shook her head again, swallowed, and placed down her pizza crust to look me hard in the eye. "She's viciously jealous of anyone who's better than her at anything. Since she's a pretty good rider, most of us don't threaten her there as long as we have flaws she can see. But in your case? Whether you ride well or not is second to the fact you're pretty and you're smart. She'll penalize you for that even if you do everything right."

Allison picked up a new slice. "Can you handle that?"

I sat back and thought. On one hand, I'd had enough of being stepped on and manipulated! On the other hand, I would always be under somebody's thumb—unless I somehow became the person in the driver's seat, like Con when he inherited his millions. Lacking that, I would spend my life choosing between lessers of evils and balancing them against pluses. Shallowkill offered multiple, huge pluses against one big minus. Just how bad was it?

"The only way to know is by trying," I answered her. "I can always quit like everyone else if it's unbearable."

"Yeah, but quitting enough jobs will pin you at the bottom forever. And quitting here will give you three not-great job endings in a row."

"True." That specter haunted me. "The other side is, I'll get nowhere if I don't take calculated risks. At least here I've got the downside being handed to me on a platter. It should be easier to deal with when I can see it coming!"

"Consider yourself warned—and I really hope you get the job and everything works out. We could have so much fun!"

I agreed. From there we returned to her trailer on Shallowkill's back forty. I lugged in my sleeping bag and conked out on the bench sofa, nervous about the morrow but secure in the knowledge I was moving away from my failures, on course to being independent. If this opportunity didn't pan out, there were many more to investigate. The knowledge let me fall right to sleep.

I appreciated the rest and recharge the next morning when I met Caryl. Mary Anne had arranged a ten o'clock appointment, giving me an hour's notice after I called in. Allison had been back at work since dawn.

Recalling Shallowkill's uniform, I donned my own blue polo shirt and khaki pants. After plaiting my hair into a tight braid, I presented myself at Caryl's office one minute early.

The woman was at her desk in an office larger and more cluttered than Mary Anne's—her papers stacked in rigid order instead of leaning and sliding all over the place like Tom's, the walls and shelves laden with ribbons and trophies—and didn't rise or offer a hand when I entered.

"You're the one who crashed a fence and went Western," she opened.

I met Caryl's green gaze with all the nerve I could muster. "Yes and no," I replied.

Caryl waited. I had trouble marshaling my thoughts against that gaze; I had heard of and read about green eyes but never seen them. Caryl's were bright and clear, with no squiggles of color in the irises, like Michael's blues, though hers lacked his dark border ring. She also didn't seem to blink.

I inhaled and said, "I got a concussion from a bad fall and had to take the summer off. My family shipped me to the Cape to stay with relatives and friends. I recovered more quickly than expected and pitched in at the local stable."

Caryl sniffed. "Western. I'm sure you've acquired some bad habits. Why did you fall?"

"I allowed myself to be distracted by personal problems and confused my horse at a fence. He refused in response. I went over his head and took down a jump."

"Stupid."

"I agree."

"Was it your own horse?"

"No."

"Was it injured?"

"No."

Caryl stared at me with no change of expression. I thought her cheekbones were so sharp they would slice washcloths when she did her ablutions in the morning.

"Have you been over a jump since?"

"No. We just took out public trail rides on the dunes."

Caryl sniffed again. "Yet you think you can just hop back into the saddle and compete."

"No, I think I need to resume training toward competing again someday."

Caryl's tone finally changed. "As home-barn staff, you'll have to buy your own lessons."

"I gathered that."

"And home-barn staff does not go to shows."

"I understand. I'm thinking long term, when I have my own horse and can move up to Allison's level."

"We'll see. It's not just a matter of money. Did Mary Anne tell you the rules?"

"No."

Caryl fired off: "Six-day week. Schedule managed by me, no arguments. One-hour lunch, immediate dismissal for three lates. Immediate dismissal for drinking, smoking, and drugs. Immediate dismissal for more than two late arrivals in the morning, or failing to complete daily chores—one time, you're out. One-year probation before benefits go into effect. Since you don't have your own horse, it's three-month probation before you can show or ride the hunt on any of ours, and only if approved by Mary Anne or Cindy. You can ride boarder horses with permission, but again, only if approved by Mary Anne or Cindy."

She stopped, waiting for a reaction. I gave none, though I understood why stable help didn't last long. The terms themselves weren't so extreme as to scare me, but the woman's manner matched the severity of her dead-straight hair, the shade of dark coffee, pulled hard into a ponytail, and her mouth a slice across her face, covering her teeth when she spoke.

"Any questions?"

I held Caryl's stare, then blinked. "When can I start?"

She did not blink. "Tomorrow morning. Six sharp. Here's the forms to fill out, a job description, and Shallowkill policies." She handed me a set of densely typed papers. "If you want to ride here, Mary Anne must evaluate you. Get a hard hat and meet us in the arena."

I scrambled, grateful that I had seen enough yesterday to know where the tackroom was and where communal gear within it was stored. I beat Caryl to the arena, where Mary Anne was finishing a group lesson over ground cavalettis that ended in a set mounted on an X for adjustable heights. Several people watched from the viewing deck—including Allison, who I pretended not to see.

Caryl led in a large brown Thoroughbred that pranced semi-sideways, reminding me of Klatawah. For the first time my control faltered, and I faced a fact I'd been dodging: I hadn't sat in an English saddle since I fell out of one, nor ridden a horse more than fifteen hands tall, save for twenty minutes on Big Buddy. Nor had I jumped anything.

While Caryl might be worried about what habits I had acquired from riding undisciplined Western, I was worried about getting onto a seventeen-hand, super-fine-tuned blood horse I couldn't reach the stirrups for. Then being judged on my performance.

But first…I greeted the big liver chestnut with a friendly voice and open hand, letting him sniff me. "What's his name?" I asked Caryl.

"Goldiggers Sonny, by Prospector out of Golden Girl. To you, he's Fudge."

I chuckled, then told Fudge he was a good boy, handsome and noble, and we were going to have a great time together.

Caryl tapped her foot. "Skip the love fest and get on."

I gave her a slitty glance and finished Fudge's neck rub with a scritch underneath his short-trimmed mane. Then I said, "Please either show me where the mounting block is or give me a leg up."

Finally the woman blinked. After handing me the reins to loop over Fudge's neck, she cupped her hands to take my knee and tossed me up into the saddle.

I landed more heavily than I would have liked, to avoid overshooting. For a second I missed Shark's high-arched neck and compact body so much that my heart panged, feeling now like I was straddling a roof peak three stories up.

But muscle memory returned as I gathered the reins and adjusted my stirrups, so that the two circuits Caryl allowed for warm-up gave me enough time to settle. Caryl then withdrew to the viewing area while Mary Anne stepped forward to direct me through half an hour of collected and extended walk, sitting and posting trot with and without stirrups, canter on both leads with flying changes, halts and reverses, turns on the forehand, then trotting passes over the cavalettis.

"I see why you had trouble at that last show," Mary Anne said while I walked Fudge on a loose rein, dazed by the return to normal from intense focus. "You give up contact just before the fence."

Those words zapped through me like an electrical shock. If my life could be summed up in a sentence, that was it.

"If you do that even now, when you're paying attention," Mary Anne continued, "it's almost guaranteed when you're not that he'll run out or refuse. We can work on that if you want to go on with lessons."

"Yes, I would," I said, hoping my pay would allow it.

"Let's give it a week, then start a program. Welcome to Shallowkill, Linny—I'll see you around, and we'll work together next week."

She strode out of the arena, followed by Caryl with a backshot glare. Allison headed across the arena while I sat atop Fudge for another moment to let my head stop spinning. Just like that, my world had changed again! Then I swung a leg over for the long slip to the ground.

CHAPTER SIXTEEN

After the most demanding and satisfying week of my professional life, I moved into Mrs. Edwards's two-room cabin on the eve of my first day off.

It didn't take long: The dwelling came spartanly furnished with a cot and dresser in the bedroom, pull-out sofa and armchair with side table in the living area, and a kitchen table with two chairs in the cooking corner. All I had to do was carry in my boxes and bags and unpack.

The last thing I did was unwrap the sixteen-by-twenty rectangle Con had slid into Jona's car the morning we departed. I had already thumbtacked up the portraits of Shark and Klatawah, and the watercolor sketch of me on Cube, where I could see them from all corners of the room; but the large picture, which I knew by feel was a canvas stretched taut on an internal frame, I had been afraid to open.

Now I sat on the saggy couch and peeled back tape, unfolded paper. Then I dropped my hands and stared at a vivid painting of myself and Con blasting through a sunset surf on Shark and Klatawah: the very moment that had caught and twirled my heart like nothing before or since.

When my lungs insisted I breathe again, I gasped and pressed a hand to my chest, which started to heave as tears stung my eyes.

"Damn him!" I blurted to the empty room. "Damn him, damn him, *damn him*!"

I laid the painting on the couch and jumped up to pace. At last in total privacy, I could not hold back my sobs no matter how determinedly I gnawed my fist and scrubbed my eyes. Finally I plunked into the wobbly hardback chair at the kitchen table, and just wept into my hands.

It all came out then: failure, doubt, humiliation, exhaustion, confusion, desperation, longing, passion, fear. Half of me wished I had Con's strong arms around me; the other half was grateful no one could see me in such a state.

I had recovered to the point of blowing my nose when the sound of a car pulling up outside startled me upright and rigid. For half a heartbeat I hoped it might be Con, then mentally shook myself for being silly. Of course it could not be him—I had not yet told anyone of my whereabouts, and I already knew from tracking Allison that Shallowkill did not give out employee addresses. Besides, this cabin had no phone, or mail delivery, so my address was an anonymous post office box in town.

But certain staff members knew where I now lived, so I dashed to the sink to splash my face with cold water before the visitor knocked. I opened the door to Allison, who stood grinning on the slate stoop brandishing a pizza box and bottle of wine.

"Happy housewarming!"

I smiled, sneaked a discreet final sniff, and waved my friend in.

"Hey, I hardly recognize it!" Allison exclaimed.

"Don't know why not—I haven't redecorated."

Allison spun around. "But you've filled it already. I never unpacked my suitcase, aside from strewing dirty clothes all over the place."

She set her gifts on the kitchen-corner table then crossed the living area to its side window, where I had hung my show ribbons across a curtain rod, and placed my one little trophy on the windowsill below them.

"I'm hesitant to do any more," I said. "It's too hard to believe I'll be here long—I mean, this is the third complete change I've had in under two months!"

"Third one's the charm," Allison quipped, handling the Breyer horse figurines half emerged from an opened but not yet unpacked box.

"Or three strikes, you're out," I returned, feeling like Sisyphus, that king from Greek mythology who'd been condemned for eternity to roll a boulder up a hill, only to have it roll back down every time he reached the top.

Allison moved on to examine my compact stereo and album stack atop a dysfunctional console TV. "Yeah, I'll grant you the endurance rate here is low," she said, "but you've got the right stuff. I'm sure it will work out fine."

"Man, I hope so!"

I scooped my coats and towels from the armchair and toted them to the bedroom, to join the clothes and sleeping bag I had already piled on the naked mattress, my riding gear on the floor. Returning to the main room, I realized with a jolt that I had left the painting in full view on the sofa.

Before I could slip it out of sight behind the TV, Allison stopped dead and stared.

"Hey, that's a nice one. You need a fireplace to put it over." She stepped closer to peer. "Hey—that's you!"

She straightened and looked at me with new admiration. "I didn't know you're an artist!"

I shook my head, my gaze still on the canvas. "I'm not."

"Then who…?"

"Um…"

Catching my reluctance, Allison recrossed the room to tackle food and beverage. "Okay. So. What are the chances the last girl left us some wineglasses?"

"About zero," I said with a sigh.

Allison tugged open cupboards above the sink and tiny counter. "Hey, here's a mug. And an iced tea glass."

Clunk, clunk. I heard her put them on the table while I stood in the middle of the room with a lance through my heart. She rinsed the drinkware and opened drawers. "Got a corkscrew?"

"No, but I've got a Swiss Army knife."

I pulled it from my khakis pocket, having not yet changed out of my new uniform, and delivered it to Allison, who said, "I hope you like red."

"I'm not fussy."

I glided back to the couch and turned the painting to face the seat back. Then flopped onto the cushion, bracing myself for the grilling to come.

Allison crossed the floor and handed me the iced tea glass full to the brim with garnet wine, then rested her rump on the sofa arm.

"Okay, so what's the deal. Who did the painting?"

"He did." I looked away.

"He—? Wait a second…"

I could almost hear the gears ratcheting in her head. She stood and reversed the painting. "This is the Cape, right? That must be your Con. You mean *he* did it? A football player?"

I got up and looked out the window at my overgrown yard. I could feel Allison studying my back, then felt the floor sag as she walked around to scrutinize my face.

"I'm putting two and two together here..." She squinted at my pink and puffy eyes. A late drip escaped my nostril, which I absently wiped with my wrist.

"Wine," Allison commanded, and sipped her own from her ceramic mug.

After I glugged some of my own, she nodded and said, "I can't stay long, since we're leaving at some god-awful hour tomorrow morning for Lake Placid. My idea was to celebrate your coming here, and a successful first week. But now I'm thinking you need to talk."

"No, not really."

"Yeah, really. Why are you crying?"

"I'm not."

"But you were."

"I'm just...tired and sad, that's all. It just caught up to me that I've left a few pieces behind, and I miss them."

"Some of those pieces big? Like, a tall, handsome blond guy?"

I nodded then shook my head. "Not just him. I miss my sister, too. We all lived together in a really nice house on the ocean. It's just...not having them to talk to. I didn't realize how much I valued that."

"Well, you've got me now."

I smiled. "Thank you."

"And if you need to keep in touch with them, there is such a thing as a telephone."

"Not here, as you well know. And we can't use the phone at work, right? I don't want to drive twenty minutes to sit in a smelly phone booth feeding coins into it."

"Then I'll give you a key to my place, and you can use my phone while I'm gone."

I squirmed. That killed any excuse to not call Jona, Con, or my parents. I wanted to talk to them all but hated making the first move. It felt like a sign of weakness right when I was trying to prove strength.

Then again...I had made a new deal with my folks and needed to honor it. They had been surprised when Jona and I had turned up; that is, surprised by the timing. I could tell by their restraint that they'd not been surprised I hadn't stuck at the Cape. After Jona went back, Mom and Dad had sat me down for The Talk, in which I told them as little as possible without being dishonest, and they had spelled out what they were willing and not willing to do.

We had all been stiff but held our tempers. Dad had quoted Thoreau—"If a man does not keep pace with his companions, perhaps it is because he hears a different drummer. Let him step to the music which he hears, however measured or far away"—by way of concession, and Mom had said, "We'll support whatever you want to do, but because we disagree with it, and you're an adult now, fully qualified for your profession, don't ask us to fund you anymore." I'd assured them I had no intention of that and promised I would let them know when and where I settled. They'd asked for a second promise: I would come home if my money ran out, and revisit the subject of school.

I had agreed because I could keep that promise. It would goad me through the challenges that would surely come. When I doubted I could meet them, I would remember how much I didn't want to go back to school, and find a way to succeed.

So, technically, I didn't have to call anyone yet. Because I still was nowhere near settled. But knowing I had a home to return to made me want to overcome my first obstacle—pride—and find a telephone. I couldn't forget that Michael had no home or people for backup, and Con had a home but a hostile family. Those handsome horsemen may have not fulfilled my romantic fantasies, but they'd taught me to value the good things life had given me.

To Allison I merely said, "Thanks, I may take you up on it," while Allison rummaged in her pockets and produced a key she dropped on the orange crate serving as a coffee table.

"Just leave it under the mat when you're done," she said.

We broke to eat. The pizza was limp and tepid, but neither of us cared. We talked more about the upcoming show while washing dinner down with wine. When we had exhausted the topic, Allison leaned back and said, "So..."

I stiffened, knowing a personal probe was coming.

"...if you're going to hide that painting behind the furniture, you might as well just burn it. Or slice it to ribbons. Or give it to me. I love it!"

"I do, too," I said, feeling heat rise. "I'm going to put it up. I just don't know where yet." *Not in my bedroom!*

"So you're not mad at him?"

"Jeesh, no. More like the other way around."

"So you had something going with him, which is why things didn't work out with Michael?"

"No, Michael two-timed me. Con is a friend."

Who had kissed me in two unplatonic ways. I shivered in remembrance then pushed on.

"It's over with Michael—and over with Con, too, I guess, even though there was never anything to end. We're still friends...I'm just not running back to the Cape for the sole purpose of seeing him. And he's too busy to come here. Doubt that he'd want to: He's into Western. He'll be moving to Montana when he gets enough money."

"I thought he was rich."

"Yes, but...not yet. He'll inherit a pile eventually, but for now he has to work, like the rest of us."

I remembered that pot of gold at the end of Con's tainted rainbow. I still envied him the reward, even though I was grateful to not have to suffer the cost. I continued to think him half crazy to put up with the conditions involved in getting it when he had so much already. That disparity between us would prevent a successful affair.

Maybe that's why he'd let me go without a fight.

And maybe—a cold zing went up my back—by walking away I'd inadvertently done the one thing that proved whatever I felt for him was not connected to his looks and money. If it were, I would have hung around and leeched. I hadn't considered that, thinking only of myself; but at least I had acknowledged true feelings for him through our kiss. We'd parted knowing that meeting each other had been an accident on a brief side trip off our chosen paths. Nobody's fault our fates weren't charted in the stars.

That eased my guilt about leaving him in the lurch, so I was able to tune back in to Allison. She was on the point where we'd left off. "Okay, yeah, I get it. My parents own a huge corporation and make such a good living I'm able to do stuff like this, but I don't have a dime in my own pocket. Still, he's a hunk in his own right, and I can't believe you're not interested. He sure beats all the good-old boys around here!"

"At least there are guys," I said. "Galeson's is the first stable I ever worked at with any at all!"

"Well, none of ours actually work in the barn."

"Yeah, but they're around." All over the place, I had discovered: maintenance crews and security guards, delivery men and transport drivers, farriers and veterinarians, husbands and sons and lovers.

Some of them had seemed good-looking from the glances I had stolen. A few were definitely single. And maybe one or two came from happy, healthy families. Only one way to find out.

But not tonight. Our visit had overextended into darkness, so Allison left to catch some sleep before her pending excitement. I didn't envy her, which surprised me. Once upon a time I would have been bouncing in glee over going to a show. What had killed that? Would I ever want to again? If not, what was I doing here?

I closed up the cabin, slack from drained tension and emotion. While brushing my teeth, I studied the painting I had extracted from its hiding place, until I had to go back to the sink. Then I left it propped up on the couch, where I could see it in the morning—but not constantly—until I figured out what to do with it. What to do about him.

The next day, after a morning in town for laundry, supplies, and a stack of books from the library, I drove to Allison's trailer and let myself in.

I drove instead of walking to save time and avoid attention. On foot along Shallowkill's field roads would have taken better part of an hour round trip from the main barn. The trailer was tucked behind the cross-country course, accessible by track between and around the turnout pastures. Few people ever walked in that area, unless they were leading horses.

Allison's place was as bare yet messy as she had lived at the cabin. I had no trouble finding the phone. I did have trouble making myself dial it. It still felt too early to report on my job tour. Shallowkill could be perfect or go wrong as fast as Galeson's, and I might be scrambling for employment for months. I wanted to impress my people with my success, to prove to them that just because they had all been right about Michael didn't mean I couldn't make a good decision. Still unsure whether I'd made a good decision, I felt vulnerable to criticism I didn't want to hear.

I timed my call for midday to catch Jona awake and scurrying in preparation for the pre-holiday parental visit. It had not been canceled just because I had left the Cape; their trip to Acadia National Park in Maine had been months in the planning. The earliest they might arrive at Con's, I'd calculated, was noon, so I delayed until twelve thirty. Then I slowly spun the dial through his telephone number.

The phone rang so many times that I was about to hang up, guiltily relieved, when Jona picked up with a breathless, "H'lo?"

"Jona? Hi…it's me."

"Linny! Finally! How are you? Where are you?"

"I'm fine. I'm working at a stable in upstate New York. This is my first day off. Thought I'd try to catch all you guys at the same time."

"Well, if you either hang on the line or call back, Mom and Dad should be here shortly. Dave and I just got back from the store."

"Con's at work, I take it."

"Of course. He's rarely not."

"Kinda like me." I summarized my new reality.

"Jeesh! You horsey types sure love punishment. And, what, you can't get a phone installed in your little cabin?"

"Well, I could, and probably will if I end up staying here." I hesitated then explained. "There's a probation period, and, you gotta admit, my life's been a bit, um, unstable lately, and I'm starting over with almost nothing, so I don't want to spend any money I don't have to, if I might be on the road again in two months!"

"Mm, see your point. The gypsy life. Definitely not for me! But…I can contact you at the stable if need be?"

"Yes. I just can't sit around chatting. It's set up the way Galeson's was. So the better plan is to call my friend Allison."

I rattled off the number along with my mailing address and schedule. "I don't know if my hours will shift around, though that's what I've got for now."

"You'll keep me posted if anything changes, right?"

"Of course."

"What about Mom and Dad?"

"Well…will you tell them I checked in?"

"Why not just call back later?"

"'Cause I'm on a borrowed phone and may not be able to get back here today."

A stretch of the truth—I still had a dozen things to do, errands to run—but I could sleep at Allison's if I wanted, for the duration of her absence, and thus make or take phone calls any time. I was just being a coward, still afraid to talk to my parents and shatter that fragile truce we had attained.

Yet it was stupid to camp at somebody else's place when I finally had one of my own. I wanted to enjoy that novelty unhindered. Besides, I had my landlady's animals to tend, which earned the rent reduction that allowed me to afford the place.

All that was just excuses. The truth was, I had reached out as far as I could for now, and any pressure would chase me back into my shell like a hermit crab.

Jona probably sensed this, because she said, "I'll tell Con for you, too. Everyone will be sorry they missed you. How about writing us all letters? That will do the job without having to play phone games."

"Yeah, I could do that…"

Jona's voice became stern. "I highly recommend it. You'll never convince anyone you're qualified for the independence you insist on if you can't face them directly."

I flinched as if slapped. Well, it *was* a slap. I wanted to slap back but recognized that I deserved it.

"I'll write," I promised, and left a long pause before adding, "Meanwhile, what's going on out there? Are you making progress on your thesis? Are you doing okay with Dave? How's Con?"

Jona returned a pause before providing, "Yes, yes, and I don't know. Con's going through the motions, but I think things are going bad at Galeson's. He's been monosyllabic at home. Lots of closed door. It would probably cheer him up royal if you called when he's here."

"I'll see what I can do," I hedged, feeling cornered. "But he can call or write me, too, you know."

We ended the conversation amicably, though a mist of resentment lingered between us. Of all people, Jona should best understand my needs, but she'd been big-sistering me for so long, she couldn't let the habit go. I decided to take her suggestion and write letters for the time being.

I closed up the trailer after leaving Allison a note recording the call number and date, so I could pay her back, then returned to my cabin on autopilot. While finishing the day's chores, I tried to tease some truth out of the tangled knot that comprised my feelings about Con.

I had never led him on, at least, not intentionally. What might have leaked out and been misinterpreted, I couldn't guess. My interpretation of *his* actions—particularly two kisses—was that he was willing to go further if I was, and he wished to be a gentleman and not prey on my emotional weakness on the rebound.

I appreciated that. A lot. But what could I offer in return?

A true platonic friendship would be impossible: One moonlit night had taken care of that. So if I called him to learn what was going on in his life, to gossip and commiserate and swap stories, as a friend would do, I *would* be leading him on. I was not willing to budge one inch off my chosen course for another man, which I would have to do if I wanted him actively in my life.

We now lived a day's drive apart, with incompatible lifestyles, dreams, and priorities. It would be painfully futile to meld them. That line about love conquering all ignored the consequences of chucking everything to be with someone, and put an unfair burden on lovers to become all to each other and stay that way forever. How could any couple hold up under that?

So in tacit understanding, we had asked nothing of each other upon parting. But then he'd said, "Till we meet again…"

How, Con? I asked him through the ether. *With only one day off a week between us, there's not even enough time to drive to each other's world and back! Even if we met halfway, the best we could do is share a meal, maybe an entertainment, both of us fish out of water because the only thing we have in common is horses. Is there anything between us that could survive without that?*

I yanked myself away from tortured thinking by composing chipper letters to my family. There was plenty to tell, between the Farm and my cabin, the local geography and climate, my duties and progress toward goals; good for many letters if I spread it out. I was practiced at this from writing home from camp and college, then writing to friends made at both places before we petered out.

But I'd never written to a man, never mind one I had no practical reason to see again. One who had brought light to my darkness. Who probably wanted to forget about me as much as I wanted to forget about him. What on earth could I say?

I stared at his paintings, then bent to my first effort. Balled it up and tried again.

He already knew about barn work, no point in talking about that. The only real difference between our horse worlds was context, and the addition of events in mine. I was sure he would enjoy comparing our environments and rituals, and swapping stories about horses and people, but those were best discussed in person, if we could ever graduate from awkward non-lovers to chatting on the phone like pals.

It took three of my days off to compose something I was willing to seal in an envelope and drop in the barn-office box. I ended up giving him the gist of things, making sure to include my mailing address and Allison's phone number, then detailed the big news I thought he would like the most:

I wasn't expecting a booby prize for losing Shark, but when I walked into the barn, there was Midnight. He could be Shark's big brother: black with a jagged white star instead of a zigzag stripe, and his white ankle on the off rear leg. He has the same arched neck and short back and high tail, but he's bigger—maybe

15.2 hands—puny compared to the blood horses here—they think he's a Morgan/Thoroughbred cross, nobody knows for sure. He's what they call a schoolmaster, doing everything right if you do, and being a contrary pain-in-the-butt if you don't. Makes him a great teacher. I ride him every time Mary Anne will allow.

Our first day was the best. The minute I swung on, he and I clicked like I've never experienced. When riding him I feel like I have a place in the universe. On other horses, it feels...uphill. Maybe you know what I mean. I always thought it might be that way between you and Klatawah.

He's like Klatawah, I think, in not wanting to be a machine for someone's sporting pleasure. Other students have trouble with him, but we get along fine because he knows I'm interested in him; I love him; and I respect him. So each time we work together, he's curious about what we're going to do and listens to my aids. Either that or he just knows I'm not afraid of him or mad at him. Which is such a change of pace, he's happy to cooperate.

I stopped there each draft of the letter, both from the ache of missing Con and confoundment on how to close on just the right tone. I had to acknowledge his parting gifts. I had to give him a clue about how I felt about him. So I wrote: "I put up all your paintings and look at them every day. Thank you very much; I treasure them."

Then, after a long hesitation, I added, "Love, Linny."

CHAPTER SEVENTEEN

With the letter off and away, I studied the August calendar. Allowing for Con to take as long to write as I had, and then for the postal service to trundle it between states, I might have to wait a month for a reply.

Then I had to stuff thought of him into a back corner of my mind, for life at Shallowkill resembled boot camp: full immersion at full tilt, with Sergeant Caryl barking orders while staff and customers griped behind her back. And there was always some event—coming or going—to help prepare for, serve at, or clean up after.

I watched and listened to all with interest, but the only thing that stopped me in my tracks was the annual cross-country event Shallowkill hosted. I was among the staff recruited to be jump judges.

That was a first for me, and probably a last: I thought I was going to faint half the time. On the ground right at different jumps I could see how huge they were; and when I felt the ground rumble and the air whoosh as the horses thundered by, and heard the clonk of their hooves against boards and bars if they didn't go clean, I understood just how violent and potentially deadly the whole exercise was—even though nobody fell.

It gave me, unexpectedly, a belated understanding of Michael. Yeah, I'd promised myself not to think about him, but during the event a memory came to me of him lying slack in bed saying, "Jumping is almost as good as sex!"

At the time, I had wondered what the heck he was talking about. Watching cross-country jumpers up close gave me a better idea. Like stadium jumpers, they had a tolerance of danger I found incomprehensible. All rode so relaxed, even while driving their mounts over fences, that they looked like

Michael. It finally clicked that he rarely fell off because he was so loose because he felt no fear; in fact, adrenaline turned him on. The higher the jump, the faster the speed, and the greater the complexity, the more he liked it. Klatawah had probably unseated him only because he'd been out of his element and not paying attention.

This difference between us, alone, would have doomed us as a couple. I was more my parents' child than I'd thought. I'd gone into hunt seat equitation because I liked its steadiness and control, and felt a sense of accomplishment from jumping modest, tidy fences at a measured pace in perfect form. Or so it had been until I galloped the Cape Cod sands and experienced heart-pounding excitement for the first time.

By then it was too late for me and Michael. I would be as doomed with Con if I didn't learn what his thrill factor was and get a solid understanding of mine. We had first connected during the high of our beach runs; was that the only basis of our attraction? Was it enough for him? Or did he need bigger, better, faster, more? If so, that would be a core incompatibility we'd never overcome.

Beyond those galloping moments, he didn't seem to have a wild streak, based on his reluctance to break family ties and his ranching/painting dreams about Montana. Then again, he might be saving it all up and would explode when chance allowed.

I wondered if I would ever find out. He was on the Cape and silent as the weeks flew past, while I was at Shallowkill relearning my seat over small fences in the arena under Mary Anne's tutelage. My body didn't want to forget that even such moderation had landed me in the hospital. Its reflex anxiety recalled Klatawah when she had seen barrels at Galeson's. *Eeek! Eeek! Danger! Danger! Fight or flight!*

Just as Con had worked the mare through it, Mary Anne coached me every step until I stopped hesitating at the wrong moment. I couldn't have done it without Midnight, whose cooperation and enthusiasm, and surefooted skill, brought back pleasure and relit my ambition. But that brought me up against another obstacle: boredom. Working in a ring boiled down to round and round, over and over. I'd lost patience for that after just a few weeks at

Galeson's. Even with the restriction of riding the same trails at a prescribed pace, I'd had more freedom there than anywhere else.

Every day had been different, and I could ride both on and off duty. At Shallowkill, I was allotted a single hour—and not one minute more—once or twice a week, for which I had to sacrifice a good chunk of my paycheck. Mary Anne was generous in letting me ride the horse of my choice during our sessions, but she couldn't guarantee that every time.

But, bless her, I didn't have to say much for her to figure out what did and didn't work for me. My timid request to go trail riding led her to organize several of her private students into a group to school on a shortened version of the cross-country course, with the jumps lowered. Just being outside revived my interest, and the jumps looked more fun than the typical hunt style and pattern I was used to. From atop a horse, they didn't look intimidating, either.

Even though I rode well that day, I knew from standing beside the jumps at full height in a real event that I didn't have the guts to turn my career in that direction. When I confessed this to Mary Anne after she caught me sulking in the lounge, she scratched her head then suggested two local events I could try. The first was a hunter pace, and second an actual hunt; in both I'd be able to ride overland while facing jumps like those I had successfully cleared, with always the option to go around. Better yet, no ticking clock. I liked the idea, and spent enough time thinking about it that I was able to ignore my empty mailbox.

Then came Jona's last letter of the summer before heading back to Providence for her final semester of grad school. Up to that point, she had dodged my inquiries about Con and Galeson's by repeating, "He'll tell you about that when he writes." This time she added: "I'm having a lonely supper tonight. Con's in Connecticut for a few days, doing something with lawyers or his parents or both. I'm not sure."

My heart jolted. The news confirmed what I'd often thought—that outside his family only I knew Con's secret—and inflamed my dormant curiosity about his affairs. It also revived my concern about his future, while comforting me about his silence. After his trip and the Labor Day weekend that would close up Galeson's for the season, he might have both time and reason to write.

His letter came shortly after, but it wasn't addressed to me.

Peggy, one of my co-workers, hunted me down to the box stall where I was holding a horse while a vet injected antibiotic into its neck. "Caryl wants to see you in her office when you're done."

I chilled. Allison had mentioned that only once had anyone emerged from Caryl's office with a promotion. Usually such a summons meant, "We no longer require your services."

After the vet left, I washed my shaky hands and tidied myself, walking casually toward the office, aware of tracking eyes. Remembering that I was dealing with someone who never changed expression, I arranged my features into my best poker face and stepped in.

"Close the door," Caryl said. When I remained standing, she commanded, "Sit."

I sat, feeling a trickle of sweat down my back.

Caryl dropped a sheaf of papers on her desk and stabbed them with a forefinger. "What do you know about this letter?"

"What letter?" I blurted, craning to see.

"This letter from one Connor Simon Winston about a horse coming here tomorrow that you and only you are to handle. Then this other letter from the Burlingames authorizing it."

"What?" I felt like a lightning bolt had just seared me to the chair.

Caryl steamed through her nostrils. "Don't play dumb. This is the son of the football Winstons—they don't just drop horses on people without a damn good reason."

"Uh, um...well, I know that Con Winston went to school with the Burlingames' son, so he probably got referred here for boarding or training."

"Where do you fit in?"

"I, uh, I guess...if it's the horse I think it is, I worked with her at Galeson's."

"What was Con Winston's horse doing at a hack stable on Cape Cod?"

"He works there. Or, at least, he used to. Maybe he doesn't anymore, which is why he's moving the horse."

Jeesh, Con—what are you doing?

"What's the matter with it?" Caryl demanded.

"Um, it's, uh, she's...ill-mannered. Unrideable by most people. Or was. I've been out of touch since June. I have no idea what's going on."

Caryl scowled. "That's too bad, because the letter gave no name, no pedigree, no performance history, no training regimen. Just one big, fat cashier's check made out to the Farm."

I dragged a hand from forehead to crown, thinking frantically. "Uh, when is she supposed to arrive? For how long?"

"Tomorrow. For the fall, and possibly all winter."

I looked away to hide my panic. Caryl pressed, "Can you ride the horse?"

I swung my gaze back around, knowing this mattered. Caryl stared with livid green eyes.

"No, I've never tried. But I'm okay with her on the ground. I'm the only one besides Con she doesn't bite. Or was, last I knew."

"I see."

Caryl waited, twiddling a pen between her fingers. I gulped and recited, "Klatawah. Mare. Age unknown, breed unknown, story unknown, rides Western only. Needs a hackamore."

Caryl sniffed and smacked down her pen. "I want a write-up of her diet, exercise, and any medical history from your term with her, with a proposed training program, on my desk, first thing tomorrow morning."

"Yes, ma'am," I mumbled and scurried away.

Allison had been watching for me and appeared out of a stall as I went by, running the heels of both hands up my forehead as if trying to shove thoughts away.

"So? Well? Are you fired or not?"

I kept walking at full pace, straight out of the barn to where I could breathe. "No. Nothing like that." I gave a reluctant smile. "Just—a walloping surprise. Can I use your phone at lunch break?"

"Sure, of course. What kind of surprise? Everything all right?"

I stopped and pivoted to face her. "Con is shipping his horse here for boarding. Tomorrow."

"No way!"

"Yes way. So I need to call him ASAP."

"Yeah, I guess so!"

"Allison!" called Caryl from the barn entrance. "Get back here, I need you. Now!"

"Coming!"

Before dashing off, Allison said to me, "Dinner tonight. Okay?"

"Yeah, fine, good." I had to run into town, anyway, to buy some Canada Mints.

The rest of the morning was an agony until I could punch out and zip down to Allison's trailer. Why was he complicating my work status again by throwing Klatawah into it? What had happened that he couldn't—wouldn't?—keep her at Galeson's?

I dialed the beach house and got no answer.

Damn! At this point I was too electrified to be nervous about talking to him. So I tried Galeson's, where Con picked up on the sixth ring.

"Hello?"

Not Galeson's Riding Stable. "Con. This is Linny."

Long pause followed by released breath. "Good, I'm glad to hear from you."

"I was hoping to hear from you more directly than what just happened. They told me about Klatawah this morning. What's going on?"

"A hell of a lot. I was waiting for it to settle before writing you back, but it keeps getting more complicated, so I figured I'd just tell you tomorrow in person."

Tomorrow! I was going to see him again! Less than twenty-four hours! Just the sound of his voice threw me into a time warp of yesterday and today, flipping back and forth.

I pulled myself together enough to ask, "So you're doing the hauling, not a service?"

"Yeah, I got someone to cover for me here. That was tough—the stable is closed now, but somebody's got to be on site, and I'm the only one."

"Where'd Tom go?"

"Back with Miriam and Magician to Colorado."

"What? Then—"

"The place is shut down. Not just for the season, but for good."

"Oh no! What happened?"

"It's a long story. I'll tell you tomorrow."

My heart did a back handspring, but I kept my voice cool. "Why here?"

"Because I had to park Klatawah somewhere in a hurry. Since that meant traveling no matter what, I decided to stash her where I know she'll be treated well."

"Well, we can do that. But jeesh! The shock factor just messed me up royal with my boss."

"Sorry. I wasn't thinking about that kind of thing—just trying to solve a big problem. I figured it would work better if it came down to you from the high-and-mighties rather than you sidling up to them and going, 'Gee, a friend of mine needs to board his crazy horse somewhere for a few months...'"

I thought this through and agreed, though, lordy, I was tired of getting blindsided.

Con's voice tightened. "You're not going to fight it, are you?"

"God, no! But you really knocked me sideways. What do you want me to do with her?"

"Keep her fit and unharassed. I don't care how."

"Do you want me to ride her?"

"If you can."

I sighed. "And what will you be doing?"

"Cleaning up a big mess."

"Did everybody just walk out and leave you holding the bag?"

"Close enough. I'll tell you the whole story later. Really."

"Oh-kaaaay..."

A windy sigh came through the line. "Look, Linny, I'm sorry, I've just got more going on than I can handle, and I don't know how to even start explaining it. Would you just...take care of Klatawah for me until I sort everything out?"

"Yes."

"Thank you. That means a lot."

We fell silent. I choked on all the things I wanted to say. I settled for: "What's your timetable tomorrow?"

"I'm loading her early in the morning. Not sure how long the drive will take."

"Long enough that she'll probably be cuckoo by the time she gets here."

"She's getting a bit of happy juice beforehand."

"Hope it lasts the whole day!"

We shared a lame laugh. My mind and heart were so overloaded that the power of speech began to fail me. I bailed out of the conversation, then sat in Allison's trailer with my hands clamped on my head.

"Well, Eagan," I said to myself, rousing to jot number and date of the call before closing up the trailer, "you wanted to know what you could offer him? Looks like this is gonna be it!"

Amazingly, I slept that night. Maybe my body knew I was going to need fortitude, and allowed me to stock up.

The next morning, Caryl informed me that Klatawah was to be housed in what used to be the quarantine pasture, atop a rise across the road from Shallowkill's main entrance. As the Farm had expanded, the inconveniently sited pasture had fallen out of use, but the maintenance staff kept it mowed, the run-in shed in good repair, and the fence and gate intact.

Whether they could also keep the hand-pumped water from freezing during the winter, I had my doubts.

But that was a question to be answered later. For now, I just had to get it ready for Klatawah's arrival sometime that September afternoon.

I roped in one of the maintenance guys to portage hay bales in his pickup truck. It was unkind of me to use the cute one who'd tried to pick me up last time the stable girls had convened at the local pub; but he was the closest set of muscles available, so I took advantage of him to help me stash the bales in the mini loft inside the shed, then check the switches and replace the lightbulbs in the shed and atop a pole near the gate. I would need light as the season got shorter, and these were connected by an iffy-looking wire I hoped would hold up.

He obliged with a smile and ease that came with being young and manly. I flicked him a smile with my thanks, then dismissed him, hoping he wouldn't be around when Con showed up.

After he was gone, I inspected the fenceline, scrubbed and filled the water trough, and placed a grooming kit and other supplies in the shed. Then I descended toward the barn, admiring the vista of the Farm before me. It both sprawled and nestled among rolling hills, a patchwork of fields and forests with long views of gold and green. The air held a liquid light, a characteristic that had given rise to the Hudson River School of painting. It was similar to the Cape Cod light that attracted so many artists.

Was that the real reason why my own artist was loath to leave the Cape? And perhaps why he craved the Big Sky of Montana? If he hung around the Hudson River light long enough, would it inspire him to stay?

Maybe I should ask him to capture this light in a horsey landscape for me.

I sighed and continued down the hill. For the next hours, time slowed down internally while it blurred by in the external world. Finally, late afternoon, a black pickup truck towed Galeson's weary two-horse trailer into the stableyard. *Thump! Thump! Wham!* came from inside.

I froze just as Caryl bellowed, "Eagan—get moving!" and slashed her arm toward the trailer. "This one's gift-wrapped just for you!"

I gulped and stepped into the parking area. Across it, the rig halted, the driver's door opened, and out stepped Con like a sunburst through clouds.

I felt movement stop behind me as every woman in the vicinity spotted him. I didn't turn to look at them, though, as my gaze was locked on his presence, too. He was tanner and leaner than three months ago, moving easily in his chambray shirt with half-rolled sleeves and open collar, tucked into snug Levi's. A gold chain I didn't recognize glinted below his collarbone, just as his hair, grown longer, glinted in the sun.

He didn't see me right away, going straight to the back of the trailer to check on Klatawah. He turned at my footsteps on the gravel and lit into a smile.

I couldn't help but smile back. My chest felt tight from all that was going on within it. I wanted to leap into his arms and hook my legs around his waist, but knew that would pay me back later because too many people were watching. For their benefit, Con and I approached each other nonchalantly and shook hands.

"God, it's good to see you," he said before any of the watchers entered earshot.

"Likewise," I returned, realizing our hands were still clasped. I slipped mine free, reminding us that business must be attended to. The scenario recalled meeting Michael at Galeson's and pretending we were associates, not lovers.

I sighed, thinking, Oh please, not again.

Caryl strode out to us, followed by Mary Anne, both wearing smiles I had not seen on them before.

"Mr. Winston?" Caryl greeted, extending her hand. "Welcome to Shallowkill. I'm Caryl Ballard, Barn Manager. I hope your trip went well. What have you brought us?"

Wham, slam! went Klatawah's hooves against the metal sides of the bullet-shaped trailer. Then, startling everyone, her nose popped out the high opening above the back door, her ears showing above, helicoptering in an effort to take in the new world.

"Uh…" began Caryl, with her question filled in by Mary Anne. "Do you always ship your horses backward?"

Con chortled. I watched his face assume the courteously smiling mask I recognized, and his voice took on its Ivy League tone. His eyes, however, were still the color of Cape Cod breakers.

"This horse, yes. When we first got her, she danced the fandango all the way home—while still tranquilized—until she broke her tie and turned herself around. Quieted right down the rest of the trip. So I loaded her that way for this trip, and she's been fine."

"Makes unloading a lot easier." I gestured with my chin toward the hill beyond the trailer.

Nobody took the hint, all still waiting for Caryl to direct. She appeared to have been struck mute, still scanning Con up and down. He feigned not to notice, while I rolled my eyes and Mary Anne stepped forward.

"We've set up for her across the road, and there's room for you to turn around at the top. So you can back right up to the gate, and we'll pop her right into the paddock."

She hiked off toward the isolation pasture, followed briskly by me—plus Allison, who had emerged from somewhere—and dazedly by Caryl. Con returned to his rig, then passed us at a ponderous crawl.

I looked after him and saw Klatawah looking back at me in a trailer designed to load two horses pointing forward. That broke my daze with a laugh, followed by a surge of love for the mare beyond the leery affection I'd known before.

By the time Con had looped the rig, Mary Anne had opened the pasture gate. He positioned the trailer so she and Allison could lower the door into its ramp configuration, then step aside as the mare surged out.

"Whee!" Allison exclaimed as Klatawah took off snorting and snapping out her back legs, showing feet still free of horseshoes. Allison and I closed the trailer, Con pulled the rig forward, and Mary Anne swung the gate closed.

Caryl caught up, Allison and I ducked back through the fence, and we women lined up on the rail while Con parked. Then he joined us to watch Klatawah curve and high-step around her new confines in a padded halter and bright blue leg wraps. That first impression I'd had of her back in May, of Lusitano or Andalusian blood somewhere in her pedigree, blinked through my mind again and vanished.

After inspecting the sheaves of hay put out for her near the shed, then dipping her nose into the water trough, she took off for a lap of the pasture. When satisfied, she dropped and rolled, heaved herself up, trotted to another spot, dropped and rolled again with grunts and squeals. Everyone chuckled except Caryl.

"Jesus Christ, what is that thing?" she exclaimed. I, like the others, looked at her while biting back any reply.

After a pause, Allison quipped, "That's a *hot-blooded* horse rather than a hot *blood* horse."

Again, no one responded. I just wished the others would go away. But Caryl, recovering her poise, said to Con without looking at him, "What are you planning to do with it?"

"Eventually, endurance trail riding. Short term, giving her a rest after a hard summer. Linny, I'm hoping, will continue working on her manners."

I wiped my brow, not only to remove sweat but in relief that I had guessed right on the report I had submitted to Caryl that morning. I had not forgotten the particulars of Klatawah's diet and stable needs, but had been uncertain about what Con considered a training regimen and had embellished according to my own logic and desires.

Caryl pushed herself off the fence. Mary Anne followed suit as Caryl said, "When you're ready, come down to the office so we can wrap up the paperwork. Mary Anne will give you a tour. I trust we'll see you at the Burlingames' tonight?"

"Yes. What time again?"

"Seven for cocktails, eight for dinner."

"I'll be there," Con said. "Thanks very much for your help."

What help? I wondered, seeing the same thought reflected in Allison's and Mary Anne's faces. But none of them spoke as Caryl marched back down the hill. Mary Anne closed with, "I'll show you where to store her tack and anything else you've brought when you come down for the tour. For now, Linny—get what you need to learn."

She, too, then exited. Allison, Con, and I relaxed. We stood in almost identical positions with one foot on a lower rail and arms leaning on the top, studying Klatawah. She had calmed enough to tug hay from the pile, but flung up her head and froze every few seconds if she had scented a wolf.

"She looks just like the paintings," Allison remarked. Con blinked and looked down at her.

"I never thought I'd see her again," I confessed, which made him swivel his head to regard me.

Under his gaze, I fell into memory of the hot sands and pine-scented breezes of Galeson's stableyard, and the salt-tinged, painted sky above the rolling surf of the Cape's outer beaches. My last image of Con on Klatawah—riding across the dunes against the wind under ominous clouds—filled my mind's eye, giving my heart a slow turn. It heaved over again, with a sharp pang, when I recalled that was the last time I had ridden Shark.

I would have thought that short segment of my life to have been a dream if not for Klatawah standing before me and Con at my side. The shock still resonated through my bones. I was starting to get over it, though, and itched to grill him about the changes. But I wasn't certain if I wanted Allison hearing everything directly or an edited version afterward.

"I get the impression," Con said, "that it won't go over well if I invite you gals to join us for dinner."

"You got that right," Allison said. "Thanks for thinking it, though. We were planning to get Chinese takeout tonight, and eat up here, looking at this horse."

"I'd rather do that," he said with a sigh.

"You're outa luck," Allison said. "They're gonna give you the VIP treatment."

Con shook his head and ducked through the rail, talking to Klatawah on a slow approach. Allison and I exchanged a look. She nodded, then took herself off.

I hesitated, then entered the pasture and walked to Con, who was standing beside Klatawah scratching the crest of her neck beneath her mane. This was my one chance to reintroduce myself to the horse with him in attendance, so I couldn't afford to be shy.

Klatawah accepted me without seeming to notice, as if us together again restored normalcy to her world. I felt the same way, on one level, but other ones vacillated.

"Want me to keep this halter on," Con asked, "or are you okay catching her without one?"

I answered by pulling the half-crushed box of Canada Mints from my hip pocket and rattling it. Klatawah's head swung around with ears at full point.

Con laughed and held out his hand, palm upward. I shook a few mints into it, then a few into my own hand, and we split to place them atop fence posts. Klatawah followed Con with a whicker.

After clearing her treats off the posts, the mare returned to her hay and settled in. Con and I stood near the run-in shed, looking first at the horse then at each other.

Con stood on tiptoe and looked past me toward the main Farm cluster. "Can anyone see us up here?"

"Only on the brow of the hill," I replied.

"Good." He started backing up into the shed while crooking an index finger to beckon me. One brow was slanted in a roguish expression that told me he wasn't worrying about being able to monitor Klatawah from below; he wanted us to be unseen.

Though I approached him slowly, my heartbeat was cantering. When I stopped before him, he took up my hands.

"It will take too long to tell you everything. I've got to get back down to your bosses, and you've got to get back to work. So here's the short version."

I waited, chewing my lower lip.

"One. I'm buying Galeson's."

I twitched in surprise, choking back a hundred questions.

"Two, *carpe diem*."

"Huh?" I tensed against something coming but let him spell it out. My fingers twined through his of their own accord.

He smiled and held my gaze. "I'm assuming that between your education and your family, you know what that means."

"Yeah. *Seize the day.* We got the words in Latin class, and had to read the book in ninth-grade Lit."

"So...I'm thinking of *carpe diem*-ing something we should have done several months ago. And might not get a chance to do again."

I didn't need that spelled out. When he drew me toward him, I flowed in. His lips felt and tasted just like I remembered.

This time I got more than a few seconds' worth. We savored the long, heavenly kiss I had dreamed of, our fronts fitting together as well as our sides had back when he had tucked me under his arm. My only lucid thought was, *Thank you, thank you, thank you...* while the rest of me melted into joy.

When our hands started roaming too far and deep, and our breathing got too steamy, I eased back, our lips separating in slow motion. My heart was almost bursting with things I couldn't say. Con looked at me with a glaze in his eyes that slowly cleared while we stared at each other. Each second brought me further back into reality, and the need to face it hardened me to speak.

All that came out was, "I, uh, uh, I—"

He chuckled and tipped his forehead against mine. "Don't bother trying."

I laughed, and we squeezed each other into a bear hug. I relished the feel of him along the length of me, hot and wanting, so impossibly strong. Against his neck, which smelled faintly of citrus, I mumbled, "And here I was hoping to just get a letter…"

"Special delivery!" he said against my hair.

I giggled. "Christmas a few months early!" But then I sobered, adding, "Though it may prove to be lumps of coal in a gift-wrapped package."

He stood back from me with creased brow, hands still on my shoulders. "Why?"

"Did you see the way Caryl reacted to you?"

"Yeah. Not the first time that's happened." He dropped his hands.

"But the first time it's happened to her. Well, I don't know that for sure, but I'll bet. This is a woman who never loses control, Con. And she just did, in front of her staff. She'll treat us all like crap from now on—especially me, because I'm the one you sent the horse to. And by your instructions, I now outrank her. Doesn't matter if it's only in this one area. She'll do her best to make me pay for the privilege."

"But…she can't fire you or anything—my paying the boarding fee depends on you handling the horse. So if there's a problem, you can go to the Burlingames."

"Oh, that's a great way to deal with your boss!"

"Damn. I'm sorry, I didn't understand all this when I planned it. And I still don't." He turned away to pace.

"I know. But it's what you've triggered."

I started tucking in my shirt and straightening my hair, thinking I really should run off and marry an ugly accountant, life would be so much simpler. But the thought of losing Con again was more than I could bear. Bad enough I was looking at his back already, as he tidied up his own façade and groped for aplomb. When he turned to stand before me, smiling, I had to lock my knees to stay upright.

"Okay," he said. "We've re-zeroed the odometer, and it's time for a new trip." He touched my face. "Think you'll get a phone now?"

"Yeah." I touched him back. "But I'm still hoping for a letter."

"You'll get one, though I can't promise when."

And I couldn't promise him anything beyond sticking with Klatawah unless pried away by other forces. I would have to be super-conscientious about Farm rules from this point on.

Con had been right to seize the moment, because visualizing any future moments was beyond me, probably beyond both of us. But Klatawah ensured we'd have at least one more contact.

Stuck for now, we both pocketed our hands and pivoted to walk back toward the gate.

"Are you driving back tonight, or staying at the Burlingames?" I hoped he would come to my cabin, even knowing he would not.

He shook his head. "As Allison said, I'm getting the VIP treatment. After a seventeen-course dinner during which everything about me and my family will be politely probed, they'll park me in some palatial guest suite with a curtained four-poster bed and six scantily clad maidens offering delicacies on a silver tray."

"If not themselves." I didn't smile.

"Um, possibly."

"I've got a cot and Cheerios."

He smiled. "I would rather."

That warmed my heart, though I doubted its truth.

He sighed with a shrug. "Morning will bring liveried servants bearing breakfast on some antique Oriental lacquered tray, or else some exquisite buffet in a dining room with a table that seats fifty. Either way, I'll have a heck of a time getting out of there before noon, which is when I'd actually like to be home."

"Tough life."

He flashed into tartness. "Try it sometime. I doubt you'd like it past the first novelty."

I flattened my voice and expression. "I'm good enough with cot and Cheerios"—mentally adding, *The only thing missing is you*.

"That's why I love ya, darlin'," he returned with a half-sided grin.

I stopped blinking and studied him. His tone had been a casual drawl, like he'd been imitating a line in some cowboy movie; but he was gazing at me intently, and his grin looked fake.

I didn't know what to say. Watching someone walk away was the wrong time to declare, "I love you."

So I kept silent and watched his mask slide into place with practiced ease. "Gotta go." He stepped forward to peck me on the mouth as if we had just concluded a lunch date. "Thank you for the *carpe*. I really will write a letter explaining all, unless you get a phone first, in which case I will tell all. For now, you might want to stay up here a little longer...your face is still as red as a stoplight."

"So is yours." I smiled. He stroked my cheek. I covered his hand with mine, then kissed his fingertips and turned away.

He hesitated, then departed. I waited until I heard him rehook the gate and get into his truck. He sat for so long I almost approached him in question, then he rumbled down the track to the Farm with the empty trailer banging like a percussion section behind.

I stood inside the gate, deep breathing, and wondering what the hell had just happened.

But deep in my belly, I knew.

I knew.

The real question was: What am I going to do about being in love with someone who's just committed to a place and business somewhere else, right when I've found a job and place that I want to commit to?

To commit to each other, one of us had to lose big.

Best I could do for now was think about him constantly and take care of his horse. Thus the next morning found me up the hill at Klatawah's pasture. I had finally slept a few hours from sheer exhaustion, but I was wide-eyed well before dawn and out the door at first light.

The mare whickered at my arrival, which lifted my spirits. I fed Klatawah, cleared away her droppings, refreshed the water trough, then groomed her as the sun rose on another fine day. Klatawah leaned into the curry comb and dandy brush, and let me remove her wraps and check her feet without fussing. After also removing her travel halter, I left a Canada Mint on the gatepost.

From my vantage point, I could hear and sometimes see other employees arriving. Sighing, I drove down to the stable and clocked in, five minutes after my assigned hour.

"You're late," snapped Caryl, halting from a brisk stride down the barn aisle.

"Sorry," I said. "New routine threw me off stride."

"That's no excuse. You should have planned for it."

"I did. I just didn't plan it quite right. Won't be a problem again."

"Well, make sure of that. Three times, you're out."

I hardened my tone to match hers. "I'll make sure of it."

Caryl resumed her march out the door, leaving me boiling. We both knew I couldn't be fired as long as Klatawah was a paid boarder and I committed no actual crime. Also that I would not abandon Klatawah. That made me a juicy target.

Damn you, Con!

Several heads of my co-workers peeked out of stalls where they had stopped work to listen. They popped back out of sight when I turned.

All morning, I noticed people skirting me to avoid political jeopardy. *Is this how it's going to be?* How could Con not realize what he caused—just as bad as Michael? In some ways he was worse, being oblivious where Michael was calculating. Once again I longed for somebody like Dave.

At lunchtime, I started the process of getting a telephone installed at the cabin, though my heart wasn't in it. I resented having to take the time, spend the money, for someone who already seemed a million miles away, in some other life—for whom I might make a fool of myself all over again. While I could scarcely spend a minute not thinking about his kisses, I was starting to realize why some cultures and religions tried to control sex. It made simple situations complicated and brought out the worst in people along with the best.

I barely made it back to duty on time, so I was unable to check on Klatawah. As I rushed through the office to the punch clock, Mary Anne snagged me by the sleeve and said, "Some mail came for you today."

I halted. "What?"

She handed me a white envelope with no stamp or return address, just my name care of the Farm. "Looks like it got dropped off," Mary Anne said. "It was in the box out by the road."

I understood immediately where it had come from. Erasing expression from my face, I folded the letter into my back pocket and said, "Thanks," before heading back to work with my heart bucking like a randy colt.

It was a busy afternoon full of students and horses and farriers coming and going, but I was able to catch a few moments in the restroom undisturbed. That's when I tore open the letter.

A cover note in Con's half-cursive, half-printed handwriting was folded around several sheets of heavy paper bearing the Burlingame crest.

4:30 a.m.

Special delivery of another sort!

No point wasting a stamp when I can just drive by. Not that I brought any with me, or the P.O. is open. I wanted to deliver this in person, but nobody's here yet—still dark, and I doubt the security guys would welcome me hanging around.

Can't swing by your cabin because you never told me where it actually is. So I'm popping this in the box and crossing my fingers. —CSW

Then came the real letter:

1:15 a.m.

Hi—I finally gave up on sleep, despite this princely bed (no curtained four-poster with nubile maidens, however—but the food and drink were great).

So, keeping with the day's theme, I've seized the night—carpe noctem—and helped myself to the bedside scribble pad they keep for guests, like at a hotel, to pen your promised letter.

Going back a few hours:

Dinner was stilted but not unpleasant. The Burlingames are kind and generous and dippy, and have either refined taste or a good decorator. They nattered about their dynasty while artfully trying to learn about mine. They seem to love horses but don't ride much aside from hunting. They invited me to join them on Opening Day.

Your green-eyed boss was very green with envy all evening. Cool and poised, but those uncanny eyes coveted everything they saw, from furniture and artwork to my butt. I felt like standing on the table and mooning her.

Her big contribution to the conversation was stories about meeting some British royalty at a big show a few months? years? ago. I might have found it interesting at a different party.

If you can keep the peace with her, yeah, you could have a great job. But after watching her up close, I see why you're concerned. That woman is so hyper-focused on controlling and impressing people that she's probably never developed a normal relationship and at this point has no idea how to start. So she's always twisting things into a her-vs.-the-world battle.

Your name only came up when she asked why I insisted on leaving my horse in your care. I told her that you're a gifted handler, and as far as I know, you're the only one Klatawah has not attacked. The Burlingames appreciated that we're not subjecting the whole staff to a crazy horse, and suggested to Caryl that she give you all the support possible.

I hope that's enough to keep her off your back. Again, I'm sorry for making your position more difficult—I wasn't thinking when I set this up. I was just desperate, and it seemed a good idea.

We hung around making nice till almost midnight, then I begged off, saying I would see myself out in the morning. Oh darn, no breakfast buffet with silver serving dishes.

Going back many weeks:

Now for the Galeson melodrama. You were smart to get out. July 4th weekend was a bonanza—full rides, great weather, everything went fine. Even Mike showed up and helped. I hate to admit he did a good job. Too bad he... well, you know what I mean. That was the last we saw of him.

But I keep wondering if he's one of those guys who create disasters everywhere they go. After what he did to you (and how many before you?), it was like he pulled a string on his way out the door and everything collapsed behind him.

Miriam regressed to a spoiled, screaming five-year-old. Tom started drinking again after multiple years dry. Then the real domino chain began. People fell off or got run away with on the rides. The weather turned lousy. Stablehands came and went in a revolving door. Horses went lame. Vehicles kept breaking, or we couldn't get them repaired. Nor could we keep up with cleaning or maintenance on buildings and equipment, and had to cut back the number of rides because we couldn't staff them. Lost money hand over fist.

Miriam shipped Shark off to her trainer about a week after you left. Then some old rodeo boyfriend contacted her, and she packed up her car and drove home mid-August instead of after Labor Day as originally planned. Tom loaded up Magician and followed the week after.

By season shutdown we were broke, had lost whatever reputation we might've had, and there I was—"holding the bag," as you put it. I called Miriam's old man and gave him hell.

He's a real estate mogul or something in Denver and is one slippery dude. Offered me the place at fire-sale price just to get it out of his hair.

Even at that price I couldn't act, for as you know my assets are tied up and Gram's money doesn't come close. Meanwhile, there were twenty-eight horses to feed and vet. I let go what remained of the staff save for Sylvie then left her holding the bag while I ran around trying to sell horses and raise money.

I ended up borrowing the funds from my father, who was willing to invest in a business venture. He thought it a sign that I'm coming around. But he couldn't see what I'd want in a rundown stable (beyond "buy low, sell high"), so I had to write an elaborate pitch and business plan showing how renovations, a name change, and an emphasis shift would draw new clientele and pay back the loan, leading to profit.

The loan is secured by the beach house, I'm afraid, but I'm pretty sure I won't lose it. The trail-riding business is doomed, because sooner or later the National Seashore will ban horses on the dunes and beaches. Galeson's—or, as soon shall be called, Spindrift Stable—has to either survive as a riding center or become another business altogether. Or else I just sell out to developers, which would double or triple my money, clear the loan, and leave cash in my pocket.

There's more—lots more—but my eyelids are finally drooping. I'll fill in the blanks next time I see or talk to you.

By now you can understand why I had to move Klatawah. On top of the chaos and the need to separate my ownership of her from the business, I now need to clear the facility so we can start tearing it apart and putting it back together.

Please keep her well for me, and ride her as soon as possible. I, meanwhile, will attempt to get a few minutes of sleep.

Love,

Con

CHAPTER EIGHTEEN

I wished I had waited until after work to read Con's letter. Trying to digest it at full speed kept me fumbling and stumbling—and grateful Caryl's attention was elsewhere for the rest of the day.

Back in my cabin, over reheated casserole, I reread the letter. So much seemed to lie between the lines, but I couldn't identify anything for sure. Did he love me, or love me not? His voice in writing was the same yet different from in person. Kind of like the surprise that came with seeing who he was in paint versus the physical man with the mask. Were they all parts of the same guy, or was his real self one or the other?

What stunned me was his buying Galeson's. That explained so much while raising so many new questions. The big one was, Why? How would that get him any closer to Montana?

I could grasp his financial strategy, sort of, but it seemed to clash with what he'd shown of his heart. Again I realized how well I didn't know him. I shook my head, thinking I should cut him off right now before I tripped down another wrong path.

Of course, he had arranged things so I couldn't move on without nasty consequences. Slick, if that was his intent. Although I believed his explanation, I fretted about ulterior motives. The situation was too loaded with head games, too reminiscent of Michael.

At least he fulfilled one promise, I thought, folding the evidence back into its envelope.

Still, it burned knowing he had been lying awake thinking about me as I had lain awake aching for him. If only I had remembered that P.O. box addresses aren't the same as road directions to the cabin!—or he had thought to ask—I might have had him in the flesh for a few hours instead of on paper a day later. Now he was hundreds of miles away again, for who knew how long.

Yet I resisted the urge to call him. Between the hassle of borrowing Allison's phone and my own need for time to think—feel—recover again from upheaval, I was willing to wait a few days until my own phone was installed.

What mattered for survival was avoiding another upheaval. Caryl could find a way to fire me if she tried hard enough. So I needed to be steady, not spazzed out from turmoil over an absentee man—especially because my three-month probation ended in just a few weeks, and I must have good status to start participating in events.

I would jeopardize that, I knew, by riding Klatawah beforehand. It was already a matter of when, not if. The mare would go bananas if not exercised more than on a longe line, and needed that sooner rather than later. How would Caryl react to expansion of what she was already angry about not being able to control?

In my report to her, I had emphasized trail riding as part of the mare's training. But we hadn't yet discussed it, and probably wouldn't, since training boarders was Mary Anne's department. I knew, however, that omitting my boss from the equation would make her more hostile. So before I did anything, I had to talk to Con.

Wet weather relieved me of immediate need for action. Things slowed for a few days, allowing me to catch up on chores and sleep. They also allowed more social life than just sharing sandwiches with my stablemates at lunchtime.

Allison had made friends with Beth, one of the boarders who shared her interest in switching from hunter/jumper shows to dressage/cross-country horse trials; and Katy, one of the grounds crew, who didn't ride but had grown up with horses and loved them. We had taken to going into town every other week to talk shop over supper and laundry; and out to the pub with the barn gang once a week to get silly.

The pub gatherings were coed, and I went along to practice mingling with different men. None, however, could compete with my handsome horseman or was different enough to approach Dave territory. If I wanted to meet academics or athletes or businessmen or anyone outside my realm, I would have to travel to Albany and beyond, where they had cities and colleges.

Instead, I stayed local and concentrated on my business. No time to date anyone seriously, anyway.

The wet spell gave me a chance for longer talks with Mary Anne. She officially observed me longeing Klatawah in the rain and agreed to accompany us on outings once Klatawah had proven stable under saddle. She volunteered to assist on my first ride on the horse.

That was the best plan, I knew. Second best was enlisting Allison for support. Worst plan was to ride the mare alone, unannounced and unmonitored. Yet I did it anyway, because what needed to be achieved between us was too personal to share. As well, Miriam and Michael had been bucked off after someone had held the mare while they mounted and fussed in the saddle, surrounded by nervous watchers. Involving anyone else might duplicate those conditions.

I chose my debut for the morning Caryl was scheduled to come in late after a dentist appointment. Right after sunrise, I drove up the hill and said "Good morning" to Klatawah, who met me at the gate with a whicker.

She had adopted me as Her Human in the absence of any other. She also knew from whence came food. I laughed and ducked through the fence, patting the mare's neck on my way by to the shed. While not sure Klatawah actually liked me, I did know she looked to me, as the only familiar thing in her life, for direction and reassurance. I was the dominant mare of Klatawah's herd. That she missed having a real herd was clear from the number of times I had seen her at the fence whinnying toward the Farm.

This morning the horse was calm and interested in what I was doing. First, breakfast, during which I cleared the area of droppings; then inspection of Con's tack. I recognized the saddle from Galeson's but he'd acquired a handsome new blanket for it, plus a hackamore in bright colors to replace the shabby one he'd originally dug up at the stable. I removed them from my car and slung the kit over the top rail of the fence out of sight from below. The discretion reminded me of my last time dodging watchers for a few heavy-breathing minutes. *Carpe diem.* I was doing it again, invisible to the workers driving in.

I groomed then saddled the mare, who nose-butted me before accepting her headgear. Then I tied up the reins and stirrups and clipped on the longe line to lead Klatawah away from the rail.

I set her to circling at walk, trot, canter, both directions. Klatawah kicked out her heels, flouncing and snorting and farting, as she normally did in the first five minutes, then settled into a steady trot—one ear cast back toward the saddle, the other toward me. When her tail stopped switching, I halted her and closed in.

Emulating Con's confidence and style, I disconnected the longe equipment and just swung aboard and asked for a walk. Klatawah tossed her head and jigged but otherwise stepped out.

I had to suppress a whoop, lest I celebrate too early. Keeping calm and loose, I directed the mare on a few perimeter laps, changing directions across the pasture. Klatawah looked around as if seeing her turf for the first time, listening to my prattle with swiveling ears. When I asked her for a jog, she hopped a few times, then cooperated. I would have liked to have followed with a lope, but feared a breakaway gallop. It was more than good enough to jog without drama, coming aware of being in a Western saddle again, too big for me, where only Con had ever sat, his crotch and my crotch sharing the same piece of leather, my fingers on reins only his hands had held.

What a weird sort of intimacy, I thought, a little disgusted. Why couldn't I just have a normal affair with someone?

I forgot him for a few minutes because of the distraction Klatawah offered. She was a narrower horse than both Shark and Midnight, so my legs felt longer and closer together; a smaller horse than Shallowkill's Thoroughbreds and hunters, but not so low to the ground as Shark, though I doubted I could mount her bareback; an inconsistent horse, in that her neck and head position changed constantly, and she didn't track in a straight line; and the tempo of her walk and jog kept varying, even though I held her to a either a four-beat or two-beat pace.

Yet she was so attuned to my presence she responded to the slightest shifts, even, it seemed, to my thoughts. I had to ride extra carefully lest I confuse her and lose her trust.

Underneath it all, her power simmered—bringing to mind Con's first description of her as an exotic, rough-tuned car, who would perform if you treated her right. Her acceptance made me feel like being admitted to an exclusive club. I couldn't wait to tell Con about it!

Wisdom said "Don't push your luck," so I returned to a walk, then halted by the fence where we had started. Klatawah bobbed her head and snorted, still wanting to go.

"Soon, soon..." I assured her, adding lavish petting and praise. Swiftly I dismounted and untacked, brushed away any saddle and bridle marks, then left mints on the fence posts. I schlepped Con's gear back to my car and got home without crossing paths with anyone. In celebration, I treated myself to a full cooked breakfast.

The rest of the day was an agony of waiting for my phone service to be installed. But finally I had my own number and a stout black telephone on the table next to my sofa. It droned a reassuring dial tone when I lifted the receiver.

That left me the guessing game of whether to call Con at home or the stable. I tried both and got no answer at either. Disappointment slumped me back on the couch. Hard after it came thoughts I had been suppressing: What was he doing? With whom?

He couldn't spend all his time painting, and I didn't want to believe he would unplug the phone for an uninterrupted session when he knew I might be calling. Maybe he was just out getting groceries.

Then again, maybe he had friends. Why not? He knew people from school, work, and social circles. Stupid to think he'd be a hermit, just because for the time I'd known him he hadn't sought extra company.

But now the easy companionship of Jona and Dave, or Miriam and Tom—even myself—wasn't available. All he had, at best, was a stable girl or two, who I could assume would be panting after him. Who else might he go out to dinner with? Who could he play with on a day off, now that he couldn't even ride his own horse? I supposed he could take out any of the trail horses still left at the stable. I'd rather he did that than take out some woman. To get a date, though, all he had to do was stand at the side of the road!

That thought made my face flame...in anger at the prospect, then shame at my jealousy. I had no claim on him—I had walked away without pause—had sworn I didn't want to compete with every damn female for any man's attention. So why wasn't I out at the bar tonight with any of the guys from the Farm who would date me in a heartbeat?

Realizing that I was pacing the room and muttering, I sat again, glared at the phone, then dialed Jona.

"H'lo?"

"Hi, it's me."

"Hi, you. How are you doing out there in Equineville?"

"Um, I'm not sure. It's getting strange."

"Oh? In what way?"

"Well, me. I'm getting strange."

"And I'm getting interested. What's any stranger about you than normal?"

I sniffed a chuckle. "I have the bad feeling I might be in love."

"That's a bad thing? Most people spend their lives looking for it!"

"It's bad when he's the wrong guy, and he lives hundreds of miles away, and you can't do anything about it without screwing up your own life."

Silence. Then: "I see."

I returned the silence for a few beats before saying, "You're not asking me who."

"I don't need to."

"Oh."

"I mean, it's obvious to me that you two were meant for each other. Doesn't sound like it's real obvious to you, though."

"No. I couldn't really feel anything for him until I got Michael out of the picture."

"And is he?"

"Yes."

"Hallelujah and praise Jesus!"

I laughed where I once would have fumed. That awareness amazed me; mere months ago, Michael had been my reason for living. Where had that desire gone? It had been so fierce and consuming, it seemed a tangible thing I could hold in my hand. Now it was just...dead.

"So where does that leave Con?" Jona asked.

"I don't know. That's the problem. I thought I was in love with Michael, but I was wrong. I was so sure!—but it came and went like it never happened. Now I feel the same for Con. How can I trust that it won't disappear the same way?"

"Sorry, I don't know the answer to that one. But…I take it he's a good kisser?"

"Uh…yeah."

"Fireworks?"

"Uh…yeah." I blushed, even though no one could see me.

"So now you're in lust."

"I—no, yeah—that's what I'm afraid of, that's all it is."

"Nothing wrong with that."

"With Con, yes, there is."

"Why?"

"Because…he wants to be loved, not lusted after. That's all he ever gets."

"Mm, true."

"And I don't know if I really love him. So I don't want to mislead him, especially since there's not anything we can do about it."

"Well, you can visit each other."

"To what end? I'm not going to marry him or anything."

"Why not?"

I skipped the family element and went straight to the bottom line. "Because he's not going to abandon the Cape or Montana to join me here, and I'm not going to give up the best job I've ever had to follow him to the Cape or Montana."

"That does pretty much kill hope."

It also shut me down. Why was I bothering to have this conversation when I already knew the obvious? Because: "He brought Klatawah here the other day."

"I know. At least, I knew he was planning to. How'd it go?"

"Well…we barely got a chance to talk to each other."

"Did he stay over?"

"Yes, but not with me."

"Why not?"

I explained about the Burlingames.

"So when's he coming back?"

"I don't know. I called when I got my phone installed, but he's not there."

"Not surprising, given all he's got with buying the stable. I can't imagine why he'd bother doing that, but to each his own. You probably know more about it than I do."

"Not really. Not yet. I was hoping to get more tonight. We really need to talk—I rode Klatawah today."

"Yeah? He'll definitely want to know that! Oh, give me your number now so we don't forget."

I recited, then listened to the faint scratch of Jona writing. Then she said, "All I can say is try him again later. I'm not going to attempt advising you because I have no idea what's the right thing to do. But I really hope you guys can work something out—I would love it. If not, at least try to stay friends!"

"I was a lot more comfortable with him when we *were* friends! Now… you can't go back to that."

"Some people do."

"I'm not sure I can. Him, either."

"Just treat him straight, Linny. Tell him what you've told me if it comes to that."

"That's the real reason I called you. How did you know that Dave was the one?"

Jona went quiet for a moment. "I didn't know he is. How do you know?"

I hooted. "Because it's obvious you're meant for each other!"

We shared a laugh, then sobered. Jona said, "It's hard to answer, because it's so stupid. I mean, simplistic and impossible to explain."

"Try."

She thought, then sighed. "I just knew."

I shuddered in recognition. I had "known" both with Michael and Con. But what, exactly, had I known? What magnetic north had my compass needle swung to? Just that they were both gorgeous riders, and I wanted them?

Was I really that shallow and sex oriented? I hated to think that of myself, but I couldn't deny the evidence of my reactions and my fantasies.

"You're right," I said. "That's not very helpful."

"Unfortunately, that's the way love is."

"You're lucky your guy reciprocates."

"I suspect yours does, too."

"Yeah, but yours is within reasonable driving distance. Do you think you'll get married?"

"I hope so," Jona said, in a small voice I hadn't heard her use in years.

"Has he proposed?"

"Not yet."

"Why not be a modern woman and propose to him?"

"Maybe I will—as soon as I graduate. If I do. You'd be surprised how hard it is to write a thesis about romance!"

I laughed. "I'm sure you'll knock 'em dead with your brilliance and insight."

"You're helping me by being a case study."

"Oh God, don't put me in your paper!"

"Don't worry, I won't. Not unless you write a book I can cite!"

We shared another laugh. I asked, "So what have you learned about romance from 1740 to 1975?"

"That women throughout time are ever unsatisfied with real men, and want an ideal."

I sighed. "I think that goes both ways."

"It's a wonder we have anything to do with each other."

"Well, I think you're a lot closer to an ideal guy than I am."

"I'm sure several thousand women would disagree with you."

"And therein lies the problem. How can you tell the difference between your body on fire with hormones in reaction to somebody's package, and your heart on fire with love of somebody's soul?"

"I'm not sure you can. It may take one to discover the other."

I fell silent to chew on that.

Jona broke into my thoughts to say, "And there's my profundity for the day. I'm overdue for food and need to get back to working. Are we done, or do you want to talk more?"

"No, I'm okay. You've helped me. Thank you."

"Good luck. Let me know if you guys elope or something."

"Hah! Not real likely."

"Remember to call Mom and Dad now that you've got your own phone."

"Yeah, I will. Maybe right now, since otherwise I'm going to walk around the cabin bumping into walls."

Jona laughed. We signed off, and I walked around the cabin for a while. I didn't bump into anything, but I spent a long time staring at Con's paintings before I picked up the phone and dialed him again—no answer—before calling home.

CHAPTER NINETEEN

In the predawn hours, I tried to calculate the best time to catch Con before work. Was his routine the same now that daylight came so much later and he didn't have to report to a job? How much time to allot to talk to him before I had to leave for my own job?

I didn't want to wake him up but didn't want to miss him, either. After feeding, washing, and clothing myself for the day, I dialed the Cape house at first light.

No answer after twenty rings, which struck me numb with disappointment—and, this time, a twinge of fear. I ran down the possibilities: He was asleep. He was jogging. He was showering. He had an early errand or appointment. He was traveling. He'd done an all-nighter and was painting with his headphones on.

He was in somebody else's bed.

He was ill or injured or dead. Living by himself now, if something happened, who would know?

I forced myself out the door to attend to Mrs. Edwards's animals, then called again when I returned. Still no answer at the house. No answer at the stable. Where the heck was he?

No opportunity to call again until lunchtime, so I trudged off to my duties. Started the day with a welcoming Klatawah, which put me back into balance. "Thanks for yesterday," I told her. "But don't tell anyone. Next time we'll both look fabulous and impress the heck out of them. Then we can get you out of here, go look at the world."

I rewarded her with mints on the fence posts, then undertook my morning chores. It felt weird to have a secret—too much like the Michael days, when I had to hide my meetings with him from my parents—and I felt childish for needing to keep it.

I would have loved to talk with Allison and Mary Anne about riding Klatawah, but everyone at the Farm, especially Caryl, would judge me poorly for having taken too big a risk.

It was extra difficult to keep my mouth shut during my midmorning lesson with Mary Anne. Fortunately, I was allowed to ride Midnight, who calmed me into deep focus for an hour. Our harmony was what I had done everything to attain, what made everything worth it. Upon dismounting, I felt as if waking from a dream.

But I also felt in command again. It must have shown, for Mary Anne said, "Next time I want you to ride Baron. You're doing so well on Midnight, we need to know if he's making you look good or you've really improved to this level."

I nodded with a smile, though I would have rather whined. There wasn't any other horse I wanted to ride! Except Klatawah. Which put a new complexion on my career dilemma. What was the point of training to show when what I cared about was specific horses, no longer the journey or the result? How could I make a living, what goals could I shoot for, in so narrow a channel?

I really should talk to Mary Anne about this, or someone else with broad experience who could counsel me. For now, however, I needed Mary Anne to help me with something specific, and myself to show delight in what I was doing so I could expand to new events and answer my own questions.

So as we walked down the barn aisle to Midnight's stall, I said, "Sounds good. In the meantime, when might you be free to supervise me riding Klatawah? She's more than ready to get back to work."

"Hmm...tomorrow early is the only time this week."

"That's fine. How early?"

"As soon as we can get here. It would be better, though, if you waited until after you pass first probation."

"I know." I led Midnight into his box and turned him around as Mary Anne latched the door. "But she's going to jump out of her skin soon, if not right over the fence."

Mary Anne's face slackened in surprise. "Klatawah can jump?"

"Don't know." I slipped Midnight's bridle off his head, at which he nose-bumped me. I patted him after hooking the browband and rein loop over my arm. "But if we keep her penned too long, we might find her in some farmer's field. She's already tried the gate latch."

Mary Anne smiled. "In that case, I'll get you clearance to start work a little late tomorrow."

"Thanks." I returned the smile while unbuckling Midnight's girth. "How about Allison? She'll want to watch."

Mary Anne shook her head. "So will everyone else. Don't push your luck."

I sobered. "Understood."

As Mary Anne walked away, I did a little happy shuffle as I finished unsaddling. I looked for Allison en route to the tackroom, but neither she nor anyone I wanted to talk to was within sight or sound.

I exchanged saddle and bridle for a box of brushes and headed back to groom Midnight in preparation for his next rider in two hours. I hated watching him go out with students, as I had ached watching Shark ride out with clumsy strangers. Somehow I had to find the money to buy and board him—was it time to tackle my parents about the savings bonds?—then convince the Burlingames to relinquish a seasoned school horse.

I would need Con's aid to approach them informally. But anything that involved using him made me shy like a horse from a flapping flag.

Lunch came late because I had to finish tasks that had built up during my lesson. Finally I was free to scoot home and again try Con on the phone.

No answer.

I made and ate a sandwich, tried again. No answer at home or stable. Perhaps he had gone back to Connecticut to sign papers or something. But wouldn't he knock that off as fast as possible and run back to the Cape rather than stay over? There had been enough time. I would have to call Jona and find out if Con had visited Dave along the way.

I tried him again that night at both stable and house. No answer, no answer, which wound me up tight.

I unwound the next morning upon mounting Klatawah. We performed superbly for Mary Anne and Caryl, which opened the door for me to ride every day. Oh, hallelujah!

I couldn't wait to tell Con, but when I called him at lunchtime, still no answer. *Damn it, where is he?* Called again from Allison's during a break, to same result. I was starting to jitter and having trouble hiding it. Dumb luck got me through the day without screwing up anything or getting hassled by Caryl. As soon as I got home, I tried Con again. No answer at house or stable.

Finally, after dinner and my chores, I tried one more time—and he picked up the phone at the house. My blood pressure relaxed several points at the sound of his voice.

"Hi, it's me," I greeted.

"Linny? Hi! Hey, are you on your own phone now?"

"Yeah, I got it a few days ago."

"Did you call then?"

"Yes, I've tried a couple times a day since." I twirled the phone cord around my fingers. "Where have you been? Are you…all right?"

"Yeah, great. I took a road trip to Vermont, just got back a while ago."

"The scenic Green Mountain State?"

"Yeah, and it's definitely scenic. They're already into foliage season. Glad I brought my camera."

"Where? Why?" I felt pushy but couldn't contain myself. After all, I would ask the same questions of any friend.

"A little town on the west side of the state, about a third of the way up. Not all that far from you, but I couldn't divert. There's a ranch up there, and I went to see if they'd take the rest of my horses. They buy, sell, lease, do trail rides, have a tack shop, run a rodeo in the summer, give lessons—quite the outfit. And great people, too. I meant to do a day trip but ended up staying two nights. They gave me lots of advice and ideas, and we've tentatively agreed for them to lease me a string next summer so I don't have to house so many horses all year."

His voice was bright with excitement. I had only heard that tone in fleeting moments during our acquaintance. It drove home that he really was buying the stable, really meant to do something with it.

I inhaled to ask him more but he spoke first, adding, "I finally got a chance to ride, too. They took me out with a trail group, so I got to experience things from the other side." He paused, then blurted, "Man, do I miss Klatawah!"

I laughed. "You'll miss her more when you hear that I rode her yesterday."

"You did! Fantastic. And—that was quick, I thought you'd take a while."

"She insisted on it, actually. I was starting to worry that she might break out."

"So how did she go?"

"She was a pussycat. I hardly recognized her."

"Told you she likes you!"

"Well, I'm still not so sure about that, but she's lonely, and I'm her only friend. Also, I made sure nobody was around to make her nervous, and just got on. We took a few laps around the pasture, but I didn't dare let her run."

"That was wise."

"Then this morning Mary Anne monitored us and gave me clearance to ride daily as long as I tell someone I'm doing it. She's going to ride with me on the trail next week."

There was a pause, in which I imagined he nodded. Then he said, "How did Caryl take it?"

"Mm, not sure. She just stood at the rail the whole time, emanating hate waves at me. I did my best to ignore her."

"If you want, I'll send written instructions for you to ride Klat on the trail."

"That would help a lot—thanks. Even better if you got specific. There's a local hunter pace next month that a whole bunch of people from the Farm are entering—boarders and employees alike. I'll have passed first probation by then, so I could ride one of the schoolies, but somebody has already reserved Midnight. I'm thinking of taking Klatawah and doing the ride-arounds."

"You mean, it's a jump course?"

"Not quite. It's a team trail ride with jumping, but like in hunting you can stay on the flat. It's timed but not a race against the clock; more like, which team gets closest to the ideal pace, which is set by a rider who goes out beforehand. I wouldn't try to compete, just ride the course as way to get Klat into the countryside and with other horses. They tell me it's close enough that we can all hack over, which is why so many of our riders go. A big play day for them."

"Sounds like fun. I wouldn't mind doing something like that, myself."

"Well...you're the owner, come on out and ride your horse!"

"But then who will you ride?"

"Whatever I can get. If not, I'll work the course. Don't worry—come if you can." I crossed my fingers.

He sighed. "Unfortunately, I can't. I take legal possession of the stable October first and will dive right into renovations. I'll be stuck here for a while."

I swallowed my dismay. "Well, okay. I'll feel pretty stupid riding Western in an English habit, but in this event looks don't count. Do you have any desire to cross-train her to English?"

There was a pause while I imagined he shook his head, then he recalled he was on a phone and verbalized, "Nope. Just work on strength and control, so someday she can go out with a group on an endurance ride."

This time I nodded before remembering to speak. "That sounds good."

I leaned back on the couch and stretched my feet out the long way, feeling relaxed with him for the first time since the moonlit beach.

"I'll come if I can," he assured me, "but it's going to be iffy through winter. If all goes well, though, I'll be able to bring Klatawah home before Thanksgiving."

"Oh..." I had been so absorbed in the present that I'd forgotten about the future. Klatawah was my bridge to him. What would we do when that was gone?

I asked a different question. "What, exactly, are you planning to do with the place?"

"I'd like to just tear it down and start over, but both the barn and the house are still sound, so it's going to be a cleanup and renovation. Starting with plumbing and wiring."

"Then fill the stable back up with what?"

"A lot fewer horses, that's for sure. Thirty is just too much. So is five rides a day. I'm thinking just one morning and one afternoon ride, and more specialty ones like the sunset."

Like the moonlight ride we never got a chance to try.

"If we're not overtaxed," he was saying, "then we can even offer lessons."

"We...?"

"Well, uh, me and the staff. I can hire fewer and better."

"If you can get them," I said, recalling Tom's constant complaint and the ease with which I had walked into Galeson's without having to prove my qualifications.

"I'm kinda hoping you'll help me with that."

I sat up and swung my feet to the floor. "What do you mean?"

A rustle came through from the background as he fidgeted. "Maybe you could come back and help me run the new operation."

I choked then stammered, "You mean, as a hand—or a partner?"

"Uh-erm." He cleared his throat. "As top hand. I can't take a partner right now...you know...those restrictions."

The rocket ship of my hope reversed and crashed down. "So I'd be your employee."

"Yeah—but only on paper," he hastened to add.

"Paper counts. You'd have to cut me a paycheck every week, deduct my taxes, and all that stuff. You'd have the power to fire me and would control my income."

"Yep. A regular job. Just like you've always had and probably always will."

I shook my head. "It's not the same. The Farm will never kiss me."

Silence. I stood and paced to the end of the phone cord. "If there's anything Michael taught me, Con, it's to keep some distance between my men and my job. Here, there was a nice dividing line until you plopped Klatawah into it. Even with that, there's still some buffer...and if things go bad at the Farm, I've got a hundred local options. But at the Cape, it's you or nothing—if it didn't work out, I'd have to haul off again and start all over again. *Again!*"

"I would hire you as my trainer," he said, at which I saw his dual motivation in shipping Klatawah to Shallowkill.

Sure, he'd needed a fast boarding solution; but also, if he publicly attached me to his horse, then fewer questions would be asked if we stayed together wherever the horse went. The idea touched me; his failure to spell it out infuriated me.

But I kept my voice even. "That might fly if I had some credentials. But think about it, Con. We'd have to play the secrecy game even worse than here, to keep your father or banker or whoever checks up on you from finding out I'm just an unpedigreed blond gold-digger you imported for your pleasure—instantly undoing the gain you got with them by going into business."

I waited for him to try persuasion, something like, "I love you and want you with me." When no words came at all, my voice hardened in anger and hurt. "Thanks for the offer, but I don't want to be part of your economic equation. For me to give up everything great here, it's got to be for love first, then we figure out how to do it. Not make a damn business plan and slot me in, hoping it works!"

He said coldly, "That's not what I'm trying to do, Linny."

"Then what *are* you doing? It sounds to me like a backup plan to Montana in case you don't get your millions."

"Yeah, that's a factor. But first I'm trying to make something for us that doesn't depend on my inheritance."

That struck me dumb. I could hear a faint crackle on the line behind his breathing. And he was puffing hard, awaiting my response.

I plunked back down on the couch, helpless to speak. A long minute later, he said, "Damn it, Linny, what do you want?"

"I don't know anymore!" I wailed.

"Well, let me know when you figure it out." He punctuated the ultimatum with a click.

The dial tone droned through my shock. *He hung up on me!* After making the equivalent of a declaration of love, he had cut me off!

I started at the handset for a second, then flung it away. It flew to the end of its cord, then yanked the phone after it, all clanging to the floor as I flopped face down on the sofa in tears.

The multiple Linnys I'd been sitting on for months rose to fight within me. Grown-up Linny said, Get over it and stop acting like a twerp! Adolescent Linny said, Love's not supposed to make you cry, it's supposed to make you happy! Sunshine and flowers! Hearts flying away on wings! Little Linnea said, Boo-hoo, he doesn't love me!

Grown-up Linny shouldered the others aside, measuring what love had brought me. Michael: I love you, but 'scuse me while I skip like a stone through other women's beds. Con: I love you, but 'scuse me while I devise a scenario without consulting you, according to my priorities and resources and family weirdness. Take it or leave it, baby.

Granted, I couldn't offer much better to him, but at least my world contained choices. Even if he abandoned his Montana dream, why tie himself to the Cape when he could more easily sell or rent his house, come here with Klatawah, and we could invent something together in a region abundant with horse opportunities?

Noooo...he had to have it his way, which made me more determined to stick with mine.

Which would be fine if I didn't have his horse to deal with. Which I could hardly abandon just for spite. *Oh Con*, I wailed internally, *you've wedged me so tight between a rock and hard place, I'll never get out!*

Whatever happened, I wondered, to *If you love something, set it free...*?

I wished I could pack up tonight and move to Montana, just to thumb my nose at him. Make him come crawling to me, instead of me capitulating to him. Oh God, more head games and power plays. That was no kind of love at all.

After pacing the cabin for a while, I settled enough to register that I held the advantage. He had asked me to make a decision and let him know. We both had forgotten about giving him my new phone number, so he couldn't contact me again without extra trouble.

That left the ball, as the saying went, in my court.

I didn't do much with it over the next month. To quiet my screaming heart, I existed in a state of critical analysis.

For every task, I opened all my senses to the experience, and compared it to the hypothetical equivalent of same at Galeson's—rather, Spindrift Stable—which I visualized as different upgrades to the rickety public outfit I had so briefly known.

While pondering what would make it attractive enough to entice me to abandon Shallowkill, I openly rode Klatawah around the compound every day, as if I owned her; which, in effect, I did; which put me, in effect, in Con's shoes.

I came to understand why trail riding appealed to him. It was a hundred times more interesting outside the ring than inside. You could work on horsemanship to the same degree but in constantly changing conditions, while feeling unconstrained. I had known this feeling from riding the dunes but had attributed it to that specific environment. Wandering around the Shallowkill lands and roads opened up new vistas in both the literal and figurative sense.

Klatawah proved herself a trail horse from her flaxen forelock to her unshod gray hooves, curious about everything, calm at surprises, instantly responsive to conditions, always looking ahead. I grew to love and trust her, though always remained prepared for a backslide.

Mary Anne cleared me for solo outings after our first two rides together and invited me on a group ride she gave to one of her classes as a preview to the hunter pace. Klatawah shone that day, even hopped over a log with her ears pricked forward, inspiring me to enter the event as soon as we got home.

While waiting for the date, I concentrated on giving the mare the most varied experience available in the landscape we were permitted to ride. For my own training, I continued lessons on Midnight, after my requisite ride on Baron.

Baron was a big bay Thoroughbred Cindy was developing for the A circuit, who had perfect hunter conformation and a steady going but was prone to choosing his own pace. I found him heavy-footed and bone-headed and couldn't wait to get off him. I even rode Trix once, at Allison's insistence, and found her nimbler of foot and softer in the mouth, always waiting for direction on what to do, but still a snooze.

Both of them, along with Fudge, Clipper, and Stella—the other school horses—grew ever more dull to me. While my friends among the stablehands and boarders talked endlessly of showing, with some attending local and regional events every other week, I focused on just riding. For some reason, I could communicate with Midnight and Klatawah in a way I couldn't with other horses, save for Shark. But all these were either unsuitable for the show ring or unavailable to me. For the money it would cost me to compete, I could no longer see value if I had to ride other horses.

What had changed within me, and what was different about those animals, I couldn't define; I knew only that what I wanted from riding had come true with that trio. They taught me so much through pleasure that I could transfer the skills to other mounts, making my form and control improve so rapidly that I gained compliments from my teachers and peers.

They encouraged me to attend clinics—which I did—and resume showing, which I resisted. It wasn't about avoiding Michael anymore. My interest had turned toward unfenced events like those I kept hearing about: the hunter pace, hunting itself, and cubbing.

I eliminated cubbing from the list once I learned it was the training exercise for hounds, horses, and prey, a ritual left over from an era when eradicating vermin was the goal. It came in late summer and early fall to condition all parties for the real hunts in October and November, and was oriented around killing foxes.

Thankfully, those local meets, especially Opening Day, were drag hunts more often than not. In these a scent was tracked across the countryside for the hounds to follow, ensuring the field a great day's ride without having to torment and murder anything.

Hunting, as Mary Anne had suggested, promised to blend all my interests into one intense experience. Having started as a show hunter, I became eager to know the real thing and compare them against each other. This gave me, finally, a new goal: to ride the Opening Day on Midnight. Not only would it be thrilling, but also it might answer the critical questions in my soul.

Con's harsh sign-off had revealed that I couldn't make up my mind about him until I understood what I needed for myself. While the dream of medals still lured, I now recognized it as a fantasy and knew I'd never have what it took to get there. So I needed to find something else that would bring the same sense of achievement, through the same process of mastery, and gain the same fulfillment, while paying the rent for the rest of my life.

While waiting, I continued doing my chores at twice the performance level required so that when my probation ended, Caryl could find no legitimate reason to deny me full employment status. She granted it with the expression of a persimmon chewing glass. I thanked her and immediately sought Mary Anne to arrange renting Midnight for Opening Day.

"I beat one of the regular students to him by twenty minutes," I told Jona on the phone.

"Wow," my sister said vaguely, not understanding the import but willing to give credit and share excitement. "What's so special about this horse that everyone wants him?"

"Not everyone, but there are so few school horses and so many people who want to ride Opening Day that everything with four legs within twenty miles gets rented by people who don't have their own horse."

"Ah. So this isn't a thing for Klatawah."

"God no. Well, maybe. If I hadn't nabbed Midnight, who's experienced and who I can ride like I was born on his back, I might have gone crazy and ridden Klatawah second field."

"Huh?"

"Second field is the non-jumpers. There are people up front who manage the hounds, and the experienced riders and horses follow them. Then it trickles back to less experienced ones who still jump, like me; another batch who follow on the flat; and I think even a trailing group who just goes out for the heck of it. One of these back groups is called 'hilltoppers,' but I'm not sure which. This is all new to me. I only know that Opening Day is the big social and show-off event around here, and everyone who isn't a member of the hunt club goes as a guest. From Shallowkill we can hack directly to the meet so don't have to trailer all the horses."

"That's a big hassle and expense, I take it?"

"Definitely, though if you've done it all your life, not so much."

"I recall you or Con saying he'd been invited to this thing by the Burlingames."

"Yeah, but he can't go. Not just 'cause of the renovation at the stable, which he's got to hang around for, but in hunting you need fancy formal dress—as well as English tack—and he doesn't have any of it. And, frankly,

I think Klatawah would go nuts and try to race everybody, violating protocol and scaring me half to death. Con might be strong enough to stop her, but if he's got a grain of sense he won't risk injury to himself or her."

"Or you."

"Yeah. But we haven't really discussed it; I'm just assuming."

"What do you talk about, then?"

"Er, nothing much lately. Not for a few weeks."

I stopped. Jona waited.

"Um, we had...words."

"Oh?"

"He wants me to come back to the Cape and work for him."

"Oh." Jona thought for a moment. "I don't suppose that went over very well."

"No, it did not."

"So...did you break up?"

"How can we break up? We've never gotten together!" I gave a bitter laugh.

"I would have thought those fireworks you told me about meant couplehood."

"Yeah, well...jeesh, how can you be together when you live so far apart? Never mind thinking so far apart."

"Where there's a will, there's a way."

"Apparently not enough will on either of our parts."

"You may be surprised."

"I would. He hasn't called or written. Me neither. We left it that I would figure out what I want to do and let him know."

"That could take decades."

"Well, I'm narrowing it down. I'll get a much better idea after the hunter pace and Opening Day. Those are coming up quick, and only two weeks apart."

Jona sighed.

I said, "Do you know about his family thing?"

"Some of it."

"Well, that's a big problem behind the scenes. What he's basically asking me to do is, for the pluses of riding the dunes and beaches and being with his wonderful self, to pay the minuses of watching the public grind down good horses every summer, relying on an unreliable income, being chained to responsibilities I never asked for, having my lover be my boss with the power of God over me, and both of us turning a lying face to the world for years until he finds out whether he's going to get his inheritance. Or else we just flaunt our relationship and guarantee him losing the money. I don't care what a big-hearted guy he claims to be, he'll blame me if that happens. How could he not?—at least in his secret heart, since he's oriented his whole life around that reward, and I'd be the element that made things different."

Jona hummed.

"I mean," I went on, "if he wants to break with his family, fine. But that's his choice—I can't demand it, and I refuse to cause it. It's one thing to make my own choice to walk the poor road, but another thing to demand it as a condition for someone else."

I would rather never have him, I realized, than force him into anything. How could we ever be equal if one's priorities and preferences dominated the other?

That would make a mockery of love. Over time, bitterness would seep in; possibly, hatred. What point giving in to love now, only to lose it later?

I fell so deep into thought that I forgot I was talking. "Sometimes I think it actually hurts more to have lost Michael because when he was there, he was all there. It's too damn bad for me that he isn't Mr. Monogamy. But Con is bound to something he's put ahead of love, not daring to open his heart until he's got his ducks in a row. He plays his cards close to his chest, and weaves plans around me like spiderwebs. If he would just step up and say, 'I love you—I want you—I need you,' then I wouldn't feel like I'm being undermined."

"I dunno," Jona said, startling me back into the moment. "It seems to me he's done that. What's more direct than asking you to come back and live and work with him? What's more symbolic than entrusting his horse to you—the thing you both value above gold? That sure beats words that get proven wrong!"

My mouth moved but nothing came out. "The thing is," I said eventually, "I miss him so much I feel like a bunch of arms and legs flailing around a hollow core. Which doesn't make sense, because I've only known him for a few months."

"Yeah, but in that time you knew him more intimately than you ever knew Michael. You lived together. Worked together. Rode together. With Mike, you always lived and worked in separate places and had to leave them to be together. That made each occasion a special event instead of building blocks."

I thought about that until Jona said, "You two need to talk more."

"Why bother? He's already said he can't marry me."

"Can't, or won't?"

"Can't."

"Why?"

"Because of all that family crap."

"What do you mean?"

"If he hasn't told you about it, then it's wrong for me to."

"You've already let the cat out of the bag."

"And that was a mistake. I'm sorry. He told me in confidence, and I shouldn't have said anything."

"It sounds like he and I are going to have a little chat."

"No, Jona—don't!"

"Why not? My fiancé's best friend is driving my little sister crazy. I think I have a stake in the matter. He can always tell me to keep my nose out."

While I spluttered, Jona added, "Maybe I'll just sic Dave on him…"

"Please, Jona, don't!"

"Hey, you're making a mess of it, and Con might need somebody to talk to. Did you ever think of that?"

No, I hadn't. I'd just assumed that guys didn't talk about love. Sex, yes; but matters of the heart? When did that ever happen?

Then again, I would never be there when they did, so how could I know?

"Listen," Jona said. "You were mad when I tried to protect you from Michael, now you're mad I'm trying to help you get together with Con. I can't win!"

"Have you considered not interfering at all?"

"No."

"Gad, you're just as bad as Mom and Dad—trying to run my life!"

"I wouldn't put it that way. Remember, elders are supposed to be wiser so youngers can learn from us. I'm not sure about Mom and Dad, but how do you think Dave and I manage to keep together?"

I hesitated then said, "You talk about all this stuff."

"That's right. And you're so freaked out about this stuff that you missed the giant boulder I just dropped in your lap."

"Huh?"

"Dave. He's is my fee-aunts-say, Linny. We're engaged!"

"Oh!" I sat down. "When did that happen?"

"Last night."

"Wow! Have you told Mom and Dad yet?"

"No, I thought you'd like to be the first to know."

"Double wow. Yeah. Thank you. Congratulations! When and where? You sure?"

"Yep. Unlike you. And, in fact, it gives me or Dave a nice reason to call Con."

"Jona!"

"Linny, I would bet my degree that you haven't told him half of what you're telling me, and it's all stuff he needs to know. You guys have a complicated situation and you need to *talk*. It's not fair for you to expect him to declare himself when you won't do it, either."

She waited for me to speak. When I didn't, she said, "What's the worst that could happen: You won't get together? You're already there, so what's to be afraid of?"

I carried that thought through the night. I had to put it aside in the morning, however, because hunter-pace day had finally arrived, and it left no room for angst.

CHAPTER TWENTY

My angst vaporized during the best time I'd had since riding the sunset beach. Not until all the horses were tucked away for the night, and all my chores were finished; not until I'd steamed myself limp and pink in my tiny shower stall after a laugh-filled dinner in town with the gang, then settled on my couch in sloppy, comfortable clothes, did I remember I had to make a phone call.

A difficult, possibly life-changing phone call.

Whatever else I and Con were to each other, I owed him a report on his horse's performance at her first known event.

I could play mean and wait until my next day off (which would only be a half day because I had to make up the hours taken for the hunter pace), or I could make him wait possibly longer by writing a letter. That seemed appropriately petty in response to the fact he'd never sent the letter he'd offered, formally authorizing me to ride Klatawah outside the Farm.

Neither had he forbidden it, so I'd ridden her to the hunter pace a few miles down the road and was so relaxed by the time the chock-full day was over that I just picked up the handset and dialed his house.

No answer! Good grief, where had he gotten off to this time? Goddamn him!

On afterthought, I dialed the stable, knowing it could be switched to ring at Tom's former residence if Con hadn't discontinued that. Maybe he was bunking there during construction, to keep a better watch on things. Maybe he had closed up the beach house for the winter to economize.

Maybe he was out for supper, or on another road trip. Maybe he'd given up on me and was out on a date.

Nope, not yet: He picked up. "Spindrift Stable."

My pulse spiked. "Hi, it's me."

He hesitated, then lowered his voice, "Hi. How ya doin'?"

"Good. Real good. I wanted to tell you about Klatawah today."

"I was hoping you would."

I was glad to learn he'd had his eye on the calendar and had been waiting around, wondering. "She went terrific. You've got yourself a first-class trail horse, Con."

"Tell me something I don't know!" He laughed.

My heart lightened further. "Okay: Klatawah can jump."

"Really!"

"Yeah. Just a few logs, but it was her idea. I was planning to go around everything, but since we ended up at the back of the pack, I let her show me how much she wanted to follow or go her own way. After looking at the first jump like it was going to bite her, she attacked it by sailing over like an Arab—head and tail in the air, feet tucked up too high—but I swear she was laughing afterward. Popped over all the easy ones the rest of the course. By the way, I think it's time to put shoes on her."

"Yeah, I was thinking about that the other day."

"Her feet aren't getting sanded down daily anymore. The farrier was here a while back, and we managed using a lip twitch to get her to stand for filing. The full ordeal of shoeing will probably be worse. But it's getting hard or slippery underfoot, with frost and wet leaves and all, and I ride her anywhere we can go. She needs better traction and protection."

"Go ahead and take care of it," he said in his owner's voice.

"Okay. Anyway, Shallowkill entered three teams of three people each, and I rode in the non-jumping class with Mary Anne, who's working a client's green horse, and one of the boarders, who's a weak rider on an old horse. Everyone else bombed away, including Allison on Trix and a girl named Pam who rides Midnight. She's really mad at me for nabbing him for Opening Day, but got her fun in today."

"Uh-huh," Con said, waiting for more.

"Our teams got first and third in the jumping group, and second to last in non-jumping. It was more fun and training than anything else, though a couple people there were real serious about it. They told me about other events in the area, but all would mean trailering."

"Hm, sorry I didn't leave the old bullet there. Can you get a tow vehicle, and do you know how to drive with a trailer?"

"I've only done it once, and I don't have anyone to borrow from."

"I might be able to enlist the Burlingames, but that would take some schmoozing. Anyone from the Farm likely to go, and you can tag along?"

I twisted my mouth. "Maybe, but doubtful. This was the only one our people go to, just because it's nearby and a community thing. Kind of like the hunt. I don't think anyone will go out of their way for another hunter pace; they're more interested in showing."

"Any organized trail rides in the region?"

"I haven't found any yet, but I'm sure there's something. I can ask around, and I've been poring through current and back issues of all the horse magazines to learn about options."

"When I was in Vermont, I came across an association that's been doing competitive trail rides for decades, as well as pleasure rides. Maybe we can arrange to do one of theirs."

I warmed. He'd said it casually, yet it sounded like an invitation or a promise. I returned, "And maybe you can borrow some togs from the Burlingames and ride Klatawah second field on the hunt."

"Whoa. That's ambitious!"

"It would be a blast. Me on Midnight, you on Klatawah..." I glanced across the room at the painting of us pounding through the surf, and a big *ker-twannng* occurred in my breast.

"Yeah, but you'd leave me a mile behind," he said.

"You might have to ride her with a double bit to hold her back," I said to keep things on safe territory.

He chuckled. "I haven't jumped since I was about fifteen."

"You don't have t—"

"I know. I'm just not sure I'm up to it, correct clothes or not."

"Well...think about it."

"I will."

"Meanwhile..." I twirled the cord around my finger, hearing Jona in my head: *Talk to him! Talk to him!* "How's the renovation going?"

"Slow and messy, but starting to pick up some steam. It's sorted out enough that I can bring Klatawah home any time."

I swallowed a gulp. "Like, when?"

He hesitated long enough to account for a shrug. "Don't know yet. But soon."

I sighed. "I'll miss her." Jona's voice again: *Tell him what he needs to know!*

I should have then said, "I miss you"—but he spoke first: "Something about buying a stable and not having a horse to ride is getting to me."

Ooomph. "Yeah, I can understand that."

I sure could! If not for Galeson's, I would have had to go horseless for three months. He was already halfway there. I could not ask to keep Klatawah longer at his expense.

"Well, whenever you come for her, you don't have stay at the Burlingames'."

"That's good to know. Couch and Cheerios?"

"My cot and Cheerios, if you want."

Long pause. "That's *really* good to know."

I went mute. I had just invited him to my bed and he had liked the idea.

Oh my God!

After another long pause, he said, "It would help to have your street address as well as your home telephone number."

"Oh! Right, sorry, I keep forgetting." I recited the data, hearing him rustle up pen and paper on the other end of the line.

"Okay," he said after scribbling the info down.

The moment approached to either say good-bye or extend the conversation. *Talk to him! Talk to him!* What could I say?

"So, what are you doing besides not riding, and bossing around contractors?"

He hesitated before answering, as if sensing my effort and evaluating it. But he answered in a relaxed voice. "Making lots of phone calls and doing lots of paperwork. Running in the morning. Cooking all my meals now that

Jona's gone. Painting when I'm not doing anything else. I've got a pretty good portfolio building up."

"I'd like to see it."

"Well, you'll have to get your little hiney back out here, because I'm not going to tote the whole thing back and forth across New England."

"Maybe if I ever get two whole days off back to back. In the meantime, can you take photos?"

"Mm, yeah, I've got a tripod...not sure how to light them..."

Before he could drift off into technical puzzles, I asked, "Do you have some friends to hang out with? It must be darn quiet out there off-season."

"That's for sure! But there's a couple I know who run a gallery in Provincetown. I'm hoping they'll show my work someday. They stay open year-round, to catch the folks who are more likely to walk in when so little else is open. We do dinner now and then. In fact, we're meeting for drinks tomorrow before their favorite restaurant closes for winter. The community gets really small then, and it's easy to meet people. I like it more now than summer."

I wondered about that, having not lived anywhere other than home, school, or the Academy during winter, all well populated. Maybe this winter things would slow down enough I could get a whole weekend off, and go see for myself.

Until then, I had run out of things to ask or say, and switching back to horse talk felt phony when I just wanted to look him in the eyes and touch him. We weren't in tune enough to switch to intimacy yet; and I didn't think I could speak my heart without it coming out garbled.

He apparently suffered the same problem, for his voice got stiff as he said, "I guess that's it for now. See you sooner rather than later."

"I look forward to it."

"Then...good night. I'm glad you called."

"Me too. Good night."

I love you. The words stuck in my throat. I wasn't sure whether to be angry at myself, or relieved.

Regardless, the ball was now back in his court. He would come or he wouldn't. He would sleep with me or he would not. I couldn't visualize further.

The thought that did push itself into the forefront was whether I should get sheets for the sofa bed before he arrived.

Work, as always, prevented me from accomplishing things at home. Although I had far fewer horses to serve than at Galeson's—about the same number as at the Academy—there were many more tasks each hand had to perform. The school horses, which fell under my purview, had their own daily routines plus scheduled treatment from vets and farriers, as well as the injuries and emergencies that went with any combination of horses and people.

The boarders, however, each had unique demands and timetables; and because they showed so often, I had to pitch in with braiding and polishing and trailering and miscellaneous other prep because it was always done in a hurry, and there were never enough hands.

On top of that was helping set up, tear down, and run around during the seminars and events the Farm hosted with regular irregularity, on top of daily care and training of Klatawah while losing light at both the start and end of the day, plus twice-a-week lessons for myself. I couldn't clock out until I'd done my share of cleaning the place until it glowed in the dark, which Caryl inspected as if with white gloves and microscopes. If she spotted a spot, we had to do the job again.

I could barely remain civil to her when she hovered, inspecting and criticizing and causing delays. The day I almost snapped, I was saved by Mary Anne, who had a genie's gift for materializing at the right moment. In this instance, she rescheduled her students into a group lesson on the outside course again, to help us prepare for the hunt.

Riding Midnight that day restored my equanimity. The grounds crew had lowered all the jumps, and Midnight bounded over them in horse glee. The different sizes, shapes, distances between, and approach patterns better approximated what we might find in the field. I jumped everything successfully, better than I had performed any time before.

I fantasized about riding with Con on Opening Day, but during the two weeks counting down to that event, I neither saw nor heard from him. Nor did word come from anyone in the office about him fetching Klatawah. I was grateful for the delay but didn't like what motives it might signify. Most likely he would just show up and sample my body, then whisk his horse away, and that would be the end.

I decided not to exert the time and effort to buy new sheets.

But when I lay in my cot at night, I imagined what might happen on either it or the sofa. Recalling that kiss in Klatawah's hilltop shed left me hot and sweaty. It disturbed me to be so thrilled yet so terrified at the thought of Con wrapped around me; I wanted him so much, yet something kept holding me back from reaching out.

I hadn't paused before leaping into Michael's arms. What was so different here?

The answer came to me in the middle of the night: familiarity. Michael was of my world, and embracing him hadn't felt like swan-diving off a cliff into the unknown, with a high chance of splatting fatally at the bottom. Whatever went right or wrong between us had been our own choices and personalities in our own context.

My equation with Con, however, involved more and bigger things and people—everything more complicated, with higher stakes. Yeah, we shared a love of horses; but the rest of his life was strange or repellent to me. I wanted him without his baggage, which was not an option.

So my choice boiled down to whether or not I could accept all that came with him. Whether I could make a major capitulation that violated my principles or my heart, or would force changing my career again. Was that sacrifice worth love? Was any love really worth it in the end?

I lost a lot of sleep over this. Finally I decided to again heed Jona's wisdom: *It may take one to discover the other.* If/when Con arrived, I would offer him myself on cot or sofa—or floor or bed of his truck—and learn what I needed to know.

Until then, the countdown went on to Opening Day. When it finally dawned, I lobbed some hay to Klatawah, then went straight to the barn.

Mary Anne and Caryl, as hunt officials—one mounted, the other not—left early to meet their peers and the pack. I joined the general scurry of stablemates and boarders braiding manes and tying up tails, grooming coats to a shine, and checking equipment, all while trying to keep clothes clean.

In the preceding weeks, I had acquired the pieces I didn't already own to make the habit required for hunting: black coat, white shirt and stock (correctly tied and pinned), black boots, and neutral, preferably buff, breeches. Hunt members added the hunt's colors to their collars; some, members or guests, wore top hats or derbies.

I skipped bringing a field kit for emergencies, settling for my Swiss Army knife in my pocket. I appreciated my coat's woolen warmth against the clear autumn morning that left frost on the foliage. Horses snorted and cavorted, raring to go.

The Shallowkill contingent trotted down blacktop toward the meet point two miles distant. The clatter of forty hooves, striking sparks with their horseshoes, jarred my teeth and sent chills along my nerves. Beneath me, Midnight arched his neck and lifted his knees and tail like a gaited show horse. Although he pulled hard against the bit, he didn't fight me. Other horses bucked and raced.

The group drew up at the village square, where thirty riders and twice that in spectators had already gathered. I held Midnight on the fringe near Allison, who was riding Trix on her first hunt, which was Allison's second. I hoped to stick with her for advice and company, and help if needed, keeping well behind the hounds.

More riders arrived, prompting Allison to say, "This is way more than last year." The officials I glimpsed were talking and gesturing nervously while counting heads. Eventually the milling, snorting, stamping, chattering crowd, all breathing clouds in the midmorning sun, settled down enough to permit stirrup cups to be distributed. Non-riding hunt members wove through the mass bearing trays of mini plastic tumblers bearing the club's logo, half filled with grape juice or wine. I took one at Allison's urging: "A bracer—you'll need it!" I agreed as I wondered how so many bodies would negotiate the trails.

The crowd quieted and then parted to accept the hunt master, the whippers-in, and various helpers, in black or scarlet coats, all following the truck carrying caged foxhounds. After this group occupied the crowd's center, the master made a speech, and a priest blessed the hounds.

I missed the presentations while trying to find the hunt secretary. As a non-member, I was supposed to pay a capping fee, but the hunters began sorting themselves into order before I succeeded. The first field followed the released hounds, and second field followed in their hoofsteps. Allison and I were swept along in between them.

During the next four hours, I lost all self-awareness. Occasionally I glimpsed Allison or another familiar face, but crash evasion dominated my reflexes and thoughts. Regular members of the hunt, and guests who rode or showed field hunters, comported themselves with reasonable control, but the guests just out for the occasion outnumbered them, introducing a chaos factor the field masters weren't prepared to manage.

We swarmed shoulder to shoulder down roads and nose to rump in field or forest, changing speed as dictated by braying hounds and bleating horns. I never saw the hounds work and almost immediately lost my bearings. The glamorous equestrians I had seen at the opening ceremonies became cursing competitors for space.

In the forest we piled up like cars on a jammed freeway when the hounds bunched to recast for scent. I was grateful for the harmony I had with Midnight, who responded to my slightest command despite his herd instinct to run. We managed to keep out of everyone's way without stumbling over roots or backing into trees, then found a place back in line when the field resumed careening along twisty trails.

Up and down, left and right, over dirt trampled to rocky paste, whipped by branches that limited sight to one horse ahead. When traffic stopped abruptly again, whether for the hounds or a surprise like a panicked deer leaping across the trail, horses bumped into and scuffled around one another while riders swore and turned red. One Thoroughbred thrashed so severely that its rider was asked to move to the back.

Presently a cry came down the line and all moved forward again. Riders warned "'Ware hound!" or "'Ware hole!" until increasing speed eroded manners into anarchy. No time to react to fallen trees or low boughs or sudden crevices of running water. I went over, under, or through as best I could, barely managing sometimes to stay aboard.

Forest alternated with field for mile after mile. The hunt gradually spread across many miles as the most experienced surged forward; novices tumbled and were rescued, to follow at a slower pace with the second field. The core of first field broke into subgroups to maintain the elbow room needed at obstacles for safe passage. My group got stalled at a water crossing by a horse who wouldn't get his feet wet. I and four others rode upstream to splash through another ford, then followed the sound of hounds giving tongue back into the woods.

By then horses were lathered and riders were panting and sweating. Nonetheless, we cantered uphill toward a crescendo of horns, shouts, and bays. The leaders came into view as my group burst into an enormous cornfield. Although harvested, it remained spiky and rutted, and sloped downhill for acres. The hunt paused for a confused moment, then the horn sounded again and the hounds took off as if catapulted. Horses followed regardless of their riders' intentions, in a maniacal stampede.

Spectators waiting along the road at the bottom watched a modern Charge of the Light Brigade thunder down at them. I could only hang on and hope Midnight didn't step into a hole. Momentum propelled us ever faster toward a rock wall inset with coops and gates peeking out between bushes and wire. The hounds arrived first and scrambled over, wagging tails and baying; the master and whips almost landed on them as they flew over in the hounds' wake.

The next line of riders jumped in ten different places, with only seven coming up on the other side. I had a clear shot over a coop if no one cut in front of me. As Midnight launched, I heard cameras snapping, capturing my face first slack and bloodless then pinched as Midnight's landing slammed my jaws together. He lurched out of the roadside drainage ditch and onto the shoulder between parked vehicles, then galloped after the pack along a dirt lane.

I let him run, holding the reins in one hand while wiping my eyes with the other. Not only were they clogged with hair and dirt and sweat and tear-water, but I had glimpsed something back there I didn't believe. A tall blond man in blue standing in the bed of a black pickup truck. His face had been masked by a camera with big lens.

It couldn't be, but it could only be. I wanted to stop and confirm, but the hunt sucked me along.

Horses cantered down the road, cut sharply into the forest before any cars came along, and once again screeched to a messy halt. This time eight riders reversed their mounts and created a separate cluster, calling it quits for the day. I voted with them and reined Midnight in.

When the rest of the field moved on, tailed by late arrivals, our group had to wrestle back our horses. One girl came off as her horse won the fight. It flew away, to be caught and led home later. The unseated rider, bruised and angry, swung up behind her friend and headed toward the road back to her barn.

I tagged behind them, blowing almost as hard as Midnight. My legs had turned to jelly and every muscle burned. To my relief, Midnight remained sound; others in the group weren't so lucky. Three limped so badly that their riders had to dismount and lead.

Back on pavement, the group split again to ride in opposite directions. Because I was thoroughly lost, I stayed with two women and a man from a stable in Shallowkill's vicinity. I longed to remove my helmet but dutifully kept it on just in case. The horses bobbed and strained at the walk until well separated from the excitement. Then they cooled down to an amble, relaxed their necks, blew through their nostrils, shook their manes.

My companions peeled off at a crossroad, leaving me alone for the last leg to Shallowkill. I welcomed the chance to regather my poise. Midnight clopped along so slackly that I doubted he'd shy at anything, so I dared remove my hard hat, unpin my stock, and wipe my face, keeping one hand on the reins. Then I shook my head and faced my new reality.

He's here. He came. By surprise, as usual—*a sandbagger, that guy!* But was he here to claim his horse or me? Would that photograph of me turn into a painting?

I had thought today would be the day that would determine my new direction in riding, but instead it would be the day I had to decide about Con. "Gee, thanks!" I said to the foliage. I was so tired I could barely sit up, never mind make important choices!

Occasional cars overtook us; I glanced back anxiously each time, hoping and dreading it would be his truck. It never was, just locals or returning spectators, who crawled past respectfully, smiling and waving.

As I neared the Farm, I passed parked vehicles along the berm—an overflow of the cars, trucks, and trailers in Shallowkill's yard. The only people around when I rode in were the skeleton crew, done with their chores and waiting for our riders to return. I was the first one back.

I slid off Midnight outside the barn, my knees buckling upon landing. Helpful hands caught me up before hitting the ground and different voices peppered me with questions as they half carried me into the lounge and plied me with drink and food. Someone I didn't see took care of Midnight.

After satisfying their curiosity with a report, I washed and changed into my uniform. Nobody knew if the hunt would end in minutes or hours, and all would have to hop into action when the riders dumped their horses and headed for the hunt breakfast. The crew chattered back and forth over the stall dividers, up and down the aisles, sharing stories and speculations. I had time to finish attending Midnight before Caryl drove in.

"So, Miss Eagan," she said, looking me up and down in search of flaws. "You weren't able to stick through the whole thing? I'm not surprised."

"No, ma'am," I said, dropping my eyes even though I wanted to lift my chin and glare. But the last thing I needed was a dust-up with my boss!

"Did you fall?"

"No, we just ran out of gas. A group peeled off, and I joined them rather than risk laming my horse." *Or killing us both.*

"Good call," Caryl said reluctantly. Then she raised her voice to carry down the aisle. "And well done, all of you, for making everything ready. The field is on its way back, and at least one of them *is* lame. The vet will be here shortly."

She spun on her heel and clacked to her office. Half an hour later, Mary Anne led an exhausted troop into the stableyard. I ran out with the crew to repeat what had been done for me, and help get mud-spattered, sweat-flecked, ravenous beasts into their stalls while the non-staff riders staggered off to the breakfast.

"Why do they call it breakfast when it's afternoon?" Allison popped in to check with me. "How long you been back? Everything okay?"

I explained. Allison responded, "We had a great time. I'll tell you about it later when we're off."

"I'm…not sure I'll be around," I said. "Con's here, and I don't know his plans yet."

"And I doubt they include me." Allison bobbed her eyebrows. "Well, we'll catch up whenever."

I dashed off to resume duty. The barn remained a-bustle for the rest of the day.

Late afternoon, things got suddenly quiet. I peered into the aisle from the tackroom to see Con sauntering in through the big main door. He was backlit by the exterior brightness, but I knew that silhouette anywhere. He started down the aisle, looking into each stall as he passed and nodding to anyone in them. I ducked back into the tackroom, frantic at the thought of facing him, then mentally slapped myself upside the head, put down my tools, and stepped out.

Just as Caryl entered into the aisle, calling, "Mr. Winston!"

He glanced back over his shoulder, then turned to face her. "Hello, Ms. Ballard."

She stopped and simpered up at him. "Good to see you again. Can I help you with something?"

"Thanks, but I'm just picking up my saddle. Figured it a good time to ride my horse."

"Yes, of course. But perhaps you can ride later, and join us at the Burlingames'? I'm just heading over there now."

I approached as quietly as I could, but Caryl spotted me beyond Con's shoulder. Her face darkened, and Con turned to see what had caused the change.

His own face lit up, and I could not help but grin at him. My knees, which had been unsteady for hours, got a little gummier, forcing me to push effort into a simple stride.

Con turned back to Caryl and demolished her with a smile. "Thanks, but I'm all set. Have a good time."

He gave her his back. I felt sorry for the woman, whose face dissolved into hurt swiftly replaced by anger. Then it screwed into hatred as she glared at me. My compassion faded, and I focused on Con, hoping he didn't sense what was going on behind his back.

As Caryl's bootheels punished the floorboards on her way out, Con and I stood a few paces apart, looking at each other. I felt the urge again to fling myself into his arms and wrap my legs around him, but with so many actual and potential witnesses, I held back.

"Glad I caught you," he opened in the same Cool Mr. Winston voice he'd used with Caryl. "How'd the hunt go?"

I struggled to match his tone and manner. "Exhilarating. Exhausting. But we made it through fine. You're going to ride Klatawah?"

"Yeah. Care to brief me?"

"I, uh, can't break right now, but I'll join you shortly."

I turned for the tackroom, beckoning him to follow. While he gathered up Klatawah's gear, I resumed the saddle-cleaning his arrival had interrupted. Thankfully, it was the last of the day. Three other stablehands found an urgent need to fetch or return brushes or bridles, or to visit their lockers. Con greeted them all with a friendly nod.

When they had gotten an eyeful and slinked away, one was bold enough to say at the door, "See you at dinner, Linny?"

"Ah, I'm not sure. The Coach House at six?"

"Yeah, though a bunch of us will be opening the bar at five."

The girl dimpled at Con and left.

He caught and held my eye until I explained. "Since any of us on duty couldn't go to the breakfast, we're meeting for dinner."

"I was hoping," he said, "to take you out."

I fluttered inside but kept my voice and gaze level. "While you're riding, decide whether you want to join a loud party or go somewhere by ourselves. Keep in mind that there are a lot of extra people in town and every place will be busy, probably needing reservations."

"Any takeout joints?"

"Chinese and pizza."

"Which would you prefer?"

"Your choice."

"I'll let you know when you get up top."

He departed with an armload of saddlery. I hurried through my remaining tasks, then scooted to my car. The parking area and drive were as empty now as they had been full a few hours earlier. Con's truck was gone, too; I could see its roofline up by Klatawah's pasture.

I drove slowly up the hill, parked and closed my door quietly, then moved to the rail, where Klatawah's saddle sat on the top bar. She and Con, riding bareback, were at the far end of the pasture circling at a jog; when he spotted me, he turned Klatawah and approached at a lope.

Those few seconds of watching him, flushed and beaming with windblown hair, gave my heart the flip-flops. Klatawah lifted her head and sucked my scent through her nostrils as he slowed her, then she whickered and trotted to the gate.

I stepped through and patted the mare's neck. "I think you made her day."

"And I think I'm damn glad I wasn't on her for that hunt," he confessed. "From what I saw, it looked wild."

"It was. Completely insane!" But it had answered one of my critical questions. If I wanted to gallop full blast on a horse, I would rather do it on the beach than over fences.

"Are they all like that," he asked, "or only Opening Day?"

"I think it calms down from here on, and they're more serious about the hounds and protocol. Today they got a lot more people than they were expecting, so it was mayhem on the trails."

"I'll bet." He slid off. Klatawah rubbed her nose on his upper arm. He scratched up under her mane.

"I've never ridden so hard or for so long," I said. "I'm utterly...depleted."

"I'll bet," he repeated, dropping Klatawah's reins to pull me into his arms.

I offered no resistance, even when he squeezed me so hard my breath got crushed away. I could feel and hear his heartbeat. If I hadn't been so drained, mine would have been galloping at the same speed.

For now, I just wanted to stay enfolded and never let go.

He eased his grip, though, so I tilted my head back. He bent to kiss me softly.

I savored it, then parted my lips in invitation. Instead, he pulled back. "Not now," he said, skimming his hand atop my head.

"Then when?" I stepped out of his arms, which opened to release me.

"Are you off duty yet?"

I shook my head. "Almost."

"Then let me pack up here, and I'll go find some dinner and bring it back to your place."

"All right."

Yes!

I kept my face neutral and turned to see where Klatawah had wandered off to. She had crossed to another section of fence and was tearing grass below the bottom panel.

"Are you taking her?" I thumbed toward the mare.

"Yes, but whether it's tonight or tomorrow morning depends on you."

We stared at each other. His eyes were dark and sober. I knew I was looking at either a beginning or the end.

"I can't wait," I said, "to hear your proposition."

"I can't wait," he echoed, "to hear your response."

"Then you go your way and I'll go mine, and we'll meet, hopefully, in the middle."

I meant it literally, but he caught the parallel meaning and smiled. Then he turned to catch his mare and unbridle her, while I returned to the stable with quaking insides.

CHAPTER TWENTY-ONE

Descending the hill, I observed the autumn leaves rustling like jewels in the setting sunlight, fluttering down to a crunchy carpet in a breeze that nipped through my shirt. At the barn, horse noses probed through barred windows, and the distant paddocks were trampled brown by their hooves.

I loved it all and wondered if I could leave it. I would likely have to someday; would it be because I'd been fired, or moved on to a better position, or run off with the guy I'd just left?

I rushed through my closing duties and back to my cabin. Con hadn't arrived yet, so I dove into the shower while I had the chance. Upon emerging, I slipped on fuzzy socks and belted into my terry bathrobe, debating whether to remain in it or change into slouch clothes, or something neat and pretty, or to just greet him at the door naked. If I'd had a naughty negligee, that would be an option, too.

Instinct told me that seduction would flop, and I would be better off behaving genuinely—which happened to be so exhausted I felt sick instead of hungry—letting him see what he was getting into. Or out of. If he chose out, I would feel less a fool being myself than if I had pretended womanly arts and failed.

Listening for his truck, I dug out mismatched and ill-fitting sheets for the sofa bed, just in case, but instead of opening it up and making the bed, I left it closed and reclined atop it for a just moment. Next thing I knew, the cabin was dark and the windows showed black around the curtains.

Oh no!

I jerked upright, looking at the clock. No multiple hours had passed;

I'd just been surprised again by the shortening days. Con was later than I expected, but not enough to make me worry. Yet.

I rose with a groan, turned on a lamp, rebelted my robe, and shuffled across the room to the kitchen corner. I absolutely had to eat something or pass out. Fastest choice was toast and jam with a cold-water chaser. Then I undertook combing my two-foot tangle of hair.

Outside, a rumble was followed by a door slam. My fingers stopped moving as I listened, holding my breath. Unless it was Allison coming to swap stories, Con had arrived and was about to deliver my destiny. My feet refused to move to open the door for him. Instead, I stood clutching my bathrobe closed at the neck until he knocked.

"Come in," I croaked.

He entered and closed the door to stand before me, impassive. The wind had splayed his hair across his forehead, and he had added a rust-colored down vest over his denims against the chill. His hipshot stance, with thumb hooked into one pocket and other hand curled around a bag emanating spicy aromas, revealed to me that he belonged in a dream Montana but would never, because of his beauty and privileged East Coast background, be fully accepted in the real cowboy world. Maybe he knew that, too, which was why he was here.

The fact he'd come was all I could wrap my mind around. If he asked anything of me that moment, I would not refuse. Yet he just stood there, his eyes hooded in shadow so I could not see into them. However, his shirt was open two buttons lower than it had been before.

He startled me by breaking into action. "It was mobbed, and I had to wait a long time," he said, depositing the bags on the table. "Then I overshot your driveway and had to turn around."

"Thank you," I said, meaning, *everything*. He looked at me still hunched in my bathrobe, reached out then retracted his hands, and turned them toward dishing out food.

I was reminded of Allison tending to me the day she'd caught me crying. Now the subject of my tears was caring for me in my own home. *My sanctuary.* At that thought, I knew I could not leave with him tomorrow, and slumped into the hard kitchen chair.

He piled food in front of me. My snack had calmed my nausea, so the Oriental aromas stirred my appetite. I tucked in gratefully—now reminded of the night he had sobered me up on the beach.

He, meanwhile, picked at his brightly sauced rice dish and watched me. Finally he said, "If half a day's ride wipes you out this bad, you're a long way from being an endurance trail rider."

I looked at him over the fork in my mouth, swallowed, and said, "Not a big deal, since I don't plan to be one."

"Why not?"

I sat up straight and challenged, "Why would I? That's more your line."

"So I hope someday. But you've pretty much dumped showing and have taken up overland riding. We can do that together in infinite variety. I'm hoping you'll help me train."

What I had swallowed almost came back from the jolt that gave me. But I kept my face blank and said, "How? You've got all the dunes and beach in the world to work out on. What difference would I make?"

"Keeping me company and giving me someone to talk about things with and ride against, help me pull all the pieces of the new business together while having some goals and fun for ourselves."

"For which you want me to leave the best job and horse I've ever had."

"Yes."

He put it so simply and unashamedly, I felt convoluted and ashamed.

I leaned back. The offer appealed; I had already visualized ways to mold it into a joint dream, and had come to this meeting prepared to discuss them, if things went in that direction.

But: "I already told you I don't want to be your employee."

"I know. But it's not the bondage you think. It's actually the way to keep your freedom. If you're my partner—in any sense of the word—then you'd be subject to the same garbage I am. As my employee, you'd be exempt from all that and free to run if you need to. In the meantime, we could still be together."

I eyed him, feeling my body absorb the food and produce energy, and my heart swell with…I wasn't sure what. All I could say was, "That's a strange and confusing offer, Con."

He gave a sheepish smile. "Unfortunately, it's the best I can do." He hesitated then added, "I'm just trying to be straight with you, Linny."

"I appreciate that. But it doesn't mean I know how to answer." I flashed my eyes at him.

"I understand," he said, and I thought he might.

After a pause I said, "Where would I live—the beach house?"

"If you want. Or the house on the property or the barn apartment, whatever. Be more credible if you resided on the premises, but I wouldn't care about that. I'm thinking of renting out the house to help defray the loan costs, and living at the stable; but whatever you wanted would be yours."

"And you would live in one of the other places."

"I would have to."

"Have to."

"For the record, yes. But it's not like anyone would be hanging around watching us."

"I get it."

We stared at each other across the table. I thought his eyes looked tight around the edges and knew he wasn't telling me everything.

"There's a big piece missing," I prompted, then gestured across the table. "You're over there. I'm over here. It's hurting your credibility."

He smiled, but his eyes turned down at the corners. "I wanted your blood sugar back up to normal before I hit you with the big one."

"Uh-oh." I rolled my eyes, then narrowed them at him. "Don't ever try to get a job in sales."

He laughed and stood, holding out his hand to me. Hesitantly, looking up at him under my brows, I took the hand and allowed him to pull me up. But he didn't pull me close. Instead, he scooped me up and carried me to the couch as if I weighed nothing. That got my little heart a-pumping. He sat me across his lap and kept his arms snug around me, nuzzling my hair before inhaling deep and saying, "It's about this couch."

I waited, my arms slackening around his neck.

"When you offered me your cot," he said, "I, well, I was real happy. But I can't act on it, Linny: I've got to sleep on the couch."

I gulped and turned my face, finding his so close he was out of focus. "Why? You've got the clap or something?"

Other, worse possibilities ran through my mind, but I didn't voice them.

"No...not that simple. Or at least, that straightforward."

"Then what?"

He waited long seconds to answer, then enunciated, "I took a vow."

"What?" I pushed back so I could see him clearly. "Are you a *monk*?" The prospect thrust a spear through my heart.

He gave a breathy chuckle. "No. But I promised myself—I swore—when I was twenty—that I wouldn't bed a woman again until my wedding night."

I jerked, not sure which was more shocking: that he could be such an old-fashioned romantic or that he hadn't had sex for two years.

"Non-negotiable?" was all I said.

He nodded.

I turned my face away, recognizing that he'd been sending signals along those lines for a while, which I had received but not interpreted. They'd been at some subconscious wavelength, only to come clear now with a hollow ache.

"It's not that I'm unwilling to...fool around," he said. "But in my head, well, you can probably figure it out."

"Yeah," I said bitterly, "I think I can."

I had been right when I'd told Jona that Con wanted to be loved, not lusted after. The only proof that would convince him was the total, lifelong, risk-everything commitment of marriage—after he'd inherited his money, of course. No room for speculators.

I squinted back at him. "So what, exactly, does 'fooling around' mean, and where, exactly, is the line that can't be crossed?"

He squirmed and dropped his gaze, not wanting to say the blunt words.

I didn't, either. We sat silent until I said, "Okay, Con, but...you've just taken away what I need to make my decision."

We both lifted our chins and stared at each other. I couldn't read what I saw in his eyes. Finally he said, "I'm sorry. But I can't help feeling...it's just—such a waste—to make love—then separate."

But what if making love motivates you to not want to separate?

As Jona had said, It may take one to discover the other.

I said neither to him, not wanting to be seen as begging for sex. So I let silence press him to explain himself.

He tightened his arms around me and said into my neck, "I believe, I truly believe, that love, sex, and marriage should go together, not be experienced in pieces, with different people."

Then propose, goddamn it! I couldn't force out those words, either. Apparently he had the same problem. His mouth opened and closed, but nothing more came out.

I pivoted to straddle his lap. He stirred beneath me. I wriggled to suggest maybe we could find where that line was to not cross, but he didn't smile.

Anger overrode hurt but I kept my voice soft. "I used to believe the same thing, Con; used to dream it. And I still do—no, I still want it, but it's not possible anymore, because I bought somebody else's line and made a mistake I can't undo. I'm glad I made it, though, because it showed me the futility of holding out for Mr. Perfect. What if you don't want the same things in bed, or it turns out you're incompatible as people afterward? It's a lot harder to take a marriage apart than put it together. Trying each other out beforehand—in the most important area—is safe, sane, honest—and fair."

"But not when—"

"That's what I'm trying to tell you! It's especially important in your case, with what you've got at stake. You can't make a mistake as big as marriage without knowing up front what you're getting into. Tonight we have a chance to find out that may never come again. You knew that when you walked in here!"

He rubbed his face. "Yeah...and I really should walk out. You don't get it, Linny. I want something more than sex. And I'm so used to waiting, I can wait until everything's right."

I felt a rock in my gut upon recognizing the bottom line. "Then I guess you're going to wait forever, because it's never going to be perfect."

Tears pricked my eyes and I started to dismount his lap, but he clamped me in place. "Yeah, maybe it's going to take a while," he said, in a voice so cold I thought he might dump me on the floor. "But I'm willing to show you where that line is."

I looked back at him, into his eyes, which were dilated beyond what the room's meager light accounted for. I could see way into them, into more layers than I would have guessed lived inside. No mask now.

"And then what?" I whispered.

He touched my cheek. "And then I sleep on the couch."

I flung back my head and yelped in frustration. Then I snapped my chin down and pummeled his chest. He laughed and grabbed my wrists with just enough strength to stop them. Then one of us twitched the other a little closer; then neither of us pulled back, or breathed for a heartbeat. Then we gave up at the same time and fell into a hard, hot kiss.

Yes!

This time, surrounded by walls, with curtains drawn over the windows, we didn't need to break off and look over our shoulders. We could kiss and kiss…and run fingers through each other's hair and hands under each other's clothes, unwrapping them, unbuttoning them, unzipping them for exploration.

For hours I abandoned thought, just felt him all over me, and me all over him, lost in happiness. *I love you. I want you. I need you,* poured out of me, more potent and sincere than I could put same into words. Con gave it all back, so different from the message I had always received from Michael: *I love sex, and I love most having it with you. Therefore, I love you.*

Not the same. Oh, not the same at all.

I forgot about The Line until we almost—almost—crossed over it. I only recognized it when Con eased me back, then distracted me with fresh ardor in a new direction.

We returned to reality on the floor in a jumble of sofa pillows and the old bedspread I'd thrown over them to cover split seams and stains. While waiting for his consciousness to resurface, I stroked his long, firm muscles, like hot velvet over granite even when slack. Presently his back started to rise and fall with a huffing that startled me until I identified it as muffled chuckling. For a second it stung me, but then I realized, when he rolled away and threw back his head in open-mouthed laughter, that he was making the only sound that could express total delight.

The same bubbled up from within me, and I joined him in giggling and guffawing. We wrapped back together then fell quiet, pondering how to escape the discomfort of the floor without facing the question of who would sleep where.

I didn't want to retreat to my lonely cot, so I suggested, "The couch pulls out into a double, you know."

He didn't answer for a moment, his breath still heavy. "You trying to get me to break my vow, Miss Eagan?"

"I'm offering a bed you might actually fit into. That just happens to be big enough for two."

He slumped onto his back and let his gaze drift upward, only then noticing his painting that I'd hung on the wall behind the couch. Something jabbed him upon recognition, which I felt through his skin.

"God, Linny, you torture me."

"You're getting me back pretty good."

That silenced us, leaving us unresolved on the too-hard, too-cold floor. I draped my free arm over his chest; he covered my hand with his. We sighed in unison.

"It might be better if I go," he said.

"No."

He neither moved nor argued. Maybe he felt the pressure building inside me, knowing I was going to say something that he'd been waiting to hear.

"I want one night with you in my arms, goddamn it!"

"Just one?" He rolled back around me and kissed my neck.

"Well, looks like that's all you're going to give me."

"That's 'cause you've given me not the slightest sign that you might marry me."

"And when have you asked?"

He rolled away. "I haven't bothered, because I know the answer."

I sat up. "You're right, if the conditions you've outlined are firm."

"I don't have a choice at this point."

"You could have created a choice. Said something to me before you bought the stable. Maybe between the two of us we could have come up with a workable idea."

"It's not like you were there to talk to." His voice had turned hard again.

I matched it. "It's not like you gave me any reason to stay."

He sat up and turned away. Bare to the chilling room, our skin started to goose pimple as sweat evaporated. At least, I thought, he wasn't putting his clothes back on and walking out.

Yet.

"It wasn't for me to argue," he said, voice still tight and cold. "All your reasons for leaving were good." But then his tone flared as he snapped his head around. "Did you want me to drop on my knees and beg?"

"I—"

He turned the rest of himself and pressed me back onto the floor by his weight atop my chest, pinning both my wrists back beside my head. "Not very modern-woman of you, if you need a man to come crawling."

I could barely draw a breath. "You could have given me a clue."

"I did. A couple of big ones. You went, anyway."

He dropped his head beside mine, still holding my arms. We panted heavily for a few moments, at loss for what to say.

Being skin to skin together made me want to bare the rest of me. "Have you ever seen that poster...*If you love something, set it free—*"

"If it comes back, it's yours. If not, it never was. Is that what this is really all about?"

"Yes. No. Sort of."

He released my arms. I shifted to my side, propped my head up with one hand, and stroked his jaw and neck with the other. He used silence as I had to compel me to explain myself.

In a whisper I confessed, "The truth is, I thought I was in love once. But I was wrong. And that scares the heck out of me, because I don't know how to tell what feeling is right. I was so sure!—but it came and went and now I feel nothing for him. I'm so afraid that will happen with you, especially since dropping everything to be with you puts so much pressure on love, I can't imagine how we'd hang on to it. All I can tell you for sure is that something is different this time, and I fell for you the first day I saw you with Klatawah, though it took me a long time to figure that out."

He pulled my hand to his mouth and kissed my fingers, closing his eyes. A trembly heat ran through me, and I didn't want to talk anymore.

Presently he opened his eyes and said, "I'm waiting for the *but*..."

"No *but*. That's all there is. Now you need to push or pull me off the fence."

He gave a bitter chuckle. "Who'd've thought that The Most Eligible Bachelor on the East Coast would have such a hard time getting a woman."

"It wouldn't be so hard if you hadn't told me about your family thing."

"That's why I did. How would you like to have been seduced into marrying me, then I sprang *that* on you?"

"Not one bit! Though I do want to know if you're ever going to tell me the whole story."

"No. I'm not telling anyone, ever. It's history, and when the waiting is over and I get my blood money, then I'll have nothing to do with them ever again."

I sucked air through my teeth and shook my head. Then slid down beside him, and we nestled in silence for a few minutes.

He broke it by saying, "That's why I like the idea of waiting, Linny. It would give you a chance to understand what you're up against, and for both of us to get used to being in love. It's tough to accept the idea that someone will be the last person you'll ever get physical with, and the one you'll wake up to every morning, and grow old and ugly with. It's a chance to see what might pull us apart, so we can break up if we need to before signing papers and joining property and having a family. It's that old idea of getting engaged—we ought to try it."

It took me a second to register that he had just proposed. Then I banged my forehead against his chest. "That completely reverses everything you said before!"

He pulled me close. "Not really. The setup at the stable would be the same, except that we'd be promised to each other. We just can't tell anyone. Yeah, it would be stupid and demeaning. But by the time it was over, we'd know for sure if we're right for each other, and marrying could be a real celebration. If not, I would have enough resources to set you up on your own, so you wouldn't feel you'd wasted your time and your love."

I sobbed silently in his embrace.

He added, "I understand what I'm asking of you. But I can give you all your dreams if you'll give me the time and the charade."

I gulped and hung on him for a while before saying, "With or without sleeping together?"

"Well, 'not' was the plan, but I'm not sure I can hold out."

"I know I can't. I won't. I'm as much a product of my family as you are, Con."

I tilted my face to see his arched eyebrows. Then explained, "I used to plug my ears when my parents blathered on about their beliefs, but I still absorbed their point. Which is, your life is your own, and you can do anything you want no matter who you are and where you come from and what color or sex you are. You just have to be willing to put in the work and face the consequences. I broke with them because they preached it but wouldn't let me live it. So now I live the consequences."

Con flopped his head back and slapped a hand onto his forehead. "Are you asking me to give up my inheritance? And everything I've gone through and still have to, in order to do exactly what you just said?"

"No. I'm asking you to help me pull out the couch, and sleep in my arms tonight. In the morning, we'll make a decision and live with it."

He flopped his hand to his side and breathed hard for a minute. I squirmed away and, with complaining muscles, got up and stood over him, letting him look at me in a new light.

Then he grunted and dragged himself upright, and we shoved everything around until we had a padded surface and pillows and coverings. The exercise gave us time to regroup, while enjoying peeks at each other in motion, naked. His beauty hit me afresh now that I could fully see it. And it engendered in me a thrilling thought: *He's mine, mine, mine!*

Even if he left in the morning and I never saw him again.

But for what remained of the night: We stood on opposite sides of the sofa bed, gazing at each other. I hesitated to turn the lights out, lest he see my desire for him glow in the dark. His desire for me was more obvious, and I doubted we could stay on the right side of his line much longer. But it was up to him to invite me across it. If he did, then my life was going to upheave yet again, to a degree I couldn't imagine.

He dropped a shoulder and slow-rolled onto the mattress, leaving me to deal with light switches and come back to him in the dark. As soon as I knelt on the bed and crawled across it to him, he pulled me into a full wrap, where we stayed for the rest of the night.

CHAPTER TWENTY-TWO

Next thing I knew, gray daylight filled the room. An arm and a leg had grown numb beneath Con's weight; I endured it a moment longer, studying his slack face in the dawn and savoring an internal glow. Then I advanced to thought—and went rigid.

Daylight. I shouldn't be able to see the room. In October, I got up in the dark. It wasn't my day off. *Oh no*—I had forgotten to activate my alarm clock and was now overdue at work!

As I scrambled out of bed, the telephone shrilled. I leaped for the handset as Con spasmed awake.

"Linny! Oh, thank God you're there!" came Allison's voice.

"I'm sorry, I overslept, but—"

"That doesn't matter. Just get here as fast as you can. Klatawah escaped, and she's down!"

"What!"

"Please tell me Con is with you—we can't find him, either."

"Yes, he's right here."

I glanced to the bed where Con was frozen partway upright, wide-eyed. We exchanged stricken looks, then he lunged forward and snatched the phone from my hand.

"What happened!" He tilted the receiver so I could hear what Allison said.

"Klatawah got out. She might have been hit by a car. Caryl—I tried to—"

"Where!" he roared.

"On the side of the road in front of the Smiths' hayfield, just past the Farm from your direction."

"We'll be right there."

Con slammed down the receiver with an explosive "*Shit!*" then stopped to look at me. I held his gaze for a fraction of a second, then dashed for my clothes as he went the other way for his.

I jammed my limbs into pants and sleeves and raced back into the living room where Con was hopping on one foot while pulling on his jeans, an empty sleeve flapping from behind his half-donned shirt. I grabbed both of our jackets as he shoved into his boots, then followed him out the door.

He was backing his truck out the driveway before I had the passenger door closed. We covered the four miles to Shallowkill in less than three minutes, not exchanging a word.

We rounded a curve a few hundred yards beyond Shallowkill's entrance and swerved past a partial blockade formed by two Farm pickups and Mary Anne's car. I saw other cars along the berm and people standing in the drainage ditch and squatting or kneeling on the upslope beyond it, half concealed by brush.

Con slammed to a halt and jumped out running. I had to get out more carefully, as the truck was tilted downhill into the rocky, pricker-clogged ditch. As I gained the roadbed, Allison pulled around in front of Con's pickup. I waved acknowledgment but jogged after Con before Allison finished parking.

His shirt showed blue through the shriveled underbrush, close to the ground near a russet mass. I heard grunts and weak squealing as I shouldered past the people looking on.

Con and Mary Anne knelt beside Klatawah. The mare lay with heaving sides just above the ditch, half on the ground and half atop a tumbledown wall comprising ancient fieldstones, rotted wood posts, and rusted barbed wire. Her legs were ensnared in a Gordian knot of wire, brambles, ferns, and fence remnants, which she must have plunged or fallen into while jumping away from a car.

Con didn't look up when I squatted next to him. I was so relieved not to find the bloody remains of a collision that it took a moment to register how badly Klatawah was tangled and bruised.

"Far as I can tell, nothing broken," Con said to me without removing his eyes and exploratory hands from the trembling mare. "More trapped and cut than anything else."

"Vet should be here any minute," Mary Anne said, standing up.

"Caryl called him," Allison added. "She was chasing Klatawah when the car came and ran back to the Farm for help."

"The vehicle didn't stop?" I asked.

"No, they took off, and Caryl didn't get a look at it."

"Where is she?"

Mary Anne snorted. "Either halfway to the Canadian border, or back in the office letting us clean up her mess."

"What the hell happened?" Con snarled.

"Not sure. Since Linny didn't show up, and last Caryl knew you were shipping Klatawah today, she went up to get her ready."

Con swore again, then returned his attention to Klatawah, who was rolling her eyes and trying to kick away the wire to stand. It just bit deeper into her flesh. "Easy, easy..." Con murmured as he stroked the matted, quivering neck. I swallowed back tears and realized my legs were shaking.

Mary Anne crunched back to the road. "I called the vet myself when I found out, plus the Burlingames. They should be right along."

"Is that a whip cut on her neck?" Allison stepped closer to peer. Nobody answered, so she answered herself. "Wouldn't surprise me. But none of us really saw anything—Caryl must've come in early and been up with Klatawah when I got in."

Con shot me a look but kept his mouth pressed shut in a line. I shuddered at the dangerous glint in his eye. He looked feral and weary and strained, with his nostrils stuck in a flare like an outraged stallion. But to me he looked beautiful, and my heart swelled when I remembered that he was mine.

He rocked onto his heels and dragged a hand through his hair so it stayed slicked back stiffly, showing a tan line on his forehead. In that same moment, I realized why I loved him: not because of his face, but because he was his face. Everything inside him shone through it, despite his efforts to hide behind his mask. At this moment, his love for Klatawah gleamed through his eyes and every muscle beneath his skin.

More cars pulled up, delivering the Burlingames and the veterinarian. I ignored their anxious greetings and, after touching Con on the shoulder to signal my departure, returned to the truck and then the barn.

Caryl's Buick was still parked outside, as were the bewildered and concerned staff who weren't milling in the aisles. I ignored all who hailed me and headed straight to the office. From within, I heard slamming drawers and staccato bootheels.

Caryl straightened from loading files into a briefcase open on her desk as I turned the door handle and entered. We narrowed our eyes at each other.

I shuddered upon recognizing jealous loathing. For a second, Caryl's eyes were tunnels into her soul, where a desperate woman, untouched and unloved for too long, raised an iron-spiked armor in defense against her cravings. From inside it she schemed to punish the younger, prettier, more talented girls who lured away opportunities and men.

Then my rage boiled over. "What the hell were you doing with that horse!"

"Helping," Caryl sneered back, her tone belying her white face. "You failed to report for work—next time you're out, Eagan—and the horse needed to be cleaned up and her legs wrapped for travel. Somebody had to do it."

"Somebody should have waited and found out what was going on, first. You know Con left explicit instructions that only I am to handle Klatawah when he's not here—no excuse, Caryl. And since he is here, you were even more out of line. How did she get out?"

Caryl placed down her papers with menacing slowness. "She jumped."

I wouldn't have believed it if I hadn't seen Klatawah jump, myself. Still, the pasture fence was substantially higher than the logs and bushes the mare had popped over during the hunter pace, and I would not have expected anything other than a trained show jumper to clear them.

I sympathized for a moment with the shock Caryl must have received, but then my rage returned. "And what provoked her to jump out after living there peacefully for so many weeks?"

Caryl's gaze dropped to the briefcase she finished stuffing. "I was trying to catch her. She came over to the grain bucket, but when I went to put on the halter, she took off."

I rolled my eyes with a hot sigh. "And she just happened to get whip welts on her neck after skipping off down the road."

Before Caryl could respond, I stepped forward to stand too close and growl through clenched teeth, "Run if you want, coward, but if that horse has to be put down, I will follow you to the ends of the earth and beat you to a bloody pulp!"

Caryl's gaze flicked past my shoulder to the riding crop lying on her desk. I had seen it from the doorway and fought the temptation to snatch it up myself. I knew I could not but didn't know what to do instead—unwilling to let the woman walk away.

I forced myself to step back and inhale, exhale, a few times before saying, "Don't even think of leaving here until you have apologized to Mr. Winston and offered him restitution."

"Don't you even think of telling me what to do, Eagan."

Caryl snapped her case shut and grabbed the handle, advancing toward the doorway with a scarlet face and wild eye. I thought for an instant she might hit me with the briefcase, and dodged back a step before standing fast. But Caryl kept coming. "Get out of my way!"

She bulldozed into me with a shoulder. I staggered and shoved back, shouting, "Don't you dare!"

"Mind your own goddamn business!" Caryl swatted my arms away.

"This is my business!" I cried through a red mist, ready to spring and strike. I would not allow another jealous, vicious woman to interfere with my horse and my man—this time to crueler effect. Only awareness of consequence, flickering dimly through my red mist, dropped my arms and flattened me against the doorframe, letting Caryl by.

The defeat left me steaming through my nostrils, stomach boiling. Tears burned my eyes. Even though I knew Caryl's quitting before she was fired removed this enemy from my life, her legacy would linger long through Con's and Klatawah's hurts. I wanted so badly to punish her that I almost followed, to drag Caryl from her car to kick and claw and scream.

I was rescued by my body, which fell into the shakes from ebbing adrenaline. That brought out the aches and stabs from yesterday's overexertions, as well. Memories of their cause finally quieted the volcano in my breast. I sagged into the desk chair and dropped my face into my hands.

What now? How would this change things? What would Con think—say—do with Klatawah so needlessly injured on my watch? Caryl had deprived us of our crucial morning-after talk. I knew how his body and heart felt about me, but we needed to speak to learn the depth of each other's minds. Where would his mind be now? Certainly not on romance!

My mind had moved beyond that, tempering love into something ferocious. Caryl had proven that pairing with Con was my only course that would prevent more events like today's. I must proudly embrace and display him as my man and own my position as his woman, never letting another person cross that boundary or hurt him. No more hesitating until things got out of hand. No more buckling under other people's rules. He and I must own and train our own horses and put together a great stable according to our own standards. If that cost him his millions, so be it. That would not matter if true love truly dwelled between us. We had plenty to work with in building a life together.

That is, if I could persuade him to give up those millions and get started on our life today.

I shook my head. It didn't matter anymore. I would go and be his employee or whatever; what mattered was being together. Let him have the millions he deserved. It was 1975, and we could live in sin without me being burned at the stake. My parents might choke upon learning that this was the door their generation had opened that I was choosing to walk through, but it was my choice, not theirs. *Reap what you sow, Mom and Dad. Just like me.*

I sighed. All that was still down the road. I must return to the real road right now and get back to my beloved man and his beloved horse.

I hastened past the stablehands who had gathered outside the office during the ruckus, tossing a terse explanation over my shoulder so they had an inkling of what drama was storming around them. I had left Con's truck with the door open and key in the ignition, so I hopped back in and returned to the incident scene.

There I found the vet busy stitching and bandaging a doped Klatawah. The mare's frantic eyes had glazed, but her nostrils remained distended and fluttering. She had stopped fighting, seeming to understand that the bipeds were trying to help.

Con remained at her head while everyone else debated how to move the horse to shelter. I held back lest I startle her, though I sought to catch Con's eye. He sensed my return and glanced up; I nodded the message, *I took care of it*. He nodded back and returned his attention to the vet, who straightened and pronounced that no tendons looked to be severed and the wounds were as under control as he could make them.

The ring of watchers released their breath. After further delay and much discussion, everyone combined efforts to coax the bandaged mare to her feet and into a trailer, in the absence of a crane with a sling. The trailer was towed at a crawl, preceded and flanked by creeping cars, down the quarter mile to a box stall hurriedly prepared for her by one set of stablehands while the other deflected incoming customers and boarders.

Klatawah drooped for nearly an hour before halfheartedly snatching a mouthful of hay. That raised a quiet cheer among the employees, who then trickled back to work, save for Allison, who joined the vet and the Burlingames around me and Con outside Klatawah's stall.

"I am so, *so* sorry this happened," said Desmond Burlingame.

"Rest assured," said Clarissa, "that Ms. Ballard will cover all your expenses, and apologize in person."

"I don't want to lay eyes on her again," Con stated.

"You won't," I said. "She got away."

"Don't worry, we know where she lives," said Desmond.

Clarissa added, "And you can be sure she won't get another job in the horse business."

"Please take your pick from our string in compensation," Desmond offered. "Or a cash settlement if you prefer."

My eyes bulged at the offer. Did they have any notion of the canyon between Klatawah's dollar value and anything in their stable? Midnight was at the bottom of that totem pole, but even he was worth many times Klatawah.

I wondered if the gesture had been made to forestall a lawsuit, or was a gentleman's graciousness, or a businessman's worry about the Farm's reputation.

Con held a bland expression and tone. "Thank you. We can discuss it later."

"How soon before he can ride her again?" Clarissa asked the vet.

He shrugged. "Depends on whether she heals without infection. Even so, it won't be for weeks, maybe months, maybe never. She might heal all right but not be sound enough for working under saddle. We'll see. I'll be back tomorrow, which will tell us more."

Con and I exchanged looks. He sighed and turned back to the Burlingames. "Obviously, I won't be shipping her today. But I do need to make calls."

"Yes, yes, of course—please use the office, or if you need more privacy, come to the house."

"Office is fine," Con said, adding to Allison, "Will you stay with her? We won't be long."

"Of course." She flicked her gaze to the Burlingames, who nodded to absolve her from shirking her normal duties. I had written off mine.

After a final scritch around Klatawah's ears, Con detached himself from the group and headed for the office. I took his hand for the walk. He cast me a sidelong glance and dim smile.

Alone with him behind the closed door of Caryl's office, I told him about my confrontation with her. Both of us noticed the riding crop still on her desk.

"Nice to know I've got a she-tiger defending me," Con said as some of the lines relaxed in his face.

"I've never come so close to killing anyone in my life! It was scary and kind of thrilling at the same time."

"Glad you didn't do it, since that would only make things worse."

I gave him a sad smile. "That's why I didn't."

He curled his hands slowly into fists. "If she'd been within reach when I first saw Klatawah..."

He shook the thought from his head and reached for the phone.

I scraped my fingers through my hair while he called whoever was covering for him and arranged a delayed return. When done, he tipped far back in the office chair and rubbed his hands over his face, leaving dark streaks. He looked down at his palms and frowned but didn't rise to do anything about them, just sagged and gazed at me with bleary eyes.

I gazed back, swallowing a lump in my throat.

"I can't stay any longer than what you just heard," he said. "I have no choice about going back, but you still do. Will you continue caring for Klat until she can travel?"

"Yes."

"Thank you. And...that'll give you time to think."

"I don't need any more."

"I—really?" He lifted an eyebrow and sat forward.

"Really."

He waited for more, eyes bright and muscles tense.

I said: "I finished thinking."

"And...?"

"Well, it depends whether your offer is still open."

"Oh, yes." A smile started to tease around the corners of his mouth. "Though it's changed some since we started."

He rocked forward to his feet and held out his arms. I stepped into them, saying hopefully yet coyly, "Oh?"

He hesitated with a solemn face and darkening eyes that searched into mine. Finally he said, "Forget the money."

I stiffened as hope shot through my veins. Con continued, "I mean, if I get it, great. But I'm not going to waste any more life and love playing games for it."

"You mean—?" I could barely breathe.

"I mean I'm hoping like hell I just slept with the woman I'm going to marry!"

Thrill geysered through me, erupting in a high laugh as I pulled his face down to kiss him breathless. Upon surfacing I infused my voice with sincerity. "You did. I don't care when or how. I just don't want to live another day without you."

We held tight another minute, trying to fuse our hearts together. I finally felt relaxed and right.

Con eased away to arms' length. "So you'll ride off into the sunset with me?"

I shook my head. "Sunrise. Let's think in terms of beginning, not end."

He grinned and engulfed me again, then held me away again, eyes moist around the edges. "If we're really lucky, Klatawah will be fit to endure a trailer ride in a few days, and we won't have to part anymore."

"Meanwhile," I said, pulling him back to me with bobbing eyebrows, "we might have an uninterrupted night toni—"

He expressed hope for that by cutting me off with a kiss.

I would have happily not waited until night but couldn't forget we were standing in Caryl's office. So I pulled away and said softly, stroking his jumbled hair, "What we're really, really lucky about is that Klatawah is standing."

Con sucked air in through his teeth. "Jeesh yes, let's thank all the gods and stars and planets for that!" Then he grinned with a devilish gleam. "There's one more piece of incredibly good luck I don't think you've picked up on yet."

"Oh?" Curiosity bubbled through the champagne already fizzing inside me.

He led me out of the office, down the barn aisle, to Midnight's stall. Stablehands bustling around shot glances at us but kept their distance.

Con opened the stall door for me and closed it behind us. Midnight looked up from his hay, ears forward, the not-quite-diamond in his forehead bright against his ebony coat.

"Behold," Con said, "the booby prize."

I stopped, looked between man and horse, and remembered. Con spoke in a fine imitation of Desmond Burlingame's voice. "Please take your pick from our string in compensation."

"Oh my g—" I clapped my hands to my cheeks. "I thought they meant one of their hunters!"

Con puffed up and said, "They own everything on four legs in this facility and two others, aside from the boarders. And this is my pick."

I shoved my fists into my mouth to keep from squealing. Then I spun to fling my arms around Con's neck—"Thank you! Thank you!"—then crossed the stall to sling them around Midnight's neck—"I don't believe it! I don't believe it!"—and back again a few times, laughing through tears.

"And this," Con said, "seals the deal."

He yanked a few hairs out of Midnight's tail. The horse jumped with a snort and looked at him. So did I, without the snort. Con pretended to ignore my puzzled gaze while digging into a pocket to draw out a wad of long flaxen threads I recognized as from Klatawah's tail.

"These were caught in the wire," he explained, aligning them into a straight clump. "Here, hold this."

I pinched my fingers onto the end of the clump as he deftly separated the hairs into three strands and braided them together. Within seconds he had fashioned a small loop that left a tail he sliced off with the work knife he produced from a different pocket.

"Now, give me your hand," said Con. "No, the other one."

I watched as he slipped the horsetail loop onto my left ring finger and dropped his voice so whoever might be in earshot no longer was. "I, Connor Simon Winston, hereby ask you, Linnea Eagan, to move back to Cape Cod and live with me forever and ride our horses into the sunrise. Will you?"

After a moment of suspended heartbeat, I grinned and laughed. "Yes! But—"

Con's smile fell at the *but*, then his whole face sagged when I pulled off the horsehair ring.

Until I lifted his left hand back to me and slid the loop onto his ring finger. "I, Linnea Eagan, ask you, Connor Simon Winston, to treat me always as an equal partner, as I will treat you, no matter what role I'm playing in your family and business as we ride off into the sunrise together. Will you?"

Now Con laughed. "Yes!" and bent forward to seal his new vow with a kiss. I placed a palm against his chest to hold him back, while extending my right hand. He hesitated a beat, confused, then got it and shook my hand vigorously. "Deal."

"In that case, you may now kiss the bride," I said, and he did. For a long time…

…until voices and footfalls approached along the barn aisle, and life picked up where it had left off. *But not for long*, I promised myself, and accepted Con's hand.

Dear Reader,

Thank you for purchasing this story. I hope you enjoyed it. If so, please let others know by leaving a review.

More of my hybrid romances are available at Borealis Books, as well as through Amazon.

The Aurora Affair
Paranormal romance and metaphysical mystery

Killer Heart
An un-cozy mystery with a love interest, set in Vermont

Open Your Heart with Gardens (nonfiction)
A volume in DreamTime Publishing's "Open Your Heart..." series which helps readers "master your life through what you know."

ABOUT THE AUTHOR

Carolyn Haley lives and breathes novels as an author, editor, and reviewer, all from her home in rural Vermont.

Through her editorial business, DocuMania, she helps other authors through editing, production, and education. She also writes articles for magazines and blogs, and reviews fiction for New York Journal of Books.

For direct correspondence, contact Carolyn at dcmahaley@gmail.com.

Borealis Books:
https://carolynhaley.wordpress.com/about/

DocuMania Editorial Services:
www.documania.us

Reviews at New York Journal of Books:
https://www.nyjournalofbooks.com/search-site/carolyn%20haley?

Blogs:
An American Editor
(https://americaneditor.wordpress.com/tag/carolyn-haley/)

Adventures in Zone 3
(https://adventures-zone3.blogspot.com/)

www.ingramcontent.com/pod-product-compliance
Lightning Source LLC
LaVergne TN
LVHW091031080826
845145LV00002B/439

* 9 7 8 0 9 8 8 7 1 9 1 3 2 *